Lisa Genova

Love
Anthony

**SIMON &
SCHUSTER**

London · New York · Sydney · Toronto · New Delhi

A CBS COMPANY

First published in Great Britain by Simon & Schuster UK Ltd, 2012
This paperback edition published by Simon & Schuster UK Ltd, 2013
A CBS COMPANY

3 5 7 9 10 8 6 4 2

Simon & Schuster UK Ltd
222 Gray's Inn Road, First Floor
London, WC1X 8HB

www.simonandschuster.co.uk
www.simonandschuster.com.au

Simon & Schuster Australia, Sydney
Simon & Schuster India, New Delhi

A CIP catalogue record for this book is available from the British Library

Paperback ISBN 978-1-47111-327-7
Ebook ISBN 978-1-47111-328-4

Printed and bound by CPI Group (UK) Ltd, Croydon, CR0 4YY

For Tracey

In memory of Larry

Love
Anthony

It's Columbus Day weekend, and they lucked out with gorgeous weather, an Indian-summer day in October. She sits in her beach chair with the seat upright and digs her heels into the hot sand. The ocean in front of her sparkles white and silver in the sunlight. There are no fishing boats or yachts in the distance, no kite surfers or swimmers near the shore, nothing but a pure ocean view today. She inhales and exhales.

Soak it up.

Her three daughters are busy building a sand castle. They're too close to the water. It'll be flooded and destroyed within an hour, but they wouldn't heed their mother's warning.

Her oldest daughter, almost eight, is the architect and foreman. *More sand here. A feather there. Go get some shells for the windows. Dig this hole deeper.* The younger two are her loyal construction workers.

"More water!"

The youngest, barely four, loves this job. She skips off with her pail, charges knee-deep into the ocean, fills her bucket, and returns, struggling with the weight of it, sloshing at least half of the water out as she walks a drunken line back to her sisters, smiling, delighted with her contribution to the project.

She loves to watch her daughters like this, absorbed in playing, unaware of her. She admires their young bodies, all in little-girl bikinis, skin still deeply tanned from a summer spent outside, skipping, squatting, bending, sitting, utterly unself-conscious.

The weather and the holiday combined have invited a lot of tourists to the island. Compared to the last many weeks since Labor Day, the beach today feels crowded with walkers and a few sunbathers. Just yesterday she walked on this same stretch of sand for an hour and saw only one other person. But that was a Friday morning, and it was foggy and cold.

Her attention becomes drawn to a woman sitting in a similar beach chair at the water's edge and her boy, who is playing by himself next to her. The boy is a skinny little thing, shirtless in blue bathing trunks, probably a year younger than her youngest daughter. He's creating a line of white rocks on the sand.

Each time the water rushes in, momentarily drowning his line of rocks in white foam, he jumps up and down and squeals. He then runs into the water as if he's chasing it, and runs back, a huge smile stretched across his face.

She continues to watch him, for some reason mesmerized, as he methodically adds more and more rocks to his line.

"Gracie, go see if that little boy wants to help you build the castle."

Outgoing and used to taking orders, Gracie bounces over to the little boy. She watches her daughter, hands on her hips, talking to him, but they're too far away for her to hear what her daughter's saying. The boy doesn't seem to acknowledge her. His mother looks over her shoulder for a moment.

Gracie runs back to their beach blanket alone.

"He doesn't want to."

"Okay."

Soon, the ocean begins to invade the castle, and the girls grow bored of building it anyway, and they start grumbling about being hungry. It's lunchtime, and she didn't bring any food. Time to go.

She closes her eyes and draws in one last warm, clean, salty breath, then exhales and gets up. She gathers a handful of stray shovels and castle molds and carries them to the water to rinse them off. She lets the water roll over her feet. It's numbingly cold. As she rinses her daughter's beach toys, she scans the sand for seashells or sea glass, something beautiful to bring home.

She doesn't see anything worth collecting, but she does spot a single, brilliant white rock peeking out of the sand. She picks it up. It's oval, tumbled perfectly smooth. She walks over to the little boy, bends down, and carefully places her rock at one end of his line.

He glances at her so quickly, it would've been easy to miss them altogether—stunning brown eyes, twinkling in the sun at her, delighted with her contribution to his project. He jumps and squeals and flaps his hands, a happy dance.

She smiles at the boy's mother, who mirrors a smile in return, but it's guarded and weary, one that doesn't invite anything further. She's sure she doesn't know this woman or her little boy and has no particular reason to think she'll ever see them again, but as she turns to leave, she waves and says with total conviction, "See you later."

CHAPTER 1

⌒⌒

Beth is alone in her house, listening to the storm, wondering what to do next. To be fair, she's not really alone. Jimmy is upstairs sleeping. But she feels alone. It's ten in the morning, and the girls are at school, and Jimmy will sleep until at least noon. She's curled up on the couch, sipping hot cocoa from her favorite blue mug, watching the fire in the fireplace, and listening.

Rain and sand spray against the windows like an enemy attacking. Wind chimes gong repetitive, raving-mad music, riding gusts from some distant neighbor's yard. The wind howls like a desperately mournful animal. A desperately mournful wild animal. Winter storms on Nantucket are wild. Wild and violent. They used to scare her, but that was years ago when she was new to this place.

The radiator hisses. Jimmy snores.

She has already done the laundry, the girls won't be home for several hours, and it's too early yet to start dinner. She's grateful she did the grocery shopping yesterday. The whole house needs to be vacuumed, but she'll wait until after Jimmy is up. He didn't get home from work until after 2:00 a.m.

She wishes she had the book for next month's book club. She keeps forgetting to stop by the library to check it out. This month's book was *The Curious Incident of the Dog in the Night-Time* by Mark Haddon. It was a quick read, a murder mystery narrated by an autistic teenage boy. She liked it and was especially fascinated by the main character's strange inner world, but she hopes the next one will be a bit lighter. They typically choose more serious literature for book club, but she could use a pleasant escape into a hot summer romance right about now. They all could.

A loud bang against the back of the house startles her. Grover, their black Lab, lifts his head from where he's been sleeping on the braided rug.

"It's okay, Grove. It's just Daddy's chair."

Knowing a big storm was on its way, she told Jimmy to take his chair in last night before he left for work. It's his "cigar-smoking" chair. One of the summer residents left it on the side of the road in September with a sign taped to it that read FREE, and Jimmy couldn't resist it. The thing is trash. It's a cedar Adirondack chair. In most places on Earth, that chair could weather a lifetime, but on Nantucket, the salty, humid air eventually degrades everything but the densest man-made composite materials. Everything needs to be extraordinarily tough to survive here. And probably more than a little dense.

Jimmy's moldy, corroded chair belongs at the dump or at least in the garage, as Beth wisely suggested last night. But instead, the wind has just lifted it off the ground and heaved it against the house. She thinks about getting up and hauling the chair into the garage herself, but then she thinks better of it. Maybe the storm will smash it to pieces. Of course, even if this happens, Jimmy will just find some other chair to sit in while he smokes his smelly cigars.

She sits and tries to enjoy her cocoa, the storm, and the fire, but the impulse to get up and do something nags at her.

She can't think of anything useful to do. She walks over to the fireplace mantel and picks up the wedding picture of Jimmy and her. Mr. and Mrs. James Ellis. Fourteen years ago. Her hair was longer and blonder then. And her skin was flawless. No pores, no spots, no wrinkles. She touches her thirty-eight-year-old cheek and sighs. Jimmy looks gorgeous. He still does, mostly.

She studies his smile in the photo. He has a slight overbite, and his eyeteeth jut forward a touch. When she met him, she thought his imperfect teeth added to his charm, lending just enough to his rugged good looks without making him look like a hillbilly. He has a self-assured, mischievous, full-out grin for a smile, the kind that makes people—women—put forth considerable effort to be the reason for it.

But his teeth have started to bug her. The way he picks at them with his tongue after he eats. The way he chews his food with his mouth open. The way his eyeteeth stick out. She sometimes finds herself staring at them while he talks, wishing he'd shut his mouth. They're pearly white in this wedding photograph, but now they're more caramel- than cream-colored, abused by years of daily coffee and those smelly cigars.

His once beautiful teeth. Her once beautiful skin. His annoying habits. She has them, too. She knows her nagging drives him crazy. This is what happens when people get older, when they're married for fourteen years. She smiles at Jimmy's smile in the picture, then replaces it on the mantel a little to the left of where it was before. She takes a step back. She purses her lips and eyes the length of the mantel.

Their fireplace mantel is a six-foot-long, single piece of driftwood hung over the hearth. They found it washed up on the shore one night on Surfside Beach during that first summer. Jimmy picked it up and said, *We're hanging this over the fireplace in our house someday.* Then he kissed her, and she believed him. They'd only known each other for a few weeks.

Three pictures are on the mantel, all in matching weathered, white frames—one of Grover when he was six weeks old on the left, Beth and Jimmy in the middle, and a beach portrait of Sophie, Jessica, and Gracie in white shirts and floral, pink peasant skirts on the right. It was taken just after Gracie's second birthday, eight years ago.

"Where does the time go?" she says aloud to Grover.

A huge, peach starfish that Sophie found out by Sankaty Lighthouse flanks the Beth-and-Jimmy picture on the left, and a perfect nautilus shell, also huge and without a single chip or crack, flanks the Beth-and-Jimmy picture on the right. Beth found the nautilus shell out on Great Point the year she married Jimmy, and she protected it vigilantly through three moves. She's picked up hundreds of nautilus shells since and has yet to find another one without a flaw. This is always the arrangement on the mantel. Nothing else is allowed there.

She adjusts her wedding picture again, slightly to the right, and steps back. There. That's better. Perfectly centered. Everything as it should be.

Now what? She's on her feet, feeling energized.

"Come on, Grover. Let's go get the mail."

Outside, she immediately regrets the idea. The wind whips through her heartiest "windproof" winter coat as if it were a sieve. Chills tumble down her spine, and the cold feels like it's worming its way deep into her bones. The rain is coming at her sideways, slapping her in the face, making it difficult to keep her eyes open enough to see where they're going. Poor Grover, who was warm and happy and asleep a few moments ago, whimpers.

"Sorry, Grove. We'll be home in a minute."

The mailboxes are about a half mile away. Beth's neighborhood is inhabited by a smattering of year-rounders and summer residents, but mostly summer people live on her route to the mail. So this time of year, the houses are empty and dark. There are no lights on in the windows, no smoke billowing from the chimneys, no cars parked in the driveways. Everything is lifeless. And gray. The sky, the earth, the weathered cedar shingles on every empty, dark house, the ocean, which she can't see now but can smell. It's all gray. She never gets used to this. The tedious grayness of winter on Nantucket is enough to unravel the most unshakable sanity. Even the proudest natives, the people who love this island the most, question themselves in March.

Why the hell do we live on this godforsaken spit of gray sand?

Spring, summer, and fall are different. Spring brings the yellow daffodils, summer brings the Mykonos-blue sky, fall brings the rusty-red cranberry bogs. And they all bring the tourists. Sure, the tourists come with their downsides. But they come. Life! After Christmas Stroll in December, they all leave. They return to mainland America and beyond, to places that have such things as McDonald's and Staples and BJ's and businesses that are open past January. And color. They have color.

COLD, WET, AND miserable, she arrives at the row of gray mailboxes lining the side of the road, opens the door to her box, pulls out three pieces of mail, and quickly shoves them inside her coat to protect them from the rain.

"C'mon, Grover. Home!"

They turn around and begin retracing their route. With the rain and wind pushing behind her now, she's able to look up to see where she's going instead of mostly down at her feet. Ahead of them in the distance, someone is walking toward them. She wonders who it could be.

As they get closer, she figures out that the person is a woman. Most of Beth's friends live mid-island. Jill lives in Cisco, which isn't too far from here, but in the other direction, toward the ocean, and this woman is too short to be Jill. She's wearing a hat, a scarf wrapped around her nose and mouth, a parka, and boots. It would be hard to recognize anyone in that getup in this weather, but surely, Beth must know who it is. There are only so many people who would be out walking in this neighborhood in this weather on a Thursday in March. There are no weekenders or day-trippers out for a stroll on Nantucket today.

They're a few yards apart now, but Beth still can't identify her. She can only see that the woman's hair is long and black. Beth prepares to say *Hello,* and she's already smiling when the woman is directly in front of her, but the woman is fixated on the ground, refusing eye contact. So Beth doesn't say *Hello,* and she feels sheepish for smiling. Grover wanders over for a sniff, but the woman skirts by too quickly and is then behind them before Beth or Grover can learn anything more about her.

Still curious after a few steps, Beth looks back over her shoulder and sees the woman at the row of mailboxes, toward the far end.

"Probably a New Yorker," she mutters as she turns around and presses on toward home.

Safe inside, Grover shakes himself, sending water everywhere. She'd normally scold him for doing this, but it doesn't matter. Just opening the door splashed a bucket's worth of water into the mudroom. She removes her hat and coat, and the mail falls to the ground. She kicks off her boots. She's soaked through.

She peels off her wet socks and jeans, tosses them into the laundry room, and slips into a pair of fleece pajama bottoms and a pair of slippers. Feeling warmer and drier and immediately happier, she returns to the front door to collect the mail from the floor, then walks back to the couch. Grover has returned to the braided rug.

The first piece of mail is the heating bill, which will probably be more than their monthly mortgage payment. She decides to open it later. The next is a Victoria's Secret catalog. She ordered one push-up bra three Christmases ago, and they still keep sending her catalogs. She'll toss it into the fire. The last piece of mail is an envelope hand-addressed to her. She opens it. It's a card with a birthday cake pictured on the front.

May all your wishes come true.

Huh, that's strange, she thinks. Her birthday isn't until October.

Inside, the words *Happy Birthday* have been crossed out with a single, confident ballpoint blue line. Below it, someone has written:

I'm sleeping with Jimmy.
PS. He loves me.

It takes her a few seconds to reread it, to make sure she's comprehending the words. She's aware of her heart pounding as she picks up the envelope again. *Who sent this?* There's no return address, but the postmark is stamped from Nantucket. She doesn't recognize the handwriting. The penmanship is neat and loopy, a woman's. Another woman's.

Holding the envelope in one hand and the card in the other, she looks up at the fireplace mantel, at her perfectly centered wedding picture, and swallows. Her mouth has gone dry.

She gets up and walks to the fireplace. She slides the iron screen aside. She tosses the Victoria's Secret catalog onto the fire and watches the edges curl and blacken as it burns and turns to gray ash. Gone. Her hands are shaking. She clenches the envelope and card. If she burns them now, she can pretend she never saw them. This never existed.

A swirl of unexpected emotion courses through her. She feels fear and fury, panic and humiliation. She feels nauseous, like she's going to be sick. But what she doesn't feel is surprised.

She closes the gate. With the card and envelope squeezed in her fist, she marches up the stairs, emphasizing each loud step as she heads toward Jimmy's snoring.

CHAPTER 2

⁓

Olivia strips down to her underwear and changes into sweatpants, socks, and her oldest, favorite Boston College sweatshirt. Drier but still freezing, she hurries downstairs to the living room and presses the button on the remote to the fireplace. She stands in front of the instant blaze and waits and waits, but it doesn't throw off any noticeable heat. She touches the glass with the palm of her hand. It's barely warm. It was David's idea to convert the fireplace to gas. Better for the tenants. More convenient and less messy.

Although they've owned the cottage for eleven years, she and David have never actually lived here. They bought it as an investment just before the housing market boomed and prices skyrocketed. David, a business major who reluctantly stepped into his family's real estate business after college, is always keeping his eye on properties with potential. He's all about location, location, location. He looks for a fixer-upper in the right neighborhood, buys it, hires contractors to renovate the kitchen and baths and to paint the interior and the exterior, then he sells it. The goal is always to flip it fast, a SOLD sign on the front lawn and a tidy profit sitting fat and pretty in his pocket.

But Nantucket was different for David. With almost 50 percent of the island designated as conservation and "forever wild," leaving only half of the almost fifty square miles buildable, David wasn't interested in flipping this house. He assured Olivia that the property value would never dip below what they paid for it. The house is nothing special, a modest three-bedroom cottage with little remarkable about any of the rooms or layout. But situated less than a mile from Fat Ladies Beach, it's a highly desirable vacation property, and David correctly guessed that they would always more than cover their annual mortgage payments with summer rentals.

It's a smart investment for our future, he'd said, back when they could so blissfully imagine a future.

They stayed in the house for a week or two each year in the shoulder seasons, usually in October, but stopped coming altogether after Anthony turned three. Pretty much everything stopped after Anthony turned three.

A violent gust of wind screams in the distance, sounding to Olivia like a small child crying out in pain. The windows rattle, and a cold breeze dances along the skin of her bare neck. She shivers. Nantucket in winter. This is going to take some getting used to.

She rubs the palms of her hands together, trying to create some friction to warm them. Dissatisfied, she wonders where she might find a blanket. She's only been here nine days, and she's still learning where everything is, still feeling like a guest in someone else's home. A stranger at the inn. She searches the linen closet, finds a gray, woolen blanket she vaguely remembers buying, wraps it around her shoulders, and snuggles into the living-room chair with the mail.

The bills are still sent to their house in Hingham, a small, suburban town on Boston's South Shore, so she hasn't yet received anything but home-repair-service advertisements, local election postcards, and coupon flyers, but today she knows she has some real mail.

Before even opening the first, she knows it's a book from her old boss, Louise, a senior editor at Taylor Krepps. The envelope has a yellow forwarding-address sticker on it. Louise doesn't know that Olivia has moved to Nantucket. She doesn't know about Anthony either.

She doesn't know anything.

Olivia hasn't worked as a junior editor to Louise in self-help books at Taylor Krepps Publishing for five years now, but Louise still sends her advance reader copies. Maybe it's Louise's way of keeping the door open, of trying to entice Olivia back to work. Olivia suspects Louise has simply never gotten around to taking her off the mailing list. Olivia's never hinted to Louise that she'd ever come back; it's been a couple of years since she's sent a note thanking her or commenting on a book, and even longer since she's read any of them. But they keep coming.

She doesn't have the heart or stomach to read anybody's self-help anymore. She's no longer interested in anyone's advice or wisdom. What do they know? What does it matter? It's all bunk.

She used to believe in the power of self-help books to educate, inform, and inspire. She believed that the really good ones could transform lives. When Anthony turned three and they were told with certainty what they were dealing with, she believed she'd find somebody somewhere who could help them, an expert who could transform their lives.

She scoured every self-help book, then every medical journal, every memoir, every blog, every online parent support network. She read Jenny McCarthy and the Bible. She read and hoped and prayed and believed in anything claiming help, rescue, reversal, salvation. Somebody somewhere must know something. Somebody must have the key that would unlock her son.

She opens the envelope and holds the book in her hands, rubbing the smooth cover with her fingers. She still loves the feel of a new book. This one is called *The Three Day Miracle Diet* by Peter Fallon, MD.

Hmph. Miracle, my ass.

She used to attend conferences and seminars. *Please, expert Dr. So-and-So, show us the answer. I believe in you.* She used to go to church every Sunday. *Please, God, give us a miracle. I believe in you.*

Sorry, Dr. Fallon. There are no miracles, she thinks, and tosses the book to the floor.

She holds up the cardboard envelope from David next, staring at it for a long moment before carefully tearing the tab and upending it.

Three white, round, perfectly smooth rocks fall into her lap. She smiles. Anthony's rocks. And three of them. She shakes the envelope. There aren't any more. He would've liked that there are only three and not one or two or four. He loved things that came in threes. The Little Pigs, One-Two-Three-Go, Small-Medium-Big. Of course, he never said the words to her, *Mom, I like the "Three Little Pigs" story.* But she knew.

She rolls the three small rocks in the palm of her hand, enjoying the cool, smooth feel of them. When she's done with the mail, she'll add them to the glass bowl on the coffee table already containing at least fifty more of Anthony's white, round rocks. A shrine in a bowl.

Anthony wouldn't have liked his rocks in Olivia's bowl on the coffee table, however. He preferred them lined up like perfectly straight rock parades on the floor, all over the house. Heaven forbid Olivia should ever clean up and put his rocks back in his box in his bedroom. But sometimes, she couldn't help herself. Sometimes she simply wanted to walk through the house and not kick through a rock parade. Sometimes she simply wanted to walk through a normal house. It was always a huge mistake. They didn't live in a normal house. And change, however small, was never Anthony's friend.

She peeks into the envelope and sees a folded piece of stationery.

Found these three under the couch.
Love, David

She smiles, thanking him for taking the time to send her three rocks, for knowing she'd want them. And the *Love, David*. She knows these words aren't throwaway or insincere. She still loves him, too.

The rest of Anthony's rocks are in his box, now in her bedroom. It was one of the few things she insisted on bringing with her on her final trip over, and it was no small feat getting it here. She lugged it, sweating and questioning her sanity, from the backseat of David's car to the ferry in Hyannis, from the ferry to the taxi in Town, from the taxi to her bedroom here. More than once she thought about dumping the rocks overboard on the way over, freeing herself from the physical and emotional burden of carrying all the damn rocks. But they're Anthony's damn rocks. Beautiful damn rocks collected from the beach and obsessively lined up in rows by her beautiful boy, now artfully displayed in the glass bowl on the coffee table.

So the damn rocks came with her. She left behind her cookbooks, her collection of books she helped edit at Taylor Krepps, all of her novels. She didn't take any of the furniture, the appliances, or any dishware. She left Anthony's clothes still folded in his drawers, his bed unmade, his Barney DVDs in the TV console cabinet, all of the educational toys he never played with, his toothbrush in the holder in the bathroom, his coat on the hook by the front door.

She brought her clothes, her jewelry, her camera, and her computer. And she brought her journals. Someday, she'll have the courage to read them.

She also left all of her photographs—her college album, their wedding and honeymoon albums, the collection of arty shots she used to take of sunsets and trees and seashells, the best of which adorn the walls of their house, Anthony's baby album. She left it all with David. She feels as if that life didn't happen to her. It happened to some other woman.

She kept only one picture. She looks up at the eight-by-ten photograph framed, matted, and hung on the wall over the fireplace, that one picture that took many hours over many days of patient waiting to get. She remembers how she sat cross-legged in front of the refrigerator, camera over her face, finger on the button, ready to click, waiting. Waiting. Anthony passed by her many times, skipping on his toes, squealing and flapping his hands. Each time she held her breath. She didn't move. He didn't look at her.

One day he sat down only a couple of feet in front of her and spun the back wheel of a toy truck with his index finger for at least an hour. She didn't get up and demonstrate how to play with the truck appropriately. *See, Anthony, the truck goes vroom, vroom.* She didn't redirect him. She didn't move. He didn't look at her.

With each attempt, her knees, arms, and ass would eventually ache and scream for her to shift position. Her mind would try to talk her out of it, too, mocking her for wasting another morning sitting on the floor like an idiot. She ignored herself and sat, silent, unthreatening, invisible.

Then finally, it happened. He looked directly into the lens. He was probably thirsty, looking to the refrigerator, wanting juice. It was probably a complete accident, but she clicked the button before his eyes darted away. She looked at the LCD display, and there they were. His eyes! Wide-open windows into a shiny, clear day. Not disconnected or wandering eyes. Deep, dark, melted-chocolate-brown eyes belonging to her little boy, looking at his mother. Seeing her.

She sits on the living-room chair with the mail in her lap and loses herself in his eyes, wiping tears from hers, grateful for the chance to look into them and see real meaning, even if she doesn't understand what that meaning is, even if it was only one moment in almost nine long years, and even if she only ever saw them like this through her Nikon lens and then on two-dimensional paper. She's grateful to have it.

She wipes her eyes again with the edge of the blanket and turns her attention to the last piece of mail, a manila envelope from the law offices of Kaufman and Renkowitz. Olivia slides out the stack of papers and reads the top of the first page.

Separation Agreement for David and Olivia Donatelli

She closes her eyes and listens to the wind and rain banging at the windows, pounding on the roof, raging all around her. She tucks the blanket over her feet and holds on tight to the three rocks still inside her hand. Like everything, this storm can only last so long.

CHAPTER 3

⌒⌒

Facing away from her side of the bed with their puffy down comforter pulled up to his chin, Jimmy is still sound asleep.

"Jimmy," Beth says loudly, just shy of shouting, startling even herself.

He lurches upright. "Huh? What?"

Jimmy doesn't wake up well, never has. His thinking is all jumbled at first, staggering around and bumping into the walls of his skull as if he'd just thrown back six beers. He wouldn't be able to recite the alphabet or the full names of his three girls within the first few seconds of waking. He might not even know he has three girls right now. She hesitates, giving him a minute to let the fog clear from between his ears. Or maybe she hesitates because she's giving herself one more minute of not going where they're about to go.

"What is it?" he asks, rubbing his eyes and nose.

"What's this?" She throws the card and envelope at him, aiming for his head. But they're like a poorly constructed paper airplane, fluttering weakly onto his lap instead of smacking him in the face. He picks up the card.

"It's not my birthday," he says, still rubbing his eyes.

"Open it." She shakes with anticipation as he does.

"I don't get it."

"Don't act dumb. Who sent this?"

"Hold on, let me get my glasses."

So now he's dumb and blind. What next? Deaf? As much as a part of her doesn't want to hear his answer, another part of her can't resist it, compelling her toward what feels inevitable.

Jimmy reaches for his glasses on the night table, puts them on, and reads the card again. He opens and closes and opens it, studying it as if it were a crossword puzzle or one of Sophie's algebra problems, like it's some kind of test.

It is a test, Jimmy. It's a test of your integrity. This is a test of your character.

She watches his face as he keeps his eyes focused on this most mysterious riddle, refusing to look up at her. He's stalling.

"It's not the tax code, Jimmy. Who sent this?"

"I have no idea."

He's looking at her now. They pause here, eyes locked, unblinking, unmoving, nobody saying a word. A showdown.

Jimmy ends it by getting out of bed and tossing the card and envelope into the wastebasket. He then walks past her and down the hall. She hears the bathroom door shut. Apparently, he's said all he has to say about the card. Incensed, adrenaline now surging through her veins, she retrieves the card and envelope from the wastebasket and storms down the hall to the closed bathroom door.

Manners stop her with her hand on the doorknob. She and Jimmy aren't one of those couples who share bathroom intimacy. She doesn't floss while he sits on the toilet, he doesn't chat with her while she's in the shower, she doesn't change tampons while he shaves. She wouldn't normally go in. They don't have that kind of marriage.

But what kind of marriage do they have? She shoves the bathroom door open and stares at him as he stands over the toilet.

"Jesus, Beth, can you give me a minute?"

"I'd like a real answer."

"Hold on a second."

"Tell me who sent this."

"Wait."

He flushes. He turns and faces her. She's standing in the doorway, arms folded across her chest, blocking the way out. He's wearing nothing but plaid boxers and glasses, his hair mussed, his hands hanging heavy by his sides, looking vulnerable, defenseless. Caught.

"You don't know her."

The joints of her legs suddenly loosen, and she leans into the doorframe, steadying herself. She feels like she's standing on train tracks, tied to the rails, staring at the oncoming train, so close she can feel the hot wind on her face from its relentless forward motion.

"Who is she?" she asks with slightly less demand and a lot more fear clinging to each word.

"Her name is Angela."

There it is. He admits it. This is really happening. He's cheating on her with a woman named Angela. She fights through crashing waves of dizziness and thickening nausea, trying to picture Angela, but she can't come up with a face. She's not a real woman if she doesn't have a face. Maybe this isn't really happening.

"Angela who?"

"Melo."

Angela Melo. It's the dead of winter on a fourteen-mile-long-by-three-mile-wide island. Everyone knows everyone. But he's right. Angela Melo. She doesn't know her. Petra will.

"Do you call her Angie?"

He sighs and fidgets his feet, his face struggling, as if only now has she asked him something too personal. "Yes."

She focuses on the blankness of the white tile wall behind him, unable to inhale. Jimmy's been having sex with a woman named Angela Melo. Angie. He's been naked with her, kissing her mouth, her breasts, her everything. She wonders if he uses a condom, but she's too embarrassed and disgusted by the thought to ask him.

She walks back to their bedroom and sits on her side of the bed, not sure of what to do or say or feel next. She wishes she could go back in time and undo this. Crawl back into bed, wake up, and start the day over. And not get the mail. Jimmy has followed her and is standing over her, waiting.

"How long?" she asks.

"A while."

"How long is a while?"

He hesitates. "Since July."

She doesn't know what she was expecting him to say. She hadn't developed any specific suspicions or scenarios in her imagination. A few stolen nights. Maybe a month or two. Since July? She ticks off the months in her head. Too many stolen nights for her to count or imagine. Hot tears start streaming down her face.

Damn it, Beth, don't cry. Don't fall apart.

She doesn't want to feel like a victim. Like a cliché. But she can't help it. She gives in and sobs on her side of the bed against her own will while Jimmy continues to stand a few feet away from her.

"Do you love her?" she asks, choking out each word, shaken and airy.

"No."

She studies her hands in her lap, her engagement and wedding rings on her finger, rings that came with vows that didn't protect her from this, afraid to look at him, to see if he's telling the truth or lying. He's been lying to her for months now, so maybe he's lying about this. Would she know the truth if she saw his eyes? What does she really know about him now? Ten minutes ago she would've said, *Everything*.

She closes her eyes and retreats into crying. Something has to happen now. She can't simply walk downstairs, finish her cocoa, and vacuum the house.

"I think you should go," she says. "I think you should move out."

He's still. Beth quiets her crying and holds her breath, holding on for his reply.

"Okay."

Then he's in motion. He's at the closet, pulling clothes from hangers, he's at his dresser, emptying drawers. He's stuffing his gym bag.

She wants to let out a scream, but her voice is too devastated for sound. *Okay?* He's not even putting up a fight. He's not apologizing or begging for forgiveness. *Okay?* He's not asking her to work on this with him, to let him stay.

He wants to go.

She wants to hit him, shake him, hurt him. She wants to throw something hard and heavy at him. She considers her iron bedside lamp. She wants to hate him. But to her shame and confusion, she also wants to hug him, soothe him, stop him. She wants to tell him that everything will be okay. She wants to go to him and kiss him the way they used to kiss. Those deep, long kisses that melted her.

Now he's kissing some woman named Angie and melting her.

He's banging around in the bathroom now, probably gathering his things from the medicine cabinet. She looks over to the indent where he was just sleeping. Was he with Angie last night before coming home to sleep and snore here?

She can't sit on this bed, their bed, for one second longer. She gets up and begins stripping it. Still crying, she tugs the comforter, the blanket, and each sheet off the mattress and whips them into a heaping, defeated pile on the floor. As she's peeling the pillowcases off the pillows, she notices Jimmy's socks lying on the floor, lazy and careless, waiting for her to pick them up and put them in the hamper. She's always picking up his stinky socks. His stinky socks, his dirty underwear, his coat, his shoes, his crumbs all over the floor from the pastrami sandwiches and chips he eats without using a plate, the gobs of dried toothpaste spit he leaves in the sink, the sand he always tracks throughout the house. She's picking up his stinky socks and wiping up his crumbs and sand and spit and doing his laundry while he's out having an affair.

Jimmy appears at the foot of the bed, carrying his gym bag and their big red suitcase, the one they bought at Kmart in Hyannis for their road trip to Disney World back in October. Back in October, when he was cheating on her with Angie Melo.

"I'll call you," he says, sounding reluctant.

"Uh-huh," she says, holding all of their bedding and his dirty socks in her arms, trying not to look at him.

He stands there, struggling to say something more, possibly hoping for her to say something more, for her to stop him. She can't be sure. She sneaks a quick glance at him. His face is pained, tears pooled in his eyes. She looks away. He doesn't say anything. She doesn't either. He turns and walks down the stairs. She doesn't move an inch until she hears the sound of the front door closing behind him.

In the laundry room, she carefully measures out the detergent. The engine of Jimmy's truck turns. She pours the liquid fabric softener into the dispenser. He backs out of the driveway. She turns the dial to SHEETS and presses START. His truck shifts into first gear and rumbles down their street. She watches the hot water pour onto their bedding. Steam fills the barrel of the washing machine. Everything begins to spin.

He's gone.

She walks into the kitchen, stands at the sink, stares out the window, and does nothing. She doesn't know what to do. With determined effort, she directs her thoughts over to her routine, hoping the comfort and safety of her daily schedule might counter the wild panic rising mightily within her.

She still needs to vacuum the house. And she can get dinner started in the Crock-Pot soon. She's making chicken-noodle soup. And she'll bake brownies for dessert. The girls get out of school at two. Sophie has drama club, Jessica has basketball, and Gracie has a playdate.

She won't tell them, of course. Not today. They won't notice. Jimmy's hardly ever home for dinner or bedtime.

She stands at the sink, motionless. The wind screams. The radiator hisses.

Jimmy is gone.

She takes a deep breath and releases it through her mouth. Okay, time to vacuum. But first, before she does anything, she's calling Petra.

CHAPTER 4

⌒⌒

I t's predawn and still dark out. Not pitch-black the way it is
on Nantucket nights that are moonless and starless, when
she can't see her hand in front of her nose. The world around
her is colored like a photographic blueprint, an anticipation-
of-morning shade of blue-gray. But it's also foggy, which is
typical at this early hour, especially near the shore, and the lack
of visibility makes it seem darker than it really is. Even with the
headlights of her Jeep on and the windshield wipers flapping
as fast as they can, Olivia is having a hard time seeing where
she's going. She drives slowly, carefully. She's in no hurry.

The Wauwinet Gatehouse is empty. She parks the Jeep, gets
out, and releases air from all four tires to 12 psi. She climbs
back in and continues, the road changing now from pavement
to sand. The sand turns soft, and her Jeep dips, bounces, and
sways as she inches along. The fog is even thicker here. She can
see nothing to either side and only a few feet in front of her.

Maybe a little over four miles into this drive—she can't be
sure, not having seen any landmarks along the way—the path
is blocked by fencing. Vehicles are restricted from further progress down the beach, an effort to protect the endangered piping

plovers who might unwittingly nest in the tire tracks. She parks her Jeep at the fence and gets out.

She hikes through deep, smooth, wind-caressed sand along the ocean that she can hear and smell but not see, the fog still obscuring everything. It can't be far now. She pulls a flashlight from her coat pocket and aims it in front of her, but the beam of light scatters, diffusing among the water molecules suspended in the air, proving useless. She presses on. She knows where she's going.

When the soft give of the sand changes to firm ground, wet from an earlier high tide, she exhales with relief. Each step is finally easy to take. Despite the cold, she's sweating, and her leg muscles burn. She licks her lips, enjoying the taste of sea salt. Still unable to see the water, she knows it's directly in front of her now and is disappointed that she can't see the lighthouse, which must be only a few feet from her path, hidden behind the wall of fog.

Great Point Light has been destroyed twice, once by fire and once by storm, rebuilt both times. A seventy-foot, cylindrical tower of white stone, it stands resilient and majestic on this fragile pile of sand, where the Atlantic Ocean meets Nantucket Sound, its existence continually threatened by erosion and gale-force winds. Surviving.

Aside from the gulls and maybe a few piping plovers, she expects to be alone here. From May to September, she imagines this seven-mile stretch of beach is probably crawling with four-wheel-drive vehicles, hikers, families led on natural-history tours, people on vacation. But on March seventeenth, no one is here. She's alone, thirty miles of water separating her from Cape Cod to the north and about thirty-five hundred miles of ocean between where she stands and Spain to the east. It's the closest place to nowhere that she can think of. And nowhere is exactly where she wants to be today.

In the past, not that long ago, being this far away from anyone or anything else would not have been appealing to her. More than that, it would've scared her. A woman alone on a secluded beach, miles from anyone who might hear her if she needed help—like most girls, she'd been taught to avoid this kind of situation. But now, she's not only unafraid, she prefers it. She's not worried for a second about being raped or murdered out here alone on Great Point. Walking through safe, suburban Hingham, surrounded by ordinary people doing everyday things—that was what had been killing her.

The chips-and-snacks aisle in the grocery store. A Little League baseball game in progress. St. Christopher's Church. Escalators at the mall. Her old friends blessed with typical children, one innocently bragging about her daughter in the school play, another unassumingly complaining that third-grade math isn't challenging enough for her son. She avoids them all.

All of those places and people and things are charged, filled with memories of Anthony or the Anthony she prayed for or the Anthony that might have been. And they all have the potential to turn her inside out in an instant, to make her cry, hide, scream, curse God, stop breathing, go insane. Any and sometimes all of the above.

She would drive many blocks out of her way to the bank or the gas station so she wouldn't have to lay eyes on her church. She stopped answering the phone. Last summer at the grocery store, she noticed a boy she guessed was about Anthony's age walking alongside his mother. Olivia was fine until the chips-and-snacks aisle, when the boy asked, *Mom, can we get these?* He was holding up a can of salt-and-vinegar Pringles, Anthony's favorite. Without warning, all of the oxygen vanished from the store. She was paralyzed, gulping for air, drowning in panic. As soon as she could move, she ran from the store, abandoning her cart full of food, and cried in her car for almost an hour before she could collect herself enough to drive home.

She hasn't stepped foot in the chips-and-snacks aisle since. It isn't safe there.

The world is littered with traps like salt-and-vinegar Pringles that swallow her whole, which would be fine with her except that they eventually spit her back out and say, *Carry on, now.* Everyone wants her to carry on now. Carry on. Move on. She doesn't want to. She wants to be here, alone on Great Point, far away from all the traps. Standing still, moving nowhere.

She squats down and writes *Happy Birthday Anthony* with her index finger in the wet sand. He would've been ten today.

She remembers the day he was born. His birth was uncomplicated but long. She'd wanted a natural childbirth, but after twenty hours of painful and unproductive labor, she surrendered and asked for an epidural. Two hours, a hint of Pitocin, and six pushes later, Anthony was born. Pinkish purple, the color of petunias, calm and wide-eyed. She loved him instantly. He was beautiful and full of promise, her baby boy who would someday play Little League baseball, star in the school play, and be good at math. She didn't know then that she should've had much simpler dreams for her beautiful son, that she should've looked upon her newborn baby boy and thought, *I hope you learn to talk and use the bathroom by the time you're seven.*

His first couple of birthdays were normal—cakes she chose and bought at the bakery, candles that Olivia blew out, presents that she and David opened and acted overly delighted and animated about. But he was only one and two years old, so this was to be expected. After two, birthdays began deviating further and further away from normal.

Anthony stopped getting invited to other kids' birthday parties when he was four, and when he turned five, she and David followed in turn, hosting private celebrations, family only. It was easier this way. Anthony didn't participate in the party games or pay attention to the birthday clown anyway. It still broke her heart.

And while the maturing interests of other little boys his age were reflected in the party themes with each passing year—from Elmo to Bob the Builder to Spider-Man to *Star Wars*—Anthony had and was perfectly pleased with a Barney birthday year after year. Sure, she could've gone with another character. But there was no point in pretending that he loved superheroes or robots or ninjas. He loved Barney, and there wouldn't be any other little boys at his parties to tease him for loving a purple dinosaur.

So each year, Olivia and David lit the candles on his Barney cake and sang "Happy Birthday." Then she'd say, *Come on, Anthony! Make a wish and blow out your candles!* And then he wouldn't, so she'd blow them out for him. She always made a wish, the same one every year.

Please don't get older. You have to talk before you get any older. You have to say "Mom" and "Dad" and "I'm six years old" and "I want to go to the playground today" and "I love you, Mom" before we put another damn Barney cake on the kitchen table. Please stop getting older. We're running out of time.

She never stopped wishing.

They went through the motions every year, but his birthday was not a fun day for her or David. Instead of celebrating like other parents whom she imagined and so passionately envied and sometimes hated, instead of marveling over the past year and how much her child had changed and grown, she and David felt only unspoken dread and desperation on Anthony's birthday. March seventeenth was the one day each year when they were forced to stare the severity of Anthony's autism straight in the eye, to be fully cognizant of how much progress he hadn't made. When she shopped for his present and considered toys for age five-plus or ages five and up, she would be forced to admit to herself that these toys would hold no interest for him, that he couldn't possibly play with any of them. There it was, printed on too many Fisher-Price boxes—Anthony was impossibly behind for his age.

So she would buy him an educational toy recommended by Carlin, his applied-behavioral-analysis therapist, or a new Barney video, or one year she wrapped a can of salt-and-vinegar Pringles. Pringles always made him happy. But the gift he loved the most each year was the card.

When he was four, she bought him the first of countless musical greeting cards. This one was a Hoops & Yoyo. She showed him first. He watched, pretending not to look. She opened the card. A song played and the characters sang. She shut the card. The music and the singing stopped.

To this day, she remembers his face, wondrous and joyful with the unexpected discovery of a new fascination, like when he found light switches. He opened the card. Music. He shut it. No music. Open. Music. Shut. No music. These cards were heaven to Anthony. The same song every time it's opened, the same music; everything the card did was predictable and entirely under his control.

He'd spend the rest of the day smiling and squealing and flapping his hands as he opened, shut, opened, shut, opened, shut. That's all he wanted every year. Unlimited time alone with his card. So this is what she and David gave to him.

She wonders how David is doing, if he's awake yet, realizing the date, thinking about Anthony. She hopes he finds comfort today. Her heart aches thinking this, wishing she could be this to him. But she can't. Comfort doesn't exist within her, and she can't offer what she doesn't have. He doesn't have it either. They know this.

Olivia sits on the beach, waiting for sunrise, listening to a gull squawking above her, sounding like laughter. The tide is coming in. With each pulse of waves, she watches as a little more of *Happy Birthday Anthony* washes away, until it's pulled into the sea entirely. Wiped clean, as if it never existed. If she still believed in God, she would ask Him to send her birthday note written in sand to her son in heaven. But she doesn't ask for this. These are only words scratched in sand with her finger, swallowed by the ocean.

In front of her feet, she writes *I love you* and waits. The water comes, steady and sure, pooling and bubbling into each letter. The words wash away, reaching no one.

The fog has started to lift, and the day begins to lighten. The metallic-gray ocean tumbles out in front of her. The lighthouse materializes to her left. The next wave crashes, dissolving into a bed of fizzing foam, and deposits a single white, round rock at her feet. Her heart stalls, then quickens. She squats down, picks up the beautiful, smooth stone, and rolls it inside her hand.

Anthony.

I miss you, my sweet boy.

The sun rises, glowing pink on the horizon over the ocean, the color of petunias, beautiful and full of promise.

CHAPTER 5

⌒ ᴄ ᴏ ⌒

B eth and Petra are sitting in Jill's living room, waiting for
Courtney and Georgia. It's book club night, but Courtney teaches yoga on Thursday evenings, and her class doesn't
get over until six thirty, so they know she'll be running a bit
late. And Georgia is always late. Jill knows this, but she's still
irritated. She's holding them in the living room until everyone
arrives because she wants the entire group to see the dining
room at the same time. She's imagining a grand entrance.

Beth is growing antsy, too. Petra's planning on outing her
tonight, and Beth is feeling less and less certain about this decision each time Jill sighs. It's not that she doesn't want her
girlfriends to know that Jimmy's having an affair and has
moved out. She doesn't want the whole island to know. And
they will—Len, the school principal; Patty, the checkout
woman at Stop & Shop; Lisa, Beth's hairdresser; Jessica's basketball coach.

But Petra's right. Beth needs to stand tall in her truth, draw
strength from the collective love of her friends, and something
else. Another platitude from Petra's pep talk earlier today
sounded good at the time. Beth can't remember it now. Petra

reads a lot of inspirational books. She also reads tarot cards and sees a shaman once a month instead of a regular therapist. A lot of people on the island think Petra's a little cuckoo. While Beth agrees that Petra can lean a bit eccentric, she also believes Petra possesses an inner wisdom that most people never know, a spiritual center that Beth admires and is drawn to and is certain that she herself lacks.

Plus, honesty, friendship, and New Age mumbo jumbo aside, it's nothing short of a miracle that Jimmy's affair isn't public knowledge already anyway. Beth knows. Petra knows. Jimmy and Angela know that Beth knows, so they're probably less careful now. Someone from the restaurant must know. And that someone will sooner or later tell someone who will tell Jill or Courtney or Jessica's basketball coach.

And the girls now know that he's moved out. Sophie was the first to notice that Dad wasn't inhabiting any of his usual spots—the bed, the couch, his cigar chair. *Where's Dad?* turned out to be a harder question to answer than *What's sex?* or *Have you ever smoked pot?* Beth teetered her way through her answer, purposefully keeping the explanation short and vague (and honest—she doesn't know exactly where he is either), a vain attempt to protect them from having the kind of father who would cheat on their mother. So the girls know that he's not living at home, but they don't know the ugly reason. Yet. Sadly, their father is, in fact, cheating on their mother, and it's only a matter of time before everyone on Nantucket, including his three beautiful daughters, knows it.

Beth picks up the copy of *Nantucket Life* from Jill's coffee table and thumbs through it, hoping for distraction while Jill frets about how late it's getting. Beth agrees. It's taking too long to get started. She feels like she's in the waiting room at her dentist's office, knowing that she needs to get her teeth cleaned and that they'll look and feel great when she's done, but the waiting around gives her anxiety and her memory too

much time to play together. She'll begin to fixate on the anticipated sound of the metal instruments scraping against her
teeth, the throbbing soreness in her gums, the shame she feels
when the hygienist scolds her for not flossing enough, the taste
of latex and blood in her mouth. If she has to wait more than
ten minutes for the hygienist to call out her name, it takes every ounce of self-control she possesses not to leave for another
six months.

Her hygienist and dentist are going to know that Jimmy is
cheating on her.

Beth tries to forget about Jimmy and her dentist and what
she and Petra talked about earlier and focus on Jill. She's telling them a story about Mickey's latest transplant project. Jill's
husband, Mickey, runs his own construction company. The
most incredible jobs he contracts aren't new construction or
elaborate additions, but the moving of existing homes a few
critical feet. The historic cottages and mansions positioned on
the cliffs in 'Sconset are all in imminent danger of tumbling
over with the eroding edge, as if each home were sitting on
a piece of pie, and every year Mother Nature carves out another bite with her fork. Mickey's crew can miraculously move
an entire house back, one hundred feet, four hundred feet,
but eventually the owner will run out of frontage. The front
door will be at the road. There'll be nothing left but crust, and
Mother Nature will still be hungry.

Mickey's now transplanting a seven-bedroom monstrosity
on Baxter Road, but this one's different. The owners recently
bought the house directly across the street. Mickey's crew
razed it, and now they're moving the cliff house to the other
side of Baxter, to an entirely new piece of pie. Only on Nantucket.

"Crazy, huh? Mickey says if he lives long enough, he'll
move that house again," says Jill.

"This is why I live mid-island," says Petra, who lives mid-island because that's where she grew up and because she can't afford to live closer to the ocean.

It's a good story, but Beth is now busy testing out the believability of different exit strategies in her head and can barely keep her butt on the couch. *I forgot my book. Gracie's not feeling well. I'm not feeling well.*

Petra, who is sitting next to Beth and somehow senses her approaching flight, reaches over and discreetly slides Beth's hand between their laps. She squeezes it, firmly but not too hard, offering both comfort and an anchor. *I love you, and you're not going anywhere.*

They hear a perfunctory knock at the door, and then Courtney and Georgia enter at the same time, a study in contrasts. Courtney's round, makeup-less face is flushed pink, her hair is loosely gathered into a ponytail high on her head, her hairline is wet with sweat. She's wearing a lavender tank top under an unzipped thrift-shop winter coat, black cotton yoga pants, and flip-flops. She has her book in hand. Bright and smiling, she takes a seat on the couch on the other side of Beth, her energy floating into the room along with her, landing softly, like an airy, white dandelion puff blown in on a gentle breeze. She smells of patchouli.

Georgia, on the other hand, is hurried and harried, wearing smoky evening eye shadow, lipstick, and bold, dangling gold earrings, clomping in on her black business heels, struggling against the weight of the stuffed leather laptop bag on her shoulder, cursing the latest bridezilla who kept her on the phone for forty-five minutes agonizing over aisle runner choices, peeling off hat and gloves and scarf and coat as she apologizes for being late. If Courtney is a wispy seed sailing in on a warm breeze, Georgia is a tree limb snapped by a hurricane wind, crashing to the earth. It's hard to imagine from the sight of them that Courtney and Georgia are best friends, but they are.

Relieved and now called to action, Jill excuses herself and runs into her kitchen. Before Georgia can sit down, Jill returns, claps her hands twice like a schoolteacher demanding her class's attention, and ushers the group into her dining room. Georgia is the first to gasp, then they all do. Jill beams, delighting in all the oohs and aahs, gratified to have elicited the exact reaction she'd imagined.

The book this month takes place in post–World War II Japan, and clearly Jill was inspired by this setting. An origami animal sits on the center of each plate—a purple crane, a white swan, an orange tiger, a green turtle, a gray elephant. A gob of green wasabi and a neat pile of fleshy, pink ginger are placed to the right of each paper animal, and each plate is flanked by a pair of chopsticks and a tiny bowl filled with soy sauce. White tea lights are scattered around the room, and two bottles of sake are on the table. California, salmon, and tuna rolls are displayed on an oval platter at the center of it all.

"Wow, Jill. Tell me you didn't roll these yourself," says Courtney.

"Of course she did," says Georgia.

"I did," admits Jill.

"And did you make these, too?" asks Courtney, holding up a purple paper crane.

"It wasn't hard. They have simple directions on the Internet," says Jill.

"It wasn't hard for you. You're amazing," says Courtney. "You must've been preparing all day."

"It didn't take that long," says Jill, taking great pleasure in all the fuss.

"You could do this for a living," says Beth.

Jill's been a stay-at-home mom for sixteen years, and she certainly doesn't need to work as long as Mickey keeps moving houses, but it's not a bad idea. She could hire herself out to the wealthy summer residents, hosting lavish book club parties. They'd love her.

"Okay, now everyone choose a seat. Each place card has the name of one of the characters, so you'll—"

"We're not talking about the book tonight," says Petra.

Beth's stomach tightens. She wishes she could at least down a glass of sake before they dive into this.

"What?" Jill smiles nervously. "Of course we are."

"No, we're not," says Petra.

Petra is five years younger than the youngest of them, but she's without question the alpha male of the group. The oldest of seven children, daughter of Polish immigrants, and owner of Dish, one of Nantucket's most beloved restaurants, Petra is tough and bossy and will say with a shameless, crooked smile that she comes by it naturally. But she's also fair-minded, and there's not a nasty bone in her tall body. If anyone can derail Jill's book club extravaganza without tears or a friendship-ending argument, it's Petra.

"And we need something stronger than sake. You have any vodka?" asks Petra.

"But that's not Japanese," says Jill, still trying to resist the suggestion of deviating in any way from the book's theme.

"Jimmy's cheating on Beth with the hostess at Salt, and he moved out," says Petra.

Again, Georgia is the first to gasp. Jill turns to Beth and absorbs the fear and apology in Beth's eyes. Without another word about Japan, she walks into her kitchen and returns to the table with a bottle of Triple Eight vodka in one hand and a bottle of Ocean Spray cranberry juice in the other.

"Will this do?" she asks as she sits down.

"Perfect," says Petra, and she begins pouring vodka into wineglasses, leaving little room for juice. "Show them the card."

Beth pulls the card and envelope out from her book and obediently passes them to Georgia.

"Oh, Beth," says Georgia after reading the card and passing it along to Courtney. "This is from the hostess at Salt? Who is she?"

"Angela Melo," says Beth.

"I don't know her," says Jill, skeptical of there being anyone on Nantucket whom she doesn't know.

"She's only been here a couple of years. She's from Brazil. Came over with her sister as summer help," says Petra. "They applied for jobs at Dish, but I couldn't use them."

"I don't know her either," says Courtney. "How long has this been going on?"

"Since July," says Beth.

"Oh my God, Beth," says Jill.

"I know," says Beth.

She takes a big gulp of vodka from her wineglass. It's warm, it doesn't have enough cranberry juice, and it scorches the back of her throat. The sake would've been better. Talking about the book would've been better. She tips down another big gulp.

"I told you not to let him work at Salt," says Georgia. "That place is too sexy. The music, those martinis. Even I want to have sex with someone after I've spent an hour in that place."

Jimmy used to scallop from October to March and bartend a few shifts here and there over the summers when scalloping is prohibited. But he never actually needed to bartend. Nantucket scallopers used to make great money. He bartended mostly to stay busy, not because he had to. Jimmy made a proud and reliable living over the years, and Beth enjoyed having him around for summer vacations with the kids.

But the scallops started disappearing from the harbor a few years ago. Then, in a frighteningly short amount of time, they were essentially gone, and Jimmy was essentially out of a job. He blames the McMansion owners with their lush, green carpet lawns laced with fertilizers that leach into the harbor, poisoning the aquatic infrastructure, killing the scallops and God knows what else.

He continued to bartend part-time in the summer, but he had no work in the winter, and for a while they had a hard time paying their bills. Jimmy moped around the house, frustrated and in denial, still hoping for the scallops to make an unlikely comeback. Then, a little over two years ago, Salt asked him to work there full-time, year-round. Year-round work of any kind is a rare and precious gem on Nantucket, and they desperately needed the money, so Jimmy the scalloper became a bartender at Salt.

"How long have you known?" asks Georgia.

"About a month," says Beth.

The longest month of her life. She's seen Jimmy three times since he'd moved out, all unannounced visits. He came by once in the morning, after the girls were already in school but before she'd had a chance to shower, to retrieve a pair of work shoes. The other two times, he came over in the evening. He milled around in the kitchen, talked to the girls, never sat down, asked if he had any phone messages. He never has any phone messages.

Each time he showed up, her heart lifted, hoping, almost assuming that he was there to tell her that he was sorry, that he'd been crazy, that he didn't want to live without her and the girls, that he wanted to come home. But he never said any of this, so her heart felt stupid and betrayed all over again. She faked indifference toward him, acting nonchalant as she peeled potatoes at the sink while he chatted with Jessica, pretending to be absorbed in a book while he bumped around the house searching for his shoes (not a chance in hell that she was going to fetch them for him, and she knew exactly where they were).

Whenever she's home now, she finds herself glancing out the windows, listening for noise in the driveway, straining her vision and her hearing, holding her breath, even checking herself out in the mirrors, making sure she looks okay, just in case.

She hates not knowing when he's going to show up next. Even more, she hates that he assumes he can simply walk through the front door whenever he wants, day or night. What if she's busy? What if it's not a good time? What if she starts having an affair, too? He can't just waltz in anymore. He moved out. She hates him for moving out. But what undoes her the most, when she allows an unguarded and honest moment to settle over her while she's peeling potatoes or looking out the window, is the thought that at some point he might never walk through the front door again.

"Do you know her?" asks Jill.

"No," says Beth.

"You haven't been to Salt yet to check her out?" asks Georgia.

"God no!" says Beth.

"I'd be dying to know who she is. You don't want to be in line with her at the bank and not know it. We should all go together and give her the evil eye. Petra, you and your witch doctor should put some kind of curse on her," says Georgia.

They all laugh, including Beth, despite her self-conscious misery. She imagines a cloth voodoo doll dressed in a miniature, black Salt T-shirt with sewing pins stuck in its eyes. She can feel the vodka now, warm in her stomach, buzzing in her head. Normally, she'd say she'd had enough. She doesn't want to feel wrecked in the morning. But she hasn't been sleeping well, and she feels wrecked most mornings anyway, so what the hell. And Petra's driving her home. She refills her wineglass with vodka.

"I don't know if I could. Maybe."

"Have you guys gone to counseling?" asks Courtney.

"No."

"Maybe you should go," says Georgia. "Phil and I used Dr. Campbell. He was good. Well, not that good, I guess, he didn't fix us. But we were beyond fixing."

Phil was Georgia's second husband, the one she loved the most. She's been married four times. Her friends will say that she's "in between husbands" now, but Georgia insists she's "divorced." End of story. She keeps a Post-it note under a refrigerator magnet at eye level: DO NOT GET MARRIED EVER AGAIN. But they all know that she will. She can't help it. She's a hopeless romantic.

As the wedding coordinator for the Blue Oyster, twice a week for at least twelve weeks a year she's surrounded by brides looking like Disney princesses in Vera Wang, grooms looking like James Bond in Armani, "Ave Maria" playing on the harp (sung or played at all four of her own ceremonies), weddings that are stunningly perfect down to the most microscopic detail. Every week each summer, she gushes about the most beautiful wedding cake she's ever seen, the most elegant bridal bouquet ever carried down the aisle, the most moving toast she's ever heard, as sincere, wide-eyed, and excited as she was for her very first bride and groom. Those weddings never get old hat to her. For Georgia, each wedding has its own real magic, a belief in true love and destiny and God that permeates her soul. Then she transfers all of that over-the-top fairy-tale romance onto whatever unsuspecting guy she's dating. Next thing they know, the Post-it note is gone from her fridge, and she's got another new last name.

"I don't know if he'd even want to," says Beth.

"Do *you* want to go to counseling?" asks Petra.

"I don't know."

"Do you want a divorce?" asks Courtney.

"I don't know."

Beth doesn't know what she wants. She wants this to be a regular book club night. She wants to drink sake and talk about Japan. She doesn't want it to be the Thursday night that everything officially and publicly changed. Her marriage, her picture-perfect life as wife and mother of three on Nantucket, is gone now. Her marriage is broken.

I'm broken, she thinks.

Tears spring from her eyes and roll down her face. Georgia

scooches her chair over toward Beth and puts her arm around her.

"I can't believe this is happening," says Beth, embarrassed to be crying in front of everyone, to have a cheating husband in front of everyone.

"You're going to be okay," says Georgia, rubbing circles with her hand on Beth's back.

"I'd divorce the bastard," says Jill.

"Jill!" scolds Petra.

"Well, he is, and I would," says Jill, looking to Georgia for support.

"You know I'd get rid of him. Already been there and done that. But I was probably too quick to end things, especially with Phil. It's something I should work on, *if* I were getting married ever again, which I'm not." Georgia lifts her wineglass in a gesture of cheers and drinks the rest of her vodka in a toast to her own proclamation.

"You have to figure out what you want," says Petra. "You and Jimmy can recover from this if you both want to. Or this is the way out. But you should decide what *you* want. Don't let him or anyone else decide for you."

Petra's right. She's always right. But Beth's head is swimming in vodka, and the only thing she can think of that she wants right now is for Georgia to keep rubbing her back.

"And we love you, no matter what you decide," says Petra.

Georgia squeezes Beth's shoulders, and everyone nods, everyone except for Courtney, who looks lost in thought, her eyebrows knotted. Beth feels drunk and embarrassed, broken and uncertain, but suddenly, surprisingly grateful.

"I love you, too," says Beth, smiling through tears, because even if Jimmy doesn't love her anymore, she feels lucky to have a handful of girlfriends who will love her no matter what.

CHAPTER 6

Mourning doves whistle back and forth in plaintive conversation while sunlight eases its way into Olivia's bedroom through the unshaded windows, bathing her in a soft and gentle glow. This is generally how she begins each day now, in synchrony with the birds and the sun. And if it's a cloudy or stormy morning and the doves aren't feeling chatty, she sleeps and sleeps, probably until at least noon. Maybe much later. She doesn't know. She's lost all track of real time. The power went out for a day last month, the first of too many times to count now, and she never bothered to reset any of the clocks. She also stopped wearing a watch. This hasn't been a problem as she has nowhere that she needs to be. She's existing outside of time.

She looks over at the other side of the bed, the comforter and the pillow unbothered, and remembers all over again that David isn't here. He's in Hingham. She's on Nantucket. Separated. She still sleeps curled on her side with one arm hugging the edge of the mattress, leaving room for him. She shimmies over to the middle of the bed and lies flat on her back, arms and legs spread wide, taking up as much space as possible. It feels strange.

She stretches and yawns, in no hurry to leave her bed, enjoying the extravagance of emerging slowly from a full night's sleep. It seems like only yesterday that she woke too early every morning to David's alarm clock or to Anthony's *eeya-eeya-eeya,* shocked into consciousness, still exhausted. More than exhausted. Eroded. A little more of her missing each day. Those mornings were just yesterday, and yet they were a million years ago. Time's a funny thing, bending, warping, stretching, and compressing, all depending on perspective.

It's April, but she only knows this because the letter she received from her lawyer the other day was dated April fourteenth. Without that letter, she would've guessed that it was still March, still winter given how cold it's been and how nothing has changed.

The springs she spent in the Boston area were unrecognizable compared to the lush, warm, green springs in Athens, Georgia, where she grew up. Spring in Boston is just another word for winter, the second half. Right about when the magnolia trees are blooming in Athens, it snows in Hingham. And not just a dusting. Snowfall in March in Hingham is school-canceling, street-plowing, where-are-we-going-to-put-it-all snow. Olivia made no secret of her hatred for March snow, but she had to admit, the white at least brightened up the barren, grim, preblossom landscape.

It doesn't snow on Nantucket the way it does near Boston. Surrounded by ocean, the air is usually too wet to support the structure of a delicate flake, and it rains instead. A couple of times here, she noticed the ground was slushy, but she never saw any actual snowfall this year and hasn't had to shovel once. She's not sure she even owns a real snow shovel here. The only shovel she can think of is in the backseat of her Jeep, kept there to dig herself out of sand, not snow, if (when) the Jeep gets stuck.

But even though it doesn't snow here like it does on the

mainland, it still doesn't feel like spring. Even on sunny days, the cold is unrelenting. And somehow everything seems tinged gray, the way the world looks through sunglasses. It's been the same cold and gray winter day for months. Time feels literally frozen here.

According to the letter from her attorney, her divorce proceedings are frozen as well. The agreement is uncontested and no-fault, their divorce being one of the few things she and David haven't fought over in a long time. She's read through the entire document three times now. She likes to linger on the words *no-fault*, typed in black and white right there on the official, legal page, as if the state of Massachusetts is acknowledging them personally, exonerating them both of any blame. The failure of their marriage wasn't really his fault or hers.

Within a few breaths of the word *autism*, Anthony's pediatric neurologist actually asked them, *How's your marriage?* Olivia remembers bristling, thinking, *What business is that of yours?* And, *We're talking about Anthony here, not me and David.* But the neurologist knew their future. He'd seen it too many times before, the comorbidity of autism and divorce.

She doesn't remember if she answered him. She doesn't remember most of whatever followed the word *autism* in that office on that day, but she's thought about his question and her answer many times since. If she managed to voice a polite reply on that day, a day she thought for sure would be the absolute worst day of her life—only to be irrefutably unseated for all time a few short and long years later—she probably said something like *Fine.* And their marriage might've remained fine had they not been pressed and pulled and gutted in ways that two married people could never have imagined when they dressed up and said *I do.*

No, they most certainly weren't fine after that day. But how could anyone be? That would be like throwing a glass vase against a brick wall and expecting it not to smash into a thousand broken pieces, acting surprised and upset that it no longer holds water. The vase will always shatter. That's what happens when glass hits brick. It's not the vase's fault.

When they were still dating after college, when they entered the "real world" and things got serious, Olivia questioned whether David was husband material. She made a mental list of necessary qualities and began checking off boxes: Handsome. Smart. Funny. Good provider. Handy around the house. Loves children. All checks. They married when she was twenty-four.

She never imagined the additional boxes she should've had on that list: Can function on little sleep for years. Willing to have his heart and will broken every day. Doesn't mind dumping all the money he earns down a bottomless drain.

Like the state of Massachusetts says—it's not his fault.

They agree on all the terms. She gets the cottage on Nantucket. He gets the house in Hingham. There's no money. They already spent all of their savings on Anthony.

Applied-behavioral-analysis therapy, speech therapy, Floortime, sensory integration, metal chelation, gluten-free diets, casein-free diets, B_{12} shots. Pediatricians, neurologists, gastroenterologists, occupational therapists, physical therapists, energy healers. From the mainstream to the alternative to the practically voodoo, Olivia doesn't remember much of any of it being covered by their health insurance. David worked more and more hours. They refinanced the houses. They emptied their IRA nest eggs. Because how could they retire with money in the bank and a son with autism, knowing that there was a therapy out there that might've helped him but they didn't try because it was too expensive?

They were about to sell the cottage.

Olivia remembers those late-night conversations in bed with the lights off, she on her side, David on his, hope and hopelessness living and breathing between them and every other word. She'd read or heard about some new treatment. *It's not FDA-approved for autism, and I agree, it sounds a bit cocka-mamy, but expert Dr. So-and-So said at this year's conference it works on a subset of kids. It costs a fortune. What do you think?* She remembers the sound of his exhale and then the silence, knowing he was nodding in the dark.

They tried it. They had to.

So there's no money left, and half of nothing is nothing. There's no alimony. And no child support, of course. That's basically it. Clean and simple. They can set each other free.

But David hasn't signed the agreement. Olivia knows he will. He just needs more time. And since time isn't going anywhere, she doesn't mind waiting.

She gets up and walks into the kitchen. She opens the cupboard and sighs. She forgot to buy more coffee.

If David were here, he'd say something like *No problem, let's go to The Bean.* Before they had Anthony, they'd make a morning of it. They'd settle into a table, hopefully the one in the corner by the front window, he'd read the *Globe,* and she'd read a book for work, he'd have two large coffees, both black, and she'd have a large latte and a blueberry scone. Every now and then he'd read part of a news story to her, and she'd share either some particularly insightful, gorgeously worded nugget of wisdom or some hideously atrocious paragraph of trash. She loved those easy, unstructured mornings, back when they were newly married.

She wishes he were here. As she stews on this a bit more, she realizes that what she's really longing for is a latte, a scone, and a leisurely morning at The Bean. She doesn't need David here for that. Seized by a sense of purpose and a desire she hasn't experienced in a long time to be out in the world, she throws on a pair of jeans and a sweater, zips her coat, grabs her hat, purse, and keys, slides her feet into her boots by the front door, and, before she can talk herself out of going, leaves the house.

DOWNTOWN IS MOBBED, crawling with cars and people. The few times Olivia has driven through Town since she arrived on the island this winter, it's been deserted, even on a weekend. The storefront windows have been darkened, sporting naked mannequins and signs reading SEE YOU NEXT SEASON. Most of the restaurants have been closed in the middle of the day. Parking spaces have been everywhere, just as anyone would expect in winter, when too few people are on the island to support most businesses.

But today everything has come alive as if it were the middle of August, not the middle of April. *What's going on here?* She can't imagine.

She turns right onto India Street, beginning to loop the block for a third time, and vows to abandon the mission if she can't find anything this go-around. She's about to give up, planning a consolation trip to Stop & Shop for a bag of coffee or maybe the Downyflake outside Town, but then she spots an opening in front of the Atheneum in between a Hummer and a Land Cruiser.

The Atheneum is Nantucket's library, an imposing white building, the front entrance flanked on either side by colossal Ionic columns. It looks like an architectural anachronism, more like an ancient Greek temple than a modern library, as if it belongs on the Acropolis and not in the heart of the otherwise quaint, New England–style, historically restored town of Nantucket. Since she's right there, and she's now imagining how nice it would be to read a book while she drinks her latte at The Bean, just like old times minus David, she decides to run inside and find something to read.

As the bumper-to-bumper traffic outside might've predicted, the library is swarming with people. There are strollers everywhere, mothers and fathers reprimanding and calling to their kids, kids yelling and running away from their parents. A baby in one of the strollers is wailing, inconsolable. The whole place is buzzing with activity and voices that echo and skip off the high ceilings. The energy feels all wrong, disrespectful, like when kids talk and goof around in church, and Olivia second-guesses her decision to come inside.

She gets as far as the front desk and pauses, wondering if she wants a book badly enough to wade through the clogged chaos before her, deciding, in the end, that she'd rather get the hell out of there. She's about to turn around and leave when she catches sight of a familiar book cover sitting alone on a TO BE SHELVED metal cart. *The Curious Incident of the Dog in the Night-Time.*

She read that book years ago, just after Anthony was diagnosed, part of her mission to read everything ever written about autism. She remembers thinking at the time how different the main character's autism was from her Anthony's. Exact opposite ends of the spectrum, like red and violet in a rainbow. In the most obvious ways, they were entirely different, yet she found subtle and surprising similarities that comforted her, restored her hope. Violet isn't blue because it also contains red.

"I'll take this, please," she says, deciding that she might be ready to read it again.

After filling out the paperwork for a library card, she hustles out the door and down the front steps of the library with her loaned book in hand, relieved to be out of there. She walks around the corner to The Bean, expecting to stroll right in, but her progress is stopped well outside the entrance by a snaking line of customers. It's freezing cold, and the line is long, yet everyone around her appears to be in exceptionally good cheer. Olivia hasn't left her neighborhood much, but when she does venture out—to the grocery store, to the bank—there are never any crowds. She hasn't waited in a single line since she's moved to Nantucket. She's become used to the quiet bubble of her life here, the convenience of getting in and getting out with whatever she needs with minimal human contact.

She glances down at her bare wrist, looking for the time, wondering how long this is going to take. It's got to be well after noon. Why are all these people here? She pulls the collar of her coat up over her chin, shoves her hands into her pockets, closes her eyes, and breathes.

At long last, the line inches forward, and she steps inside. The café is exactly as she remembers—the worn wooden floor, the teardrop crystal chandelier, the antique copper and pewter teapots on the shelves, the glass canisters filled with biscotti. But her air of enjoyment in the familiar surroundings deflates when she notices every seat in the house is occupied.

"Can I help you?" asks the girl behind the counter.

"I'd like a large latte and a blueberry scone, please."

"We're all out of scones."

"Oh, okay, just the latte then."

"Milk or soy?"

"Milk."

"Regular, two percent, or nonfat?"

"Uh, regular. What's going on today?"

"Sorry?"

"Why are there so many people here?"

"The daffodils."

Olivia thinks. "Is that a band?"

The girls looks Olivia up and down, sizing her up, the way young people look at older people who don't have a clue. "The flower? You don't know? Why are you here?"

"I live here."

"Huh," says the girl, not believing this at all.

"So all these people are here to see some daffodils?"

"Yah, there's like three million in bloom all over the island."

Three *million*. Really? She hadn't noticed any. And is someone actually counting these? Olivia suspects that this girl must be exaggerating, the way young people do. "So, what, people drive around and look at flowers?"

The girl hands Olivia her latte, and Olivia pays for it.

"There's like a whole festival, the parade, the tailgating—"

"Tailgating?"

"Over in 'Sconset."

"Is there a football game?"

The girl laughs.

"Excuse me, are you done? There's a long line here," says the guy behind Olivia.

"Sorry."

Olivia steps out of the way and looks around the room one last, hopeless time. No seats. She nudges her way against the incoming line back outside and returns to her car. As she bounces over the cobblestones of Main Street and then turns onto the smooth pavement, she notices, for the first time, all the daffodils—planted in gardens and window boxes, lining fences and front yards, "wild" crops of them dotting the sides of the road. They're everywhere. How did she not notice any before?

Daffodils and tailgating. Curious, she decides to take a quick detour over to 'Sconset. She and David used to tailgate with their friends before every home football game at Boston College. Everyone wore BC sweatshirts and jackets and hats. Someone always brought a grill and a couple of kegs—charred cheeseburgers and Milwaukee's Best in plastic cups. David and his friends would talk in passionate detail about the players, and someone would invariably compare the quarterback to Flutie, and they'd argue over who was better. They'd all be rowdy and drunk by midmorning, well before kickoff.

As she approaches Main Street in 'Sconset, there they are, the tailgaters, parked one after another along the strip of grass between Milestone Road and the bicycle path. She's in a thick parade of traffic now, but she slows down even more than she needs to for a better look. A car parked on the grass ahead of her begins to pull out as she's approaching it, and she decides to take the spot.

She grabs her mirrored sunglasses, gets out of her Jeep, and begins walking. Main Street is blocked off to car traffic, so she walks down the center of the road. The tailgating cars are now mostly antiques or fancy convertibles and must've had special permission to be here. Most of the license plates are from New York or Connecticut. These people aren't year-rounders.

All of the cars are decorated with daffodils—huge bouquets tied to mirrors and roof racks and hoods. The people are decorated in daffodils, too. Hats, leis, corsages, boutonnieres. Most everyone is dressed for the occasion, casual but festive in some combination of yellow clothing with daffodil accessories, but some of the women are wearing elegant spring dresses and heels, and a few of the men are wearing seersucker suits and ties, as if they were out for tea in the English countryside. It feels like a Mardi Gras parade thrown by the Kennedys.

There are no kegs. There are wineglasses, champagne glasses, and martini glasses. There are Bloody Marys with green olives and sticks of celery. There are lawn chairs and card tables adorned with tablecloths and, of course, centerpiece vases bursting with daffodils. The tables are also piled with food, and not hamburgers and hot dogs, but beautiful food, food that could be served at a wedding. Baskets of bread, boards of cheese, fried clams, sushi, salads, and chowder.

It's all very civilized. Although everyone appears to be drinking in public, and she's sure that plenty of these people are feeling tipsy, none of them is drunk enough to be a public nuisance. No one's calling the campus police here. No one is reliving a Hail Mary pass or doing keg stands or puking. No one has taken off his shirt and finger-painted GO EAGLES or YOU SUCK on his chest.

These people aren't here to cheer on their beloved home team or celebrate a winning season. These people have packed up their suitcases and traveled hundreds of miles by plane or car and ferry, they've prepared picnic baskets full of crackers and cheese and lobster and wine, gotten dressed up in their wacky yellow outfits, and driven over to 'Sconset to sit by the side of the road on a freezing-cold day in April to celebrate a flower. These people are crazy.

Olivia avoids eye contact and walks at a brisk pace down the middle of the road, as if she's on her way somewhere specific, looking for someone she knows, and doesn't have time to stop and visit. The air smells like wet earth and buttery-sweet flowers, ocean and garlic. Her stomach growls. She wishes she had that blueberry scone. Or a bite of that woman's lobster roll.

Satisfied that she's seen all there is to see at this bizarre roadside holiday, she turns around, returns to her car, and heads to the other side of the island, enjoying the cheery sprays of yellow that decorate the landscape all around her as she drives. Back in her driveway, she spots six daffodils in her own front yard, three gold and three white, fully open and bobbing in the wind as if they were nodding and happy to see her. She wonders who planted them. She smiles, feeling not only hungry now, but also strangely inspired.

She heats up a bowl of clam chowder in the microwave and shakes a heap of oyster crackers on top. She grabs a spoon, her latte, a blanket from the couch, and her library book and sits on the rocking chair on her front porch. Cold coffee, three-day-old chowder, and six of the three million daffodils all to herself. Her own private tailgating party to celebrate Daffodil Day, or whatever they call it. Perfect. Or at least, not bad.

She eats a spoonful of chowder and studies her flowers shivering in the wind, impossibly bright and fragile and brave against the cold grayness of April on Nantucket. It must be hard to be a daffodil here. They probably wish they could stay in the ground another month. But they have no say in the matter. Some biological alarm clock inside them tripped the germination switch, telling each bulb to sprout and go forth, whether it's sunny and seventy in Georgia or still feeling like winter in April on Nantucket. They come, year after year.

She takes another spoonful and thinks about all the people partying in 'Sconset months before the weather has welcomed them to celebrate the daffodils. What's the big deal? She finishes her chowder and drinks her latte. She continues to sit on her porch, facing the flowers and the sun, feeling the warmth on her face through the frigid air. She closes her eyes, soaking in this small pleasure.

Maybe it's the promise of summer. After a long and bleak winter that often extends straight through spring, maybe the daffodil is a sign that summer will come again. The earth will spin and turn around the sun, and the clocks will tick even if Olivia doesn't reset hers, and time will move along. Winter will end. This, too, shall pass. There's the promise of a new beginning. The daffodils will bloom by the million, and life will return to the island.

And whether Olivia wants it to or not, life will return to her as well. She sits on her porch, tailgating before her daffodils, and notices that the sun has moved across the sky past her bedroom windows. It must be nearing midafternoon. Time passing.

Time heals, they say.

She reads the back cover of her library book. She's definitely ready to read about autism again. She feels ready to face what happened, to remember it all, to try to understand Anthony's life and why he's no longer here, to begin healing. But if she's feeling brave enough to face autism again, it shouldn't be through fiction. She carries her library book back into the house and returns to the porch a minute later with something else.

Rested and full and feeling like today, Daffodil Day, might just be as good a time as any, she opens one of her journals to the first page and reads.

March 19, 2001

We had Anthony's one-year doctor appointment today. He's 29 inches and 21 pounds, the 50th percentile for height and weight. He had a bunch of shots—my poor baby boy. I cried right along with him! I can't stand to watch him in any kind of pain. I was so proud to show off that he's already walking. Dr. Harvey says we can switch him over to whole milk now. It's going to be SO nice to not have to deal with buying formula anymore.

I can't believe he's already one! He's growing up so fast. He's always on the move now. He only lets me hold him to give him his bottle, otherwise he wants to get down and explore. He's not my snuggly little baby anymore. He's officially a toddler!

This must be what happens. He's already beginning the long process of growing up, pulling away, becoming an independent little person. It's what he's supposed to do, but I wish it didn't have to happen so soon.

This is why mothers have more babies. We forget about the pain and discomfort and wild inconvenience of pregnancy and childbirth so we can feel that heavenly feeling of holding a warm baby snuggled and content against our chests again. It's like nothing else in this world. Maybe David and I should start trying. We want a big family, and I'm not getting any younger.

I told Dr. Harvey that Anthony's not talking yet and asked if we should be concerned. He said that not all babies talk at a year and that we should start to hear some words by around fifteen months. So not long now. But Maria's kids all talked before one. I remember Bella saying "mama" and "dada" and "moon" and signing "more" and "all done" before her first birthday.

Dr. Harvey said girls usually talk a little sooner than boys. He said not to worry. But it's there. The worry. I can't help it. It's like telling me not to have brown eyes. I have brown eyes. I'm worried. Why isn't Anthony talking yet?

David's not worried at all. He says I worry too much about everything. I know he's right. I do worry a lot, but this feels different from my normal, everyday neuroses about switch-plate protectors and sterilizing his pacifiers and the possibility that his formula could be contaminated with bugs.

I wonder if his hearing is okay. Anthony doesn't seem to hear me. When I call his name, he doesn't look at me. In fact, he really almost never looks at me. The other day, I clapped my hands as loud as I could, and he didn't even turn his head. He just kept sitting on the floor looking out the slider glass doors at the leaves blowing around on the deck. It was as if I didn't exist.

Is he deaf? He's not. I know he's not, which is probably why I didn't mention it to Dr. Harvey. I see him bounce to music when we have it on. He loves reggae. And the other day, I dropped a pan in the kitchen, and I saw him startle, and then he cried. So he's definitely not deaf. So why does a part of me keep hoping that he is? What a crazy thing to think. God, what's going on with Anthony? Please tell me everything's okay with him.

What am I worried about? Dr. Harvey says he's fine. David thinks he's fine. I'm sure he's fine.

I'm such a liar.

CHAPTER 7

Beth has been staring vaguely into her bedroom closet for twenty minutes, about nineteen and a half minutes longer than she typically spends in this position. Her closet is a modest, rectangular pocket in the wall, enclosed by two doors that slide past each other. A single rod runs the length of it, and a single shelf sits above the rod. Nothing fancy. Beth's side is on the left, and Jimmy's is on the right. Or rather, it was.

She slides the doors to reveal the other side—the bare rod, the empty shelf, those nasty dust bunnies on the floor she needs to vacuum. She complained about their lack of closet space to Jimmy for years. She practically drooled over the walk-in that Mickey built for Jill (there's even an ottoman in the middle of it for sitting—for sitting!). Now Beth has what she wished for, twice as much space, but she can't bring herself to spread her hangers out onto his side of the bar or to walk her shoes over to his side of the floor. She can't.

She slides the doors again and returns to the problem at hand. What to wear. Like everything else in the house, Beth's side of the closet is tidy and organized. All of the hangers are the same—white, plastic, and facing the same direction.

Hanging from left to right are tank tops, then short-sleeve shirts, long-sleeve shirts, dresses, and skirts. A short stack of sweatshirts and sweaters are folded on the shelf above the rod, and two rows of shoes are lined up along the floor. One pair of each—sneakers, snow boots, leather boots, clogs, low heels, sandals, flip-flops. With the exception of the sneakers, which used to be white but are now many-years-old gray, all of her footwear is black.

Most everything in her closet is black. Not edgy black. Not New York City, metropolitan-chic black. Not even Gothic black. Everything is blah black. Safe and boring, nothing-interesting-to-see-here black. Invisible black. What isn't black is gray or white.

She thumbs through her shirts, cotton and boxy crewnecks and turtlenecks. The sweaters are shapeless and long. They all cover her butt. She holds an androgynous, black T-shirt up to her neck that might look okay with jeans. But her jeans aren't dressy enough for Salt. Her jeans are baggy, practical, and comfortable, good for driving the kids in the minivan or cleaning the house or sitting on the couch or gardening, but not good for going out to Salt. Not good at all.

She pulls out her only two dresses and lays them side by side on the bed. They're both black, but neither can be described as a "little black dress." The first is the dress she wears to wakes and funerals—high neck, long sleeves, no waist, hem at her ankles. She originally bought it for Jimmy's dad's funeral because it looked respectful and nondescript, and she liked that it didn't call attention to her in any way, but as she's inspecting it now, she's embarrassed by it. It looks like a costume for a school play, and the play is about a seventeenth-century Quaker spinster.

She turns her attention to the other dress, hoping it might be her savior. It's a scoop neck, short sleeve, Empire waist, with a flowing skirt hitting just below the knee. It's not bad. It could work. It's actually kind of cute. She holds it up and studies herself in the full-length mirror on the back of the bedroom door, trying to figure out if she looks cute, but suddenly she remembers the last time she wore it, and any possibility of pulling off cute flies right out the window. She checks the tag. Mimi Maternity. She was nine months pregnant with Gracie the last time she wore this dress. She can't wear a maternity dress to Salt, even if it is the sexiest thing she owns, and no one will see the tag.

She chews her nails as she scrutinizes her only two dresses, hating them. She returns them to their spot on the rod on her side of the closet and searches through her black clothes. Her old, dowdy, stupid black clothes. She can't do this. She can't go. She can't.

She grabs the phone from her bedside table and dials.

"I can't go," she says to Petra.

"Why not?"

"I have nothing to wear."

"What are you, sixteen? Wear a black top and a skirt."

"I need to go shopping first. Let's go next weekend."

She needs time for a trip to the Hyannis mall, an involved and expensive excursion requiring ferry tickets and bus schedules. Even if she could afford to shop downtown, which she most certainly cannot—hell, even if they were giving the clothes away for free—she wouldn't be caught dead wearing ninety-nine percent of it. She'll never understand why women who can afford anything and everything would *choose* to wear pineapple-print dresses, Pepto-Bismol-pink tops sporting sequins and embroidered dogs, skirts patterned with starfish and whales.

"Next weekend is Figawi, we'll never get in. Come on, you've been putting this off all month. Put on some jewelry and some makeup, you'll look great."

She's right. Next weekend is Memorial Day weekend and Figawi, an internationally celebrated sailboat race from Hyannis across the sound to Nantucket harbor. It's also the grand, official kickoff to Nantucket's summer season. There are clam-bakes, fancy fund-raisers, award ceremonies, and parties all over the island. And all the restaurants will be jammed.

"I don't know."

"You want to check this woman out or not?"

"I think so, but—"

"Then let's go check her out."

"What does she look like?"

In the infinite pause that follows, Beth presses her fingers to her lips and holds her breath. Her heart pulses in her temples. She's wanted to ask Petra this question so many times since book club last month, but her fear of every conceivable answer has always shoved it down, silencing her. If Angela is beautiful, then Beth must be ugly. And *ugly* is being kind. *Hideous* is the word Beth has been trying on for size, feeling as if it might fit her perfectly, better than any black thing hanging in her closet. And if Angela's not beautiful, then she must be sweet or funny or attractive in some other compelling way that Beth is not, else Jimmy wouldn't have to stray to find it. So if Angela is beautiful, Beth is ugly, and if Angela is ugly, then Beth is a bitch, either way redefined by whatever Jimmy sees in this other woman.

"That's what we're going to find out tonight."

"Yeah, but you've seen her. What do you think?"

"I think she doesn't hold a candle to you."

Beth smiles, but then her eyes return to her closet. "How about after Figawi?"

"How about tonight?"

"Petra, I don't have to go at all."

"True."

"But I can't stand not knowing who she is."

"Well then."

Beth chews her thumbnail. "Can I borrow your turquoise necklace?"

"You got it. I'll be over a little before seven. You okay?"

"Yeah."

"It's not even noon. You should get out of the house. Step away from the closet."

"I will. Once I figure out what I'm wearing."

"Black top, skirt, turquoise necklace. You'll look great. See you tonight."

Black top and a skirt. She pulls out her white peasant skirt and considers it. She walks into the hallway and stops in front of their most recent family photo hung on the wall, the one taken last summer on Miacomet Beach. She wore this skirt. She, Sophie, and Gracie wore white skirts and black tops; Jimmy and Jessica, who won't wear anything but pants, wore white shorts and black tops. It's a beautiful photograph. They're all sitting in the sand, beach grass, wispy white clouds, and soft-blue sky behind them. Jimmy has his hand on her knee, touching her skirt, this skirt now in her hands, touching her so easily, so naturally.

She remembers those days early on, when they were dating and first married, when he touched her, even in passing, and she felt it. Really felt it. That magnetic, electric heat of his hand on her. That invisible, magical, chemical connection. Where did that go?

He was cheating on her when this picture was taken. Beth pinches her eyes shut and swallows, trying to keep it together. What does Jimmy feel when he touches Angela? Does he feel an invisible, magical, chemical connection? What doesn't he feel when he touches Beth? When he used to touch her. She opens her eyes and steps back, taking in the whole wall—seven years of family portraits and a black-and-white photo of her and Jimmy from their wedding day. She looks at everyone's smiles, her happy family. Her life. She clenches her teeth and blinks back tears. Her life is a fraud.

She straightens two of the frames that were tipped just slightly to the right of level, returns to her bedroom, and crawls back into bed. The bed feels good. The bed feels safe.

And she knows how to dress for bed. She's wearing her old, pink flannel pajamas, covered in nubs, the most colorful things she owns. She should go to Salt in her pajamas. Then she'd really make an impression. Not the kind of impression she wants to make though.

But what kind of impression does she want to make? She wishes she didn't have to make one at all, that she could go in disguise, sporting a wig and dark glasses, so she could see and not be seen. But she also fantasizes about going and being noticed by everyone. She'd strut into Salt, looking confident and sexy (tastefully sexy, not trashy sexy), and shy of that, at least better than Angela, a difficult goal to set since she has no idea what Angela looks like. She's terrified of giving this woman any reason to feel any more superior to Beth than she probably already feels. Unfortunately, realistically, there's an awful good chance of this. Beth's not feeling confident or sexy. And she never struts. She looks into her pathetic closet, rolls over, closes her eyes, and tucks the blankets up to her chin.

Behind her closed lids, she envisions Jimmy shaking a martini, then stopping midpour, struck by the sight of her as she *struts* into the restaurant with her friends. She imagines him pulling her aside, telling her that he feels like an idiot for leaving her. She imagines him begging her to take him back right there at the bar, right in front of Angela.

She directs the entire Salt scene, smiling as it plays out in her head. She's even cast a fictitious Angela, devastated and defeated, with sleek black hair, thick eyebrows, severe makeup, and a spandex dress (trashy sexy). The only person she can't see in this little fantasy is herself.

Damn it, what am I going to wear?

It occurs to her that she's on the other end of this ridiculous question at least once a week with Sophie, her thirteen-going-on-eighteen-year-old. The other two girls will be dressed and ready and waiting at the front door, and Sophie will still be in her room, half-dressed, crazed and crying, clothes tossed everywhere. *I can't go to school! I have nothing to wear!*

Worried more about the girls' being late for school than Sophie's fashion crisis, Beth typically offers something quick and admittedly too glib.

You look beautiful. Just be yourself and it won't matter what you wear. C'mon, let's go!

Now Beth gets why Sophie rolls her eyes and cries harder. She owes her daughter an apology and a trip to the Hyannis mall.

She tries for a moment to take her own advice. *Be yourself.* But who is she? She's Jimmy's wife, and she's a mother. And if she gets divorced, if she's no longer Mrs. James Ellis, and she's only a mother, then is there less of her? She fears this and feels it already, physically, as if a surgeon has taken a scalpel to her abdomen and removed a whole and necessary part of her. Without Jimmy, she doesn't recognize herself. How can that be? Who has she become?

She rolls over and looks into her closet. It's organized. That's her. But otherwise, she's not in there. She sits up and looks at herself in the mirror on the back of the bedroom door, her blond, chin-length hair a matted mess, her blue eyes deeply set and dull, her pajamas pink and nubby. *That's not who I am.*

She gets out of bed and returns to face the pictures on the wall in the hallway. The most recent portraits offer her nothing more than wife and mother. She'd always approved of how she looks in these pictures, her hair not too frizzy from the humidity, her makeup subtle, her nails polished, her clothes pressed. But as she studies herself now, her smile appears forced, unnatural, her posture stiff, like she's a cardboard cutout of herself. Like she's posing. She moves back in time and visits the oldest family photo and the portrait from her wedding. Here she sees more of the woman she thinks of as herself. Her smile contains an unself-conscious abandon, her eyes are bright and happy. Where did that woman go?

For some reason, she looks up at the ceiling, and there it is, as if the answer were delivered to her from above. The attic!

She stands on her tiptoes, pulls the dangling white string, unfolds the wooden stairs, and climbs up. A wall of dense, stagnant heat greets her in a hurry at the top. Nearing the end of May, the days have been sunny, but it's remained cool, only in the sixties, yet the trapped heat up here feels like summer against her skin.

She pauses before fully committing to going in. The roof is pitched and low, and the wooden ceiling is riddled with protruding nails, making it both impossible and dangerous to stand up straight. And the floor is unfinished, with only a few planks of wood running the length through the center, like a bridge crossing a sea of pink insulation.

Beth doesn't like coming up here for fear of either forgetting about the low ceiling and impaling her head with a nail or accidentally stepping off the planks and falling through the fluffy fiberglass floor into the living room. Because of this, she normally visits the attic only twice a year—the day after Thanksgiving to take the Christmas decorations down and New Year's Day to put the Christmas decorations back. Up and in, out and down, she's never dallied in here.

Jimmy's got a bunch of his stuff strewn all over the far end—fishing rods leaning against the angled ceiling, two of them fallen over, tangled nets, tackle boxes, one of them open, a collection of golf clubs crisscrossed and loose on the floor like a pile of pick-up sticks, the empty golf bag, a single golf shoe, a surfboard, a clamming rake and bucket.

"Jimmy."

With her hands on her hips, she scolds him in her head and has to resist the urge to tidy it up. That's not why she's here.

Separate from his mess are three standing fans and two

window-box air conditioners. Six plastic storage tubs, all labeled in her printing with a black Sharpie on masking tape, sit in a neat row, two each: CHRISTMAS, HALLOWEEN, WINTER.

The winter boxes are both empty. She and the girls have still been wearing their winter coats in the morning and at night, and they've also been getting good use out of their winter boots, the ground finally fully thawed, the height of mud season. Each year, about a week or two from now and under Beth's directive, Jimmy carries all of the winter gear up to the attic and comes back down with the fans and air conditioners. She sighs, recognizing that this will be her job from now on.

One last tub, apart from the others, way at the back, is labeled BETH. The lid is coated with dust. She hasn't opened this bin in at least a decade. Feeling both excited and scared of what she might discover inside, she sits cross-legged next to it and opens the lid.

First, she pulls out a red Frisbee signed by everyone on her ultimate Frisbee team, turning it over in her hands as she studies each note and signature. Johnny C! Her four-year, unrequited crush from Reed College. She hasn't thought about him in years. He was such a sweet guy. He was premed. She wonders where he is now. He's probably a successful doctor somewhere, not cheating on his wife.

She finds a stack of ticket stubs held together by an elastic band. Rolling Stones, *Stomp*, *Rent*, Cirque du Soleil, the Metropolitan Museum of Art, an airline ticket from Portland to New York, another to New Mexico, even movie stubs, each labeled with the names of the friends or boyfriend who went with her. She can't remember the last concert she's been to (it might've been the Stones), and her last plane trip was from New York to Nantucket, one way. She misses vacations to new places, Broadway shows, and museums (and the trips with each daughter's third-grade class to the whaling museum don't count).

She shuffles through her college ID cards, photos from parties and summer vacations. She laughs at her huge hair and aqua-blue eyeliner. The nineties!

Then she finds a stack of birthday cards, and she hesitates, gathering emotional courage. Eight birthday cards from her mother. She reads through them all, starting with sweet sixteen, treasuring each handwritten word, each *Love you, Mom,* wiping her eyes with her pajama sleeve every time the words get too blurry to read through her tears.

Her mother had a lumpectomy the summer before Beth moved to Nantucket. Her doctor said they got it all. She had radiation and chemotherapy after the surgery. Everything was standard procedure. Everything looked good.

Her hair was gone when Beth moved to New York in September. It was her first job out of college, an editorial assistant for *Self* magazine. Her mother insisted she go and start her life and assured her that she would be fine.

But she wasn't fine. They didn't get it all. In November, she went back into surgery, this time to remove the whole breast and some lymph tissue. Beth's heart tightens. If only they'd done this in the first place. Again, the doctors said they got everything. She and Beth celebrated over Thanksgiving weekend, relieved and grateful.

But they shouldn't have celebrated anything because some microscopic flecks of cancer had already broken free of her breast before the doctors removed it, and they floated off into her mother's body, looking for a new residence. They found her liver first. And then her lungs. She died in January.

Beth holds the last birthday card, the last *Love you, Mom.* It was her twenty-third birthday, and she never imagined her mother wouldn't be here to see her turn twenty-four, thirty, thirty-eight.

She's often wondered if she'd be married to Jimmy if her mother hadn't died. She found getting out of bed and going to work nearly impossible after her mother's funeral. She remembers feeling utterly unable to do her job, even though it only consisted of fairly mindless office duties such as answering the phones, checking faxes, and scheduling meetings. She remembers trying to hide a torrent of tears at so many unprofessional moments. She needed some time off. She clawed her way through each week until June, then she quit and left New York City. She quit and went to Nantucket.

She had inherited a little money from her mother, enough for her to rent a cottage with three friends for the summer and attend graduate school in the fall. She'd been accepted into Boston University's MFA program in creative writing. Other than that, there was no plan. She didn't plan on meeting Jimmy and falling in love with him. And she certainly didn't plan on marrying him and starting a family instead of going back to school.

But this is exactly what she did. On Labor Day, when her friends got on a plane and flew back to the real world, Beth stayed. A year later, she and Jimmy got married, and a year after that, Sophie was born.

She's often wondered what her mother would've thought of Jimmy. She probably wouldn't have liked him. She certainly wouldn't be a fan of his right now. Her mother never had a high opinion of men. She and her father divorced when Beth was three, and they never saw him again after Beth turned four. She doesn't remember her mother ever dating. She was entirely devoted to making a living and raising her daughter, her only child.

Beth digs through the tub, now looking for a specific picture. She knows it's in here. She finds it at the bottom of everything, the only picture she has of her father. He's wearing a men's white undershirt and black-rimmed glasses. His light brown hair is receding. He's smiling. His arms look strong. He's holding Beth in his lap. Her blond hair is in pigtails, and she's wearing a pink party dress. It's her second birthday. She's also smiling. They look happy together. She has no memory of this man or of herself as this little girl, but she believes that it's them. The writing on the back of the picture, her mother's writing, reads *Denny & Beth, 10–2–73.* She breathes a dense sigh and discards the photograph back to the bottom of the bin.

She presses the stack of birthday cards from her mother against her chest. She misses her, especially now. She smiles and dabs her wet eyes with her sleeve, lost in a bittersweet thought about her own daughters. Her mother may not have cared for Jimmy, but she would've loved her grandchildren.

Beth returns the cards to the tub and pulls out a paperback book. *Writing Down the Bones* by Natalie Goldberg. The book that made her believe she could be a writer someday. Why is this book in here and not on her bookshelf in the living room or on her bedside table?

When she first moved here, she wrote event pieces for *Yesterday's Island,* nothing earth-shattering, but she was writing and getting paid for it. After she had Jessica, she landed a better job as a staff writer for the *Inquirer and Mirror,* but after she had Gracie, she found working and raising three young girls too much to juggle, and she quit the paper. But still, for a while, she kept her pen active.

She finds her essays, poems, and short stories. She finds her notebooks—ordinary, spiral notebooks, floppy and worn, every inch jammed with blue ink—writing exercises, ideas for short stories, vignettes, her imagination, her thoughts and emotions, her tender, naked insides laid out on the eight-and-a-half-by-eleven, college-ruled pages. She flips through them and becomes absorbed in reading one in particular, a short story about a peculiar boy who lives strictly within the confines of a bizarre yet beautiful imaginary world. She remembers when she wrote that story. It was about six or seven years ago after a morning on the beach with the girls, inspired by a little boy she saw there playing with rocks by the shore. She used to find inspiration in her everyday life here, and she used to write about it. When did she stop writing? When did her life become uninspiring?

One of the notebooks she finds is brand-new, untouched. She holds this notebook in her hands, makes a promise to herself, and sets it aside.

Next she comes to the clothes—the faux-leopard-print coat that was her mother's; leather pants (rock-star black); her Goldie Hawn, pink-and-orange, geometric mod dress. She used to *love* that dress. She wore it everywhere—parties, dance clubs, weddings, first dates. Her first real date with Jimmy.

She carefully strips out of her nubby pajamas and slides the dress on over her head without hitting the ceiling. Miraculously, it fits! She doesn't need the mirror in her bedroom to see if it looks cute. She knows.

She finds piles of cheap jewelry—huge silver-hoop earrings, chunky and colorful plastic bangle bracelets, lots of rhinestones, a bunch of tangled necklaces, all very Madonna circa *Desperately Seeking Susan*. She slides a moonstone ring onto the middle finger of her right hand and admires it, wondering why she ever packed it away.

She wonders why she packed any of this away. Some of it has to do with moving from New York to Nantucket and wanting to fit in here. Year-rounders on Nantucket wear oversized L.L.Bean fleece jackets and hip waders, not Goldie Hawn dresses and mood rings. And some of it has to do with the swelling and weight gain that comes with being pregnant three times. Those skintight, leather rock-star pants haven't been humanly possible in years. But leather pants aside, these things, the notebooks and clothes and photos and cards, are pieces of herself, her history, her sense of adventure and style, her dreams for her future.

This is me, she thinks, staring into the bin.

She and Jimmy used to throw impromptu parties with nothing in the house but a bag of potato chips, a six-pack of beer, and a cheap bottle of wine. Everyone would bring something, and they always had plenty. They always had fun. She and Jimmy haven't thrown a party in a long time. The parties somehow changed, no longer arising spontaneously from the quick and playful thought, *Hey, why don't we invite some friends over tonight?* Instead they required planning and cooking and cleaning the house. Everything had to be *just so.* They became work, and she doesn't remember the fun, only the fights between Jimmy and her ignited over some stressful aspect of getting ready, her anger and resentment sticking to her ribs long after the last guest went home.

She used to wear blues and greens and orange. She used to have moxie. She used to skinny-dip at Fat Ladies Beach and dance to the music she liked. Now she always wears a loose and large cover-up over her bathing suit at the beach, and she only listens to whatever the girls want to hear, usually Britney Spears or some Bambi-eyed teenage girl from the Disney Channel.

She used to write.

She can't believe she stuffed so much of herself into a box, banished to the attic for so many years. At least she didn't donate herself to Goodwill or, worse, throw herself out. She continues to dig through the box, skipping down memory lane with each item until she picks up the locket, the first gift Jimmy ever gave to her. She opens the smooth, tarnished silver heart and holds it in the palm of her hand. She and Jimmy kissing. She and Jimmy in love. She studies this picture of herself and Jimmy, and it's as if she were seeing two other people, as if they were old friends she was so fond of once, friends she's long lost touch with and who have moved far away. Her heart sinks. She wore that locket every day for years and loved it.

Then, at some point, she doesn't remember exactly when, the silver heart began to tarnish, and what once looked new and romantic and sophisticated to her suddenly felt old and boring and childish. She grew tired of wearing it and packed it away.

Careful not to stand up straight or step too far to the side, Beth drags her bin to the top of the stairs, then carries it down and into her bedroom. Balancing the bin on her hip, she slides the closet door open and plops the bin on the floor of Jimmy's side. She gathers *Writing Down the Bones,* her old notebooks, including the one that's blank, and sets them on her night table. She nods. Then she clasps the locket around her neck, rubs the silver heart between her fingers, and turns to check herself out in the mirror on the door.

There I am.

Ready for Salt.

CHAPTER 8

It's the hour before sunset on Fat Ladies Beach, and Olivia is walking with her camera in hand. She's been walking this beach every evening and has come to appreciate why photographers call this time of day the magic hour. Lighting this patch of earth for the last minutes of the day from across the horizon rather than from directly overhead, the sun coats everything in a soft, diffuse glow. Colors look more saturated, golden, romantic. Magical.

Olivia had been walking without her camera, uninspired, all spring. Everything everywhere was gray. But then the pervasive gray seemed to lift and vanish for good this weekend, as if it finally became warm enough for Nantucket to unzip and peel off its gray winter coat, revealing the remarkable beauty of this place, especially at this hour. The astonishing blues of the sky melting into the ocean, the crisp, apple-green blades of beach grass, the glittering sand, and soon the showstopping sunset, an intensifying blood-orange sun sinking out of view, trading places with a sky increasingly drenched in hot pink and lavender, unbelievably more magnificent than it was just seconds before. It all begs to be photographed.

Olivia loves the feel of her Nikon in her hands. She admits that the teeny, deck-of-cards-size pocket cameras would be more convenient to carry, and technically they can do most of what she wants from a camera, but they feel like cheap toys. She prefers her bulky Nikon, the responsive click of the button beneath her index finger, the dialing action of the manual focus, its overall heft.

It reminds her of how she used to love the feel of one of her new books hot off the press, the culmination of years of writing by the author and months of editing by her, its smooth and shiny new cover, maybe with embossed lettering, and the satisfying weight of it in her hands. She still loves the feel of a new book. While she appreciates the convenience of those thin, slick e-readers, they don't give her the three-dimensional sensory experience that comes with a real book.

She walks along the water's edge, stopping now and then to snap a wide shot of the horizon, a macro of a seashell, a sandpiper, the silhouette of a woman walking her dog in the distance. Unlike the previous months when she could walk here for as long as she wanted in complete and almost guaranteed solitude, other people are always on the beach now. The island is coming to life, and as Olivia walks, she realizes how out of step she is with the world around her. The pervasive gray surrounding *her* hasn't lifted; it's still winter in her heart. She feels that she's witnessing her life more than she's actually living it, this woman who lives on Nantucket, drinks coffee, reads her journals, goes for walks, and takes pictures, as if she were watching a movie, a boring movie about a boring woman where nothing much happens, a movie she'd like to shut off or change to a different channel, but for some reason, she's glued to the screen. If she keeps watching, something will happen.

In one respect, something does have to happen soon. She needs to find a job here. Even with her meager existence, there are the expenses of daily living. David agreed to pay for her first six months, which means she only has a little longer left on his dole. Either she'll need to make a living here, or she'll have to sell the house and move, probably back to Georgia to be near her mother and sister, Maria, and her family. Or maybe she'll sell the house and run away to somewhere even more remote, some island in the South Pacific where she can disappear.

She's thought about it, about really disappearing. Several suicides on Nantucket have been reported in the paper since she moved here. Counselors and psychologists weighed in as to why suicides are more common on Nantucket than elsewhere, pointing fingers at depression and seasonal affective disorder layered onto the extreme abyss of winter on this isolated speck of land. She's imagined her own name in print, the star subject of a similar newspaper article. She gets it. An almost unbearable emptiness unfolds before her every morning. And then come the questions.

Why?

Why was Anthony here?

What was the purpose of his short life?

No answer.

Why am I here?

Why?

No answer. There are never any answers, not in her prayers or dreams, not so far in her journals or in the faith she used to have in God and the church, not in the magic of a sunset on Fat Ladies Beach. A part of her has accepted that these questions will never find their answers, that there is no point to this life, but another part of her continues the search, asking these questions over and over, with the deepest sincerity, repeating this inquisitive loop many times a day, perseverating.

Like someone with autism.

The silence that follows the last *Why?* of the day always hangs in the air, echoing for a long moment before floating off into infinite nothingness, leaving her so utterly and painfully alone that she often wishes she could dissolve right there and disappear with her question into that nothingness. But something deep inside her insists on holding on, enduring. Witnessing and waiting. And soon, finding a job. But a job doing what? What can she do here?

Why am I here?

Why?

She squats down low, looks through her viewfinder, adjusts her focus, and clicks a photo of the shore, the white foam, the wet, metallic sand, the layers of liquid blue. She looks up and sees the slick, black head of a seal in the surf. She zooms in and clicks. Still zoomed in, she can clearly see the seal's round, black eyes, and it appears to be looking directly at her. She lowers her camera, and they hold each other's gaze for a long moment before the seal dips below the water's surface, disappearing, leaving her alone.

Behind her, a bunch of voices tumble onto the beach. She turns and looks. Two boys are running toward the ocean, toward her, laughing. Their mother, weighed down by a large beach bag on one shoulder and a toddler on her hip, unable to give chase, yells after them, warning them not to go in the water. The father walks beside her at first, then begins to run. They're all barefoot and wearing matching light blue shirts and khaki pants.

The father catches the older two boys, scoops them up in his arms, one in each, just before their toes hit the surf. The boys scream with laughter. The father spins them all dizzy and falls to the ground, and the three play-wrestle in the sand.

"Are you Rebecca?"

"Sorry?" asks Olivia, not because she didn't hear the mother's question, but because she can't quite process it, so unaccustomed to any human voice directed at her on this beach, to anyone penetrating the gray layer that is wrapped so tightly around her skin.

"Are you the photographer?" the mother asks, nodding down to Olivia's Nikon.

"Me? No."

"Sorry. I thought you were her." The mother looks back over her shoulder at the parking lot and sighs, hoisting her toddler, who is aiming to get down, higher on her hip. "I don't know how long I can keep all three clean and dry. Max! No!"

Max is the middle boy, Olivia's guessing around five, and he's now chasing a seagull down the beach. He's fast, ignoring his mother. The father goes after him.

The oldest boy, around eight, wanders over to his mother, no longer interested in the cold water without a brother to race. He stands by her side and holds her free hand.

All three of these boys are familiar and foreign to Olivia, two sides of the same sword, each equally capable of carving her in two. They are the size and shape of Anthony—his feet when he was two, his legs when he was five, his eight-year-old hands.

Max, the boy running down the beach not heeding his parents' calls to stop, is just like Anthony. And yet, he's nothing like Anthony. This boy leaps up and takes off with a glint in his eye and the devil in his smile. He's playing, and he's involving his parents in the game. *Chase me!* And he'll delight in being caught.

When Anthony ran on the beach, he ran to feel the impact of the solid ground compressing his joints, to feel the cool wind on his skin, to feel the hot, granular sand between his toes, to get to the water he loved more than anything else. He ran and didn't listen to her or David's calls to stop, but it was never a game that included them in his world.

The photographer arrives, the father returns with the middle boy, carrying him tucked under his arm like a football, and the mother gathers them all together, encouraging the boys to smile.

"Look at me," says the photographer, and unexpected chills tremble through Olivia's center.

Look at me.

How many hundreds of thousands of times did she hear those three words, spoken by her, by David, by doctors, by a series of applied-behavioral-analysis and speech therapists.

Anthony, look at me, while she held a Pringle to her nose.

Anthony, look at me, while she held her breath.

Anthony, look at me, while he did not.

The toddler is throwing his head back and stiffening his limbs, crying, his face puffed and red, his eyes squeezed shut. The mother hands him over to the father. She pulls a toy still inside its packaging from her beach bag and hands it to the photographer. It's a truck. A bribe. She's smart.

"Look at the truck."

It works. The toddler's attention is drawn to the truck, which the photographer has strategically placed on the top of her head. The toddler stops crying and points. The toddler points and says, "Mine."

Until that moment, Olivia wondered if he were on the spectrum. She'd already decided that the other two were neurotypical, but she wasn't sure about the toddler on his mother's hip. After Anthony's diagnosis, every boy she saw—preschoolers and teenagers, sons of women she knew and sons of strangers, boys sitting in front of her in church and boys playing on the playground—she observed for signs of autism. Even now she can't look at a boy and simply see a boy. She has to see or not see autism, too. Like looking at the letters of a word and reading the word, she has to do both. They are inextricably linked.

And where she feels an unspoken bond, a compassionate kinship, with mothers of children on the spectrum, she often feels all sorts of unflattering emotions toward the parents of typical boys and girls. Jealousy, irritation, hatred, rage, grief.

Their normal, blessed, easy, unappreciated lives flaunted right there in front of her.

Look at them, she'd usually think, jealousy, irritation, hatred, rage, and grief consuming her, poisoning her.

But today, quite unexpectedly, she feels none of this. Instead she feels relieved and hopeful that this mother will get at least one decent picture with her whole family smiling and looking at the camera. The toddler continues to point at the truck while sitting on his mother's hip, his older brothers are yelling, *"Cheeeeeese,"* and the father has his arm around his wife, his other hand on the shoulder of the oldest boy while the photographer clicks away, still saying, "Look at me."

Olivia pulls her Nikon up to her eye and looks at this family through the viewfinder. It's almost sunset now. The light on their faces is warm and flattering. Click. Click. Click. She looks down at her LCD, at the last image she captured. She sees the saturation, the brightness and contrast, the composition, and approves. It's a good picture. Then something shifts, maybe some of the gray surrounding her lifts, and she forgets the technical aspects of the photograph. She looks at the image on her LCD, and she sees joy, intimacy, family, love. Magic captured.

I could do this.

CHAPTER 9

⁓

Beth and Petra meet up with Jill, who is waiting for them, always early, in front of Salt. Courtney's not coming because she's teaching two yoga classes tonight, and Georgia can't come because she's overseeing a wedding down the street at the Blue Oyster. But with Petra and Jill by her side, Beth has more than enough girl power in her corner, and she's feeling confident and ready in her Goldie Hawn dress. But as Petra walks up the steps, leading the way, Beth realizes that her heart is beating way too fast, urging her body to spring into some kind of large physical action to match her racing pulse. *Run!* She focuses on the back of Petra's neck, on the clasp of her turquoise necklace, the one Beth asked to borrow but didn't wear, as she forces each forward step, walking behind her friend, slowly, deliberately, against her heart's instinct, into the lion's den.

"Hi, welcome to Salt."

Before Beth can notice anything else, there she is, smiling at Petra. Salt's Saturday-night hostess. Angela.

She's younger than Beth, possibly in her late twenties. Her hair is long, curly, and dark brown. She's wearing a plain, bor-

ing black top, but on her it's tight and has a plunging V neck-
line. That and a small gold cross at the end of a long gold chain
draw Beth's eyes, and probably everyone else's, to her big, exciting boobs. Of course. Twentysomething and big boobs.

Beth rounds her shoulders and folds her arms over her own
chest, already neatly covered by the thick polyester blend of her
Goldie Hawn dress. Even pushed up and in to the best of her
Victoria's Secret bra's ability, even before pregnancy stretched
them and breast-feeding sucked the bounce out of them, her
boobs never looked like *that*. Angela's eyes, big and black and
unnervingly beautiful, are still smiling as they move to include
Jill, but then they stumble when they see Beth.

She already knows who I am.

Angela clears her throat and pulls her fake, professional
welcome smile back on. "Table for three?"

"No, thanks," says Petra. "We're going to sit at the bar."

We are? Beth wants to correct Petra, to say that they'd prefer
a table, please, one facing the street and not the bar actually,
but a sour-tasting panic has risen at the back of Beth's throat,
and she can only manage to swallow. Like a lamb being led to
slaughter, she follows Petra and Jill to the bar and takes the
empty seat between them. And there's Jimmy.

He at first greets them with a neutral cheerfulness, the way
he might acknowledge any three women who sit down at his
bar, clearly without really seeing them. But then it registers.
His smile softens on Beth, becoming genuine, but only for the
slightest moment before it's replaced by a tensed grin, holding
surprise and uncertainty between his teeth, and then finally his
jaw clenches tight to keep him from saying what he's probably
thinking. *Oh, shit.*

"Ladies."

"Jimmy," says Petra.

"Beth," says Jimmy.

"Hi," says Beth.

"So what are you ladies up to tonight?"

"This," says Petra. "We're here to spy on you."

Jimmy laughs and shakes the martini he's making with noticeably extra vigor. Beth wipes her hands on the lap of her dress. She didn't know her hands could sweat.

"Not exactly subtle, are you, Petra?" he asks.

"Never," says Petra.

Direct and fearless, Petra would never tap a nail gently a hundred times with a rubber mallet when she could whack it once with a sledgehammer and get the job done. While Beth admires this quality in Petra, Beth has never been comfortable with the trait herself. She's too afraid of missing the nail head altogether, of creating a huge and ugly hole in the wall next to her intention.

"What can I get for you?" he asks.

"What do you recommend?" asks Petra.

"What are you in the mood for, beer, wine?"

"Something stronger. Something you make," says Petra.

He pours off some of the drink he's just mixed into a small glass and places it down in front of Petra, who takes a sip.

"That's good. Espresso martini?"

He nods.

"I'll have that," says Petra.

"Me, too," says Jill.

"Try some?" asks Petra, offering what's left in her glass to Beth.

"No, no, I—" says Beth.

"Can't have caffeine after four," says Jimmy, knowing her answer. "She'll be up all night."

Beth shifts in her seat.

"How about something sweeter?" he says, already pulling bottles.

It's strange to see him mixing all these fancy drinks. Jimmy's a beer-in-the-bottle kind of guy. And not the new kinds of beers infused with nutmeg or pumpkin or blueberries. He likes "real" beer. Budweiser and Coors. He reluctantly admits to liking Cisco's Whale's Tale, but only because the brewery is down the road from their house.

And this isn't Jimmy's kind of bar. He likes a guys' place, not necessarily a sports pub, although the Red Sox, Patriots, Bruins, or Celtics had better be playing on the flatscreen. He likes a bar that's dark and dirty, a glass jar of hard-boiled eggs and bowls of peanuts on the counter, wooden floors warped from years of soaking in spilled beer, Def Leppard playing on the jukebox. The menu might have mozzarella sticks and buffalo wings but certainly not anything with foie gras or truffle oil. There's a pool table and a dartboard and a bouncer because at least one sloppy drunk is going to throw a punch at somebody before closing.

Salt is the opposite of Jimmy's kind of bar. The coppery-orange globe pendants glow against the tin ceiling, giving off a romantic light. The mixed crowd here—some locals, most not—is more women than men, and everyone is dressed well, refined looking, out for a civilized evening. Beth reads the list of cocktails on the drinks menu and gasps at the prices. At $20 a pop, everyone here is out for a civilized and *expensive* evening. She looks down the length of the bar, at the men and women seated next to them, trying to get a sense for who comes here. She notices nothing worth mentioning until she sees the large Nantucket basket purse perched on the bar, owned by the blond woman next to the bald man in the seersucker suit jacket. Too expensive for anyone actually from Nantucket to own; Beth has seen Nantucket baskets much smaller than that sell for over $1,000.

The bar itself is a honed, rugged stone slab embedded with amber-colored pieces of sea glass. Beth slides her hand over the cool surface. It's beautiful, a piece of art. The music is techno and loud. No one will be singing "Pour Some Sugar on Me" here.

"Here you go," says Jimmy, presenting Beth with a martini glass brimming with pink liquid. "The best drink on the menu."

Beth takes a sip. It's sweet and spicy with a strong but not unpleasant kick, the kind of drink she could easily get drunk on.

"It's good. What is it?" asks Beth.

"Vodka, rum, chili, lime, and ginger. It's called a Hot Passion martini."

Hot Passion? What is he doing? Beth feels embarrassed, indignant, and then strangely flattered.

"What's with the beard?" asks Petra.

"Just trying it out," says Jimmy, scratching the hollows of his newly hairy cheeks with his fingers. "You like it?"

"No," says Petra.

He's been growing the beard for about a month now, and Beth thinks it looks good on him, rugged, masculine. It makes up for his weak chin. And she knows him, that he's not just trying it out. Jimmy stops shaving whenever he's going through a hard time—when his dad died, when scalloping dried up and they couldn't pay the bills, when Jessica had surgery on her ears in Boston. And now. Beth smiles to herself, pleased to realize that at least their separation ranks up there with the death of his father, that she still matters to him. And he stops shaving not simply because he's too distracted and overwhelmed with the stress in his life to bother, but mainly because his beard makes him feel protected, hidden. Jimmy wearing a beard is like Beth wearing one of her big, black, shapeless sweaters that covers her butt.

But she's not wearing one of those sweaters tonight. She's wearing her Goldie Hawn dress, and Jimmy's wearing a beard. Interesting. It hadn't occurred to her that he might be having a hard time without her. Maybe this isn't what he wants. Maybe he's suffering, too.

Angela wiggles her way behind the bar and says something to Jimmy that Beth can't hear. Angela laughs, and he smiles, flashing those crooked, charming teeth. It's quick and then guarded, but there it was. She made him smile.

Keep suffering. Keep hiding. I hope you end up looking like Grizzly Adams.

Jill leans into Beth. "I think he's trying out enough new things at the moment."

Jimmy turns his attention to the couple next to Jill and begins opening a bottle of wine for them. Beth sips her martini, aware that Angela is a few feet behind her, that her estranged husband is inches in front of her, that she is sitting between them. This is too weird. She downs her drink. She hates the thought of Angela looking at her right now, checking her out, without her knowing. She feels self-conscious, exposed. Beth rubs her arms as if she's cold and checks her phone. No messages from the girls.

Unable to watch Angela, which is what she thought was the entire point of this outing, she sits and watches Jimmy instead. She can't remember when she last looked at him for this long. Before he moved out, they slept facing away from each other, a habit that began because of his snoring and his cigar breath. Because of his schedule, they rarely ate meals together, and when they did, it was usually in the living room with their plates on their laps while they faced the TV. And she withheld regard for his very existence whenever they were in a fight, which for the past few years was often.

Now she has a front-row seat with nothing to do but watch him. She's never seen him bartend before. He's in constant motion back there, in command, at ease. His hands, uncorking wine bottles, pouring martinis to the rim, muddling limes, are confident, efficient, graceful. He knows where every bottle and bar tool is. He knows from memory how every drink is made. He's good at this, and he enjoys it.

She didn't know any of this. She feels surprise and a twinge of hurt to discover that there's anything about Jimmy that she didn't know. He's not exactly a complex guy. Work, sleep, TV, kids, cigars. Not that bartending is brain surgery or race-car driving, but still, he's got skill and talent. The bar is the hub of this place. Everything revolves around it, and Jimmy is keeping the cogs moving, keeping the customers happy.

This is vastly different from scalloping, which was solitary and outdoors, a job she thought suited him well. But here he is, in a crowded restaurant, confined to a small indoor space, chatting up strangers, mixing "girlie" drinks, and appearing to love it. He looks so at home.

But he's not dressed the way he dresses around the house. At home, he wears jeans or shorts that used to be jeans—frayed and uneven where he cut them with scissors at the bottom— T-shirts, a Red Sox hat, and work boots. Here, he's wearing a button-down shirt with vertical blue and white stripes. It's even ironed. He's wearing it untucked with the sleeves rolled up to his elbows and unbuttoned one button more than most men would wear it, revealing the top of his chest. He has a handsome, muscular chest. The beard, his smile, his forearms, his chest—he looks relaxed and, she could kill herself for thinking this, sexy. Fueled at least in part by the Hot Passion, she's at once helplessly attracted to him and completely pissed at him.

How is it that he can be present and engaged and so competent here, whereas at home he drags himself around, too exhausted to do anything but lie on the couch? How is it that he can pull himself together, look handsome and cleaned up for work, but at home he only wears T-shirts stained with barbecue sauce on the front and sweat under the arms? How can he save this alive and fun part of himself for work and not share it with her and his girls?

"So, Jimmy, is it always this busy?" asks Petra.

"This? This is nothing. Wait another hour, it'll be three people deep behind you."

"Huh," says Petra.

Her restaurant, Dish, does well, but not three-people-deep-behind-the-bar-without-a-seat well, not this time of year anyway.

"How was your drink?" he asks Beth.

"Okay."

"You want another?"

"No, thanks," says Beth, thinking that she's had quite enough of his Hot Passion.

"You didn't like it?"

"I did, I just want to try something different now."

"How about a glass of wine? You'd like the—"

"I can decide what I want without your help."

"Okay."

"I'll have an espresso martini."

"You sure?" asks Jimmy.

"Really sure."

He shrugs his shoulders, acquiescing. He grabs two bottles and inverts them over a stainless-steel martini shaker. "How are the girls?"

"Good."

"How was Jessica's game?"

"It was long. They lost."

"And Soph?"

"She's upset about a math test, thinks she failed it, but I'm sure she did fine."

"How's Gracie?"

"Good." *She misses you. They all do.*

"Good."

"Don't you want to know how Beth is?" asks Petra.

"Of course. How are you, Beth?"

"Good."

"You look good."

"Thanks."

"I like your necklace."

She places her hand over her locket. Her face flushes hot. She almost forgot she was wearing it. Before she can respond, Angela is behind the bar again, this time showing Jimmy something on her phone, capturing his interest. She laughs and touches his forearm. Angela's hand on Jimmy's arm. Beth could stomach the laughing and the smiling and the flirting and the boobs, but something about that small touch, the intimacy of it, undoes her.

"You okay?" Jill asks Beth in her ear. "You look a little pale."

Beth nods as she clenches her teeth and swallows. She can't speak. If she talks right now, she'll cry. Whatever goal she had for tonight, the goal now is to get out of here without crying in front of Jimmy and Angela.

"You probably just need to eat."

Beth nods again, rubbing her silver locket between her fingers, disgusted with the foolish girl who put it on a few hours ago.

Jimmy serves Beth her espresso martini and then all three women their dinners. Petra ordered the grouper; Jill, on a sushi kick ever since that April book club, got the spicy tuna roll; and Beth got a burger with fries. Truffle-oil fries.

"How is everything?" asks Jimmy after a few minutes.

"Good," says Petra. "The food is really good, Jimmy. Who's your head chef?"

While Petra and Jimmy discuss the restaurant business, and Jill is texting her boys, Beth stays focused on eating and drinking. After finishing her second martini, she notices that she doesn't feel like crying anymore. She mostly feels numb now, as if a thick layer of fuzzy static is wrapped around her like a cocoon, impenetrable, more effective than a beard or a black sweater.

She's on her third drink, another espresso martini, when she hears someone yelling her name from behind her. She turns around. It's Georgia, waving and weaving her way through the crowd, knocking into bodies and glasses and splashing drinks as she pushes toward the bar, leaving a sea of hostile faces in her wake.

"I'm so glad you're still here!" she says, out of breath. "How's it going? Where's the Salt mistress?"

Beth, Petra, and Jill look at each other and then at Jimmy, who definitely heard that. Petra laughs.

"You mean *hostess?*" Petra asks.

Georgia laughs. "Whoops, yes! And I haven't had anything to drink yet. Where is she?"

"You didn't see her on the way in?" asks Petra.

"No, where?"

"Behind you. By the door."

"Where?"

"The dark, curly hair."

Georgia stands on her toes and squints her whole face.

"The one in the black shirt," says Petra.

Georgia shakes her head, still searching.

"The one with the boobs."

"Ah, got her!" says Georgia. "Bimbo. I never pegged Jimmy for a boob guy."

Beth presses her hand over her own insulted boobs. It's true that Beth's are unremarkable, and Jimmy is more of a leg guy. Beth has great legs, long and toned. She's always walking, at the beaches, at Bartlett's Farm, all over New York City before she moved here.

It occurs to her that she's never heard of a man referred to as an eyes guy or a brains guy or a personality guy. She downs the rest of her martini. Guys suck. Maybe this is a blessing. Maybe she's better off without Jimmy. No man in the house. Her home will stay clean and organized, and it will smell pretty.

And no more fighting. It's been peaceful since he left. Somewhere in her brain, Marilyn McCoo is singing "One Less Bell to Answer," a song her mother used to like when Beth was a young girl and that Beth hasn't heard or consciously thought of since.

"Not that there's anything wrong with yours," says Georgia.

"Just wait until she has babies," says Jill. "Hers will be hanging like the rest of ours."

The fuzzy numbness of Beth's martini armor must have a chink in it because that comment punched right through and knocked the wind out of her. What if Angela gets pregnant? Beth thinks about how easily she conceived. Each and every time they pulled the goalie, it was one shot—score! She feels dizzy. The edges of her vision turn dim and blurry. She's got to get out of here.

"Hello, Georgia," says Jimmy.

"I'm not happy with you," says Georgia.

"I know."

"But I'll forgive you if Beth does."

"That's fair," he says, looking to Beth for input like he's looking for an opening in a window, even the slightest crack.

"Beth, you're looking pale again," says Jill.

Jill is sitting right next to Beth, but her voice sounds as if it's coming from way off in the distance somewhere.

"Beth, you okay?" asks Petra.

"I don't feel well," says Beth with more air than sound.

"I'll take her home," says Petra.

"I'll stay and have a drink with Georgia," says Jill.

Petra pays her and Beth's part of the bill, and Georgia hugs Beth as she gets up.

"She's a bimbo," says Georgia.

"Thanks."

"And you're a queen."

Beth smiles.

"And I love your dress."

"Thanks."

Jill gets up and hugs Beth.

"You did great. I'll call you tomorrow."

Beth nods. She looks up at Jimmy before she turns to leave.

"Good night, Beth," says Jimmy.

"G'night, Jimmy."

Petra takes her by the hand, and they worm their way through the crowd, leaving Salt. Leaving Jimmy. Leaving him there with Angela. Leaving him feels so wrong. Somewhere beneath the static fuzz and above the Marilyn McCoo song still playing in her head, a voice is screaming, *Don't leave him! Don't leave!* But it's late, and she's had enough to eat and more than enough to drink, and she's had enough of seeing Angela's boobs and Jimmy's smile, so there's nothing left to do but leave.

"Have a good night," says Angela's voice from somewhere behind her.

It sounds as if Angela's smiling, maybe even gloating, but Beth doesn't know. She's already out the door, and she doesn't look back.

PETRA PULLS INTO Beth's driveway. The house is dark. The girls forgot to flick on the porch light. At least they went to bed.

"You okay?" asks Petra.

"Yeah."

"You're too quiet."

"I'm fine."

"You don't have to hold it together in front of me."

"I'm not holding anything. I'm fine," Beth says, having some difficulty enunciating *holding anything*. "I'm a little drunk, but I'm fine. I'm drunk and fine."

"You guys really need to talk soon and figure out what you're doing."

"I know."

"Drink some water and go to bed."

"I will."

"Love you."

"Love you, too."

Beth follows the beams of Petra's headlights to the front door. It must be a cloudy night because Beth can't see the moon or any stars in the sky. Outside of Petra's headlights, the whole world is pure darkness. The air is cool and smells of salt and fish and forsythia. Spring peepers shriek in a loud and noxious chorus all around her, sounding not unlike the techno music from Salt still ringing in her ears. She hears Petra pull away as she opens the front door and turns on the hall light.

She walks upstairs and opens the door to each of the girls' rooms, checking on them, asleep in their beds. Sweet, beautiful girls. She shuts off Sophie's computer and tosses her dirty clothes into her hamper; she hangs Jessica's wet towel on a hook in the bathroom; and she pulls the covers up over Gracie. She walks downstairs and into the kitchen and pours herself a tall glass of water.

Back upstairs, she pauses in the hallway and stares at the pictures on the wall. She looks at Jimmy touching her skirt, and she relives Angela touching his arm, and an anger colored with humiliation rises up inside her, swelling. In another picture, she's wearing the locket he gave her, the one she's wearing now that he noticed on her tonight.

She can't take it. She can't take one more walk down this hallway, looking at his smiling teeth, his hand on her, the locket around her neck, the lie of their perfect marriage, his deception mocking her every time she walks from the living room to her bedroom, from her bedroom to the bathroom. She's had enough of this. Enough.

She starts with her wedding picture. She loosens the latch, removes the back plate and the cardboard filler, yanks out the photo, and returns the empty frame to the wall. She does this methodically, breathing hard, with each picture until she has them all in a nice, neat stack.

Sitting on the floor in the hallway, she flips through them. She gets to the most recent one, the one from last summer, and studies it. Some reasonable part of her not affected by the vodka and rum and humiliated anger urges her to put the pictures in a drawer, that she'll regret what she's about to do. But she's too furious and drunk and hopped up on caffeine to hear reason, and she's tired of feeling like a passive doormat.

The first tear is slow, hesitant, and then deliberate, straight through Jimmy's smiling face. Then the rips come fast, one after another, after another. There's no stopping now. She tears and tears until the shreds are too small to rip any further, and now she's sobbing, hating him for making her do this. She hears one of the girls sneeze. She stops crying and listens, afraid of waking them. She can still hear the techno music from Salt buzzing in her ears, the spring peepers shrieking outside, and she can feel-hear her heart thumping in her chest and pulsing in her fingers, but the girls are quiet. She wipes her eyes and exhales.

She collects the heaps of torn paper, shreds of what was her happy family, and throws them into the wastebasket in her bedroom. She then returns to the hallway and looks at the wall, to witness what she's done. There. Eight framed, matted pieces of cardboard. He's gone. There's no undoing it now. Like his infidelity. This is what is real.

She adjusts two of the frames so that they're level, flicks off the hall light, and returns to her bedroom. She strips out of her Goldie Hawn dress and slides into her pink, flannel pajamas. She crawls into bed, forgetting the locket still around her neck, facing the side where Jimmy used to sleep with her, her feet restless and her eyes wide-open.

Awake all night.

CHAPTER 10

⌒⌣

Everything changed in June, and Olivia, naïve to this time of year on this tiny island, never saw it coming. It started with Memorial Day weekend, when the cocooned and quiet simplicity of her daily life became bombarded on all sides by the rapid and sure-footed influx of invaders. The summer people. It took her a couple of weeks not to feel like she needed to hide inside her home, not to feel threatened or violated by their presence, to regain her composure and reestablish a routine. But after a couple of weeks, she finally exhaled, thinking, *There, this isn't so bad.*

And then came July. June did so little to prepare her for July. June is a gently sloping hill in the Berkshires, and July is Mount Everest. The roads are now crammed with mopeds and Jeeps and monstrous SUVs, engine exhausts and radios spewing their pollution into the sweet summer air. The previously desolate, private-feeling beaches are now cluttered with families and their chairs and umbrellas and boogie boards and their picnic garbage and constant conversation, and every rental house is full, every bedroom and driveway, the occupants celebrating their week's vacation with outdoor parties and cookouts night after night.

These are the real summer people, and they came by the tens of thousands, quintupling the island's population. They came by air, and they came by sea, and they came with their kids and their dogs and their nannies and their assistants and their personal chefs and their houseguests. And everyone (except the dogs) brought a cell phone. Olivia imagines the geological shelf that Nantucket sits on, fragile and precarious, and worries that it might actually crumble under the weight of all the tourists and their stuff, causing the island to sink to the bottom of the ocean. A modern Atlantis.

Even the sky is crowded. Commuter planes and private jets from Boston and New York roar overhead every few minutes. All day long.

If she adjusted in June, she's merely coping in July. She feels a kinship with the other locals, easily identified and distinct from the summer people, like picking out wild horses from circus zebras, even though she knows that the feeling is one-sided. Although she's earned some level of respect for having lived here through part of the winter and an entire spring, she hasn't lived "on island" a full year yet. She's not a real member of the herd. She hasn't put in enough time. But even after a full year—in truth, even after fifty years—she'll always be viewed as a wash-ashore, a transplant, never a true local, and absolutely never a native (a person has to be born here to own that title).

She's made some adjustments already that have become her summer laws for living:

Never go to the beach between the hours of ten and three. That's when they all go.

Avoid Town at all costs. If you must go, do not drive downtown at lunchtime or anytime after 6:00 p.m. There will be no parking anywhere.

Never go to Stop & Shop anytime Friday through Sunday. Allow an extra thirty minutes for everything.

She's written these rules out on a piece of paper and taped

it to the wall by her front door, a cute but serious reminder in case she should grow forgetful or cocky. Which is why she's cursing herself right now, as she stands at the edge of the pasta aisle in front of Newman's Own marinara sauce near the end of a discouragingly long checkout line in Stop & Shop on a Saturday afternoon.

She needed more coffee and eggs and thought it would be nice to have a salad for dinner without thinking about the calendar or her summer laws. She didn't realize what day it was until she pulled into the crowded parking lot and knew immediately. She hesitated, thinking she should forget about the salad and go home, but then the woman in the Land Rover behind her honked, urging Olivia to move along, and so she did, thinking, *How bad can it be?*

That was over an hour ago. She counts the items in her basket. Fourteen. If she reshelves the loaf of bread and the toilet paper (she can get by on what she has until Monday), then she can move over to the express line, but that line is even longer and appears to carry more hostility in its ranks.

"This is taking forever," mutters the woman in line behind Olivia. "I'm definitely going to be late."

Olivia's grateful that she's at least not in a hurry. She has no beach-portrait session tonight. The family she had scheduled for this evening canceled this morning.

Becoming a professional beach-portrait photographer ended up being far easier than she imagined it would be. First, she did some research by calling around to the other portrait photographers on the island, inquiring about their rates. Then she did the math and figured out that if she could do four sessions a week from June to Labor Day, she'd make enough money to live the whole year. More than enough.

But then she had the problem of how to get *any* customers, never mind four a week, to hire her, an unknown with no professional training or experience, just a good eye and a natural facility with a camera. To address this rather big problem, she did two small things. First, she printed flyers and posted them all over town—the Visitors Center, Young's Bicycle Shop, The Bean, the library, the Chamber of Commerce, the Hy-Line and Steamship Authority docks, even here at Stop & Shop. And second, she made sure to set her price at $200 cheaper than the "cheapest" going rate.

The calls and e-mails started coming in, and she's booked more sessions than she thought possible, four to six times a week, often twice in the same evening. She's already scheduled one family for Labor Day weekend. The prints are all ordered online through a separate company, so all she has to do is shoot with her digital camera, edit with Photoshop on her computer, and upload the images to the ordering website. Payment is online, by credit card. There are no paper invoices to send, no waiting to receive checks in the mail. She has no overhead other than Internet service. It's clean and simple.

The women in front of her have calmly been chatting the whole time, seemingly unfazed by the long lines and the increasingly impatient mood surrounding them. One, the natural-looking blonde, is wearing a black cotton tank with no logo, no embellishments, a plain white cotton skirt, and flip-flops, and the other is wearing yoga clothes. No flashy jewelry, no designer labels, their fingernails aren't manicured, and their purses look like they cost less than $50. Locals.

"Is it weird that I don't want to hire Roger?"

"No, of course not."

"He's done all the others and has always done a great job. I don't know, I feel like I'm being disloyal, but it'd just be too weird showing up without Jimmy."

"I get it."

"He'd be like, 'Where's Jimmy?' And then I'd have to admit that he's not coming, and that would be weird."

"So don't hire Roger. He won't even know."

"Everybody knows everything here."

"True. So then he probably already knows about you and Jimmy."

"I guess, maybe."

"And you know, he wouldn't even care. These things happen. I think he just got divorced, didn't he?"

"I don't think so."

"He did. His wife left the island, moved to Texas."

"Oh, yeah, that's right. So who would you hire?"

"I don't know, you should ask Jill. They used someone last summer."

"They used Roger."

"Oh."

"I know I shouldn't spend the money, but I need the pictures. They're going to be a visual reminder that my life is fine without him, that I still have my beautiful girls, and I don't need him to be happy."

"Visualization is good."

"This is my first step in really moving on."

"You manifest what you envision."

"Yeah. And I need to do it soon. Those empty frames in my hallway look depressing."

"Why don't you have Gracie draw some cute pictures, put those in the frames for now?"

"I asked, she wouldn't. None of them would. They're all mad at me for ripping up our family photos. I don't blame them. Such a stupid thing to do."

"Jimmy cheating on you was a stupid thing to do. You get a free pass."

"Shhh."

"What?"

"We're in Stop & Shop, someone will hear you."

"Oh, for God's sakes. Kevin Bacon knows Jimmy cheated on you."

"You're right, I know."

Olivia touches her purse, knowing she has a beach-portrait flyer inside. She should tap this blond woman on the shoulder and offer her the flyer, but as she imagines doing this, it feels too aggressive. And she doesn't want to interrupt or admit to listening to their personal conversation. She decides to keep to herself and hopes that the blond woman will notice her flyer pinned to the bulletin board on the way out.

Their line is finally out from the pasta aisle, and Olivia can now see every checkout line in the store. To her left, she notices a woman and her son. He's about six or seven, and he's sitting in the toddler seat of the grocery cart. His long, tan legs dangle down, almost reaching the floor. He's spinning a pinwheel, which he has pressed up against his nose. Autism.

He's so completely pulled inside a spinning world of blurred metallic color that he doesn't seem at all affected by the long line, the crowds of irritated people around him, the harsh lights, or Michael Bublé singing Tony Bennett over the speakers. Then something changes. Maybe he realizes he's hungry, or he's bored, or he hates Michael Bublé, or the tag on the back of his shirt is itching him at last more than he can stand. Who knows why? He throws the pinwheel to the ground, and he starts screaming, thumbs in his ears, his eyes squeezed shut.

His mother retrieves the pinwheel and spins it, holding it up to his face, trying to lure him back into its magic spell, but he won't open his eyes. She tries to soothe him with her voice, straining to remain calm, reassuring him that they'll be home soon, but his thumb-stopped ears are unavailable to logic or lies. She doesn't attempt to touch him. Olivia knows this would probably make everything worse. A lot worse.

Then it appears as though she's doing nothing. She's ignoring him.

Olivia sees the looks and hears the murmured judgments being passed around like mints among people in line.

He's too old to be acting like that.

My children would never be allowed to behave that way.

Spoiled.

What kind of mother?

They don't get it. Olivia does. Shy of picking him up and carrying him out of here, that mother is doing what any mother of a child with autism and a cart full of groceries would do. She's breathing, holding on white-knuckle tight to her cart and her courage, and praying to God.

God, please help him calm down.

God, please, before I lose it, too, get us out of here.

God, please.

"I don't blame him," says the woman in the yoga clothes. "If this line doesn't start to move a little faster, I'm going to start screaming, too."

"Not very Yogi of you," says her blond friend, the one who needs the pictures.

"True. But it sure would release all the negative energy I've been absorbing in this place. Stop & Shop is totally clogging up my fourth chakra."

The blonde laughs. Olivia smiles. The blonde stares at the boy and his mother while they wait in line. The expression on the blonde's face as she watches them doesn't seem to carry a trace of judgment, but rather an intense interest, even wonder. Olivia would love to know what she's thinking but says nothing.

At long last, Olivia reaches the checkout. She greets the cashier with a friendly hello, bags her own groceries, carries her canvas tote to her Jeep, and drives home.

Thirty minutes later, she is there.

AT HOME, OLIVIA boils two eggs. She slices the tomatoes, cucumbers, and a red pepper. She shreds the lettuce and tosses it all into a large bowl. She adds olives, Vidalia onions, Parmesan cheese, croutons, and, when they're done, the eggs. She drizzles on a touch of olive oil and red-wine vinegar, a pinch of salt and pepper. A glass of cold sauvignon blanc, a slice from the ciabatta loaf, and she's done.

She carries her dinner, a citronella candle, and one of her journals out onto her backyard deck. She sits with her well-earned feast, opens her journal, and begins to read where she last left off.

July 5, 2003

My life right now is all about communication, or rather, the lack of it. I spend all my waking hours demanding communication from Anthony. Anthony, say JUICE. JUICE. JUUUUICE. Say the word. Tell me what you want. Say I WANT JUICE. Say SWING. Say I WANT TO GO OUTSIDE AND SWING ON THE SWING. Please. Look at me, Anthony, and tell me what you want. Tell me what you're feeling. Tell me why you're screaming. I can usually tell if it's happy-excited screaming or frustrated-panicked screaming, but right now, I'm too tired, and I can't figure it out. Why are you screaming? How can I help you if you won't tell me what you want?

And then there's me and David. We don't know how to communicate either. We don't look at each other anymore. I can't stand to look into his eyes and see his despair, his exhaustion, sometimes the blame, and too often the wish that he'd stayed at the office another hour. Maybe I'd be in bed by then, and he wouldn't have to deal with me and what's in my eyes.

We don't talk to each other anymore. Not really. We say plenty about what has to be done. Did you buy Anthony's

JUICE? I'm going to the grocery store, do we need JUICE? Will you push Anthony on the SWING? He's screaming because he wants to go outside and swing on the SWING. Will you take out the trash, go to the store, do the laundry, pay the bills? The bills, the bills, the bills.

We say all these words, but we don't talk about anything. It's all meaningless. Blah, blah, blah.

I don't tell David what I'm thinking, that we're the parents of a permanently disabled child and our marriage is crippled. I think this every day, but I never say the words. I don't tell David.

We don't have sex anymore, and I don't want sex anymore, but I miss the part of me that used to feel connected to David, that felt horny and wanted sex. We don't talk about this.

And who would want sex after the days I have? I'm exhausted from worry and the physical job of taking care of Anthony. I have bruises from his pinches and kicks, and bite marks all over me. I look abused. I feel abused, but I don't tell David.

I don't really feel abused by Anthony, I feel abused by this life. What happened to my life? My life is all about autism. If I'm not living it, I'm reading about it or talking about it, and I'm just so damn sick of it, I could puke. I'm scared that this is all it's ever going to be. Anthony has autism, and he won't say JUICE or SWING or why he is screaming, and David and I aren't speaking, roommates in the same prison cell.

Or at best we're colleagues, self-trained therapists working on the same patient, a beautiful boy named Anthony, trying to fix him. Only we're failing. We're not fixing him. His autism isn't going anywhere, and it's this huge pink elephant in our living room, and we're not talking about what's real, that we're going to be living

*with autism for the rest of our lives, and we need to accept
this. As much as I want to scream and cry and break
everything in this world, as much as I want to resist and
fight and beg, we need to accept Anthony with autism.*

*Why can't we talk about this? Why don't we tell each
other how we feel, what we want, what we're afraid of,
that we still love each other? Do we? Do we even still love
each other?*

*What great role models we are for Anthony, huh? Hey,
Anthony, TALK. See how Mommy and Daddy DON'T
do it. We have Anthony in therapy for thirty-five hours a
week to learn to communicate. I wonder how many hours a
week David and I would need....*

SHE AND DAVID never went to couples counseling. Maybe they
should have. But between all the occupational and behavioral
and speech therapists for Anthony, the parent support groups,
and then the grief counseling, none of it effective, they weren't
exactly jumping at the idea of inviting yet another counselor,
and another expense, into their already therapy-saturated lives.

Olivia closes her journal and thinks with her eyes shut.
She's been going through her entries a little each day, reading
her past, trying to come to terms with it all, looking for peace.
She opens her eyes. Not today.

She sighs and returns to the kitchen for another glass of
wine. As she opens the refrigerator door, she hears a shrill ding.
She pauses, trying to decipher what it was. She's always hearing things in this house, eerie, unexplained noises that used
to spook her when she first moved here, but now she's grown
more curious than afraid.

The fog that often settles over the island usually insulates
sound, muffling it. The silence of a thick fog on Nantucket can
be palpable. But sometimes, and she has no idea why, the fog

amplifies, warps, and scatters sound, sending it miles away from its source. She swears she's heard fishermen talking on their boats from her bedroom. And she sometimes hears a creepy, melodic moaning that she likes to think is the sound of seals barking offshore.

A fog is rolling in tonight, so the ding might've been a neighbor's wind chime, a kid's bicycle bell from around the block, an ice cream truck at the beach. But the ding sounded louder, more immediate. More *here*. She pulls the wine bottle from the refrigerator, and there it is again. Is it the doorbell?

She sets the bottle of wine down on the counter, wipes her wet hand on her shorts, walks to the front door, and opens it.

"Hi, Liv."

She gasps. She didn't actually expect to find anyone there. And she certainly didn't expect it to be him.

"David."

CHAPTER 11

It's nine fifteen, and Beth has already dropped the girls off at the community center. Gracie and Jessica love it there, but Sophie hates it. She showed signs of outgrowing the games and crafts and activities toward the end of last summer when she was twelve, complaining that camp was "boring." Well, if last year was boring, this year is pure agony. But it's where all the other kids who are still too young for summer jobs go for camp, and Beth would rather she be in agony at the community center than skulking around the house all day, bored and in agony at home.

When Beth pulled into the community center parking lot, she said to all three, "Have fun!" Jessica and Gracie smiled and waved, but Sophie replied, "Don't worry, I *won't!*"—and slammed the car door. Ah, thirteen.

Camp runs until two. Jimmy has the night off and offered to pick them up, spend the afternoon with them, and then take them to dinner at the Brotherhood. He said he'd have them home by eight.

Beth has the next almost eleven hours stretched out in front of her to do whatever she pleases. A completely free day.

A week ago, she would've used that time to clean, a big project such as washing all the windows, or bleaching the mold and mildew off the deck furniture, or weeding. But she's been re-reading *Writing Down the Bones* and going through her note-books, her old poems, her short stories, her many unfinished vignettes, enjoying them all. And she's started dreaming again.

So she's letting the mold and mildew and the pollen spots and pesky weeds be. Instead, she's gone to the library for a quiet place to write, free of distraction. Today, she feels ready to dust off that creative part of her that she boxed up years ago and see if it still works. She's finally giving herself the space and the time to explore that expressive voice inside her that became unconsciously stifled, lost first to the demands of young moth-erhood, then seduced into ennui by her daily routine.

She walks up to the second floor and sits in an armless Shaker-style wooden chair at a substantial wooden table, much larger than the one in her own dining room, facing a window that is also oversized, at least eight feet tall. The window is open, and a fresh-smelling morning breeze fills the air in the room. Nine other matching chairs surround the table, all unoccupied.

She pulls out her blank spiral notebook, the one she bought years ago, and opens it to the first blank page. It's been a long time since she's written anything other than checks to pay the bills. She feels excited, nervous. She pulls out her favorite pen and stares at the page, trying to think of how to begin. Begin-nings have always been difficult for her. She taps her teeth with her pen, a habit she developed as a teenager whenever she was stuck on a homework problem, and she can hear her mother's voice in her head saying, *Stop that, Elizabeth,* and so she does.

She looks up at the clock on the wall. It's nine twenty-five. Like the window and the table, the clock is larger than most. It's oak with Roman numerals on an ivory face. The wood has elaborate scrolls carved into it that look like curled ocean waves. The clock appears old and probably is, and it probably has a story and historical significance, but Beth doesn't know what. It's quiet in the library today, so quiet that she can hear the clock ticking.

Tick. Tick. Tick.

Why is the library so empty today? She looks out the window. Blue sky, no clouds, a gentle and steady breeze. It's a perfect beach day. That's what she could do with her free day. She could go to the beach! She slides her chair out, but before she caps her pen, she recognizes the real motivation behind this impetuous idea. Fear. Fear of this blank page in front of her. Plus, it's a stupid impetuous idea, going to the beach in the middle of the day in July, fighting the summer people for a square of sand. That's where everyone is. She knows better than to put herself through that madness.

She slides her chair back in, tucking her legs under the table, and tries to get comfortable. Okay. Begin. But begin what? Does she want to expand on one of her unfinished short stories? She should've brought those with her. Should it take place on Nantucket? Maybe New York? The questions keep coming, echoing in her head, paralyzing her hand.

She looks up at the clock. Nine forty-five.

Tick. Tick. Tick.

Maybe she should do one of the exercises in *Writing Down the Bones*, get the pen moving, the ink flowing, grease the rusty wheels a bit. She remembers now that this is how she used to begin.

She unzips her purse, a big, bulky, worn, black nylon bag. Someone gave it to her. Was it Georgia? It's so long ago now, she can't remember. It was a baby-shower gift. Her purse is really a diaper bag. Jill thinks it's really a disgrace.

Beth admits that it's not the prettiest thing, and, yes, the girls have now been potty-trained for some time, but she likes the wide shoulder strap, that it's water resistant and wipes clean of pretty much anything, that it has tons of useful pockets. The pocket for the baby bottle is now where she keeps her water bottle. The wipes pocket now contains her wallet. The zipped compartment she used for pacifiers is now where she keeps her cell phone. The middle compartment is where she dumps everything else.

Everything else, it seems, but *Writing Down the Bones*. It's not in there. She forgot to bring it. Damn. Maybe she should go home and get it. She looks down at her notebook.

Blank.

She has to go get it. But if she leaves, she knows she won't come back. If she leaves, she'll be wearing yellow latex gloves and carrying a bucket of bleach in twenty minutes. She plants her feet flat and heavy on the floor as if they were two anchors and breathes. She's staying.

She thinks she wants to expand on the short story she wrote about a boy who found comfort and meaning inside an imagined world where colors had emotions, water could sing, and the boy could become invisible. But then she remembers the boy she once saw on the beach, the curious intensity and joy he showed, even for a child, as he created a line of white rocks, and the briefest moment they shared that felt like an exquisite secret between them. She feels compelled and captivated by both boys. Maybe she can combine them. But how?

She taps her teeth and thinks of the saying *Write what you know*. What does she know? She looks down at her blank page.

She looks up at the clock and sighs. Ten twenty-five. Maybe she should go to the The Bean, get a coffee and a snack. Maybe that's what she needs, some caffeine, some food, and a change of scenery. Maybe the atmosphere here is all wrong. She looks around her—the many bookcases painted creamy white, packed with hardcovers; the Persian rugs; the oil paintings of famous writers like Ralph Waldo

Emerson, Henry David Thoreau, and Herman Melville on the walls; that damn clock. It's all too serious, too scholarly, too intimidating. Too much pressure.

She has enough reasons to leave, excuses absurd to valid, and yet she stays. She wants to write. She looks around her, at the books on the shelves. Hundreds of books, each one written by somebody. She chooses to feel inspired instead of intimidated. Why not somebody like her?

Her eyes settle upon a book positioned face out on the bookcase closest to the window, second shelf from the top. *The Siege.* The cover is gray and white and has a black-and-white photograph of a young girl on it. The girl maybe looks a bit like Sophie when she was a toddler, but that slight resemblance isn't what's catching her attention. None of it—not the title, the cover, not even the picture of the girl—feels remarkable or particularly interesting to her, yet she feels drawn to it, oddly pulled by it.

She forces herself to look away, browsing the other bookcases from her seat. She finds no other books facing out on any of the shelves. Not one. She returns to *The Siege,* feeling again as if she can't look away, not because it's a distraction like the clock or her purse, not to avoid looking at her blank page, but because she feels strangely *compelled* to look at it.

It's the same feeling she had when she met Jimmy. It was a late night at the Chicken Box, Nantucket's legendary dive bar. She couldn't stop looking at him. It wasn't because he was attractive, although he was. Plenty of attractive single guys were all over Nantucket that summer, everywhere she looked. And it wasn't because she was drunk on beer and Jell-O shots, although she was. That night, there was only Jimmy. The whole bar was static, and Jimmy was a clear channel. She felt almost spellbound by him, as if he were a magnet pulling her to him.

Now this book on the shelf feels the same way. She stares at it, mesmerized by its nonmesmerizing, simple cover, and wonders what it's about. With considerable willpower, she shakes off its spell and returns to her blank page.

Blank. Blank. Blankety-blank.

Tick. Tick. Tick.

She looks up at the book, now feeling as if the girl on the cover were staring at her.

Oh, for God's sakes.

She walks over to the bookcase and brings the book back to her seat. *The Siege* by Clara Claiborne Park. She reads the front and back covers. It's a true story, written by a mother about her autistic daughter. Beth enjoyed *The Curious Incident of the Dog in the Night-Time,* but autism isn't a subject she would normally read about on her own. But she's obviously not going to begin writing the great American novel today. And she's *not* going back and cleaning the house. She caps her pen, opens the book, and begins to read.

HOURS LATER, SOMEONE taps her on the shoulder, startling her. She looks up. It's Mary Crawford, the librarian.

"Sorry, Beth, I didn't mean to startle you, but we're closing in five minutes."

Beth looks up at the clock. It says four fifty-five. She looks out the window. The light coming in is softer, more diffuse, suggesting longer shadows and evening. She looks at her watch. Four fifty-five. How did that happen?

She looks down at her notebook.

Blank.

"I'm sorry, I got completely caught up in this book."

"Would you like to borrow it?"

"Yes, please."

Beth didn't write anything, and she didn't clean anything, but at least she found a good book to read.

BACK AT HOME, she still has plenty of time left in her free day before the girls come home. She could clean something or eat something. She chooses the second. She's famished. She hasn't had a thing to eat today since breakfast.

She fixes herself a ham-and-cheese sandwich and, in celebration of her free day, decides to make herself a real drink. She pours vodka, lime juice, cranberry juice, and a splash of ginger beer into Gracie's lunch thermos because she doesn't have a martini shaker. She adds ice, shakes, then pours some into a wineglass. She takes a sip and smiles. It's good. See? She doesn't need Jimmy. She can make her own passion.

The air in the house is hot and stale. No one was home today to turn on the air conditioners or open the windows. Beth takes her meal and drink and her library book out onto the deck, and she sits in one of the mildewed chairs.

The moldiest chair of them all, Jimmy's cigar-smoking chair, is pushed off to the side, facing the corner of the deck, as if it'd been sent there for misbehaving. Beth asked Jimmy to get it out of here, once and for all, weeks ago. It was bad enough before, but she's certainly not going to keep his cigar chair here while he shacks up with another woman. She angles her own chair so that his disappears from view. She eats her dinner and reads.

She's still absorbed in reading and on her third Passion à la Beth cocktail, which she feels she's now perfected (less lime, more vodka), when she hears the front door open and shut.

"Hello?" she yells.

Sophie and Jessica appear on the deck.

"Where's Gracie?" asks Beth.

"In the kitchen, working on a project for camp," says Jessica.

"Oh, what project?" asks Beth.

"I dunno," says Jessica.

"What did you have for dinner?"

"Hot dog," says Jessica.

"Hamburger," says Sophie.

It frustrates Beth that they live on an island and none of her children will eat fish. She loves seafood but can't cook it in the house without the girls pinching their noses and complaining about the smell.

"Where's your dad?"

"He left," says Sophie.

"Oh," says Beth, strangely disappointed that he didn't come in. Must be the vodka talking.

"How was camp today?"

"Lame," says Sophie.

"Can you please change your attitude and not wreck it for your sisters? You loved it when you were their age."

"Fine. It was *delightful*!" says Sophie, delivering the word *delightful* in a high-pitched squeal, her face stretched and dimpled in a too-sugary-to-be-real, Shirley Temple smile.

"Okay, okay. How was dinner?"

Sophie says nothing and looks to Jessica.

"It was *delightful*!" says Jessica in the same tone and manner as her older sister.

"It totally sucked," says Sophie.

"Hey! Language," says Beth.

"*She* was there," says Sophie.

"Oh," says Beth.

"I don't like her," says Sophie.

"Me either," says Jessica.

Beth tries to summon some kind of maternal wisdom or politically correct advice or at least something positive for her girls, but the Passion à la Beths are working against her, and so she goes with something honest. "I don't like her either."

"Yeah, but you don't have to spend time with her like we do. I wish we didn't have to see her," says Sophie.

"I wish Dad would come home," says Jessica.

Beth's heart breaks.

"He's not going to, is he?" asks Sophie.

"No, I don't think so," says Beth.

Tears pool in Jessica's eyes, fury in Sophie's.

"I'm sorry, sweeties. I'm so sorry. This does totally suck."

"I miss him, Mom," says Jessica.

"I miss him, too," says Beth.

"I thought you hated him," says Sophie. "I thought that's why you ripped up the pictures."

"That wasn't why, and sometimes I do hate him. I miss and hate him at the same time. It's complicated."

"Do you hate him more or miss him more?" asks Jessica with big, wet, hopeful eyes. Beth wipes Jessica's face with her hand and kisses her cheek.

"Miss," says Beth, having compassion for her sensitive middle child.

"Well, I hate him," says Sophie.

"Soph," says Beth in the tone that typically begins one of her lectures.

"Why do you get to hate him and I don't?"

It's a good question, but Beth doesn't say anything. She doesn't say because even if he's no longer her husband, he'll always be Sophie's father. She doesn't say because it's not good to hate anyone. But is it okay for Sophie to hate her father if that's how she feels? It can't be healthy to stuff those honest feelings down. Beth should probably make appointments with the school's guidance counselor for all three girls to talk about all this stuff.

"Because I'm the mother," she says finally, waving that irritatingly vague, all-powerful parental wand over the whole discussion, ending it. "It's getting late. Go get ready for bed."

Sophie rolls her eyes and walks back into the house. Her younger sister follows. Before Beth goes into the house to see how Gracie's doing and to direct the process of going to bed, she reads just a few more pages.

SHORTLY AFTER THE girls go to sleep, Beth brings her book with her to bed, more tired than she has any reason to be after such a luxuriously free day. She hopes to finish the next chapter, maybe even the whole book, but her eyes close before she turns a single page.

As she falls into a deep sleep, unprocessed thoughts about the autistic girl in the book she's reading search out similar elements learned some months ago about the main character in *The Curious Incident of the Dog in the Night-Time*. Detached from people. Bewildered by emotions. Enthralled by repetition. An uncelebrated intelligence. A primal need for order. A row of blocks. A series of numbers. A sensitivity to sound and touch. Persistent. Silent. Honest. Brave. Misunderstood.

These elements combine while she sleeps, blending into something new, something that can no longer be distinguished as belonging to either the girl in *The Siege* or the boy in *The Curious Incident*. It is a prethought, a shadow of an idea forming.

The shadow travels through her mind, gathering energy, weaving through the short story she once wrote about a peculiar boy's imaginary world, merging with the image of a spinning pinwheel and the sound of a scream, absorbing the memory of a small boy and the joy in his eyes as he lined up rocks on the beach. And now, having collected the elements and the power they needed, through a neurological alchemy not yet described in any book, these many images and sounds within the shadow in her mind assemble, first into a chorus, and then, finally, into a single voice. The shadow is no longer a shadow. It has become inspiration.

That night, a brown-haired, brown-eyed boy inhabits her dreams, a boy who sees and hears and feels the world in a unique and almost unimaginable way. She doesn't know him, yet her mind does. She sees him clearly. He is vivid and real. She understands him. She's still dreaming about this boy when she is awakened in the morning by her alarm clock.

At nine, she drops the girls off at the community center and tells them to have a great day, and Sophie slams the car door. Beth then drives directly to the library.

She goes upstairs and looks up at the clock. It's nine fifteen. Sitting in the same seat she sat in yesterday, she opens her notebook, uncaps her pen, takes a deep breath, and begins to write in the voice of the boy in her dream.

CHAPTER 12

I am lying on the deck in the backyard, looking up at the sky. Looking up at the sky is one of my favorite things to do, especially on a no-cloud day. On a no-cloud day, I stare at the blue sky, and I love it. I stare at the blue sky for so long, and I love it so much, that I leave my skin and scatter out into it, the way rain puddles return to the sky on a hot day.

I leave the boy lying on the deck, and I become the blue sky. I am blue sky, and I am high above the earth and the boy lying on the deck, and I am floating and free. I am blue sky, and I am air, gliding on waves of wind, swirling and blowing, weightless and warm under the sun, above the earth and the boy on the deck.

I am blue sky, and I am air. I am everywhere.

I am blue sky and air blowing into lungs. I am breath. I am air moving in and out of squirrels and birds and my mother and father and the green leaves on the trees. I am air turning into energy inside bodies, becoming pieces of what is living inside. I am hearts and bones and thoughts, unspoken words inside the head of the boy lying on the deck, my father's muscles, my mother's sorrow. I am blue sky and air and breath and energy, a part of every living thing around me.

I look up into the no-cloud sky, and I am everywhere, connected to all living things. I look down at the boy lying on the deck. He is happy.

CHAPTER 13

David follows Olivia into the kitchen, hanging back and looking around as he walks, probably inspecting the condition of the floors and the window casings, assessing the current value of the place. He can't help it. She pours him a glass of wine and hands it to him.

"The cottage looks good."

"Thanks. You hungry? I made a salad," she says.

"No, I had a lobster roll on the way over. Wine is good. Here, I brought you this." He hands her a small, white paper bag.

"Aunt Leah's," she says, smiling, shaking the bag, knowing even before she opens it and sees the hunk of chocolate fudge.

"You look good," he says.

"You, too."

He does. He's wearing a plaid, cotton, button-down shirt, unbuttoned and untucked over a gray T-shirt, jeans, and black, Italian leather shoes. His hair, black but graying at his temples and in his sideburns, is much longer than he used to wear it. Thick and straight when it's short, this new length, uncombed and tousled, reveals its natural waves and cowlicks. She likes it.

Everything else is the same David. His olive skin, his dark-rimmed glasses, his pronounced Adam's apple, his brown eyes, like hers but blacker. Like Anthony's. Then she notices his hands, his bare hands. No ring.

"I'm sorry I didn't call first, but I felt like I really needed to see you, and I thought you might tell me not to come."

"Let's go sit in the living room."

He follows her, and they sit down next to each other on the couch, a polite distance apart. David looks up at the wall above the fireplace, at the photograph of Anthony. Love and joy and grief wash over David's face, all at once and in equal parts, as if each emotion is fighting to possess him. He blows out a long, audible breath, trying to shake it off. He drinks some of his wine.

"I'm moving."

"Where?" asks Olivia, immediately fearing that he's going to say *here*.

"Chicago."

She's still catching up to the surprise of this unannounced visit, to David's being here, sitting with her on the couch in the living room. And now this. Born and raised on Boston's South Shore, educated at Boston College, and running a real estate business with his parents and brother ever since, David has ties to the Boston area that are knotted good and tight. If she was surprised at the front door, she's shocked now.

"Why Chicago?"

"Not sure. Sully's there, and he's always saying I could come work for him. Mostly because it's not Hingham. I need to get out of there. Everything reminds me of losing Anthony."

He looks up at the picture over the fireplace, as if he's including Anthony in the conversation, and then back to Olivia.

"And you, Liv. Everything reminds me of losing Anthony and you."

The room becomes still. Olivia doesn't drink her wine or eat her fudge. She stares into David's eyes and waits, remaining still, hoping not to scare away what he's finally ready to say.

"I gotta go somewhere new, where I don't see you and Anthony in every room. If I even walk by his bedroom, I'm done for the day. It's awful. And it's not just the house, it's everyone. My parents and Doug, they all talk to me in that sad, careful voice and look at me with worried eyes, and it's what I would probably do if I were them, but I can't take it anymore. I can't be that sad guy all the time, you know?"

She nods. She knows.

"I can't be that guy every single day. I want to be David Donatelli." His voice evaporates when he says his own name. He wipes his eyes. "I can barely remember who I used to be. I thought it would get easier, but it's not. It's not even close to getting easier."

"I know, David. I know."

"I even had to change laundry detergent because I smelled like you guys. Isn't that crazy?"

She shakes her head. It's not crazy at all. She did the same thing.

"So, Chicago," he says, as if it were the obvious answer, *four* in solution to *two plus two*.

"Moving helped me. It'll help you."

Nantucket has saved her from seeing anyone she used to know, from bumping up against everyone's good-intentioned but devastating well wishes and pitying stares, from smelling Anthony's pillow and holding his shoes in her hands, from living inside the pretty-colored walls of what was supposed to be their happy home. She's amazed that she and David have experienced so many of the same feelings. She's even more amazed that he's sitting here now, able to articulate these feelings so well, communicating.

If only.

"Plus, I'm a single guy in a four-bedroom house in the sub-urbs. It's time to move on to something that makes more sense, right?"

"Are you selling the house?"

It's a bad market to sell right now, and she's guessing that David will hold on to it, rent it, and wait for the market to improve.

"I already listed it with Doug. I can leave your things with him for now if you want."

"Yeah, okay."

"What about you? Do you think you'll move?"

"Where would I go?"

"I thought maybe back to Georgia, near your mom and sister."

She used to think that she'd eventually return home, back into her mother's arms and her childhood bedroom, especially during those first cold weeks in March. But now, she knows she won't. She'll return to Georgia to visit, but she'll never move back there. She'd end up running into the same thing David is now running from—the well-intentioned pity, the relentless reminders of grief and loss.

"No, I like it here," she says.

"How are you doing? Moneywise. I know we said six months, but if you need more—"

"I'm okay. I've been taking pictures again. I do beach por-traits. I make enough for now."

"You sure?"

"Yeah, it's plenty."

He looks up at Anthony again. "I bet you're good at it."

She smiles. "No one's demanded a refund yet."

He looks around the room, again with his Realtor eyes, but maybe also to avoid looking at Olivia next to him and An-thony on the wall. "I thought you would've done more with the place."

"Hey."

"No, it's nice. I mean, it doesn't look like you yet."

In Hingham, she painted every room as soon as they moved in. Golden yellow, bird's-egg blue, sea-foam green. Warm and cozy walls embracing every room. Here, all the walls remain unpainted, white. And the furnishings, artwork, and knick-knacks are sparse and neutral, the same items they hastily filled the place with right after they bought it, in time for the first tenants.

"I like this," he says, referring to the glass bowl on the coffee table, filled to heaping capacity with white, round rocks. She finds them everywhere.

"Thanks."

"I like it here. I always thought we'd end up here. Together. Someday."

"Me, too."

"We had all kinds of great dreams, before . . ."

Before. The word hangs in the air alone, refusing further company.

He leans over the table and picks up one of the rocks from the top of the pile. He holds it in his fist and closes his eyes, as if he's making a wish. He then opens his eyes and his hand and returns the rock to the bowl.

"It's getting late," he says, checking his watch. "I've got to go if I'm going to catch the last ferry."

"You can stay, if you want."

He tips his head and studies her, not quite understanding the invitation.

"The guest-room bed is already made. It's no problem."

He looks relieved. And disappointed. "You sure?"

"Yeah, we can go to The Bean in the morning before you go, like old times."

He smiles. "I'd like that. And more wine if you have it."

IT'S LATE. OLIVIA'S been in bed for a couple of hours now, and she's still awake. She hears the guest-bedroom door open and David walking in the living room. Then she hears the creak of the back door opening. She hears the screen door thwap shut. She waits and listens. She waits and hears nothing. She gets up, walks through the living room, opens the back screen door, and steps outside. David is lying on his back on a blanket on the grass, staring up at the sky.

"David?"

"Hey."

"What are you doing?"

"I couldn't sleep."

She walks over to him and lies down on the blanket next to him. It's a small blanket, and she finds it difficult to lie next to him without touching him. She pins her elbows to her sides.

"The stars here are awesome," he says.

"Yeah. I love the sky here."

"I've never seen them like this. And that moon. It's incredible."

The moon is just shy of fully round, bright yellow-white and glowing, the man-in-the-moon face on its surface clearly visible, the sky immediately around it lit daytime blue. The rest of the sky is ink black, dotted all over with brilliant white stars. She finds the Big Dipper first, then the Little Dipper, and Venus. That's all she knows. She should really learn more about the constellations.

They continue to stare at the sky. Her eyes adjust, and more stars appear. And then, unbelievably, more. Stars behind stars, dusty hazes of light, layered galaxies of energy existing, burning, shining, unfathomable distances away from them. She pictures David and herself in her mind's eye as if viewed from above—two tiny, breathing bodies lying on a blanket on the grass on a tiny island thirty miles out to sea. Two tiny bodies who once dreamed of a life together, who had a beautiful boy together, now lying side by side on a blanket on the grass, observing infinity.

"See that?" He points, drawing the letter *W* with his finger on the sky. "That's Cassiopeia."

"Amazing."

A clear night sky on Nantucket truly does amaze. If it's even noticeable enough to draw attention upward, the sky at night doesn't amaze in Hingham. It won't amaze in Chicago either. She thinks about David living there, surrounded by skyscrapers and city lights, walking along the edge of Lake Michigan and looking up at the sky on a clear night and seeing only darkness when Olivia can see all of this.

It's a cool night with no mosquitoes thanks to a steady wind. Olivia shivers, needing more than her sleeveless, cotton nightgown. David moves closer to her so that their shoulders, hips, and legs touch. He laces his ringless fingers through hers; her hand accepts his. The touch of his body, the heat from his hand, familiar and comforting, warms her.

"I miss you," he says, still staring up at the sky.

"I miss you, too."

"I signed the papers."

As she has witnessed before, it takes David longer to arrive at acceptance, but he eventually gets there. And here he is.

She squeezes his hand.

"I needed to see you, to be sure you're okay before I go," he says.

"I am."

"You are."

"You will be, too."

They hold hands and watch the night sky. The moon, the stars, the heavens, the universe. It's a sky that could almost make her believe in God again, that the incomprehensible is actually divine order, that everything is as it should be.

If only.

CHAPTER 14

⊷ ⊶

Startled awake, Beth sits straight up in bed, holding her breath, eyes wide, listening. *What was that?* She looks at her alarm clock: 3:23 a.m. There it is again. Her nerves jump. She sits straighter, eyes wider.

Someone is walking around downstairs, someone heavy-footed, someone big, not one of the girls. She hasn't locked anything, not the house or the car, since she moved here. No one she knows does. Only summer people lock their houses and cars on Nantucket. Anyone could walk right in. There it is again. Someone is here. A thief? A rapist?

Jimmy?

She leaves her bedroom, her heart pounding, wishing she weren't the only adult in the house, that she could send someone else to investigate the sound. She stops at the top of the stairs and listens. She doesn't hear anything. Maybe she imagined it. She's been having such vivid dreams lately. Maybe she dreamed the sound. As she turns to go back to bed, she hears the floorboards creak. Not imagined. Not a dream.

Before braving the stairs, she notices Jessica's tennis bag in the hallway. She unzips the bag, pulls out her daughter's tennis racket, and holds it in front of her as if it were a sword. She's not sure what good a tennis racket will do her if she finds an actual thief or a rapist in the house (she's never had a strong serve), but it feels at least mildly reassuring to hold on to something.

Aiming her racket-sword in front of her, she tiptoes down the stairs, through the dark living room, and into the kitchen. At the count of three, she flips on the light, and there he is, smiling, looking caught. And really drunk.

"Jimmy, what the hell are you doing?"

He blinks and squints and cups his hand over his eyes like a visor, trying to adjust his vision to the bright kitchen lights after fumbling around in total darkness. His face is sweaty, his Red Sox hat is on backward and crooked, and he reeks of cigars and booze.

"I came to give you this." He holds out a white, greeting-card-size envelope.

"Oh, no. You can go tell your girlfriend that my birthday is in October, and I don't want any more cards from her, ever."

"It's from me, and she's not my girlfriend."

Beth's heart stops. If he says, *She's my fiancée,* she'll beat him to death with this tennis racket. She swears to God she will.

"We broke up. I moved out."

Blood returns to her head. She loosens her grip. "Well, I'm sorry it didn't work out for the two of you, but you can't just come back here."

"I'm not. I just wanted to give you this." He thrusts the card toward her.

Apprehensive of touching whatever is in that envelope, she cautiously holds out her racket-sword, and Jimmy drops the card onto the head. Extending the racket well out in front of her as if she were carrying a dead mouse or something gross and potentially poisonous, she walks the card across the kitchen and flips it onto the table.

"There, I have it. You can leave now." She points her racket-sword at the door.

"Can we talk first?"

"No, you're in no condition to talk about anything."

"I'm fine."

"You don't smell fine."

"Please."

"It's the middle of the night."

"I need to talk to you."

"You've had *months* to talk to me. You only want to talk now because your girlfriend kicked you out."

"She's not my girlfriend, and she didn't kick me out. I left. I ended it."

"You have to leave," Beth says as forcefully as she can without raising her voice. She doesn't want to wake up the girls.

"Will you open the card before I go?"

"No." She turns to walk out of the kitchen. If he won't leave, she will. It's the middle of the night. She's going back to bed.

"Beth." He grabs her free hand, stopping her. "Look at me." She does.

"I miss you."

"Good."

"I really do."

"You only miss me now because you're alone."

"I've missed you the whole time."

"You have to go."

Still holding her hand, he pulls her into him and kisses her.

He tastes like sweat and beer and cigars. She should be re-pulsed and offended. She should kick him out on his sorry, drunk ass. She should whack him over the head with her racket-sword. But for some illogical reason, she drops her weapon and melts into his kiss.

Now he's pulling her nightshirt off, and she's letting him. He's still kissing her, scratching her face with his beard, and she's kissing him back, and somewhere in her head, an outraged part of her is screaming, *WHAT ARE YOU DOING?!* But another part of her is quite calmly replying, *Shhh. We'll talk about it later. Now be quiet and unzip his pants.*

The next thing she knows, they're on the kitchen floor. She's naked, and his pants are down below his knees, his shoes and shirt still on. In the fifteen years that they've known each other, they've never done it on the kitchen floor. In fact, Beth's never been naked anywhere in the house but in her bedroom and bathroom.

The whole shebang is urgent and hungry and straight to the point and, despite the pain of the hardwood floor against the bones of her spine and its being over in about a minute, surprisingly good. Completely foolish and probably regrettable, but surprisingly, undeniably good.

Her ears prickle. Did she just hear one of the girls upstairs? Oh my God, she and Jimmy made too much noise, and now one of the girls is probably on her way downstairs to see what's going on. Beth pushes Jimmy off her and scrambles back into her underwear and nightshirt.

"Quick, I think the girls heard us," she whispers. "Pull your pants up."

He listens and doesn't move. "I don't hear anything."

He's right. Everything's quiet.

"You have to go."

"Okay, but can we talk?" His pants are still around his knees.

"Not now. Another time. When it's daytime, and you're not drunk, and you have your pants on."

He smiles at her, that crazy smile that still undoes her. "Okay."

"Now go."

"Okay, okay. Where's my hat?"

"There." She points to the counter where she threw it.

He fixes it onto his head, forward and straight this time. "I missed you."

"Go."

"Okay." He walks to the front door. "I'll see you later, right?"

She nods, and he leaves. She hopes he's sober enough to drive wherever he's staying. She wonders where he's staying. She wonders what he wants to talk about. She wonders what on earth just happened here.

The part of her that will have to face Petra and the rest of her friends, even Georgia, feels ashamed and stupid about what just happened. The part of her that has felt constantly threatened, like it had been thrown unasked into an unfair competition with that tramp Angela, feels victorious about what just happened. But the rest of her doesn't know what the hell to make yet of what just happened.

She walks over to the kitchen table, picks up the card, and opens it.

Beth, I'm sorry. I love you. Please take me back.
Yours, Jimmy

It's ten thirty in the morning, and Beth is in the library. She's writing. What she's writing began as a short story, inspired by a dream, but it's fast growing into something else, something more substantial, either a collection of related stories or a novella or maybe even a novel. She doesn't know yet.

She's writing about a boy with autism, but his story is different from those of *The Siege* or *The Curious Incident of the Dog in the Night-Time* or any of the other books that she's now read about autism. The story she's writing is about a boy with autism who doesn't speak, and yet she's telling it from his point of view, giving a voice to this voiceless child.

This morning, she is writing in her notebook instead of on Sophie's laptop. She can write significantly faster than she can type, but even with a pen, she's struggling to move her hand as fast as the words appear in her imagination, gripping her pen so hard her fingers cramp. She pauses to shake out her hand and look over what she's written about how her character believes his mind works.

I'm always hearing about how my brain doesn't work right. They say my brain is broken. My mother cries about my broken brain, and she and my father fight about my broken brain, and people come to my house every day to try to fix my broken brain. But it doesn't feel broken to me. I think they're wrong about my brain.

It doesn't feel like my knee when I fall outside in the driveway and break the skin, and the broken skin bleeds and hurts and sometimes turns pink and white or blue and purple. When I fall and break my skin, it hurts and I cry, and my mother sticks a Barney Band-Aid on my broken skin. Sometimes the Barney Band-Aid loses its sticky in the tub and comes off, and the skin is still pink and broken, and I'll get another Barney Band-Aid. But after a few tubs, the Barney Band-Aid will come off, and the broken skin will be fixed.

My brain doesn't hurt, and my brain doesn't bleed. My brain doesn't need a Barney Band-Aid.

And it's not broken like the white coffee mug I knocked off the table yesterday that split apart into three pieces when it hit the floor and that my father said he could glue back together but my mother said to *forget it, it's ruined,* and she threw the three pieces that used to be one white coffee mug into the trash. Broken things are ruined and go into the trash.

My brain didn't fall on the floor, it didn't split into three pieces, and it doesn't belong in the trash.

And it's not broken like the ant I stepped on and cracked and flattened so it couldn't move anymore, making it dead. Dead things are broken forever. That ant is broken, but my brain isn't. My brain can still think about the ant and remember the sound of its body cracking under my shoe, so that is my brain still working.

My brain isn't dead like the ant.

I wish I could tell them that my brain isn't broken so they could stop crying and fighting and people could stop coming to my house to fix me. They make me tired.

My brain is made up of different rooms. Each room is for doing a different thing. For example, I have an Eyes Room for seeing things and an Ears Room for hearing things. I have a Hands Room, a Memory Room (it's like my father's office, full of drawers and folders and boxes with papers), a New Things Room, a Numbers Room (my favorite), and a Horror Room (I wish this room would be broken, but it works just fine).

The rooms don't touch each other. There are long, looping hallways in between each room. If I'm thinking about something that happened yesterday (like when I knocked over the white coffee mug), I'm in my Memory Room. But if I want to watch a Barney video on the TV, I have to leave the Memory Room and go into Eyes and sometimes Ears.

Sometimes when I'm in the hallways traveling to a different room, I get lost and confused and caught In Between and feel like I'm nowhere. This is when my brain feels like maybe it's a little bit broken, but I know I just have to find my way into one of the rooms and shut the door.

But if too much is happening at once, I can get into trouble. If I'm counting the square tiles on the kitchen floor (180), I'm in my Numbers Room, but if my mother starts talking to me, I have to go into my Ears Room to hear her. But I want to stay in Numbers because I'm counting, and I like to count, but my mother keeps talking, and her sound is getting louder, and I feel pressure to leave Numbers and go inside my Ears Room. So I go into the hallway, but then she grabs my hand, and this surprises me and forces me into Hands, which isn't where I wanted to go, and she's talking to me but I can't hear what she's saying because I'm in my Hands Room and not in Ears.

If she lets go of my hand, I can go into Ears. She's saying, *Look at me*. But if I look at her, I have to leave Ears and go into Eyes, and then I won't be able to hear what she's saying. So I don't know what to do, and I'm wandering the halls, and I can't make a decision on where to go, and I'm In Between, and that's when I get into trouble.

If I hang around in the hallways too long and don't get safe inside a room, I can get sucked into the Horror Room, and it's not easy to get out of there. Sometimes I'm locked inside that scary room for a long time, and the only way out is to scream as loud as I can because sometimes my really loud scream can pop open the door and push me straight into Ears.

The sound of my own voice screaming is the only thing that can get rid of everything else.

My voice makes screams and sounds but not words. But this isn't a broken room inside my brain. I talk to myself with words inside my brain just fine. I think I might have broken lips or a broken tongue or a broken throat. I wish I could tell my mother and father that my voice is broken but my brain is working, but I can't tell them because my voice is broken. I wish they'd figure it out on their own.

CHAPTER 16

January 25, 2004

Yesterday was not a good day. I had a huge, ugly meltdown. That's happening more and more. My therapist thinks I should go on an antidepressant. I think this is some kind of perverse joke. I've been searching and begging and praying for a medication that will fix everything, and this is the answer to my fucking prayers? Anthony has autism, so give ME an antidepressant—problem solved!

How about a medication for HIM?! How about that? And one that actually works, please. How about a prescription for him that will make him talk and stack blocks and stop flipping the light switches and moan-shrieking and grinding his teeth? And how about one that doesn't turn him into either a doped-up zombie or a raging psychotic on crack? How about that? How about one that doesn't make him puke all over his sheets and the rugs and me? How about that?

But, no, let's medicate ME. There. Everything's all better now.

Anthony has at least one meltdown a day, and now I'm having at least one meltdown a day, and we can't manage his, so let's manage mine. Let's fix me, and then everyone can cope with Anthony's autism.

My therapist wrote me a prescription for Celexa last month. I threw it out. I see her logic, and I hate it. I'm trying not to hate her. If I'm depressed, so be it. Feels like a pretty normal reaction to my life right now. If she had my life, she'd be depressed, too. Anyone would. She can keep her nice and tidy solution to all my problems. I'll stick to wine, thank you.

So yesterday's meltdown. I went to the grocery store alone, and David stayed home with Anthony, and I was in a good mood. I love going to the grocery store alone. Then I got home, and first thing I saw when I opened the front door was Anthony standing in the middle of the living room. He shot me a sideways glance and then started jumping up and down, elbows tucked at his ribs, flapping his hands, screeching. This is Anthony excited to see me. And the first thing I thought was Hi, Anthony. I'm happy to see you, too.

And then I thought, Maybe I should try it. If he won't mimic us, maybe I should try copying him. I dropped the bags of groceries and forced a loud screech, and I jumped and flapped.

So there we were—David on the couch watching the football pregame and Anthony and I shrieking and jumping and flapping. It felt so unnatural and weird, like I was making fun of him. It felt wrong. This is not how people express joy or excitement or love. And I thought, This is what retarded looks like. And I felt so ashamed for thinking that word. I hate that word.

Why can't he just smile and say, Hey, Mom, glad you're home? Because he can't. Because he has autism. I HATE autism. He shrieks and flaps and looks retarded instead, and this is Anthony showing joy, and I can't join in and feel joy along with him.

And then I thought, This is it. This is all I'm ever going to get. No hugs and kisses. No "Hi, Mom!" No "I love you, Mom." No Mother's Day cards made by him. He jumps and flaps and screeches, and that's how he shows joy. That's how he shows love. And that's it.

On some days, I can be grateful for this. I can. But yesterday, I couldn't take it. I was purely pissed. Rationally, I know it's the best he can do, and I love him for it. I wasn't pissed at him. I was pissed at God.

I left Anthony and the bags of groceries, and I called Father Foley on the phone and unloaded on him. What kind of horrible God would give a boy autism? What kind of God would afflict a small child with this kind of suffering? Why? Why can't Anthony talk to us? Why can't he look at me and smile and say "Mom!" and come running into my arms like other little boys? Why does he have to live like this? What did he do to deserve this kind of life? What did I do to deserve this? Why?

Father Foley then said a bunch of completely useless words, something about the permissive will of God and manifestations of evil and original sin. I don't really know. It all turned to meaningless static. I didn't say anything. I was still holding the word WHY in my mouth, waiting for a real answer.

Then he said, Keep praying, Olivia. God will hear you if you pray to Him.

And here's where I had my meltdown. I said something like I don't want Him to HEAR me. I want Him to DO something. I want some fucking ANSWERS. I'm so sick of praying. Fuck praying. I'm done praying. I'm done with God.

And I threw the phone across the room and shrieked and
wailed like I was being murdered, like this is killing me.
And you know, I think it is.

This is killing me.

David missed the first half of the football game trying to
calm me down. I drank a bottle of wine while he watched
the second half, and I went to bed without dinner.

Today I woke up with the worst headache of my life. I
swallowed four Motrin with a tall glass of water, and the
worst headache of my life was gone by lunch.

We have pills for headaches. We have antidepressants for
sadness. We have God for believers.

We have nothing for autism.

OLIVIA HAD FORGOTTEN about that meltdown entirely, stuffed
it in a box, locked it up, and buried it in the basement of her
mind, but after reading her journal entry earlier this morning,
she remembers it now as if it were yesterday. Those powerful
and ugly emotions that took hold of her that day six years ago,
awakened by the memory, stir inside her again, but they feel
softer and misplaced now, like a shadow belonging to someone
else.

It's now late morning, and she is walking among the
throngs of tourists in Town, an attempt at distracting her from
herself. She doesn't have an exact destination in mind, maybe
The Bean or the library or Aunt Leah's for more fudge, or
maybe she'll simply walk. Walking is the plan.

When walking is the plan, she typically goes to Fat Ladies
Beach or Bartlett's Farm, places where she can move freely and
lose herself in nature. So it's strange that she's chosen to come
here, confined to the narrow brick sidewalks, her natural pace
impeded by the crawl of tourists in front of her, bombarded on
all sides by shoppers and one-sided cell-phone chatter.

She feels her own phone vibrate inside her purse and stops walking to search for it. She grabs it on the fourth ring.

"Hello?" She waits. "Hello?"

She looks at the area code and doesn't recognize it, but that's not unusual. People come to Nantucket from all over the world. She's already shot beach portraits for families who are from as far away as California and Germany. She begins to worry that she's forgotten a portrait session scheduled for this morning, and the family is anxiously waiting for her on some beach. But the worry isn't real. She knows she has today off.

She looks up and notices that she's standing in front of St. Mary's Church. It's a pretty church with a white clapboard exterior, large, polished-teak front doors, and a two-story tower with no bell. A simple statue of Our Lady, sculpted of white marble, stands on its front lawn, welcoming parishioners with wide, outstretched arms.

But Olivia is not a parishioner. Mary isn't welcoming *her* inside. Olivia vowed the day she had that meltdown that she'd never go to church again. If God was going to turn His back on her, she would do the same to Him. Two could play that game.

But even though she stopped attending Sunday mass and receiving the sacraments, even though she blamed and hated God, she still prayed. She didn't make a show of it, and she stopped making the sign of the cross, but she still whispered her prayers for Anthony. She prayed in the shower, while she brushed her teeth, while stopped at red lights, while she stood in line at Costco to buy diapers for a six-year-old, before dinner, before bed. She kept praying because even though she'd turned her back on Him, her boycott of God was more posture than real conviction. She still believed.

Until last year, when she stopped believing in Him altogether.

She continues walking down Federal Street. People are everywhere, taking up every conceivable outdoor space. They're eating and drinking at outdoor tables, pedaling bicycles, walking their dogs, sipping iced coffees as they sit on benches, window-shopping as they walk and talk on their phones. A continuous stream of people in their cars inches along every road, breaking the line only to allow clumps of pedestrians to cross at the crosswalks.

She pauses for a moment, debating whether she should return to her Jeep and go somewhere with fewer people or keep walking here. As she considers a hike on Bartlett's Farm, someone bumps into her, knocking her sideways.

"Watch it, lady," says a tall, lanky man over his shoulder as he continues past her, not even breaking his stride.

YOU walked into ME, she thinks.

She plants her feet in the middle of the brick sidewalk, partly as an act of defiance and partly because she doesn't know where to go, holding her ground as dozens of people weave around her in both directions, as if she were a rock surrounded by wild river rapids. She feels oddly stuck in this spot and, at the same time, a building anxiety over remaining there.

She should've gone to the beach.

Then she registers where she is. She's standing in front of St. Mary's Church. Again.

She knows she vowed she'd never return to the Church, but she also vowed to love and honor David until death parted them. And now she's getting divorced. So she's already a vow-breaker.

And maybe she does still believe in God. Ever since David left for Chicago, she finds herself talking to Him again. She came to this island to disconnect from everyone and everything, to be alone, and her self-imposed isolation has been a needed salve for her battered soul. But knowing that David was still in Hingham was a lifeline she held on to with both hands. She could go back. Maybe not back to David or their marriage, although, if she's being honest, there was that possibility, too, but back to their house, her home, her life. Now David's in Chicago, and there's nothing to go back to. There's nothing connecting her to her old life, to before. Before is gone.

Some other family will be living in their house, where Anthony was supposed to grow up, to become the best Anthony he could be, whatever that might've been, where David and she were supposed to grow old together. Maybe someone else will have that life there. Someone luckier than her. Someone blessed.

When David was still in Hingham, she could consider her life on Nantucket to be a trial run, a visit, a sabbatical, a temporary state of isolation. It was practice, pretend, a rehearsal. Now it's real. This is her life. She is alone on Nantucket, and there is no undoing it.

She has become an empty space, and despite her grief and resistance, God has wandered back in. She finds herself talking to Him while cooking in the kitchen, as she's doing the laundry, while walking on the beach. She recognizes that she's not simply talking to herself. She's talking to God. And so, there it is. If she's talking to God, she must believe He exists.

She's asking the same familiar questions, waiting in silence for answers. And in those silences, her loneliness feels too sharp, like it might slice her in half. It's not loneliness for David or even Anthony. She's not lonely for her old home or friends. She's lonely for answers. Answers are the company she seeks.

And whether or not she still believes in God, she has always believed in signs. Someone or something is calling her into this church. She hastens by the marble Mary, climbs up the steps, and, with more than a little reluctance, pushes open one of the shiny teak doors and walks inside.

This church is smaller than St. Christopher's in Hingham, probably seating about three hundred at a Sunday high-noon mass. It's dimly lit, and after her eyes adjust, she notices that everything looks brand-new—the red carpet, the polished pews, the gorgeous pipe organ, the woven Nantucket collection baskets. And it's air-conditioned. The money on this island trickles everywhere.

No one is here. The daily mass would've been said earlier in the morning, and confessions are heard on Saturday afternoons. Before walking to the front of the church, she kneels at a table of prayer candles. The candles here aren't real. They're plastic, battery-operated lights in the shape of candles. The town of Nantucket has burned down so many times that everyone on this island is, if not openly fearful, at least a little superstitious about fire, even, it seems, the Catholic priests.

She flips one over, clicks the button to ON, and replaces it on the table. It glows orange, but it's not nearly as satisfying as a real flame. She "lights" another candle for Anthony as she always used to, and then one more. One for David. She closes her eyes and tries to pray, but she can't find any words. She hasn't prayed to God in church in a long time. She presses the palms of her hands together and tries again. No words.

Maybe she should go with someone else's words, a ready-made prayer like a Hail Mary or the Our Father. She begins whispering a Hail Mary but stops after *the Lord is with thee*. The words feel memorized and meaningless, like she's reciting a nursery rhyme. These are not the words that drew her inside here. Leaving her three "lit" candles, she wanders to the front of the church, behind the altar, and finds a closed door. She stands there for more than a minute before she finds enough courage to knock.

"Yes? Come in."

Olivia opens the door to a small sitting room. A priest is sitting in the center of a brown sofa directly under a brass crucifix hung on the wall. He's holding a closed book in his hands. A reading lamp to his left is turned on. An untouched cookie on a white plate centered on an ivory doily sits on a small wooden table to his right.

"I'm sorry to disturb you," she says.

"I'm not at all disturbed. Please come, sit."

There are two chairs, one modest and covered in a floral slipcover and the other a Queen Anne upholstered in a bright peacock blue. She chooses the Queen Anne and sits with her hands clasped in her lap. She stares at the floor for a moment. It's tiled in black and white hexagons. Anthony would've loved this floor.

"I'm Olivia Donatelli. I haven't been to this church before."

"Welcome to St. Mary's. I'm Father Doyle."

Father Doyle has a full head of silver hair and a bright pink face, flushed from within rather than from a sunburn. He's wearing a short-sleeve, black T-shirt, black pants, black sneakers, and no collar.

"I'm not exactly sure why I'm here."

Father Doyle waits.

"I left the Church five years ago, but I've been praying."

"You haven't left the Church if you're communing with God."

"Well, I wouldn't call it communing. There's no conversation. I'm asking questions and not getting any answers. It's just me talking to myself, I think."

"What are your questions?"

She squeezes her hands together and takes a deep breath. "My son had autism. He was nonverbal and couldn't make eye contact and didn't like to be touched. And then he died from a subdural hematoma following a seizure when he was eight. So what I want to know is why? Why did God do this to my son? Why was he here and then gone so soon? Why did I have him? What was the purpose of his life?"

"These are hard questions."

She nods.

"But they're good questions. They're important questions. I'm glad you haven't given up on asking them."

"What do you think?"

"I don't know a lot about autism, but I know that every human being is made as an expression of God's love."

She's received this kind of pat, Catholic-textbook response before from the priests in Hingham, and it was always the end of the conversation. A vague reference to God's universal love isn't helpful. If anything, it used to intensify the violent storm that was already raging inside her. She would normally be up and heading for the door after "expression of God's love." But for some reason, maybe because she doesn't feel affronted by Father Doyle's soothing voice, maybe because today she possesses more patience than rage, maybe because she likes the blue chair she's sitting in, she stays in her seat.

"Every night of his life, I always tucked him into bed and said, 'Good night, Anthony. I love you.' And I don't know if he ever understood what that meant. I mean, it's not that he didn't understand us. He understood a lot, but love, I don't know. He was good at concrete things, black-and-white rules and routines. He liked order. But social things, people, shared emotions, he didn't seem to notice or care much about these. So I don't know."

She knows that he loved his rocks and Barney and swings, but loving things is different from loving another person. Reciprocal love is different. He wouldn't let her hug or kiss him. They couldn't stare into each other's eyes. He couldn't tell her what he felt. He couldn't say the words *Good night, Mom. I love you, too.*

"But you loved him anyway."

"Of course. I loved him desperately."

She grinds her teeth together and swallows, trying to hold back her tears, but it's no use. There's no stopping them. Father Doyle passes her a box of tissues.

"I don't know if he felt loved."

"Children who are deaf and can never hear or say the words *I love you* feel love. Children who are born with no limbs or who lose their arms and can't hug still feel love. Love is felt beyond words and touch. Love is energy. Love is God."

"I know. And I know other parents have children born with disabilities or who have cancer or a tragic accident, and I know I'm not special or deserve anything better, but I still don't understand. I feel like those other parents at least get to say that they love their child and it's mutual, it matters. And there's comfort in that.

"At least those other mothers get to hug their children and cradle them in their arms and say, 'It's okay. I'm here. I love you.' And those kids can see their mother's love in her eyes and feel it. I never had that with Anthony. If Anthony was suffering, he'd scream and cry and we couldn't know what was wrong or how to fix it. We wouldn't know if he had a stomachache or a toothache or if he wanted to go on the swings or if I'd accidentally moved one of his rocks out of place. I felt like I could never reach him close enough to comfort him."

"And what about you? You needed love and comfort, too," Father Doyle says.

She nods and wipes the tears from her face. "And now Anthony is gone, and his father and I are getting divorced, and there's nothing left. There's nothing."

"There is you, and there is God."

"So where *is* He then? Where has He *been* for the past ten years?"

"I know it can be difficult to keep faith. These kinds of hardships can either strengthen our faith or destroy it. Even Jesus on the cross said, 'My God, my God, why have you abandoned me?' As difficult as it can be for us human beings to comprehend, He is always present."

"I feel completely alone."

"You're not alone. God is with you."

"I don't hear any answers to my questions."

"You won't hear Him with your ears. You have to listen with your heart, with your spirit. His answers are there, within you."

"I don't know," she says, shaking her head.

"Keep asking your questions. Keep communing with God and try listening with your spirit."

She nods, but she's skeptical and unsure of what exactly she's agreeing to. She thanks Father Doyle for his time and tells him that she has to leave. He puts his hand on her shoulder and tells her to come and see him anytime.

She walks past the altar, past her three lit candles, and back outside. The bright sunlit day assaults her vision, forcing her to squint her eyes shut and wait. And in those few seconds with her eyes closed, she pictures Anthony—his uncut brown hair, his deep brown eyes, the joy in his smile. She smiles, loving him.

Then, before she descends the church steps, she thinks. If she can see Anthony without her eyes, maybe she can hear God without her ears.

God, why was Anthony here? Why did he have autism?

She opens her eyes and tries to listen with her spirit as she walks onto the crowded sidewalk below her.

CHAPTER 17

Beth showers and dresses and makes pancakes for breakfast. She packs three lunches, washes the table and the dishes, and waters the plants. She drops the girls off at the community center, drives downtown, and finds a parking space on India Street without a problem, grateful as she always is that tourists sleep late. Everything about this morning is typical until she enters the library. And then everything is different.

Someone is sitting in her seat.

The offender is an older woman, at least seventy, with short, brilliant white hair and thick glasses attached to a beaded chain looped around her neck. Pencil in hand, she's working on what appears to be a Sudoku puzzle. Balls of yarn, knitting needles, and a paperback peek out from the top of a quilted bag on the floor next to her. Good God, this woman could be parked here all day. Here in Beth's seat.

Of course, Beth understands that the chair doesn't belong to her. It's not "her seat." But she's sat in this chair every morning since she began coming here to write at the beginning of the summer. She likes sitting with her back against the stacks of books, facing the window, able to see the clock. She likes the left corner of the table, with plenty of room to her right to spread out her notebooks and papers and laptop. And if she's being honest, she believes in the magical powers of that seat. In that particular seat she's been writing page after page without second-guessing her prose, without ridiculing her dialogue, without becoming seized with fear, without stopping. As long as she sits in that wooden chair at that wooden table facing east, the boy's story keeps coming, and she keeps writing it down.

And now some elderly woman with bad vision is using up its magical powers for solving Sudoku puzzles.

She considers her options. She could sit in the chair next to the woman, slide it too close, blow her nose, clear her throat, chew gum, and tap her pen on her teeth until the woman is annoyed into finding a new location. She could ask the woman in a polite and nonthreatening voice if she would kindly move to another chair. She could go home and clean. Or she could be a mature adult and find another place to sit.

She picks a chair on the other side of the table, a respectful distance but close enough that she could gather her things in a heartbeat and regain her rightful spot should the woman decide to leave. She opens Sophie's laptop, which Sophie is now begrudgingly sharing with her mother, and stares at the screen. She's facing west, and her chair wobbles. She taps her teeth with her fingernail and sighs, resigned to the obvious truth. There's nothing magical about this seat.

After a while, she twists around and looks up at the clock. She's now been here for an hour and has done nothing but read what she's already written. And as she feared, the woman is now knitting. Maybe Beth should go home. She stares at the cursor, willing it to produce something as if it were a planchette on a Ouija board. No words appear, but a reflection of a woman emerges within the screen. She spins around in her ordinary chair. Courtney is standing behind her, smiling.

"Hey, have a seat," says Beth, relieved to have a distraction. "What are you doing here?"

"Had to come into Town for something. Thought I'd stop by and see how you're doing. How's it coming?" Courtney points to the blank, white nothing on Beth's computer screen.

"Good, good, I think. We'll see when it's done."

"Do you have a title yet?"

"Not yet."

"We should all read it for book club when you're done. Wouldn't that be fun?"

Beth smiles and nods, loving the idea if her book actually turns out to be "good," imagining her unbearable humiliation if it sucks.

"This is for you." Courtney hands Beth a book.

Mending Your Marriage by Johanna Hamill. As Beth flips through the pages, she notices passages underlined in pen, handwriting in the margins. Courtney's handwriting. She looks over at her friend, confused, wondering.

"It's my copy. I thought it was pretty good, better than most of the crap out there on how to save your marriage."

"But, so, you read this? Why?"

"Steve cheated on me."

"He *did*?"

The old woman looks up from her knitting.

"When?" asks Beth, lowering her voice.

"Four years ago."

"What? My God, I thought you were going to say 'last week.'"

Beth stares without focus down at the cover of the book and shakes her head, unable to decide whether she's more stunned by Steve's infidelity or that Courtney has kept it a secret for four years.

"Who?"

"Some rich-bitch divorcée. He was working with Mickey's crew over in Madaket, remodeling her bedroom and master bath. He said she came on to him, which I believe. You know how some of those wealthy summer biddies act like they're entitled to everything. He said they only did it once."

"So you're okay? You've forgiven him?"

"Well, not at first. I wanted to kill him. That lasted awhile. Then I stopped wanting him dead, but I couldn't forgive him. I read all these books, and that one might help you, but none of them helped me. I couldn't forgive him. I couldn't trust him. The power balance was all wrong. He had all of it, and I had none."

Beth nods, following her, empathizing.

"So I cheated on him."

"You *did*?"

The old woman looks up from her knitting again, this time really meaning it, down her nose, disapproving. Good. Maybe either the subject or the volume of their conversation will drive her out of here. Courtney nods and smiles.

"With who?"

"Some twentysomething, young thing. His name was Henry. I picked him up at 21 Federal. It was just a one-nighter." Courtney grins, knowing she's blowing Beth's mind. "The next day, I told Steve. And I said, 'Now we're even. No more.' And we promised that was the end of it, and we moved on."

"That's crazy."

"I know. It was, but it was the only way I could stay with him, and I wanted to stay with him. I love Steve and our life here. I didn't want to lose him. So I'm just saying, if you want to take Jimmy back, read the book, and if that doesn't do it for you, I say, go have your own Henry."

"But Jimmy cheated on me for a whole year, I don't think—"

"You only have to do it once. Once makes it even."

"Is *that* in the book?"

"I'm just saying. Marriage isn't only about whether you love each other. You have to have mutual power, mutual trust. Do you trust Jimmy?"

"No. But sleeping with someone else is going to help?"

"It worked for me."

Beth shakes her head, struggling with the math of this adultery equation, to imagine that cheating on Jimmy would accomplish anything but giving them both reputations for being unfaithful scoundrels who should never be trusted. "I keep thinking, 'Once a cheater, always a cheater.' Who said that, Oprah? Dr. Phil?"

"I don't know. Not the case with me and Steve."

"So you guys were just a onetime thing."

"Yeah."

"And you're happy."

"Yeah, we really are."

"And you trust each other."

"Enough. You're always at the mercy of the people you're in a relationship with, right? Anything can happen. But I trust him enough."

"What if he cheats again?" asks Beth.

"I'd kill him."

"No, really."

"I don't know, maybe another Henry."

"I don't know, Courtney. I don't think I could."

"Do you want it to work out for you and Jimmy?"

Beth used to think that Jimmy and she were soul mates. They had so much in common when they first met. They're both only children, raised by single parents. His father died of lung cancer the year after her mother's death. Independent and somewhat fearless, they both held a fierce determination to follow their dreams, to do something they loved for a living. For Beth, that was writing. For Jimmy, it was scalloping.

Jimmy grew up in Maine. His father was a lobsterman who saved every penny so Jimmy might go to college, hoping for his son to discover a more reliable, less backbreaking way to earn a living. Jimmy attended the University of Maine and after graduating got the desk job of his father's dreams at a small software company. But Jimmy hated his desk and his cubicle, and he hated being trapped indoors, and he admired his father's life as a fisherman.

He went to Nantucket the following summer, after he'd been at his "soulless" job for a year. It was supposed to be a long weekend, a vacation with friends. Like Beth, he fell in love with the place. He decided to stay, but instead of lobstering, which he knew, he learned how to scallop, which was where the big money was at the time.

They loved the same music, the same food, Nantucket. They loved each other. And now, here they are. Jimmy gave up scalloping, and until recently she forgot about writing, and Jimmy's been sleeping with another woman, and she doesn't know what they both love anymore.

She looks over at the old woman. Beth's still young. She could start over, and not necessarily with another man. She could regroup, redefine her life as a single mother. She could finish this book, maybe move off-island, get a job at a newspaper or a magazine, maybe somewhere with mountains or a city, maybe back to Portland. Somewhere with no sand or fog or tourists. Somewhere with no Angela Melo.

The possibilities, even contemplating the words *I could*, feel exhilarating. She could do anything she wants. But what does she want? She's happy that Jimmy wants her back, but she doesn't entirely trust her own motivation for feeling good about this. He picked her. She wins. She beat Angela. So maybe she feels more victorious than happy.

And who's to say that he won't change his mind in a week, in a month, next year, that he won't someday show up in Angela's kitchen at three in the morning with a card in his hands and his pants around his knees? No, she has no desire to be strung to that yo-yo.

Maybe there are no soul mates. Maybe husbands are simply men women eventually put up with so someone is there to haul air conditioners in and out of the attic, to love their children, to keep them company. But Beth can haul the air conditioners herself, her friends provide her with plenty of company, and he can still love their kids even if she doesn't love him. But there's the thing. She might still love him.

"I don't know."

"Look, Jimmy's got all the power now. It's not just about whether you can love each other again or trust each other again, it's about evening out the power."

As Beth thinks about these ingredients of marriage, about love and trust and power, her mind wanders over to truth and takes an east-facing seat. A marriage should have truth.

"I had sex with Jimmy the other night."

"I know, Petra told me. That's why I brought you the book."

For a second, Beth feels indignant at Petra for betraying her confidence, but she shrugs it off. "That didn't even out anything, did it?"

"Right idea, wrong guy."

"He wants to talk."

"That's impressive for Jimmy."

"I know."

"You could try counseling."

Beth wonders if Jimmy would agree to go.

"If you do, go to Dr. Campbell."

"The guy with the falcon?"

"I know, but the only other option is Nancy Gardener."

Nancy Gardener is a twice-divorced marriage counselor whose sister is Gracie's fourth-grade teacher.

"I don't know," says Beth.

"He's good. Jill and Mickey go to him."

"They do?"

Courtney nods, eyebrows raised knowingly.

"Why? What's going on with them?"

Courtney shrugs. "Everyone has stuff, Beth."

Courtney looks over at the clock on the wall and gets up. "I've got to run. Read the book, go see Dr. Campbell, go find your own Henry. Or be done with him. That's a fine choice, too."

Courtney leaves, and Beth is alone again in her wobbly chair staring at her blank computer screen. She looks over at the old woman whose knitting is fast taking the shape of a mitten. Magic seat.

She sighs and shuts off Sophie's laptop. She packs her notebooks and pens into her bag, holding on to Courtney's book for an extra second, considering it, before she tosses it into her bag, too. As she's leaving the library, feeling defeated, she thinks about love and trust and power. And truth. As she walks down the front steps, she thinks about what is true in her life, and four simple, honest thoughts jump up and raise their hands.

1. She's not going to read *Mending Your Marriage*.
2. She's not going to go have her own Henry and call things even.
3. She'll make an appointment with Dr. Campbell if Jimmy is willing to go, and she hopes he is.
4. That old woman had better not be in her seat tomorrow, or she's going to lose it.

CHAPTER 18

Beth didn't write anything yesterday, and the words she didn't write have been gathering and growing louder inside her, building to a crescendo, feeling full and urgent, like floodwaters pressing against a failing dam. She woke up this morning at dawn with this boy's words already in motion, rushing at her, through her, insistent, dogging her everyday, routine thoughts until each and every one of them surrendered. She can now think of nothing else.

She arrives at the library only seconds after it opens, hurries upstairs, and is relieved to see no one there. No one sitting in her seat. She sits down, opens her notebook, uncaps her pen, and writes.

I wake up, and it is daytime. I get out of bed and say Good Morning to the tree outside the window, to my box of rocks, and to the calendar on the wall. Yesterday was Sunday, and today is Monday. Danyel comes after lunch on Tuesdays.

I stand on every step with both feet until I do all twelve, and I'm downstairs. I walk into the kitchen and sit down on my seat at the kitchen table. My Barney cup is filled with purple juice, and my fork and white napkin are on the table, but there are only two French Toast sticks with maple syrup on my blue plate, and there are always three.

I can't eat two French Toast sticks because breakfast is three French Toast sticks. I can't eat two because three is finished, and two is stopping in the middle, and stopping in the middle hurts too much. I can't eat two French Toast sticks because then I won't ever be done with breakfast. And if I don't finish breakfast, then I can't brush my teeth in the bathroom and play with water in the sink. And then I can't get dressed in dry clothes on the bottom step. And then I can't go outside and swing. And I can't have lunch if I haven't finished breakfast. And Danyel won't come because she comes after lunch.

If I don't have two plus one equals three French Toast sticks for breakfast, I'm going to be stuck at this table forever.

I NEED ANOTHER FRENCH TOAST STICK!

I run over to the freezer and open it. The French Toast sticks box is gone. There is always a yellow box of French Toast sticks in the freezer. And now there isn't. Something terrible has happened. I'm getting tingly shivers in my hands, and I'm racing around in my head trying to think about how to make the French Toast sticks box come back into the freezer, but I'm breathing too fast, and my hands are too tingly, and I can't think.

My mother is now standing between me and the freezer, showing me an empty French Toast box. Empty is zero, and zero French Toast sticks is a disaster. I flap my tingly hands and moan.

My mother walks me back over to the table and says

something in a loud and pretend happy voice, but I can't hear what she said because I'm looking at my blue plate. One of the two French Toast sticks has been cut in half, so now there are two Medium-size sticks and one Big stick, which is even worse than before because two is in the middle and one is the beginning, and none of this can be eaten because this is not breakfast. Breakfast is three of the SAME French Toast sticks. I cannot eat this.

The French Toast box has zero, and my blue plate has one Big stick and two Medium sticks, and nothing has three. Everything is zero or the beginning or the middle, and I can't eat breakfast because it can't be finished if it doesn't have three. I can't get dressed and go outside and swing because getting dressed and going outside and swinging happens AFTER breakfast and I can't have breakfast until I have three French Toast sticks.

I know how to solve this. If my mother would cut the one Big stick in half and get rid of one of the halves, then I'd have three Medium-size sticks. And then I could eat breakfast. Or she could cut one of the Medium-size sticks in half and get rid of one of its halves, and then there would be a Big, a Medium, and a Small stick. This is not as good as three SAME-sized sticks, but it's a three that I can handle. I could eat a Big, a Medium, and a Small French Toast stick breakfast because that is three, and three is finished and safe. Then I could eat breakfast and brush my teeth and play with water in the sink and get dressed and swing outside and see Danyel.

But I can't tell my mother my solutions because my voice is broken. And I can't cut the Big or Medium French Toast stick myself because I can't feel my hands anymore. I can't go into my Hands Room because I'm stuck in Ears. I'm stuck in Ears listening to the sound of someone screaming.

While I listen to the screaming, I lose my body. I have the distant and dreamy feeling of leaving the kitchen, moving through air. I don't want to move through air. I want three French Toast sticks. But I don't have a voice, and I don't have a body. I have the distant and dreamy feeling of struggling, hot and angry, then sweaty and cool. But mostly, I'm in my Ears, listening to the sound of screaming.

Now I'm back in my body. I'm in the bathroom, watching water run in the sink, when I realize that the someone screaming is me. I scream louder, and I lose my body again. I keep screaming so I can become the scream, and then I am the sound of how I feel and not a boy in a body who is in the bathroom without having eaten three French Toast sticks for breakfast first.

CHAPTER 19

⁓ ⌒ ⌒ ⌒

Beth checks her watch. They still have five minutes before they need to leave the house. Gracie and Jessica are ready, wearing identical gauzy, white shirts and faded blue jeans, waiting at the kitchen table, but Sophie is still upstairs fussing with herself.

"Sophie!" Beth yells. "Two minutes!"

She steps into the bathroom for one last quick check in the mirror. With her fingers she smoothes down a section of hair threatening to frizz and wipes a bit of shine from her forehead. She fake-smiles. Nothing stuck in her teeth. Even though she knows she should stay out of the sun with her fair skin and tendency to freckle and burn and, more recently, wrinkle, she's been lying out on the deck for an hour each day for the past week, trying to achieve a healthy glow. Her cheeks are pink, and her eyes look bright. Mission accomplished.

She found a beach-portrait photographer with cheap rates on a flyer at Stop & Shop and the perfect beach-portrait shirt online at Old Navy last month. She ordered four, one for each of them, and she laundered and ironed the matching shirts weeks ago. Last night, they all painted their toenails the same shade of peacock blue. They're all wearing tiny pearl earrings and matching silver bracelets. They're perfectly coordinated from head to toe. Beth smiles, congratulating herself on being so organized, for thinking of everything.

"Mom!"

The urgent shrill in one of her daughters' voices sends Beth running into the kitchen. She looks Jessica up and down. No blood. No tears. She looks fine. But then Beth turns her attention to Gracie. The entire front of her beautiful gauzy, white shirt is drenched in red fruit punch. Gracie, teary-eyed and shocked, is holding a tall and mostly empty glass in her hand. Not fine. Not fine at all.

"My God, Gracie! What did you do?"

"Jessica did it! She pushed me while I was drinking!"

"I didn't push her."

"You did!"

"It was an accident," says Jessica.

"Why were you even drinking anything?" asks Beth. "I told you we were leaving in two minutes."

"I was thirsty."

"Come here."

Beth doesn't wait for Gracie to move. She yanks the shirt over her daughter's head and leaves Gracie in the kitchen, naked from the waist up and crying. Beth runs into the laundry room, pours a capful of detergent onto the shirt, and scrubs it under running water. The stain lightens from deep red to pink, but it's still there. And now the whole shirt is soaking wet. Gracie can't wear this. Beth checks her watch. They need to leave the house *right now*.

Think. Think. Think.

Beth scrubs the shirt again. Still pink. Still wet. There's no time. She has to accept it. They can't wear the beautiful matching gauzy, white shirts. That dream is gone.

She has to come up with a plan B. Okay, they won't all be in the same style white shirt, but they can still all be in white.

"Gracie!" Beth calls. "Go to your room and put on a white shirt!"

"Which one?"

"Any! Go!"

Beth takes a deep breath and blows the air out slowly through her mouth, trying not to freak out. She walks back into the kitchen and eyes Jessica, who is standing awkwardly still, as if she were afraid to blink.

"Why did you push your sister?"

"I didn't mean to."

"Fine. Just stay there, and don't touch anything. And don't drink anything."

Gracie returns to the kitchen wearing a white T-shirt with the words GIRLS RULE, BOYS DROOL written in puffy, purple lettering on the front.

"No, no, no," says Beth, crazed impatience curling into her voice. "Not that one. No words. It can't have words on it. Go get a plain white shirt!"

"I don't have a plain white shirt!" says Gracie, still crying.

"You must."

"I don't."

"Then go get one of Jessica's!"

"It'll be way too big!"

Beth scans through a mental catalog of the girls' wardrobes. Gracie's right. All the white shirts are graphic T-shirts. Beth looks at her watch. They're late. She's never late. She likes to be early. Her face feels hot. Her soft, sun-kissed glow is now blazing red with stress.

Plan C.

"Okay, listen. Everyone has a solid-color tank top. I don't care what color, no words, go find one and put it on. Go! Go! Go!"

Gracie and Jessica skedaddle up the stairs, and Beth races right behind them.

"Sophie!" Beth yells through the gauzy, white fabric of her beautiful white shirt as she disrobes in her own bedroom. "Change into a tank top!"

"What? Why?" yells Sophie.

"Just do what I say!"

All of Beth's tank tops are black, so she re-dresses in a flash. She waits for her girls at the top of the stairs, in the hallway of sad and lonely picture frames, each second smacking the center of her forehead as it ticks by. Sophie, surprisingly, is the first to join her. She's wearing a red tank top, no words, and she looks great, except for her face.

"Excuse me, are you wearing makeup?" asks Beth.

"Only a little."

"Where did you get it?"

"Alena. *Her* mother lets her wear it."

"Well, *your* mother doesn't."

"So not fair."

"Life's not fair. Come here."

Beth looks at Sophie's made-up eyes, which are a striking blue and only a couple of inches below Beth's. She won't be able to keep her oldest daughter from wearing makeup for too much longer, but she can at least keep it off for this picture.

She resists the urge to lick her hand and wipe Sophie's face with her own spit and instead grabs her by the hand and pulls her into the bathroom. She pumps some hand soap into a face-cloth, wets it in the sink, and scrubs Sophie's eyes and cheeks clean.

"Ow, my zit!"

"Sorry. You can keep the lip gloss on, but that's it."

The other two are now in the hallway. Gracie is in a pink tank top, and Jessica is in blue. No words. No stains.

"Okay! Let's *go!*"

They run down the stairs, Beth claps and calls for Grover to follow them, and they all race into the car. Beth eyeballs her girls in the backseat through the rearview mirror as she slides the key into the ignition. Gracie's eyes are puffy from crying. Sophie's face is splotchy from being rubbed too hard with the facecloth, and she does have one honker of a zit on her cheek. Jessica's jaw is clenched, and her arms are folded. She looks angry, but Beth can't imagine why. They're all wearing different colored tops, and Beth's face still feels red-hot.

They're all supposed to be wearing white. They're all supposed to be calm and happy. They're supposed to be on time. And Jimmy. It's their family portrait. Their family is supposed to include Jimmy.

Maybe she should call and cancel. She thinks about the beautiful gauzy, white shirts and her hallway of sad and lonely frames. She looks back at her three girls again and then at the empty passenger seat. This is her family. She takes a deep breath, blows it out through her mouth, shifts the car into reverse, and drives her late, mismatched, puffy, splotchy, zitty, angry, Jimmy-less family to Cisco Beach.

CHAPTER 20

~ ⌒ ~

Olivia checks her watch. Her client is late. This, she has already found in her brief experience, is typical. If it isn't the entire family, then it's a stray cousin who didn't get the directions, or it's an indispensable sister who is coming straight from the ferry, or it's a father who is actually here, but he's still in the car wrapping up a call from work. He'll be done in a minute. Or thirty.

This is why she started toting a beach chair to these portrait sessions. She doesn't mind waiting on a beautiful beach if she has somewhere to sit. Today was overcast, threatening rain all day, and Olivia doubts that the beach was crowded at any point. It's mostly emptied out now. There are more seagulls here than people.

Olivia likes the seagulls on Nantucket, which resemble the seagulls on Nantasket Beach—the beach she always went to when she lived in Hingham—only in that they're both white-and-gray shorebirds. Those gulls from Nantasket are insatiable, thieving rats with wings that prey upon anything labeled Nabisco or Frito-Lay. They stalk the edges of beach blankets, waiting for an unguarded moment to peck open a sealed bag of potato chips or fly off with an entire tuna sandwich.

The seagulls here pay little attention to people and their processed food. She watches one nab a crab from the shallow water, then settle into a warm dimple of sand, where it rips off the legs and devours the meaty body. She watches another fly overhead to the parking lot, where it drops a clam on the pavement, cracking open the shell. Why settle for cheese puffs when an abundance of fresh seafood is on the menu? These gulls are handsome and respectable birds.

Olivia follows the flight of another seagull across the cloudy horizon and wonders if it's possible ever to grow indifferent to this view. The water closest to the S-shaped shoreline is a metallic blue dance of rippling waves, but as her gaze travels out to sea, everything goes still and flat and almost white. A laser-sharp line of crisp, dark blue separates the ocean from the blushing pink sky at the horizon. Gorgeous.

The gull disappears in the distance. Olivia checks her watch. At thirty minutes late, she makes a point of calling the clients to verify that they are in fact coming and haven't forgotten or changed their minds. As she digs through her camera bag for her schedule sheet and phone, she sees them walking toward her, the mother and leashed dog leading the charge, three girls in different-colored tanks and jeans lagging behind.

"Olivia? Hi, I'm Beth Ellis. Sorry we're late."

"Hi, Beth. No problem."

"We had a wardrobe issue. I know everyone normally matches. Do you think this will look okay?"

Beth's right. Every family always wears matching outfits, like uniforms on the same team. All faded-blue shirts and khakis or all white shirts and Nantucket reds. The matching theme looks nice, but it's hardly necessary. She wonders who came up with this very autistic rule about family portraits.

"You look great."

Beth rolls her eyes. "We looked great a half hour ago. I'm hoping for not too embarrassing."

"No, the colors are fun."

"Again, so sorry. Before we get started, my oldest would like to know if you can Photoshop out her pimple."

"Mom!" says the oldest.

All three girls are now gathered behind Beth. Olivia glances down at her schedule sheet. Sophie, Jessica, and Gracie.

"Consider it gone, Sophie. No one will ever see it," says Olivia.

Sophie smiles just enough to be polite. That pimple looks painful.

"Can you get rid of this line right here while you're at it?" asks Beth, pointing to a deep vertical crease between her eyebrows. "And anything that looks over thirty-five around my eyes?"

Digital plastic surgery. Olivia can erase all evidence of dark circles, crow's-feet, and age spots with a few precise clicks of her computer mouse. Whatever else her photographs have going for them—magic hour, the correct f-stop, composition, meaningful expressions captured at just the right moment, everyone smiling with their eyes open—her ability to subtly edit years off a woman's face is probably her most marketable skill.

"You won't look a day over thirty. Let's start over by the water."

Olivia has developed an Eat Your Veggies First philosophy when it comes to beach portraits. She always takes the most difficult shot first. Ninety-nine percent of the time, this is the photo of everyone in front of the ocean, the one necessary photograph her client came here for, the one her client will be pissed about if it isn't perfect. All the other pictures, individuals and pairs and combinations of various people and pets and backgrounds, are bonus. Those are the Dessert shots.

Today, the Veggie shot will be easy. Three well-behaved-if-a-little-grumpy girls, a mellow dog, and a mother. No crying babies, no sugar-crazed toddlers hell-bent on running into the ocean, no preschoolers who refuse to smile, no preschoolers who refuse to do anything but smile, freezing their faces into the most unnatural-looking *Cheese*, and no husband.

Although couples don't openly fight right there on the beach in front of her, and Olivia never witnesses the actual argument, she's seen it too many times now. Irritation, blame, contempt, the negative energy between husband and wife over whatever skirmish they had earlier still simmering, bleeding through their eyes and smiles, as obvious as the zit on Sophie's cheek. And there's not a tool in Photoshop that can edit that out.

It's also a small group, much easier to catch eight eyeballs open than twenty. Groups of ten and more are truly difficult. Someone is always misbehaving, not looking at the camera, out of place, blinking. Four is a piece of cake. She'll snap about six hundred shots with the expectation of producing about two hundred quality pictures for Beth to choose from.

They line up in a straight row in front of the incoming tide.

"Smile. Look at me," says Olivia.

They all do, except for the middle girl.

"Sorry, in the blue, what's your name?" asks Olivia, looking up over her camera.

"Jessica."

"Jessica, give me a big smile."

"She won't," says Beth. "She has braces. She won't show her teeth."

"Uh, okay," says Olivia. "How about just less angry?"

"Jess, look happy," says Beth.

"But I'm not," says Jessica.

"Then fake it, please," says Beth through a clenched smile, in a threatening singsong voice.

"Fine."

Jessica pulls her pursed lips into the shape of slight amusement. Close enough. Olivia clicks away. She checks her LCD display and scrolls through the images. Veggies done. Now on to Dessert.

She shoots the girls in all possible combinations together without their mother, with and without the dog, sitting and standing. She shoots Beth with each daughter, then each girl alone, then the dog alone.

"Now how about just you?" asks Olivia.

"Me? By myself?" asks Beth.

"Yeah."

"No, I don't need one of just me."

Olivia has also learned this—a client can't purchase a shot that doesn't exist. Get every shot.

"Let's shoot it anyway. You don't have to decide if you want it now."

She might want a headshot for her job, whatever it is that she does. She's a young, single mother. She might want it for Facebook or Match.com.

"Okay," Beth says.

"Great. Look at me. Chin up, shoulders down."

Click. Click. Click.

After Olivia finishes with Beth, they all move over to the dunes and smile at the camera in a similar round of poses. Even though the Veggie shot comes first, Olivia has often found that the second round of pictures is better. Everyone is more relaxed in the new location, and true personalities and relationships begin to emerge here. She can now see that Sophie and Jessica are close, that Sophie is edgy and bossy, and Jessica idolizes her. Gracie is goofy, and despite being around nine or ten, she is still Beth's baby girl. In the solo shots of Beth up against the dunes, Olivia sees a resolve peeking through a well-worn uncertainty, an openness in her posture, an authentic happiness alive in her smile.

After an hour and 652 images in the camera, Olivia declares that they're finished.

"Girls, go walk Grover for a few minutes while I talk to the photographer. Here's a baggie."

Beth follows Olivia over to Olivia's camera bag and beach chair.

"So when will the photos be ready?"

"I'm running about six to eight weeks."

"Wow, that long?"

"They might be sooner, but, yeah, probably at least six weeks."

To her own pleased amazement, Olivia's had steady business all summer. She's done an average of five portraits each week, which means she's actually earning a living. But the editing piece of this beach-portrait-photography gig is more labor-intensive than she anticipated, and she's now considerably backed up. Editing the large family portraits is particularly time-consuming. She had one family of thirty-two who were gathered on Nantucket for the grandparents' fiftieth wedding anniversary. Editing that session was a beast. And erasing any signs of aging on all these women takes time.

"And that's when we'll get the proof book?"

"Yes, I'll e-mail you the link."

"Link?"

"Yes, it's all online."

"Oh, so we don't look through an actual book?"

"No, I do it all online."

"Oh," says Beth, sounding disappointed.

"It's great. You'll like it. You can choose the size, black-and-white or color. It's easy to navigate, but if you have any questions, feel free to get in touch."

Olivia places her camera in her bag and zips it shut. She folds her beach chair. It's time to go. She will happily hold

Beth's hand via phone or e-mail through any step of the purchasing, but this is the end of the face-to-face part of this relationship.

"Okay. Thanks. Sorry about Jessica's sour puss."

"She was fine. She'll look great."

"I think she was upset that her father wasn't here. We separated this winter, and it's been hard on them."

"I'm sorry." Olivia stands with her heavy camera bag over one shoulder and her beach chair tucked under the other.

"It's been hard for me, too. Do you see this a lot? Families without the father?"

Struck by something familiar in Beth's question, Olivia pauses in her haste to leave. She studies the expression on Beth's face, and it registers. The need to feel normal. The desire to be accepted.

"All the time," Olivia lies.

Beth smiles, grateful.

Olivia senses something else familiar in Beth but can't quite put her finger on it. And then, there it is, like looking in a mirror. Loneliness. Olivia decides to wait with Beth until her daughters return with their dog.

The sky has completely clouded over now, and the sun is just about to set. The air is noticeably chillier than it was only five minutes ago. Beth grabs a sweatshirt from her bag. As she's pulling it over her head, Olivia notices a marriage self-help book sitting faceup at the top of Beth's bag.

"That's my book," says Olivia aloud instead of to herself as she'd intended.

"What?"

"I mean, I helped edit that book. I used to work at a publishing house."

"Oh. I haven't read it yet. It belongs to a friend."

Both women stand in awkward silence. Beth turns and looks down the length of the beach. Her girls are three dots in the distance. She turns back and rakes her toes through the sand. "So you used to work in publishing?"

"Five years ago. Feels like even longer."

"I know this is a little forward, but I'm writing a book. It's a series of related stories, or maybe it's a novel, I'm not really sure yet, but I'd love for someone professional to take a look at it."

"Oh, I edited self-help, not fiction—"

"That's okay. I'd really appreciate your feedback, if you have the time."

Outside of her job, Olivia's never offered to read anyone's anything. She's never wanted to be the one to tell someone not to quit her day job, to crush someone's dream. She looks down at Beth's bare feet, at her blue-painted toenails, at her copy of *Mending Your Marriage,* at the wedding and engagement rings she still wears on her finger, at the hopeful expression hung on her lonely face. She sighs. She has time.

"Sure. I'd be happy to take a look at it when you're done. Just let me know."

"Thank you so much!" says Beth, her face lit up.

Olivia smiles. She adjusts the beach chair under her right armpit. It felt light when she first picked it up, but now it's feeling heavy and unwieldy. And the strap to her camera bag is digging into the bare skin on her shoulder. She didn't bring a sweatshirt, and she's cold in her sleeveless sundress. She looks over Beth's shoulder.

"Here come your girls."

Beth turns and sees her daughters and her dog walking toward her. "Oh, okay. Thanks again. I knew there was a reason I picked you to do our pictures."

Olivia extends her somewhat free hand to shake Beth's, but Beth maneuvers around this formal gesture, the camera bag, and the beach chair and gives Olivia a sincere hug. Chills run down Olivia's arms, but not because she's cold. It's been a long time since anyone has hugged her.

"You're welcome."

The girls file in next to Beth. Sophie is holding a huge seagull feather in one hand and the dog's leash in the other, and Jessica is holding a bag of poop.

"Mom! Look what I found for you!" yells Gracie, smiling, excited.

She holds out the palm of her hand, displaying the amber-colored exoskeleton of a baby horseshoe crab.

"Cool, sweetie," says Beth.

"And this is for you," says Gracie, extending her other palm toward Olivia.

Olivia offers her somewhat free hand to Gracie, and Gracie rolls a white, almost translucent, wet, oval pebble into Olivia's palm. Chills run down her arms again.

"It's a pearl," says Gracie.

"Thank you," says Olivia, her voice catching at the back of her throat. "I love it."

"Okay, we're off. Thanks again," says Beth, and they all begin walking toward the parking lot.

"We'll talk in six weeks?" Beth asks at her car door.

"Six weeks," says Olivia, even though it could easily be eight.

Beth waves, disappears into her car, and drives away.

Olivia tosses her camera bag and chair into the backseat of her Jeep and gets in. The warm air inside feels like a thick blanket wrapped around her bare skin. As she backs up, it begins to rain. She turns on her lights and wipers, relieved that the weather held for her portrait session. She pulls out of the parking lot, grateful for Gracie's gift still in her hand, smiling as she drives down Hummock Pond Road in the pouring rain.

When she gets home, she adds Gracie's rock to her growing collection in the glass bowl on the coffee table. She then connects her camera to her computer and retrieves one of her journals from the kitchen table. As the images from today's shoot are downloading onto her computer, she sits in her living-room chair and thinks about Beth and her three daughters, about her loneliness and her book. Olivia wonders what it's about.

Then she opens her journal and reads.

CHAPTER 21

⟨∼ ⌣ ∽⟩

April 12, 2005

I spent today back in eighth grade. It started at the playground. We got there late morning, and Anthony ran straight to the swings, as usual. His body is way too big for the toddler bucket seats, but he refuses to even try the big-boy swings, so I hoisted him into one of the buckets and pushed my five-year-old next to another mother pushing her two-year-old. She smiled nervously at me and said nothing.

It was finally warm out today, and the playground was crowded. There were lots of kids Anthony's age playing with each other. Two boys and a girl were chasing each other up and down the slides, laughing, having a blast. A line of four kids were playing Follow the Leader, moving across the field of grass next to the playground, all arms up, then down, all jumping, then crawling, then clapping. Another group of kids were playing under the jungle gym.

A couple of girls were selling wood-chip ice cream. The customer kids waited their turn at the "ice cream stand,"

*placed their orders, paid with wood-chip money, and "ate"
their delicious treats. They went back for seconds and thirds.
It would've been adorable to watch if it didn't make me
want to sob.*

*Anthony is light-years away from any of this. Interactive
play. Imaginative play.*

Friends.

*All these things that other kids do spontaneously and
naturally would have to be broken down into discrete
behavioral pieces, and Carlin would have to work on each
one with Anthony for hours and weeks and months before
he might learn to pretend that a wood chip is vanilla ice
cream. But it wouldn't be for the pure, innocent joy of it.
He'd do it to get the Pringles he wants or to get Carlin to
stop bothering him about it, to be finally left alone already.
Because that's what he wants. To be alone. That's what
gives him joy.*

*All Anthony wants to do at the playground is swing.
But I see these other kids playing, and my heart wants
more, and I get bored just standing there, pushing him over
and over. I stopped his swing a bunch of times and asked
him if he'd like to try the slide, if he'd like to play with the
other kids, if he'd like to go over to the sandbox. He loves
sand. But nothing rivals the swing, and he wouldn't budge.
So we stayed there, swinging. I felt self-conscious and
defeated.*

*Why can't I just be happy that he's happy alone on the
swing? Why do I have to insist that happiness is doing
what I want him to do? Because the world is full of people,
Anthony, not swings, and I want you to be happy in the
world and not just happy in a swing. Is that too much to
want? Is it selfish to want this?*

*Because the other kids at the playground can play
independently and don't stay on the swings all morning,*

*the other moms were free to sit together at one of the picnic
tables. I pushed Anthony on the swing and listened at a
distance to these moms chatting and laughing, having a
grand old time. I felt like I was in eighth grade all over
again—the awkward outsider, not part of the "in" crowd.*

*They say 1 in 110 kids have autism now, but I don't
know any other mothers in town with an autistic kid.
Where are they? I've been out of work entirely now for
six months, and I miss adult company. Conversation.
Morning meetings.*

Friends.

*Carlin and Rhia are over every day, but they're
Anthony's therapists. They don't count. And David acts like
I'm asking him to re-shingle the roof every time I ask him
the simplest question. I know I'm probably being sensitive
because I've got my period, but I felt how lonely I am while
I watched this group of moms. A group I won't ever be a
part of. Like the popular girls in eighth grade with their
perfect Farrah Fawcett hair and their fancy Jordache jeans.
I hated them and wished I could be one of them in the same
breath.*

*We'd been at the swing for over an hour when the moms
called their kids over to the picnic table for lunch. The kids
came. The moms opened pretty, insulated lunch bags and
passed out sandwiches, yogurts, orange slices, string cheese,
Goldfish crackers, and juice boxes.*

A fun picnic. Not for us.

*It was time to go. I gave Anthony a 1, 2, 3 warning,
which sometimes helps, but not today. He gave a quick
screech and flapped his hands when I stopped the swing, but
when I didn't immediately return to pushing and instead
began lifting him out, he lost it. His body went stiff and
his screeching escalated to an I'm-being-murdered decibel.
I had to use all my strength to pry him out of the bucket,*

to carry him, forty-five pounds of dead weight screaming in agony over being separated from a swing that he'd just spent the last hour and a half on, to not look back at the moms at the picnic table who I'm sure were looking at me the whole time, judging me, thinking, *Thank God I'm not HER.* Just like eighth grade.

I got Anthony in the car and turned on Barney as fast as humanly possible, and he calmed down. God bless Barney. Then, I stupidly decided to stop at CVS on the way home. I just got my period this morning, and I only had a couple of tampons left. For any of those other mothers at the playground, it wouldn't be a stupid idea to go to CVS when you have your period and only two tampons left. They'd breeze in, zip out, no problem. They might not even remember the quick errand by the end of the day. But for me, this was a colossally stupid idea. And I'll never forget it.

We always go straight home after the playground, and I always take Center Street to Pigeon Lane, but CVS is the other way. I hoped Anthony wouldn't notice. I hoped it wouldn't matter. It would only take a few minutes. *Stupid girl.*

As soon as I went left instead of right out of the parking lot, Anthony started screeching. When I kept going, he started kicking. I should've turned around then and there, but I kept going. He started screaming, whipping his head and flapping his hands, fighting against the buckle of his car seat as if he were being repeatedly stabbed with a knife.

Fueled by sheer and again stupid determination to run a simple and necessary errand, I got all the way to CVS, but there was no way I could go in. There's no way I could physically carry him given the state he was in; I would never leave him alone in the car, and there was absolutely no way to reach him with a rational explanation.

Mommy needs tampons, sweetie. Please stop freaking out. We'll be home in five minutes.

So I drove home.

By dinner, I was out of tampons. But I wasn't going to risk another meltdown in the car, so I had to wait for David so I could go to CVS alone. I made a homemade pad out of wadded toilet paper to hold me over until he got home. But David was forty-five minutes late (with no phone call), and the wad of TP was no match for my period, and I bled through onto my favorite skirt.

Eighth grade all over again. At least my accident happened at home and not at the playground in front of the "in" moms.

It occurred to me while I was driving to CVS for the second time today that I've spent my whole life since eighth grade terrified of being the outsider, doing almost anything to fit in, always desperate to belong. Anthony doesn't worry about any of this. He doesn't mind being by himself. He enjoys it. He doesn't care what people think. He's not going to get caught up in wanting expensive designer clothes or the latest $100 sneakers. He's not going to drink or smoke pot to look cool. He's not going to do anything because everyone else is doing it.

He doesn't care what other people wear or think or do. He likes what he likes. He does what he wants to do. Until I say it's time to go and rip him out of his swing.

I thought about those kids playing Follow the Leader today. Anthony will never be a follower. He won't be the leader though either. This thought would normally shred my heart and make me weepy, but as I drove to CVS, I felt unexpectedly at peace.

He's simply not playing that game.

CHAPTER 22

—— ❧ ——

I am swinging on the swing at the playground. I love swinging. Swinging puts me in my body.

I usually know I have hands, but if anything interesting is going on, if I'm counting or thinking or watching TV, my body disappears from me. I don't have a voice, so people sometimes treat me like I also don't have a body, like I don't exist in the world. And because most of the time I'm not aware of my body, I think they might be right. Maybe I don't really exist in the world.

Swinging makes me exist in the world.

My thinking often gets stuck repeating. If I find a thought I like, I think it again so I can keep enjoying it. These kinds of thoughts are like Pringles. Pringles are so yummy, I never want to eat just one. I want to eat another and another and another. If I find a yummy thought, I want to think it again and again and again. But if I think it too much, then I don't just want to think it. I NEED to think it because I'm afraid if I don't always keep it with me, I might lose it forever. So my thinking gets stuck a lot on the same idea again and again and again. And when this happens, nothing else exists.

The other day I got stuck on Three Blind Mice. I said these three words inside my head, loving them for a whole morning. Nothing else existed. Not even me. I became those three words. Three Blind Mice.

But I don't get stuck on Three Blind Mice right now because I'm swinging. When I swing, I am no longer my repeating thoughts. When I swing, I am a repeating body. I am moving through air, forward and down and up, backward and down and up, forward and down and up, backward and down and up. I am Anthony's body, repeating this perfect rhythm. I swing, and I am here!

I am forward and down and up, backward and down and up, feeling the cool air tickle my face. My face is smiling. My face is real.

Then my mother stops the swing and says something about going over to the sandbox. I flap my hands and make a noise to let her know that I don't like her idea. I don't want to get off the swing. I flap and make a noise because my voice won't say the word NO.

My mother understands me and starts the swing moving again.

I love sand. I love to scoop up as much as my hands can hold, raise my hands high, and let the sand spill down. I love the feel of the sand moving through my fingers, how it drizzles and sparkles in the air like music as it falls. It's almost as good as water.

But sand in a playground sandbox is not like sand at the beach. Sand in a playground sandbox is always too close to other kids. When I play with sand in a playground sandbox, another mother will tell me I can't play with the sand. She'll say, *Please stop doing that, the sand is blowing into people's eyes.* And my mother will take me out of the sandbox because I won't stop doing that, and I also don't know how to *share the sand.*

My mother stops me again and wants me to go over to the slide. I make a noise and flap my hands, and she starts the swing moving again. Forward and down and up, backward and down and up.

I don't like the slide. Sometimes kids will walk up the slide on their feet instead of sliding down the slide on their bottoms, and that is breaking the rules. If I'm at the top of the slide and another kid starts climbing up the slide, then I don't know what to do. I can't slide down because the kid is in the way, but I can't climb back DOWN the steps because the slide steps are for climbing UP. That is the rule. So on the slide, I might have no solution to my problem, and I don't want that.

And out on the playground, a kid might hit me or push me or ask me a question. The mothers always ask me a question, invading me with their eyes and an UP sound at the end of their voices. *What is your name?* But my voice doesn't work, so I can't even tell them that I don't want to answer their questions.

On the swing, I feel protected from all of this. No one can touch me, no one wants me to say my name, and no one is telling me not to play with sand. I only want to swing.

My mother stops the swing again, but this time she doesn't say anything about the playground. She starts taking me out. I make a loud noise and flap my hands, letting her know that this is not okay with me. She keeps taking me out.

NO! More swinging! I'm not done. I want to stay in the swing! I want to stay in my body! NO! I want to exist in the world! I need to keep my body repeating or I might lose my body forever. I might be gone forever!

I scream really loud, trying to show my mother that I need to keep swinging or I might die, but for some reason, she doesn't understand what I'm showing her. I go stiff, trying to keep my body in the swing, but she's too strong and she doesn't understand, and she grabs my body away. I squeeze my eyes shut so I won't see my body leaving the swing. I scream even louder so everything about my stolen body and the swing disappears, and only the sound of my screaming exists.

The next thing I know, I'm not outside anymore. I'm in the car, watching Barney. I'm watching Barney and his friends, and they're doing what I know they should be doing. I stop screaming. I'm not dead because I'm watching Barney. I'm okay.

But then I'm not okay. The car is going the WRONG WAY. The way the car is going is not the way home. The way home is by three white houses, then one brick house, then a street, then one yellow house and two white houses, then a red light/green light. Then church, the trees, one brown house, one white house, one gray house with peeling paint, then Pigeon Lane, the street that HOME is on.

But we did not go this way. This way is a sign with a picture of a girl on it, then a brown house, a white house, a blue house, then a street, a building, a parking lot, a red light. This is not the way HOME. We ALWAYS go HOME after the playground, and this way does not match the map in my head that shows the way home.

I don't know where we're going, but we're not going home. I am not going home to have three chicken nuggets with ketchup on my blue plate with juice in my Barney cup for lunch at the kitchen table. I'm not going to see Danyel after lunch because Danyel comes to my home, and I will not be home. I will be somewhere else.

Maybe we are lost, and maybe I will never see my home again. The rule is we ALWAYS go HOME after the playground, and this is breaking the rule. If this rule can break, then anything can break. Maybe the world is breaking.

I am screaming. I want to go HOME. I want to get out of this car that is going the wrong way, but I am trapped in this seat. I am screaming, filling with hot, scary liquid. The hot, scary liquid keeps filling me, until I'm too full and burning on the inside. I shake my hands to spill some of the hot, scary liquid out through my fingers, but the hot, scary liquid keeps filling me, too huge and hot and fast for my fingers to empty.

I close my eyes so I don't have to see the wrong houses and buildings and streets. I'm screaming as loud as I can so I can become the sound of my scream and not a boy trapped in a car seat who is no longer swinging but going very fast in the wrong direction.

When I open my eyes, I realize I'm no longer screaming. I'm lying under my Barney blanket in my bed. I see the tree outside the window, my box of rocks, the calendar on the wall. I know this is good because this means I am home, and this also means that the world didn't break, but I don't feel good yet. I feel sweaty and tired, and I still feel too much hot, scary liquid bubbling and sloshing around inside that needs to leak out to make room for feeling good.

I lie in bed and wonder how we got home. There must be a different way. I wonder why we went a different way.

Today is Monday. It is sunny and warm. I am wearing brown pants and a red shirt. Maybe on sunny, warm Mondays when I wear brown pants and a red shirt, after my mother says I'm done swinging at the playground, we go a different way home. Maybe on sunny, warm Mondays when I wear brown pants and a red shirt and we leave the playground to go home, we go by the sign with a picture of a girl on it, then a brown house, then a white house, a

blue house, a street, a building, a parking lot, and a red
light. Maybe this is a new rule.

I'm hungry now. I go downstairs with both feet on all
twelve steps and into the kitchen. My three chicken nuggets with ketchup on my blue plate, my Barney cup with
juice, my fork, and white napkin are all on the table for
lunch, just like they always are. My mother isn't sitting at
the table, but I feel her nearby. I flap my hands and jump
and let out one of my happy sounds, getting rid of the last
drops of the hot, scary liquid inside me.

I sit down and eat my lunch. I feel good. But then I have
a thought I don't like. I didn't know there were a NUMBER
of ways home from the playground. Now there are TWO
ways to come home from the playground. I don't like that
number two. Two is in the middle of things. Two is unfinished. Two is in between, and I don't like in between.
I wish there were THREE ways to come home from the
playground.

The first way, which is the old way, goes by three white
houses, then one brick house, then a street, then one yellow house and two white houses, then a red light/green
light. Then church, the trees, one brown house, one
white house, one gray house with the peeling paint, then
Pigeon Lane. The second way, the new way we go on
warm, sunny Mondays when I wear brown pants and a
red shirt, is by the sign with a picture of a girl on it, then a
brown house, then a white house, a blue house, a street,
a building, a parking lot, and a red light, and some other
stuff I didn't see before Pigeon Lane because I had my
eyes shut.

There has to be one more way. There have to be THREE
ways on the map from the playground to home. But what
if there are only two ways, and that is it? What if we are
stuck with two?

I feel the hot, scary liquid rushing at me again, but I see it coming this time. I shut the door on it before it can even touch my toes, before it has the chance to flood me.

Three Blind Mice. Three Blind Mice. Three Blind Mice. Three Blind Mice. Three Blind Mice. Three Blind Mice. Three Blind Mice. Three Blind Mice. Three Blind Mice.

CHAPTER 23

A fter finishing another chapter, Beth left the library early and is now sitting on a couch in Dr. Campbell's office, which is really the living room in Dr. Campbell's house, wishing she'd waited in the car. She's on time, and Jimmy's late, and she feels unbearably self-conscious sitting alone on a marriage counselor's couch with nothing to say.

And the couch isn't helping anything. When she sat down, she sank deep and back into the cushion, her knees forced apart and up, her feet lifted off the ground. She tried to reposition herself without looking as if anything was wrong, but the more she wiggled, the deeper she sank. Dr. Campbell's couch is quicksand.

Dr. Campbell is sitting opposite her in a sturdy leather chair, sipping his coffee, studying her, saying nothing. Maybe this is some kind of psychological test. He told her to "have a seat" and waved her over here. Maybe he's judging what type of person she is based on how she reacts to being swallowed by a couch cushion. Does continuing to sit like this mean she's an easygoing, well-adjusted woman, or does it mean she's a doormat who will silently endure anything? Should she politely ask for a different seat?

She decides to keep quiet. She waggles her feet in the air as if to the beat of a playful melody and browses the room, trying to act normal.

Dr. Campbell has long, wavy, gray hair, glasses, and a beard. He'd look like Santa, but he's rail thin. He's wearing a gold wedding band. That's good. A marriage counselor should be married. It's always bugged her that the girls' pediatrician has no children. Textbooks and degrees from expensive universities are great, but for her money, there's no better school than real life.

He's drinking coffee from a large, white Starbucks mug. This interests her. She's never seen a Starbucks. She left New York City just before the first one there opened. She only knows they exist because she's been stopped many times over the years by tourists asking her, *Can you tell me where the Starbucks is?* She'll never forget the look on the man's face when, that first time, she replied, *What's Starbucks?* As if he were talking to a woman who'd just been released from an insane asylum. Now she simply says, *There aren't any here,* and she points their astonished faces to The Bean.

She wonders where Dr. Campbell got the mug. He must travel off-island. She wonders where he goes—Boston, New York, exotic parts of the world where they have Starbucks coffee.

Despite there being no bookshelves in the room, books and magazines are everywhere, piled in teetering towers as tall as Beth up against the walls, on either side of Dr. Campbell's chair, on random spots in the middle of the floor. It's a library constructed by Dr. Seuss. Several towers look as if they're one magazine or book shy of collapsing, like a book version of the game Jenga just before someone loses.

The white walls are bare but for one picture, an elaborate family tree drawn in calligraphy on tea-colored paper meant to look old. As she traces the branches, she realizes that it is

Dr. Campbell's family tree and that, if the tree is true, he's a direct descendant of Edward Starbuck, one of the original 1659 settlers of Nantucket. She's impressed and surprised that she didn't know this about him.

Island lineage carries a lot of status here. Jimmy's lived here for twenty-one years, and she's been here for fifteen, but they'll both always be considered "wash-ashores." Outsiders. Peasant people. Their children were born here, so Sophie, Jessica, and Gracie are natives, but only first generation. Insiders, but direct descendants of peasant outsiders. Dr. Campbell is a native whose ancestors go all the way back. On Nantucket, Dr. Campbell is royalty. It's an understated royalty, without the paparazzi or a castle or pomp and circumstance or even any real wealth, but it's recognized. It's there.

She wonders if the Starbucks coffee store has anything to do with the Starbuck families of Nantucket. Probably not, else the island would surely have one. She doesn't ask.

By far the most interesting thing in the room is the falcon in the enormous cage next to the fireplace behind Dr. Campbell. The bird is about the size of a small hawk with dark gray wings, a white belly flecked with gray, and gray feathers that wrap around its creepy black eyes like the mask of a villain. One of its wings looks as if it might be mangled, broken. The falcon is perched on a piece of driftwood, almost motionless, staring at Beth. It looks menacing, like it wants to peck her eyes out.

"That's Oscar. Don't worry, he's domesticated. He won't bother us," says Dr. Campbell.

Beth nods, bothered.

The doorbell rings. Thank God. Dr. Campbell gets up and lets Jimmy in.

"This is for the bird," says Jimmy, handing Dr. Campbell a black trash bag.

Dr. Campbell peeks into the bag and smiles. "Wonderful. Have a seat. I'll be back in a minute."

Nantucket locals love to barter. Beth and Jimmy used to pay for car repairs with scallops. Jill's husband, Mickey, does construction work in exchange for dental work. Dr. Campbell accepts roadkill as a copay.

Jimmy sits on the opposite end of the couch, an empty cushion between him and Beth. He sinks just like Beth did, but he doesn't look nearly as uncomfortable as she feels. His feet still reach the ground.

"You're late," she whispers.

"I had a hard time finding something."

"What was in the bag?"

"Squirrel."

"Ack. Gross. Why didn't you just get some pet food at the grocery store?"

"Because the whole point is to save twenty bucks. Kinda defeats the purpose if I go *buy* him food."

"Where did you find the squirrel?"

"Milestone Road."

"Did you wash your hands?"

Before Jimmy can answer, Dr. Campbell returns with what she can only assume from the smell is dead squirrel, opens the birdcage for a moment, latches it shut (she's careful to notice), then settles back into his leather chair. He slaps his thighs and smiles.

Is anyone going to wash his hands?

"Let's begin," says Dr. Campbell. "Why are we here?"

No one answers. Beth and Jimmy sit, comfortable in their respective, familiar silences, uncomfortable in their respective, sunken seats. Beth looks over at Jimmy, who is staring into his germy, roadkill-covered hands. She looks over Dr. Campbell's shoulder at Oscar, who has a bit of squirrel slime hanging from his yellow beak, his black, predatory eyes still sizing her up.

"Jimmy," says Dr. Campbell. "Let's start with you."

"Well, ah, we're separated. We've been married fourteen years, and we're separated, and we're trying to get back together."

Jimmy clasps his hands and waits. That's it. That's his summary.

Get him, Oscar. Gouge his eyes out.

"We're separated because he *cheated* on me, and I don't know if I want to get back together."

"Okay," says Dr. Campbell, not at all visibly outraged or moved to her side, as Beth would've hoped. "Jimmy, why did you cheat on Beth?"

Jimmy fidgets and sinks a little deeper into his cushion. A black cat with white paws struts into the room, brushes against Beth's dangling feet as it walks by, and curls up in a sunny spot on the floor by one of the windows, just outside the shadow of one of the book towers. Jimmy is allergic to cats.

"I dunno."

"Beth, why do you think he cheated on you?"

Salt is too sexy, Angela is too sexy, I'm not sexy enough, he isn't attracted to me anymore, he doesn't love me anymore, he's a jerk, he's a liar, he's a cheater, he's a man. "I'd really like to hear Jimmy's answer."

Beth and Dr. Campbell look at Jimmy and wait. Another cat, this one gray, runs into the room and chases the black cat off its sunny spot on the floor. They both disappear behind the couch. Oscar chirps and flaps its one good wing against the cage. Jimmy rubs his nose and clears his throat.

"Look, I know I was wrong. I'm the bad guy here, and I'm really sorry. I was hoping we could put it behind us and start over. Wouldn't rehashing all this stuff just hurt Beth all over again?"

"*Re*hashing would mean that we've already hashed it. We haven't talked about this at all," says Beth.

"Beth, have you forgiven Jimmy?"

"No."

"Are you ready to put his infidelity behind you and start over?"

"No."

"If you're going to get back together, it's important for both of you to understand why this happened and to make some sort of peace with it. If you stay unconscious to why this happened and get back together, it'll likely happen again. So you're going to have to risk talking about some things that are uncomfortable and a little painful for both of you, yes?"

The phone rings somewhere in Dr. Campbell's house. Dr. Campbell sips his coffee as if he doesn't hear it. The three of them sit in silence. The phone stops ringing. The three of them sit in silence.

"She was always unhappy with me. I can't remember the last time I came home and she was happy to see me."

"You get home at two a.m.! I'm asleep, Jimmy. I'm sorry I don't wake up and throw on a smile and something pretty and greet you at the door with slippers and a cigar."

"Even before the bartending job, you hated having me around."

"You weren't working. I hated you not working. You were miserable, moping around the house, making messes for me to clean up all day, like the house was your hotel, and I was housekeeping."

"Everything in that house has to be exactly how she likes it. Everything has to be perfect. I'm not perfect, Beth. No guy is."

"Not looking for perfect, Jimmy. Something in between miserable cheating bastard and perfect would be great."

He says nothing. She folds her arms over her chest and waggles her foot, satisfied to have delivered the last word there.

"Okay, Jimmy. Let's get back to the question," says Dr. Campbell, redirecting the two the way a parent might talk to a pair of preschoolers. "You felt unwanted and unhappy. Did you talk to Beth about how you were feeling?"

"No, but it was obvious."

"Maybe, maybe not. By not telling her, you didn't give her the chance to help you or change anything. You have to communicate what you need, open yourself, give Beth the opportunity to understand what's really going on with you. Unfortunately, we humans can't read minds."

Jimmy nods.

"Beth, were you unhappy with Jimmy?"

"Before I found out he was cheating?"

"Yes."

"Well, yeah, anyone would've been. After he stopped scalloping, he was out of work. He wasn't fun to be around."

"You weren't exactly supportive," says Jimmy.

"What does that mean? How wasn't I supportive?"

"Everyone we saw, she had to talk about me being a bum."

"I never said that. I only mentioned it to people so they'd know to call you if anyone had any work."

"And how about you? I didn't see you out looking for a job to help us."

"I checked all the papers. None of them had any positions open. And I did work. Remember I did caretaking for those summerhouses?"

"That was like a couple hundred dollars a month, that wasn't a real job."

"What am I supposed to do here, Jimmy? I quit my *life* fifteen years ago to marry you and have these kids and live on this godforsaken island. I was supposed to go to school and become a writer."

"I never stopped you from writing."

When Gracie was a baby and Jessica and Sophie were preschoolers, Beth could barely manage to take a shower, never mind write anything creative. This was probably when all of her essays and short stories and writing notebooks went into the attic. She didn't have the time or space. But the girls got older and more independent. They went to school, and Beth had plenty of time for showers. She had plenty of time and space to write again, but she didn't. Something stopped her, but it wasn't Jimmy.

"Well, I'm writing now," she says, like it's a threat.

"Do you think it's my life's dream to be a bartender?"

"You love it."

"I didn't at first. And I'd still rather be on a boat."

"And I'd rather have a husband who wasn't screwing the hostess."

Her voice is now hollow and shaken with anger. She blinks back tears. She hates that she always cries when she's angry, as if her emotional wiring is crossed. Her heart is pounding to support her anger, her red-hot face feels her anger, and her mind understands the reasons for her anger, but her eyes take in all this information and conclude, *She's sad. Make tears.* It's infuriating.

"I'm sorry," says Jimmy.

"You should be."

"Is the affair over now?" asks Dr. Campbell.

"Yes. She wanted me to get a divorce and marry her, but that was never going to happen. The whole thing was a huge mistake. It's over, I promise, and it'll never happen again. Beth, I don't want to lose you."

"Beth, do you believe him?"

Beth thinks. She doesn't know what to think. She'd like to think that he leaves Salt alone now, that he goes straight to his friend Harry's apartment, sleeps alone in Harry's extra bedroom until noon, spends the afternoon feeling bad about what he's done, then goes to work again.

But *she's* at Salt. Beth thinks about the two of them there. She imagines a smile, a laugh, a touch, *her* hand on his arm, a kiss. Those pictures in Beth's head are easier to envision, more vivid and real than imagining Jimmy alone in some apartment she's never seen. She pictures Angela's necklace dangling between her big boobs and breathes in a powerful whiff of dead squirrel and something else. Cat pee? She feels physically sick.

"I don't know what to believe. They spend every night together."

"We don't 'spend' the night together. We work at the same place."

"Fine. She works where he bartends. I don't know if I can trust him again."

"I promise, it's over."

"Yeah, well, clearly you don't always keep your promises."

Dr. Campbell lowers his Starbucks mug and cocks his head. Everyone waits.

"Did you hear that?"

Beth shakes her head. Jimmy says nothing.

"Listen," Dr. Campbell says.

Beth hears Jimmy sniffling and a car drive by outside.

"Excuse me, I'll be back in a second," says Dr. Campbell, and he rushes out of the room.

Beth and Jimmy sit in silence, staring straight ahead, expecting Dr. Campbell to return within a few seconds. When this doesn't happen, Jimmy starts to fidget. He clears his throat, much louder than he would if Dr. Campbell were still in the room. Beth picks at her cuticles. Jimmy checks his phone. She checks hers.

She didn't hear any noise. Maybe this is some kind of test, some kind of time-out for misbehaving couples. Maybe the "listen" was meant for them.

Well, it's not working. They don't know how to talk to each other. They don't know how to listen. This is why they're here. In addition to feeling ridiculously wedged in Dr. Campbell's couch, stalked by a falcon, angry at Jimmy for betraying her, embarrassed that she cries when she's angry, and sick at the thought of Jimmy and Angela still seeing each other, she now feels abandoned and manipulated. This therapist doesn't know what he's doing.

Dr. Campbell doesn't come back, and the silence between Jimmy and her expands. Dr. Campbell is gone, and the silence develops, forming itself into an actual presence in the room as real and as predatory as the falcon. It has its own evil eyes, pursuing them, uncaged in Dr. Campbell's absence, licking its chops, waiting for the right moment to attack. The silence between Jimmy and her would like nothing more than to devour them, as it's been aiming to do for years.

Finally, after what seems like their entire session but was probably only a few minutes, Dr. Campbell returns to the room, sits in his leather chair, and sighs.

"My apologies. The dogs got out. Now, let's go over where we're at. Jimmy, you need to feel wanted and that you make Beth happy. Beth, you need to be able to trust that if Jimmy is feeling unhappy, he'll come and talk to you about it and that he'll never be unfaithful again. Yes? Does this sound fair?"

"I don't think it's fair to say that Jimmy's the only one who feels unwanted. He cheated on me. That's not exactly wanting me. I didn't go out and 'want' another man."

"Yes. True. Okay, let's add that in. You both want to feel wanted, happy, secure, and loved, yes? Fair to say?"

"Yes," says Beth.

"Yes," says Jimmy.

"Then this is what we're going to work on," says Dr. Campbell, slapping his thighs.

"But shouldn't those things come naturally if you're right for each other?" asks Beth.

"Some of it does, and some of it requires communication and effort."

Jimmy sneezes. Beth says, *Bless you,* in her head and offers Dr. Campbell a tight-lipped, timid smile.

"Okay," says Dr. Campbell, checking his watch. "Here's your homework. I want you each to get out four pieces of paper, one for *wanted,* one for *happy,* one for *secure,* and one for *loved,* and I want you to write down specific actions and words that you need to see and hear in order to feel each of these things. Come up with as many as you can. Don't hold anything back."

"Uh, like, what do you mean?" asks Jimmy.

"Well, these four feelings are necessary to both of you, but they probably mean different things when actualized. For example, feeling loved to you might mean a hug and kiss from Beth every time you come home from work. It might mean cigars and slippers. It might mean sex. For Beth, it might mean the same things, probably not the cigar and slippers, but it also might mean something else. Love for Beth might show up as doing the laundry or taking her out to dinner."

Beth nods.

"Love, happiness, security, feeling wanted—these are the basics, yes? And because they're so basic, people often assume that they should happen automatically. But what floats your boat might not float hers. We're all different. Unless you *communicate* the specific and quirky ways that make you feel loved and happy, your partner can miss the mark. And then we feel unloved and unhappy. Yes?"

Jimmy nods.

"Okay, that's it for today. Good work," says Dr. Campbell.

Jimmy pops up like a boy who just heard the recess bell. He pays Dr. Campbell in cash for the session, minus the twenty dollars for the fresh roadkill, while Beth rocks herself up and out of her hole. Beth thanks Dr. Campbell and smiles with her hands in her pockets, and she and Jimmy walk out to the driveway.

"What did you think?" she asks once she's sure they're out of earshot.

"I think that guy is really odd."

Beth laughs.

"He probably needs therapy more than we do," Jimmy says, smiling.

"Really though?" she asks, needing something more from him than a laugh.

"Therapy's not really my thing."

She nods.

"But it's worth it if it works, right?" he asks.

She nods.

"All right. I gotta go do my homework," he says, smiling. "See ya."

"See ya," she echoes.

She gets into her car and laughs, more a nervous release than over anything funny. That whole experience was odd. The living room, that couch, the roadkill copay, the falcon's black eyes, the cats, the "noisy" dogs.

She thinks about her homework assignment as she drives back to the library, already itching to begin the next chapter. Wanted, happy, secure, loved. What does she need to feel wanted? What does she need to feel loved? What will Jimmy's four pages look like? What does the boy in her book need to feel these things?

Her mind wanders through their therapy session, replaying it as she drives.

Trust. Anger. Silence. Communication. The falcon. That couch. The smell. The cats and dogs.

Her thoughts then shift to the brown-eyed boy in the book she's writing, wandering through the chapters she's already written.

No spoken words. The blue sky. Repetition. His mother.

Wanted. Happiness. Security. Love.

Dr. Campbell might be odd, but he's also brilliant.

CHAPTER 24

I am lining up some of my rocks in the living room. This line is made up of rocks that I've collected in the past week. It is a line of new rocks. The line stretches from the coffee table to the wall. It will be a line of 128 rocks when I am done. I'm picturing the line of 128 rocks in my head before I get to the wall, and I'm already excited.

This is why I stopped lining up plastic animals and dinosaurs. I never had enough. I could line them up by type or size or color or in order of what animal could get eaten by another or by who can run the fastest, but the line never stretched all the way from the coffee table to the wall. I always needed more animals and dinosaurs.

I had to wait for my mother or father to buy more plastic animals and dinosaurs from the store, but they never bought enough, and sometimes they wouldn't buy any at all. Even if I went to the store with them, and I begged them for more, they didn't always get me the animals and dinosaurs that I needed:

No. You have enough elephants. Not today. You don't need any more dinosaurs.

But they were wrong. I didn't have enough elephants and I did need more dinosaurs. And their *No*s and *Not today*s would make me feel like exploding, to leave those animals and dinosaurs I needed at the store when I had lines of animals and dinosaurs at home that didn't even reach the wall.

So I decided to stop needing those animals and dinosaurs. The rocks are much better. My mother takes me to the beach almost every day, and I can always find more of the rocks I need there. My mother can even forget to bring my green bucket and that's okay because I can fit twenty-one Big rocks in one pants pocket and forty-eight Small rocks in the other. And if it's cold, and I'm wearing a coat, I can fit twenty-seven Big rocks in one coat pocket and fifty-four Small rocks in the other.

My mother never says *No* or *Not today* at the beach. The rocks at the beach are free. I can collect and bring home as many rocks as I need.

There are rules for collecting rocks. They have to be mostly white and mostly smooth and mostly round. I am the judge of what is *mostly*.

Sometimes I collect a candy-corn-shaped rock, which really isn't round. It's really a triangle. But if it's very smooth and very white, I will collect it. If a rock is really good at being round, but it's a little too yellow or has a few bumps or cracks, I will collect it. My mother would call these *exceptions to the rule,* but I just call them part of the rule, and that makes it okay.

At home, I like to count them, organize them, and arrange them into lines that stretch across my bedroom floor, the living-room floor, the kitchen, or, if it's warm outside and not too cold or snowing or raining, the deck. The kitchen floor is difficult because of the tiles. I have to think and plan ahead to make sure the entire line will space out so no rocks fall into the grooves in between the tiles. Every rock has to be on a tile, and I can't break the line with a big space to jump over a groove, because then I've really made two lines and not one. And I don't like that number two.

The kitchen is also a difficult place to make my rock lines because my mother is usually walking around in there, but I don't notice her until it's too late. She sometimes walks through my line of rocks and kicks some of them out of place, or she tells me to *Clean this up and get these rocks out of the way,* and in either case the line gets ruined. And if my rock line gets ruined, I get ruined. So I like to line up my rocks somewhere where they and I won't be disturbed or kicked or cleaned up or ruined.

Once I get to know my rocks, they can be lined up in all kinds of ways. They can go by size, from smaller than a pea (these are also usually my roundest and whitest) to the size of my hand (always oval). They can go by smoothness, from no cracks or bumps to cracked and bumpy. They can go by roundness, from perfect sphere through every egg and glob and candy corn to perfect oval.

They can line up by whiteness. People call my rocks *Anthony's white rocks,* but this isn't fair to call them Anthony's white rocks because it's not the whole truth. A few of my rocks are only white, but most of my rocks are mostly white, which means that there are other colors, like yellow and gray and pink, living inside. If you take the time to get close to them and really see them, you will understand that most of my rocks have more inside them than only white.

I was so excited the day I learned the names for the different mostly whites. On Sunday, August 22, my mother and father were getting ready to paint the wood around the windows and doors, and my mother spread out a bunch of paper tickets across the kitchen table. Each ticket had six rectangles on them, all different mostly whites! Just like my rocks! I was so thrilled to see all those mostly whites!

My mother saw my excitement about the colored rectangles on the tickets, so she pointed to each one and told me their names. Super White. Decorator's White (white with gray). White Dove (white with yellow). Atrium White (white with orange). Antique White (white with yellow and orange).

More yellows: Linen White. Navajo White. Cameo White. Ivory White. Seashell. Grays: Bone White. China White. Oxford White. Paper White. Cloud White. Dune White. Blues: Fanfare. Blue Veil. Pinks: White Opulence. Alabaster. White Zinfandel.

I spent the rest of August 22 in my Memory Room, and I memorized the names of all the mostly whites. This made me so happy because now I have names for the colors of my rocks. So I can line up all the Alabaster rocks. Or I can line up all the yellow-white rocks by name. White Dove comes first. Seashell comes last.

Today the sky is cloudy. I have made a line of Super White, Cloud White, and Dune White rocks to match the color of the clouds in the sky. The line begins with the smallest pebble rocks at the coffee table and ends with the biggest rocks at the wall. There are 128 rocks in the line. There are 11 Super White rocks, 78 Cloud White rocks, and 39 Dune White rocks; 36 are Small, 80 are Medium, and 12 are Big.

Eleven are Super White and Small, 0 are Super White and Medium, and 0 are Super White and Big. Twenty are Cloud White and Small, 50 are Cloud White and Medium, 8 are Cloud White and Big. Five are Dune White and Small, 30 are Dune White and Medium, and 4 are Dune White and Big.

I lie down with my head on the cold wooden floor at the corner of the coffee table and look down my line of rocks. It's so beautiful. My fingers fill with happy.

My mother sometimes looks at my rock lines and has something to say about them:

That one looks like the bones of a dinosaur tail.

That one looks like my pearl necklace.

That one could be a row of clouds in the sky.

I don't know why she says these things about my rock lines. They are rock lines. Sometimes I organize them according to a certain rule. Sometimes I make a line that is all oval or all White Dove (the color painted around our windows and doors) or all Medium. But they are always rock lines. And they are always beautiful.

My mother also says my rocks are very old and came from volcanoes. She says the energy from the ocean water is what made them so smooth. But I think she's making up a funny story because volcanoes make something called lava, which is orange, hot liquid that turns into rock that is black and not white. And I've taken some of the bumpy rocks into the sink and turned the water on them for a long time, and they're not any smoother. So I don't think volcanoes or water made these rocks. I think my mostly white rocks were just born this way.

I move from the corner of the coffee table to the middle of the line. I get down with my eyes on the ground again and look across my line of rocks. It's perfect. I smile and let my eyes go blurry, so the rocks go on forever.

But in the edges of forever, something is happening. Another rock line is forming. I rub my eyes because I think they might be tricking me, making another line of rocks inside my head and not really on the living-room floor. Then

I notice a hand. The hand is adding more rocks. I know that hand. That's my mother's hand!

My mother's hand is adding more rocks in a straight line next to my line. Her line contains rocks that are Ivory White, Cameo White, and Linen White and are all Small and mostly round. Her hand stops. The line stops growing. My mother's hand is done. There are 21 rocks in this yellow-white, small, mostly round line.

As I am admiring this new line of rocks, I see my mother's nose and mouth and chin on the floor behind the rocks. I quick look and see my mother's eyes. I put them together and see my mother's face. My mother's face is on the ground just like mine.

Your line of rocks is beautiful, Mom! Does it make you calm and happy, too? Do you love lining up rocks, too?

I wish my voice weren't broken, so I could ask her. But then I look more closely at her mouth, and I see my mother's face is smiling, and I don't need a voice to know her answer.

CHAPTER 25

⸙

It's the beginning of October, a new page on the calendar and the first real chilly day of fall, but the change in season, the shift from summer life to something markedly different, felt as if it happened a month ago. The summer families with school-age children evacuated the island in a mass exodus immediately after Labor Day. On that Monday holiday, the island was mobbed and bustling as usual, but by Tuesday afternoon, it was eerily empty and quiet, as if the island itself could be heard exhaling. Olivia can now relax again, go to Stop & Shop any day of the week, turn left without waiting several minutes, and walk on the beaches alone; but strangely, just as the influx of summer people had required a large and conscious adjustment, so did their abrupt absence.

A full month after Labor Day, Olivia still finds herself trapped in a funk. She enjoys solitude, prefers it even, but for some reason, when everyone left Nantucket in September, she felt abandoned, like she literally missed the boat. She has no more beach portraits scheduled. The pages of her calendar for October, November, and December are unmarked. She has plenty of photo editing still to do, work that should keep her busy for at least the next month, but she wakes up each morning feeling as if she has nothing to do. No routine. No purpose.

She thinks about Anthony all the time, experiencing vivid sensory flashes of him in unanticipated moments. She closes her eyes, and she sees the curl of his hair against his neck, his small hands and fingers that looked exactly like hers, his knobby shoulders, the peaceful stillness of his face asleep. She listens to the crickets in the evening, and she hears the sound of his bare feet running across the floor, the melody of his laugh, his *eeya-eeya-eeya*. She inhales the crisp fall air, and she smells his skin the way it smelled after a day in the sun or after a sudsy bath.

She's still trying to understand the why of it all, praying, still trying to listen for answers from God with her spirit, still completely unsure of how to do this. She feels like she's trying to smell with her eyes or hear with her nose, or even more impossible, like she's trying to cajole some part of her anatomy or being she's not even sure exists into becoming an antenna, a satellite dish capable of receiving wisdom from heaven. It feels unproductive and more than a little crazy.

Today is a good day though, a distraction from unanswered prayers and aimless solitude. Today she is the assistant photographer to Roger Kelly at a wedding at the Blue Oyster. Roger is *the* sought-after wedding photographer on island. His assistant had some kind of family emergency off-island that left Roger scrambling. Olivia shot the Morgan family beach portrait in July, and Mrs. Morgan is the bride's maid of honor's mother's best friend, and through this last-minute, word-of-mouth reference, Olivia got the job. It's a long day and doesn't pay much, barely more than a portrait session, but she won't have to edit anything, and she's grateful to have something to do.

Roger has asked her to capture the more documentary-style, photojournalism shots that are trendy these days, while he makes sure to get the posed, more formal and traditional pictures. He's in charge of the Veggies, she's in charge of Dessert. She scrolls through some of the images already in her camera, pausing and nodding at her favorites. The father of the bride kissing his daughter's cheek. The bride laughing. The groom whispering in his bride's ear. The preschool-age flower girl lifting up the tulle of her dress to see her patent leather Mary Janes.

The ceremony took place on the Blue Oyster's modest, man-made beach overlooking the harbor, and the reception is now in full swing on the hotel's terrace. It's evening now, and the sky is lit with a bright moon and twinkling stars. A blazing fire in the stone fire pit and outdoor heaters positioned like lampposts among the tables keep the nippy night air from penetrating the edges of the elaborate white tent. Olivia shoots the moon over the harbor, the tea lights and glass bowls filled with cranberries on the white linen tablecloths, the bride's white-rose bouquet next to a glass of champagne.

The action is now taking place on the dance floor, but Olivia's attention is drawn to a boy sitting alone at his table for six. He looks to be seven or eight, he has long, surfer-shaggy, blond hair, and he's dressed in a white shirt, khakis, and boat shoes. He's adorable. His index fingers are plugged into his ears, his elbows jut out sideways, and he's rocking back and forth in his seat. Click, click, click. Olivia looks at the LCD display of her camera. His gaze is far-off, unfocused.

The band finishes playing "Love Shack," and the boy's mother returns to his table to check on him. She kisses the top of his head. Click. Click. Click. She returns to the dance floor. He continues rocking with his fingers in his ears.

The band is loud. People have to yell to talk. The singer's voice amplified over the microphone, the thumping bass, a hundred people yelling to be heard, the dancing, the lights, the smell of the fire—it's all too much. This little boy is fighting against an onslaught of stimuli, doing his best to block it all out, rocking to create his own stimulus to zone in on, a soothing back-and-forth rhythm, a cradle.

The father comes to the table and sits down next to his boy. Click. Click. Click. The father finishes his drink and stays for another song. The mother returns to the table, sweaty and happy. She says something to her boy. He rocks and doesn't look at her. She pulls the father by his hand. He smiles. Click. Click. They return to the dance floor.

Olivia feels her stomach tighten and realizes that she's been holding her breath. She exhales. She's been here. She's lived this. That sweet little boy is only going to be able to cope for so long. What is celebration to everyone else is misery to him. None of this is fun for him, and Olivia wishes that his parents had left him home with a babysitter or that they'd call it a night and leave early. But she also understands their desire to include him, to dress him up like any other boy invited to the wedding and bring him along, to risk one more song, to enjoy themselves, to be a whole family here together.

She and David eventually stopped going to weddings and birthdays and holiday parties with Anthony because it was easier and safer to leave him home than to risk what might happen in public. Autism and noisy parties do not mix well, and if this boy's parents stay too long, it's not going to end well. At some point, rocking in his seat with his fingers in his ears won't be enough, and his nervous system is going to freak out, unable to tolerate one more second of this madness. He'll either melt down or bolt. Fight or flight.

Olivia assumes his parents well know the dice they're rolling, and while she's holding her breath again, worried about their boy, she's also rooting for them, hoping they manage to get through at least one more dance as husband and wife before the fuse on this invisible time bomb detonates, before their entire world transforms from a lovely evening at a wedding reception to a harrowing escape mission. But for now, they dance, seemingly oblivious to the hissing fuse. Olivia checks her watch, knowing it's getting late.

The band changes the mood with a slow song. The boy's father gathers his wife into him, and she snuggles her head into the nook of his neck. The two sway back and forth, pivoting in a small circle, and although they're surrounded by a crowded dance floor, they appear totally focused on each other, on the singular rhythm they've created together, as if no one else exists but them. Click. Click. Click.

Olivia lowers her camera and observes the couple without the mask of her lens between them. A wave of emotion swells in her throat, and she swallows several times to push it back down.

David.

Why couldn't they do that? Why couldn't they hold on to each other and block out the world? Why couldn't they surrender to what they couldn't control? Why weren't they brave enough to celebrate a life that included autism? She wanted to, and she thinks she eventually got there, but it took her too long. Just as she was ready to dance, the music stopped playing.

She glances back over at the boy's table. He's gone. Panic floods her every cell, paralyzing her for a second, but then a powerful and well-trained instinct kicks in.

Where are the exits? She eyes the door to the hotel that leads to the parking lot. He wants to go home, and the car is how to get there. The car is familiar and safe. Or maybe they're staying at the hotel. Either way, he'd have to worm through the crowds of people going in and out to use the restrooms, milling around in the loud lobby, by the concierge and the front desk.

She looks the other way, away from the people and the tent

and all the noise, down the lawn, to the windy path that leads to stairs, to the beach, to the harbor. To the water. If Anthony were here and bolted, that's where he'd go.

Olivia forgets everything and runs. Her heels sink and stick with each step into the soft earth beneath the Blue Oyster lawn, slowing her down. She kicks them off and races barefoot down the cold stone stairs, praying to God that he'll be there when she rounds the corner and sees the beach.

CHAPTER 26

⁓

Beth is peeking out the kitchen window, watching Jimmy and the girls drive away, feeling left behind. It's late Saturday afternoon, and Jimmy popped by about an hour ago, said he had the night off, and offered to take the girls for a hike at Bartlett's Farm and then dinner. She hesitated to allow it at first, not because she had other burning plans for her and the girls, but because she wasn't included.

When in past months an unannounced Jimmy visit would've unnerved or angered her, today she quite enjoyed his company. He wiped his feet on the doormat before coming in the house, he changed the burned-out bulb in the overhead living-room light, he told her he'd line up the chimney sweep, and he asked the girls all kinds of questions about school. And he asked Beth lots of questions about autism and the book she's writing. He was considerate, useful, and sincerely engaged in conversation.

Before they left, he made a proud point of telling Beth that he'd finished Dr. Campbell's homework and looked more than a little crushed when she admitted she hadn't started hers yet. She needs to do the assignment. She knows she's been avoiding it. She's also been avoiding asking herself why she's avoiding it.

She finds a sheet of printer paper and sits down at the kitchen table. She draws a cross, dividing the paper into four squares, and writes one word at the top of each quadrant: *Wanted. Happy. Safe. Loved.* Her eyes go unfocused as she stares at the page. She taps her teeth with her pen and daydreams for several minutes. She snaps out of it and returns to the task. *Wanted. Happy. Safe. Loved.* Blank. Blank. Blank. Blank.

She sighs, folds the paper, and stuffs it into her pocket. She'll do it some other time. Later.

She's grateful this kind of writer's block is limited to her personal life and not to her novel, still untitled. She still goes to the library almost every day, excited every morning to be there. The story has been coming easily, and she's proud of what she's written so far, fully believing when she rereads her chapters that she's somehow able to capture the voice of this fictional boy with autism.

A pen still in her hand and scenes from her novel now running through her mind trigger an almost compulsive urge to write. She checks her watch. She looks out the kitchen window at the spot in the driveway where Jimmy's truck was parked a few minutes ago. With a sudden burst of intention, she gets up, grabs her keys and her bag, and leaves the house. Instead of doing her marriage-counseling homework or cleaning the bedrooms or crashing on the couch in front of HGTV for the rest of the evening while she waits for the girls to return, she's going to the library to write.

She bounds up the steps to the second floor, but then her heart sinks. Four people are sitting at her typically empty table. Eddy Antico from the Chamber of Commerce is sitting in her seat, and Pamela Vincent is reading aloud at the podium on the stage. Beth steps over to Mary Crawford at the reference desk.

"What's going on?" Beth whispers.

"It's the twenty-five-hour reading of *Moby-Dick*."

"Really? What hour are they on?"

Mary looks up at the clock and counts to herself. "Six hours, forty minutes. You want to read? We can fit you in pretty much anytime between four and six a.m."

I'm sure you can!

Mary shows Beth the roster. Rose Driscoll, head of the garden club and at least seventy years old, is scheduled to read at 3:00 a.m. Mary Crawford is signed up at six.

"No, no thanks," Beth says, trying not to laugh, unable to imagine why any sane person would actually plan to be at the library to read or listen to *Moby-Dick* at four in the morning, or at any time for that matter. Excitement on Nantucket during the off-season is a highly subjective experience.

Beth looks around the room, searching in resigned vain for a way to stay and write, wishing she didn't have to leave. She could try writing downstairs or at The Bean, or she could write at the kitchen table in her quiet house, but she's become more superstitious than a baseball player on a hitting streak about where she writes. She has to be in the library, sitting at the long table in the seat closest to the stage, facing the window. She knows her complete faith in this set of rigid conditions borders on diagnosable, and it can't really be true, but she believes in it. It is true. This is where she feels the inspiration. This is where Anthony's story comes to her. This is where the magic happens.

Reluctantly, she walks outside and zips her coat. She hesitates at her car door. She came all the way downtown and doesn't want to turn around and go home without accomplishing anything. What else could she do here? Maybe Georgia is at the Blue Oyster. Maybe she'd be up for a break and a drink at the hotel bar. A perfect plan.

She makes a brisk walk out of the four quick blocks, excited about seeing Georgia and a deep martini, but as she arrives at the edge of the Blue Oyster property, she spots a wedding ceremony in progress down on their fake little beach, and she stops walking, deflated. A wedding means Georgia is busy and won't be free for a drink. Now what? She's come all the way downtown and walked all the way over to the Blue Oyster.

She sees Georgia standing well behind the two neat rows of white folding chairs and decides to sneak over to her and at least say a discreet hello.

"Hey," whispers Beth, now standing next to her friend.

"Hey!" whispers Georgia.

Georgia's face is flush with admiration and weepy joy. She dabs her eyes with a tissue. "They wrote their own vows. I love it when they do that."

Beth looks over at the bride and groom and strains to hear them. She can hear the groom's voice, but because he's facing the other way, she can't make out what he's saying. The bride's face is young and glowing. Beth wonders if her own face looked anything like that when she married Jimmy. She believes it did. She glowed on her wedding day. But sometime down the married road, she can't pinpoint exactly when, the glow disappeared. Jimmy's right. She hasn't been happy to see him in a long time. In bed, on the couch, at the kitchen table, walking through the front door—no glow. Can she get it back or is her Jimmy glow gone for good? Did she feel a little of that glow rekindled today?

She looks over at Georgia, who can't possibly decipher what the groom is saying, and she looks like she's glowing with his every word. But it doesn't take much for Georgia. She glows over Cotton commercials.

"I should go," says Beth.

"Why? Stay. I'll be done soon, and then we can go get a drink."

"Okay." Beth smiles, pleased that her friend has read her mind.

The bride and groom kiss, and everyone claps.

"Come with me. I have to herd them over to the terrace."

Georgia ushers the guests over to the tented terrace, where they are met with passed hors d'oeuvres, champagne, and live music. The bride and groom are still at the beach, posing for the photographer. Beth and Georgia stand at the back of the terrace, behind the dance floor and the tables, near the door to the hotel.

"We just need to wait for the bride and groom. Make sure they get settled over here before I can leave."

"Okay."

"Such a lovely ceremony, wasn't it?"

"Yeah. Seems like a million years ago that that was me and Jimmy." A million years and yesterday.

"What's going on with you guys?"

"I don't know. We're seeing Dr. Campbell. I don't know though. What do you think I should do?" asks Beth, already sure of Georgia's answer.

"If you can forgive him, I'd take him back."

"What? You've never taken any of them back!"

"I know, but I wish I did. I wish I knew how to love through all the messy stuff. I've never had that love-conquers-all kind of love. Wish I did, but I don't think it's in me. I can't love someone no matter what."

Georgia has always wanted the fairy tale, the happily ever after. But so far, her princes haven't possessed the kind of character and stamina it takes to reach a proper storybook ending. Prince Charming doesn't go and sleep with the village tramp, he doesn't make a habit out of drinking twelve beers before noon, and he doesn't stop doting on his beloved. But even after four failed princes, Georgia still deep down believes marriage can be a Disney movie. If only she could find the right prince.

What does Beth believe in? Does she believe in Jimmy, that he'll never cheat on her again? Does she believe that she'll get her own happily-ever-after ending? Will Jimmy be there with her? Does she believe in love?

"I don't know if I can either."

"But I never had any kids to consider, so it was easier for me to end things and not look back."

"I can't stay with him just for the girls, right?"

"No, you shouldn't. But I think it would make me hang around longer to work on things."

"So you'd take Jimmy back?" questions Beth, not believing this for one second.

Georgia tilts her head as if she were giving this real consideration but quickly gives up the charade and laughs at herself. "No, I couldn't do it. I'd be done. But I'm not saying I'm right."

Beth could argue that restoring her marriage is the right thing to do. Forgive Jimmy, take him back, and everything can go back to normal. Forgiveness is good. Normal would be bliss. The girls would get their father back. They deserve to live with their father. It feels like the kind of selfless decision a good mother would make for her children. It would be big of her.

For the sake of the children, take him back!

But the argument against taking him back is ranting with just as much volume and confidence, heated words scratching against some thin inner membrane of her wounded heart, barely containing her spite and self-loathing.

Are you kidding me? If you don't divorce his ass, you're a pathetic, spineless martyr with no self-esteem!

She imagines Pamela Vincent whispering to Debbie McMahon in the Atheneum while Eddy Antico reads the seventh hour of *Moby-Dick. Did you hear Beth and Jimmy Ellis got back together after he cheated on her for a year? What a fool!*

She imagines Jill and Courtney gossiping over goblets of iced chardonnay. *Those poor girls, to have to grow up without their father. Beth didn't even give him a chance. We're all human. We all make mistakes.*

She worries that everyone she knows will judge her either way. She shakes her head and closes her eyes, trying to ignore all arguments about what she *should* do, what everyone else thinks, even her kids, to clear it all away and focus inward, to discover what is real and true for her in her own once-glowing heart. It's a simple question really.

Does she love Jimmy enough to take him back?

She opens her eyes. The bride and groom have made their grand entrance at the reception and are now dancing their first dance as husband and wife. The groom's face is tight and concentrated, and their movement together across the floor is hardly fluid, the obvious product of not quite enough dance lessons, but the effort, despite its being awkward, is sweet. Beth and Jimmy didn't even try to learn actual steps for their wedding. They just sort of waddled back and forth like teenagers at a school dance.

The bride is relaxed and beaming. Her clumsy groom probably took dance lessons with her, probably one night a week, and he probably loathed every second of it, but he did it. He did it because he loves her. He's willing to dance like a fool in front of a hundred people for his darling's happiness. Fast-forward ten years, and she'll be lucky if he's willing to replace the toilet paper or use a plate.

"I love a man who can dance," says Georgia.

"He's not exactly Gene Kelly."

"He's trying. I love it."

The first dance is then followed by the other traditional dances—the bride with her father (he can't dance either), the groom with his mother, and then the groom with his grandmother, which generates even more adoration from Georgia. If he hadn't just got hitched, she'd be all over him. The dance floor is now open to everyone. The five-piece brass band is festive and loud. Unable to hear each other without yelling, Beth and Georgia have stopped chatting. Georgia checks her watch. She snatches a glass from a tray of champagne flutes.

"Here, stay and have some champagne! I have to take care of one quick thing, and then we can go!"

"Okay!"

Beth leans against the wall, sips her champagne, and people-watches, self-conscious now that she's alone, keenly aware that she's wearing jeans and attending a wedding reception she wasn't invited to. She avoids eye contact with every stranger who walks past her on the way to the restrooms, hoping no one talks to her or asks her how she knows the bride and groom or, God forbid, asks her to dance.

She becomes interested in watching a young boy sitting alone at one of the front tables. He's blocking his ears and rocking in his seat. Autism. She knows enough about autism now, from both the books she's read and the book she's writing, to recognize it anywhere. And like an obscure vocabulary word she'd never heard of, once learned, she sees it everywhere.

But her writing has done more than simply allow her to recognize it. When she notices a child with autism now, like this cute little boy sitting at the table, she feels a compassionate connection, a softness in her heart, like they're friends who share an intimate secret. Before she began writing her book, she would've looked at this boy and thought, *He seems odd. Something's wrong with that boy.* And then she would've intentionally looked away. Now she smiles as she watches him and thinks, *I know, it's* way *too loud in here. I want to get out of here, too.*

The boy's parents keep checking on him, but he's not paying them any attention. Good boy. He's smart. If he acknowledges their presence, if he listens to what they're saying, if he cracks open the door to receiving input from outside himself, it might swing wide-open, and then the trumpet and the trombone and the singing and a thousand other aggressive sounds would stampede into him along with the voices of his parents. And that would be disastrous.

He's rocking faster now. His eyes, although still mostly unfocused, have started glancing around. His defense mechanisms aren't doing the job. He's starting to come undone. She can feel it.

Just as she guessed he would, he hops off his chair and bolts. He runs right out from under the tent and onto the lawn, into the night. Beth scans the dance floor and finds his parents in each other's arms, slow-dancing, oblivious.

Without thinking, Beth loses her champagne flute and runs after him. He's fast, scrambling down the stone path, back toward the beach where the wedding ceremony had been. She loses sight of him as she slows down on the stone steps, careful not to fall, but reassures herself as she keeps going that he'll be at the beach when she gets there and not gone. If he's not on the beach, he could be anywhere.

She reaches the sand, and there he is. He's up to his knees in the water. He dips his hands beneath the surface and then raises them overhead, creating a splash. He smiles and squeals, flapping his wet hands, spraying water from his fingertips. He throws his hands back into the glassy, calm water, creating an even bigger splash. He squeals and laughs. He repeats the process.

Beth stands with her hands on her hips, catching her breath, relieved the chase is over and the boy is safe, asking herself what the plan is now. She wishes she'd alerted his parents before she took off, but by now they've probably noticed he's missing. She'll simply stay with him until they come.

The boy is walking parallel to the shore and doesn't seem to want to go any farther out, any deeper than his knees. Good. Beth has no desire to plunge into the freezing ocean to save a drowning boy. He's unbothered by Beth, who is now standing quite close to him, still delighting in his splashing hands, when Beth hears someone coming down the path. She turns around, expecting to see the boy's parents, but instead it's a woman. Beth knows her, but maybe because she was expecting someone else, she can't at first place who it is. Then she notices the serious camera in the woman's hand, and it registers. It's Olivia, her photographer.

Olivia runs straight to the water, her face pale with dread. But the boy is squealing and laughing. He's totally fine. Olivia stops at the water's edge and breathes hard with her hands on her hips, smiling as tears stream down her cheeks.

"Olivia."

Olivia startles, placing her hand on her heart. "My God, Beth, I didn't see you," she says, wiping her eyes and face. "Do you know his parents?"

"I know who they are, but I don't know them."

"Same. Will you go find them while I wait here with him?" asks Olivia.

Beth agrees, but just as she turns around, his parents appear at the edge of the stone steps.

His mother, already barefoot, runs straight into the cold water, soaking the bottom of her black dress. "Owen! You gotta stop taking off! We don't want to lose you!" She picks Owen up by his armpits and spins him, dragging his feet across the surface of the water, drawing circles around them. His face is pure joy.

Happiness.

Olivia aims her camera. Click. Click. Click.

"Thanks for looking after him," says his father to Olivia and Beth. "I thought for sure he'd be in the parking lot."

"No problem," says Beth.

The boy's father, Beth, and Olivia stand next to each other for the next many minutes in silent relief, watching the boy and his mother splash and spin and laugh together in the bright moonlight. Glowing.

Loved.

Click. Click. Click.

"There you are!"

Beth looks over her shoulder and sees Georgia waving and teetering in her heels on the last step of the stone stairs. Georgia slips out of her shoes and walks over to this small, unlikely gathering, visibly unable to piece together why they're all here. "Is everyone okay?"

"Yup," says the father, removing his shoes and rolling up his pants. "We're all good now."

Safe.

"Great," says Georgia.

Probably dizzy, the mother has stopped spinning her boy and now hangs behind him as he splashes. The father joins them and holds his wife's hand.

Wanted.

Click. Click. Click.

Happiness. Loved. Safe. Wanted. Beth can identify these qualities, these necessary ingredients for a relationship that works, so readily among this family in front of her. She sees each one in this little boy with autism as easily as she sees the bright moon in the night sky, yet she still can't form a specific image of what these elements look like in her.

"I thought you ditched me," says Georgia.

"Never. You ready to go?" asks Beth.

"Yeah, let's."

Before Beth ascends the stone path, she looks back toward the harbor to say good-bye to Olivia, but she's squatting at the edge of the water, photographing the boy and his parents, and Beth doesn't want to interrupt her. Beth smiles, imagining how beautiful those pictures will be. She can't wait to see her own portraits. They should be ready soon. She meant to ask about them.

As they walk up the steps, Beth wonders what motivated Olivia to chase after the little boy. It was probably the concern any adult would have who notices a young child who takes off alone toward open water. But as she walks with Georgia across the lawn of the Blue Oyster, she remembers Olivia's panic-stricken eyes and the tears on her blanched face and wonders if it was something more.

She'll have to ask her when she sees her again.

CHAPTER 27

B eth's been champing at the bit all morning, dying to get to the library, but she had too many household chores that couldn't be ignored, and now she's at Jessica's soccer game. Jimmy is there, too. Alone. They're both watching Jessica run up and down the field, standing separately but next to each other on the sideline in awkward silence.

"So how's your book coming?" asks Jimmy finally, still staring at the field.

"Good. It's coming along," says Beth, similarly not averting her eyes from the game, but not because she's worried about missing a play.

"That's great. It's really great that you're writing again. I'm proud of you."

"Thanks," she says, unexpectedly flattered.

She turns to look at him. He's watching her now and not the game, smiling.

"I'd love to read it."

Her face flushes hot, and she diverts her eyes down to her black shoes. She's been pouring her heart and soul into her writing, weaving everything she feels and knows and believes into this story. Jimmy's sudden and unsolicited interest in her book, in her, makes her happy. But the thought of Jimmy reading her heart and soul, of revealing herself so intimately and completely to him now, pokes at something inside her not yet ready to be touched. Trust.

She lifts her eyes to meet his and flashes a timid smile before forcing herself to focus on the girls on the field.

When the game ends, Jessica goes off with Jimmy, and Beth drives straight to the library. She walks up to the second floor and peeks through the doorway. Eddy Antico and Pamela Vincent are gone. No one is reading *Moby-Dick,* and no one is in her seat. She smiles and gets settled.

She dreamed about her book last night and woke with the next chapter fully formed, vividly detailed, waiting for her, like a gift. She was thrilled but then increasingly anxious every second that it lived only as knowledge likely to vaporize at any moment in her head and not as letters written down in ink, safe on a page. She opens her notebook, uncaps her pen, and writes as fast as she can to release the words before they vanish.

My one name is Anthony. When I was a smaller boy, I used to think I had two names: Anthony and YOU.

My mother and father would say things like:

Anthony, come here.

Do YOU want to go outside?

Do YOU want some juice?

Anthony, here's your juice.

Can YOU say TRUCK?

Anthony, say TRUCK.

Anthony, put your shoes on.

Go ahead, YOU do it.

YOU can do it.

Anthony, do it.

So it's easy to see the cause of my earlier confusion. These nickname words—YOU, I, ME, WE, HE, SHE—they can still confuse me, but I'm mostly okay with them now even though I don't like them. Nickname words depend on the situation, and I've never liked things that depend on the situation.

This is why I like numbers. 6 + 3 = 9. Always. 6 + 3 Pringles or 6 + 3 doughnuts or 6 + 3 rocks in a line or 6 + 3 silver minivans in the parking lot. The answer is 9. Always.

But YOU can mean Anthony or my mother or my father or Danyel or a total stranger in the parking lot.

How are YOU?

YOU is my mother if my father is talking and my mother is there, but YOU is Danyel if my mother is talking and Danyel is there, but if both Danyel AND my father are there, then YOU could be my father or Danyel or BOTH of them. So the owner of YOU depends on who is talking and who is there to be spoken to. Like I said, YOU depends on the situation. YOU follows a Depends Rule, and this is not the kind of rule I like. I like Always Rules, rules that always stay the rule no matter where you are or who is talking.

Always Rules are perfect because they always follow something called cause and effect, and this makes me calm and happy. I used to think light switches were an Always Rule. If I flipped the switch up, the light turned on. If I flipped the switch down, the light turned off. Over and over and over. Always.

Until light switches turned into a Depends Rule. Last winter a big storm came, and the *power went out,* and I flipped all the light switches in the whole house up and down and up and down and nothing happened. The lights stayed off.

So light switches turn out not to be an Always Rule, the kind I like, but a Depends Rule. Flipping the switch up will turn the light on as long as the power hasn't been stolen by a big storm. Light switches depend on the weather. I stopped loving light switches after that big storm last winter.

Eyes are also a Depends Rule. Eyes can be happy or angry or interested or sad, they can be awake or asleep, bright or tired, they can stare or move away. Sometimes eyes cry. Eyes are always something different depending on the situation. Some days when my mother and I go to the grocery store, her eyes are bright, but other times at the grocery store, her eyes are tired. And sometimes at church, her eyes are happy, but other times at church, her eyes cry. So even the same situation can't tell me what eyes are going to do. This is why I don't like eyes.

Things that are Depends Rules like YOU and light switches and eyes are bad because they can't be trusted. I can't know for sure what is going to happen next with YOU and light switches and eyes, which means that ANYTHING can happen next, and anything is too much. I end up wandering the halls in my brain, not knowing what room to go in, scared and confused. I usually end up hiding in the corner of the Horror Room if I'm dealing with a Depends Rule.

So I avoid Depends Rules like eyes and light switches. But there was no avoiding the nicknames like YOU. Nicknames like YOU are everywhere, so I had to learn to accept YOU.

But mostly, I only like Always Rules. I like cause and effect. Something makes something else happen, and I know what's going to happen before it happens because it always happens. This makes me feel good.

When something is a Depends Rule, anything can happen, and this makes me scared. It makes me scream and cry.

I have a thing called AUTISM. My mother and father don't understand the cause of my autism, and this makes them scared. It makes them scream and cry. They must like cause and effect and Always Rules like I do.

Being a boy doesn't mean having autism because most boys don't have autism and some girls do. Getting shots doesn't mean having autism because lots of boys and girls get shots and they don't have autism. So having autism must follow a Depends Rule. Autism is not like math. Autism is like YOU and depends on the situation. So I avoid thinking about autism because I don't like Depends Rules.

All this thinking about YOU and light switches and eyes and autism has me wandering the halls. I'm going into my Counting Room now.

I'm counting the tiles on the kitchen floor. 180. There are always 180 tiles on the kitchen floor. Always.

Always makes me feel good.

Always makes me feel safe.

Always.

CHAPTER 28

Olivia sits in her living-room chair with one of her journals in her lap and stares out the window at the trees in her yard. She doesn't like the trees here, the scrub pines and the scrub oaks. They're too skinny and too short. They appear brittle and emaciated to her, as if they're undernourished or sick. But that's just the way they are. The trees back in her old yard in Hingham are real trees—huge, several-hundred-year-old oaks with trunks thick enough to hide behind and branches that spread across the sky. This time of year, the leaves would be red and gold and breathtaking. She sighs as she looks out the window at the rusty brown leaves on the tiny scrub oaks in her yard, daydreaming of fall in Hingham.

October 1, 2006

I think I want to stop Anthony's ABA therapy. I know it's helped with a lot of things. His attention span is better. They've used it to teach him how to stay in his seat, do puzzles, stack blocks, get dressed, brush his teeth.

I have to admit, it does work. Anthony performs a desired behavior, or in the beginning, a close approximation to what we want him to do, and he gets a positive reinforcement. Reward for good behavior. Pick up a puzzle piece, get a Pringle. Stick your head in the middle hole of your shirt. Pringle. Put your feet inside your shoes. Pringle.

I remember not liking the idea of ABA at first. Scientists use this same kind of behavioral conditioning to get pigeons to peck a button for food pellets. Anthony's a boy in a house, not a pigeon in a cage. But it works. ABA has given Anthony so many skills I worried he'd never master.

But lately, instead of adding skills, Carlin's been focused on eliminating undesired behaviors. The ABA language for this is "extinguishing." I'm not at all comfortable with that word. I picture a candle burning, glowing orange in the center of Anthony, and Carlin is huffing and puffing like the big bad wolf, trying to blow it out. Trying to extinguish him.

They've been working on trying to get rid of Anthony's most prominent autistic behaviors, the stimming ones that most get in the way of his functioning or appearing normal. Hand flapping is the biggest offender. HANDS DOWN. Carlin says this every time he flaps. She places his hands by his sides to prompt him, and if he keeps his hands still at his sides, even for an obvious second, Pringle.

The stated rationale for "extinguishing" the hand flapping—it's a crutch. Anthony is hand flapping instead of talking to communicate what he wants and feels. If we eliminate flapping as an option, he'll have to find some other way, hopefully spoken words, to communicate.

The unspoken motivation for trying to get rid of the hand flapping is that it just looks weird. It tips everyone off. He looks like a regular, if aloof and quiet, kid until the flapping starts. Then I notice the looks. Something's wrong with that kid. Parents are careful to keep themselves and their children at a safe distance once they see the hand flapping. It might be contagious.

When Carlin first spoke to me about the agenda for extinguishing Anthony's hand flapping, something in me resisted, but I didn't have the words yet to explain it. Plus, she's the therapist. She's the expert. She knows what she's doing. So I went along with it and made a joke instead.

"He's Italian. Of course he talks with his hands!"

Carlin smiled and then proceeded to outline the precise plan for silencing Anthony's hands.

But here's the thing. I don't think his hand flapping is a crutch. I don't think, Oh, if only Anthony weren't flapping his hands, then he'd talk to us! He can't talk, and thank God he flaps his hands. Anthony communicates through his undulating bundle of ticking screeches and flapping. This is how he tells us what he wants and how he feels.

Granted, it's a limited form of communication, but this is what he has. And I've become pretty fluent in this bizarre language. I know when his hands mean This is TOO good or This is the best thing I've ever seen or I don't like what's happening or It's too noisy in here or I want MORE swinging or I want to go home right NOW. Like with any language, the quality and emphasis of the flapping plus the context communicate the specific meaning.

HANDS DOWN. Are we silencing an already muted whisper? Shouldn't we be doing the opposite? Hands, tell us more!

Another behavior on the "extinguish" list is his obsession with Barney. Anthony still insists on watching Barney, and only Barney, over and over and over. If I try to redirect him before he's done watching, or if I shut off the TV because we need to leave the

*house or it's time for his ABA therapy, he loses his mind.
"Perseverating" and "addiction" and "obsession" are the
words his therapists and teachers and doctors use, and
so I've been using them, too. And again, like the theory
that removing Anthony's hands might force him to use
his voice, the hope is that by eliminating Anthony's
preoccupation with Barney, this will make room for
other, more age-appropriate interests.*

*At first, I was on board. Barney drives me crazy. I wish
Anthony would move on, even to a new obsession. I like his
rock obsession much more. At least this lets us spend time at
the beach, and even I enjoy combing for beach rocks, so it's
an activity we sort of do together. I don't understand the joy
he gets from lining them up, but I don't mind the rocks. But
the purple, singing dinosaur, he can go.*

*I thought about our contribution to his Barney
obsession. We buy the DVDs, record the show on the DVR,
and at least once a day I actually encourage him to zone out
in front of the TV, in need of thirty minutes of peace. And
today's technology really does feed this symptom of autism.
When I was a kid, there were no DVD players, no On
Demand, no DVRs. I'm sure I would've been obsessed with*
The Sound of Music *or* The Wizard of Oz *if I could've
watched them every day instead of only once a year. So it's
easy to enable this kind of addiction today. And I've been
his dealer, happily handing him his drug of choice each and
every day.*

*Carlin said we could go cold turkey if we wanted.
We could simply throw out all the Barney DVDs, stop
recording it, delete all the existing episodes, get rid of his
blanket and all the Barney toys. That'll end it. Or she could
work with him using ABA to wean him off it. That seemed
more humane to me. The methadone-clinic approach to
Barney rehab.*

But yesterday, when he was in hysterics in front of the blackened TV screen, Carlin refusing him access to the remote control, I had a different thought. We've been calling this thing with Barney a "perseveration," an "obsession," an "addiction." What if instead we called it "love"?

When I watch Anthony watching Barney, he's completely enamored. Delight dances all over his beautiful face every time the little, purple, stuffed animal turns into the giant, live Barney. He squeals, Eeeya-eeeya-eeeya, and flaps his hands.

This is too good!

He recently discovered the REWIND *button on the remote, and he's learned how to replay the same thirty seconds over and over and over. He laughs a deep belly laugh every time and flaps his hands.*

I love this so much!

Anthony LOVES Barney. How can we take away something he loves? Don't we want to encourage love? Why would we extinguish love?

I wish he loved something other than Barney. I really, really do. But why should we get to pick what he loves? I love books and the beach and cooking. David loves football and hockey. What if someone decided that I spent too much time at the beach and reading and cooking and insisted that I give up these things I love? What if someone "redirected" me and insisted that I love hockey instead? Instead of reading and going to the beach and cooking, I had to watch hockey and learn the rules and play it. I hate hockey. I'd be miserable. I wouldn't be me.

I know getting rid of the flapping and Barney would probably help Anthony in some ways. He'd appear more normal. It'd be easier for him to be mainstreamed in school, to engage with other kids his age (there's not a neurotypical six-year-old kid on this planet who loves Barney).

But here's the thing. Anthony isn't normal. There. I wrote it down, and the world didn't end. I didn't die, and neither did he. He's not normal. He has autism, and his autism makes him flap his hands instead of saying *That noise you're not even aware of is making me crazy* or *I love Barney so much!*

So I don't want to extinguish Anthony's hand flapping or his love of Barney, but I'm afraid to tell David this. He's going to disagree. He's going to say it's giving up on Anthony. Not long ago, I would've said the same thing. But now I don't see it that way. The way I see it, we can look at Anthony's hand flapping and see an abnormal behavior that needs to be eliminated, or we can see our son bravely communicating what he wants and feels the only way he knows how to. We can look at Anthony rewinding Barney over and over and call it an obsession that needs to be treated, or we can call it love.

David's going to say, *If we don't get rid of these autistic behaviors, then he'll never be normal. He'll always be different.*

And my answer to this is going to be Yes. He will always be different.

And the world won't end, and I won't die. And Anthony will be in the living room, loving Barney.

CHAPTER 29

I t's now November, and the island continues to thin out, shedding the fat, each passing week seeing fewer weekenders and day-trippers. Olivia can go for long walks on the beach or along the roads of her own neighborhood without seeing anyone. Downtown is still open for business, but only because the merchants are all hanging in there for Christmas Stroll, one final bonanza chance to squeeze big dollars out of the tourists before winter officially sets in. After December, she knows most retailers will shut their doors for at least three months. Until the Chamber of Commerce invents some kind of organized excuse for people to come in the winter—the Nantucket Ice Sculpture Festival in January, the Nantucket Winter Olympics in February, the Nantucket Coffee Festival in March—no one will be back until spring. Nantucket is a quaint and seasonal island playground, not a winter destination, and certainly not a place any reasonable person would live year-round.

Olivia's professional life is about to close for the season as well. She has one portrait session left to edit and then no more work. Her days are becoming lean and slow, unpressured and simple, and she now welcomes the change.

It's late afternoon, and she is walking to her mailbox because she forgot to go this morning before breakfast and after reading from one of her journals as is her routine. Reading and rereading her journals these past many months has given her the gentle time and space to go back to what happened with compassionate eyes and a loving heart, to discover what she didn't know then, what she couldn't have known because it was all too raw, too immediate. She was too inside the emotions and the journey then to see them, never mind understand them. Now she does.

She sees her denial and then the scary anger that replaced the denial. She sees her despair and David's, too, and the boundless chasm that grew between them. But more than anything, the thing that she sees now with the most clarity that stays inside her for hours and days after she closes her journal, is Anthony. Not the denial of Anthony's autism or the anger about his autism or the despair over his autism. Not even Anthony and his autism. Just simply Anthony.

She sighs, wishing she knew then what she understands now.

She strolls alone in the middle of the road over long shadows, mindful of the sounds of seagulls overhead, wind chimes in the distance, the rhythm of her footsteps scratching sand against the pavement. The air is wet and salty and cold. Walking feels good. It enlivens her brain, convincing scared and buried thoughts that it's safe to come out of hiding, inviting incomplete thoughts to show their jagged edges, welcoming the wandering and the weak. When she walks, her thoughts line up in her mind like white rocks where they can be clearly seen and cared for. Today, as she walks, she's thinking about her sister and mother.

Maria wants her to come home to Georgia for Thanksgiving. It would be good to see her. Olivia misses her older sister. But the work of packing, leaving the island by ferry or plane, enduring at least one connecting flight, sleeping on the couch in Maria's living room, all feels impossibly overwhelming.

And despite her substantial and growing guilt over not having seen Maria's kids in ages, Olivia's still not ready to spend time with them, her beautiful niece and nephew, Anthony's cousins, older now, thriving, so capable. Alive. And it's not just the kids. It's Maria's entire life. Maria has always, effortlessly had it better, easier. She had the better grades, the cuter boyfriends. She attended a more prestigious college, landed a higher-paying job. She's taller. And now look at her, happily married with two healthy children. Olivia knows this comparison isn't fair or productive, but if she goes to Maria's house for Thanksgiving, it's also inevitable.

And she's definitely not ready to deal with her mother, who, according to Maria, is still going to church every day, clad head to toe in black, where, in addition to still praying for Anthony, she now prays for Olivia's divorced soul. She's also probably saying a few rosaries to clear her own name, to be sure God knows she's in no way responsible for Olivia's shameful and sinful act against the Church. Olivia doesn't have the strength to go home and be judged by her religion and her mother.

Maria says Olivia can't stay in hiding forever. This is without question why Olivia came here in March, but without intending to, and just as the rest of the island prepares to go into hibernation, she feels the possibility of emerging, of beginning a new life. Maybe Nantucket isn't simply a temporary asylum for her, a shelter from her grief and the life she didn't get to live. Maybe this is her home.

Her remote residence is also the perfect excuse, her refuge from dreadful air travel, unbecoming jealousy, and eternal damnation. No, she's not going to Georgia for Thanksgiving. She's staying home on Nantucket, grateful to be here.

She arrives at her mailbox, opens the door, and pulls out a

small stack of mail. As she turns around, she sees a woman and her black dog walking along the side of the road. Olivia pauses with her mail in hand, realizing the woman and her dog are walking directly toward her. It's Beth Ellis.

"Hey!" says Beth, smiling. "You live *here*?"

"Yeah, I'm on Morton."

"You're kidding. I'm on Somerset. We're neighbors. How could we not know this?"

Olivia shrugs. Beth's dog sniffs Olivia's shoes and jeans for a few seconds before turning its feisty attention to her crotch. Beth pulls on its leash.

"Grover, no! . . . How long have you lived here?"

"Since March."

"Really? Tough month to move here."

"Yeah."

"Are you married?" asks Beth, not finding an answer on Olivia's gloved hand.

"Divorced."

Olivia watches Beth digest this bit of information as she opens her own mailbox and retrieves a thick stack of catalogs and envelopes.

"Do you have kids?" Beth asks.

"A son."

"Oh, how old?"

"Ten." *He would be ten.*

"Same age as my Gracie! Is he in fourth grade with Mrs. Gillis?"

"No, he doesn't live here."

"Oh."

That ended the inquisition, but Olivia can sense the additional questions tumbling in Beth's mind. *What can that mean? Does he live with his father? What kind of mother doesn't live with her child? Where is he?* Before she can verbalize any of them, Olivia changes the subject, hoping Beth will follow.

"Funny, I was just about to e-mail you. Your pictures are ready. Sorry it took so long."

"Oh, good! I was getting worried. I can't wait to see them. I want to use one of them for our Christmas card."

"I'll e-mail you the link as soon as I get home. They're great. You're going to love them."

The two women begin walking.

"I think my book is almost done," says Beth after an apprehensive silence.

"That's great. Congratulations."

"But I'm not sure. This might be a stupid question, but how do you know when it's done?"

Endings are difficult. Wrapping everything up in a tight, elegant bow. Leaving the reader with a satisfying *The End*. Saying good-bye.

"It has to have all the essential elements, a beginning, middle, and end. You just feel it. It's intuitive, I think. When you're done, you know."

"I don't know what I know. I've read it so many times now, my eyes skip over the words. I can't see it anymore."

"Maybe take some time away, then go back to it with fresh eyes."

Beth nods as she walks.

"I'd still like your feedback if you're still willing."

"When you're ready, I'd be happy to read it."

"Thanks so much," says Beth, smiling. "I'll put it in your mailbox when I know it's perfect."

"Don't aim for perfect. Aim for complete."

Perfection is an unattainable illusion.

"Okay," says Beth, uncertainty in her voice, as if she doesn't quite understand the difference. "I will."

They pause, facing each other at a fork in the road. Beth is staying straight, and Olivia is turning right. Beth waves, smiling, then walks away.

Olivia gets back to thinking as she walks home. She thinks about Beth and her novel. She wonders what it's about. She forgot to ask. She thinks about endings and intuition. She thinks about her marriage, how she and David both knew it was over, how they both saw their ending spelled out long before they arrived at the final page. She's thinking about the last time she saw him, lying under the stars and holding hands, when she reaches her front door and thumbs through the mail in her hand.

Tucked between the electric bill and a newsletter from the library is a letter from David.

CHAPTER 30

Beth is sitting in her seat in the library, holding the printed pages of her novel in her hands, reading. She thinks it might be done, but then again, whenever she approaches this thought, an itch flares up inside her chest, nagging her from within like a burning-hot rash. Something's not quite right. Even if she doesn't aim for perfect, only complete, she can't declare her book finished.

Today she's reading what she's written, enjoying the story, but she's yet to identify what might be missing. She's on Chapter 10 now, the one about the Three Little Pigs.

I love when my mother reads the Three Little Pigs book to me. I love Three Little Pigs, but it's not the story about a wolf and pigs that I love. I'm not "obsessed" with pigs, and I'm not afraid of that big bad wolf. It's the music of my mother's voice, singing in threes. There are perfect threes all over that story:

Lit-tle pig. Lit-tle pig.

One-two-three. One-two-three.

Let. Me. In.

One. Two. Three.

Even the title makes me smile. Three words AND the number three.

My mother reads Three Little Pigs, and I feel the big drumbeats inside those words thump-thump-thumping. I jump to the sound of the book's drum, thumping in perfect threes:

Knock. Knock. Knock.

One. Two. Three.

Jump. Jump. Jump.

My mother reads Three Little Pigs, and she sings a waltz. I spin and dance to her beautiful song.

> *Not by the*
> *Hair on my*
> *Chinny-chin-chin.*
>
> *Then I'll huff.*
> *And I'll puff.*
> *And I'll blow*
> *Your house in.*

My mother finishes the story and closes the book. I jump and squeal and flap my hands, begging her to sing it again. She says she's tired of the Three Little Pigs book. She says I'm getting too old for this story. She wants to read something else.

She pulls two books that are not Three Little Pigs from the bookcase and shows me their shiny covers. But I don't want to hear those books that are not about the sounds of three.

My mother sighs and puts those books I don't want away. She opens Three Little Pigs and reads again:

Lit-tle pig. Lit-tle pig. Let. Me. In.

One-two-three. One-two-three. One. Two. Three.

My mother reads my favorite story, and my world sings.

CHAPTER 31

"So why aren't you writing today?" asks Petra.

Beth and Petra are sitting at a corner booth at Dish, splitting a heaping plate of sinfully rich and fattening lobster mac-n-cheese. It's early afternoon on a Wednesday in November, and the restaurant is dead. The two people who came in for lunch left an hour ago. This is how it goes midweek in the restaurant business on Nantucket in November. Petra will limp along until Christmas Stroll, then close down until April 1.

"I think it might be done," says Beth.

Petra's eyes widen, excited.

"Really? You finished your book?"

"I don't know, I'm not sure. I'm taking some time away from it so I can see it clearly and then decide if it's really done."

Petra mutters a laugh through a mouthful of lobster and macaroni.

"What?" asks Beth.

Petra swallows.

"What you just said. Are you talking about your book or your marriage?"

Interesting. Beth wonders if the two are in any way related.

"I have this homework assignment from our marriage counselor that I haven't touched that I should've done like two months ago. I made Jimmy cancel our next appointment because I didn't do it yet. I don't know what my problem is."

"Maybe you're afraid of what you'll discover."

"Maybe."

"Probably."

Petra looks straight into Beth's eyes, straight into Beth in a way that most people never do. Her gaze is focused, unrushed, unafraid to stay there, and kind.

"I think I'm scared he'd cheat on me again."

"He might."

"If I take him back, I'd wake up every morning and think, 'He could cheat on me today.'"

"He could, but that was true before he actually did, you know. Every day is a commitment and a choice, for both of you."

"I know, but he chose to cheat. I'd worry after every little fight that he'd be off with someone again. Every time I see him, I think, 'You slept with another woman.' And I picture them together. It's disgusting, and I can't help it. I feel obsessed about it. I wish I could erase it."

"Do you still love him?"

"Yeah, but I hate him, too."

It's true. Beth loves him, and she hates him. She misses him and never wants to see him again. She's disgusted by the thought of him, yet she can't stop thinking about that night on the kitchen floor.

Petra sighs.

"I just wish I knew what to do," says Beth.

"Do what you're doing with your book. Take some time away from thinking about it, guilt-free. Then go back to it with a clear mind and fresh eyes when you're ready."

Beth nods. She discovers a big hunk of lobster hidden in the creamy cheese and stabs it with her fork.

"But what do you think?" asks Beth.

"About what?"

"Jimmy. Do you think I should take him back?"

"Only you can answer that."

"But what would you do?"

Petra scrapes a crusty, caramelized section of macaroni and cheese from the side of the dish and eats it. She drinks her water and wipes her mouth with her napkin. Beth waits. Petra smiles with her lips closed.

"Petra? Really, I want your advice."

Petra raises her eyebrows and says nothing.

"That's what I'd do," she finally says. "Stop all the chatter. Stop looking outside yourself for the answers. Get quiet and still and ask yourself those homework questions you're so afraid of. Whatever you find in that space, that's the truth. That's your answer. That's what I'd do."

Beth sighs, disappointed but not surprised. She should've known that Petra wouldn't do her homework for her.

"You're too wise to be single."

Petra laughs.

"That's exactly why I'm single! No, I'd love to share my life with someone, have a family. I will. I just haven't invited it yet. I've been so focused on Dish and all these people who need their jobs and taking care of my mom and dad. But someday. Someday, I'd like to have what you have."

"Had."

"And have. I'd be lucky to have what you have."

Beth smiles, grateful for the reminder. She has three beautiful, healthy girls, a lovely home, great friends, and a possibly finished first novel. She has so much. She checks her watch.

"Oh my God, I have to go! I have to pick up the girls."

Beth wraps her bright purple scarf around her neck, grabs

her bag, and hugs Petra good-bye. "Thanks for an amazing lunch."

"Anytime," says Petra, hugging her back. "So good to see you."

"You, too." Beth rushes for the door, not wanting to be late.

"You'll figure it out," says Petra, but Beth is already outside and doesn't hear her.

IT'S TUESDAY EVENING, the week of Thanksgiving. Beth and the girls have just finished eating macaroni and cheese for dinner, but Beth doesn't feel at all satisfied. Petra's lobster mac-n-cheese has probably ruined the Kraft version for her forever. She browses the refrigerator for something else, maybe something sweet, but nothing appeals to her.

All three girls are in the living room. Sophie has the remote control and is in charge, scrolling through the On Demand movie options while Jessica and Gracie yell out different titles. They have no school tomorrow and nothing going on tonight—no basketball practice, no play rehearsal, no homework. Beth is grateful to have a relaxed night with no schedule and no one to drop off or pick up, and, if they can ever make a decision, a movie to watch with her daughters.

She starts a fire in the fireplace and pops a bag of popcorn in the microwave. The girls are still watching trailers, undecided. Beth grabs a blanket and tries to get settled on the couch next to Grover, but she's feeling inexplicably restless. She stands up and looks out the kitchen window. It looks cold and dark and entirely uninviting, yet, for some reason, she needs to get outside. She grabs her coat, hat, scarf, gloves, and a flashlight.

"I'm going for a walk. I won't be long. Don't start the movie without me."

"Okay!" says Gracie.

Hypnotized by the TV, Sophie and Jessica don't even acknowledge that their mother has said anything. Gracie can tell them where she is if they ever wonder.

It's a dark night with no moon, but the stars are amazing, and it's not as cold as she expected. She points her flashlight in front of her and walks, not conscious at first of a destination, but after a couple of minutes she has one. Fat Ladies Beach. It's a bit farther than she'd planned, but she'll walk fast.

She's walking on the dirt road, focused on the uneven ground within the beam of light in front of her, the visible puffs of her breath, the tempo of her breathing coordinated with her pace. She can't see anything to either side of her, but she knows her surroundings well, the flat, grassy, uncultivated, and mostly treeless landscape that looks like African savanna. It feels good to walk, to move. She spends most of her days, her entire life really, sitting—at the kitchen table, in her car, in her seat at the library. Sedentary. Stuck.

Her exposed nose and cheeks are freezing cold, and her eyes are watering from the wind on her face, but otherwise, she's bundled well. She feels her heart beating hard, the muscles in her legs burning. She's both hot and cold, holding two opposing energies at once, sparking something within her that feels unfamiliar but exciting.

She reaches the beach, which feels far enough without walking along it, but before turning straight around, she stops for a minute to simply take it all in. She turns off her flashlight and listens to the waves, which sound to her like the earth itself breathing. She tips her chin up and stares at the starry sky, at its vast, complicated, unfathomable enormity but also at its simple, accessible beauty, its existence explained by the logical laws of physics and, at the same time, ultimately, utterly unexplainable.

She's the only person here. She's completely alone, yet she

feels strangely and beautifully connected to everything. Two opposing energies, held within her, sparking something.

It's time to go home, to blankets and popcorn and a movie with her daughters. She's off the beach and back on the dirt road when her flashlight catches two glowing white lights, like two fallen stars hovering just above the earth, and she stops fast in her tracks. It's a deer, an adolescent, positioned directly in her path only a few feet in front of her. They both stand still, face-to-face, breathing and bearing witness to each other for at least a full minute. Beth observes its black nose, its perky ears, its long, erect neck and wonders what the deer sees of her. And then, without warning, it takes off into the dark and wild Nantucket savanna.

Back at home, the girls had grown equally annoyed and worried by Beth's absence. They're ready now. They've been waiting. But first, Beth makes root-beer floats for them and a mudslide for herself. Then they all settle into the couches under blankets and watch *Marley & Me*, a movie they already own and have all seen at least three times.

It's late when the movie ends, and Beth goes to bed shortly after she tucks her girls in. It normally takes her a while to fall asleep, at least a half hour of tossing, the day replaying, tomorrow already tugging at her sleeve, but tonight, the walk and fresh air must've tuckered her out because she falls straight to sleep.

An hour later though, her eyes pop open. She's fully awake, her heart pounding, demanding something of her. She gets out of bed. She finds a sheet of paper and a pen. She draws a cross, creating four squares, and writes. She can barely write fast enough. Words she didn't know she had within her pour out.

When she finishes, she looks over the four squares. She reads the entire sheet three times. There it is, her homework assignment completed. Her answer. She reads it one more time and knows what she needs to do.

WHAT I NEED TO FEEL WANTED

Choose to spend time with me (instead of sleeping late, smoking cigars outside alone, staying out past closing, sleeping with other women)

Be happy to see me

Compliment me every now and then, something more specific than "you look nice"

Never cheat on me again

WHAT I NEED TO FEEL HAPPY

My girls

My friends

My writing

For you to see and appreciate the love and care I give to our family/household

A neat house

Spending time off this island, in a big city or near mountains

Believing I deserve to be

WHAT I NEED TO FEEL SAFE

Knowing my girls are okay

Not going into debt ever again and always being able to pay the bills

You never seeing Angela again

Believing you would never cheat on me again

WHAT I NEED TO FEEL LOVED

Hugs and kisses

Hearing you say the words "I love you"

CHAPTER 32

Olivia stands over the kitchen counter where two dozen glass jars filled with hot, homemade cranberry jelly are cooling in pans of water. She's been in busy motion for two weeks, ostensibly preparing for winter. She stored the deck furniture and the grill in the shed. She raked the yard and turned off the water to the outdoor shower. She ordered a dozen books and a case of her favorite merlot. And she's been cooking.

She's made old favorites—pasta fagioli, clam chowder, butternut squash risotto, and black bean soup—and she's tried new recipes, Pad Thai and lobster macaroni and cheese, insane quantities of food for a woman who lives alone and never has company. She's been cooking every day, creating gallons of savory dinners that are barely tasted before being aliquoted into plastic containers and stacked neatly in the freezer. Once the freezer was full, she turned her attention to cranberries— cranberry-walnut bread, orange-cranberry muffins, and now cranberry jelly.

She tells herself that all this cooking is good planning. If it's a harsh winter, if it's a season of nor'easters, if she gets snowed in (she still only owns that one, small sand shovel), she won't need to leave the house for food. But this is just what she tells herself. In truth, the cooking has been necessary for other reasons.

She started cooking right after she read the letter from David. The first recipe she turned to was the pasta fagioli, the one she knows by heart, the soup her mother used to make on Saturdays. Her eyes burned as she chopped the onions, and she welcomed the stinging tears. She cried while she chopped the garlic and the celery and the tomatoes. She sobbed while she stirred in the broth and the beans, then she stopped when the soup was done. She did the same thing while making the black bean soup, the tomato bisque, and the meatballs, but when she got to the onions for the butternut squash risotto, she ran them under cold water, wiped her eyes with her shirtsleeve, and finished the recipe without weeping.

She's done crying, emptied out, but she keeps cooking. It seems the only thing to do to keep herself sane. Fill a pot, fill the void. She keeps her hands moving, stirring, chopping, pouring. Her hands move through the steps for making cranberry jelly, and she can think about David and his letter without becoming leveled by it. She's read through it, dissected it, and cried over it so many times now, she knows it as well as her mother's recipe for pasta fagioli.

Dear Liv,

I wanted to write you rather than call. It seems somehow more proper, and I wanted you to hear this news from me before anyone else. I'm getting married. Her name is Julie. She's a math teacher. I met her here in Chicago. I know it's fast, but it feels right. I feel ready.

I wish I could've gotten back to this place with you, Liv. I'm sorry that I didn't. I know I didn't give my best self to you and Anthony. I guess I got a bit lost in all that

we went through. I forgot how to be happy. I think we
both forgot.

I hope this news doesn't hurt you, but I know it probably
will. That isn't my intention. It never has been. I wish every
day that you're okay, that you find happiness again, too. Call
me if you want.

> *Love,*
> *David*

Now that the initial shock of the letter has worn off and
onions no longer trigger hours of soul-scrubbing tears, other,
less explosive feelings have been taking their due turns. Where
she'd felt content to be alone the minute before she opened
David's letter, she now feels abandoned in her solitude. She
checks to see if the jelly lids have sealed, and she feels scared of
being alone forever.

A math teacher named Julie. She sounds young. And pretty.
And for some reason, blond. Olivia removes the jars one at a
time from their water bath and wipes each one dry against her
apron with her jealous hands.

They'll probably have children. She pictures David holding
a baby swaddled in his arms, a house full of kids who belong to
him and not her, a big family. These pictures in her mind, vivid
and achingly beautiful, punch the air right out of her, as they
always do, and she wishes she could somehow stop imagining
them. She holds on to the edge of the kitchen counter and
waits to either breathe or cry. Today, she breathes.

She reads the letter in her mind again, and it's the sound
of David's voice she hears. His voice is light and happy. He's
happy, and he's found a woman named Julie he can share his
happiness with.

He's right. She forgot about happiness. At first, it wasn't
a priority. Anthony had autism, and every ounce of energy
went into saving him. Her happiness was irrelevant. Then it

didn't seem appropriate. How could she be happy when they were living a tragedy? And then, just when she was starting to realize that happiness and autism could coexist in the same room, in the same sentence, in her heart, Anthony died, and happiness was no longer a concept she could fathom.

He died, and for a long time after that worst of all mornings, she replayed his death in her mind, unleashing the massive sorrow that still clings to those images, consuming her in a tsunami of devastated grief every day. She thought she would do this forever, that she should do this forever. Her grief was her daily duty, her misery a humble tribute to her son.

But reading her journals has helped her to remember more than that morning. There was more to Anthony's life than his death. And there was more to Anthony than his autism. So much more. She can think about Anthony now and not be consumed by autism or grief.

But not being consumed with grief is a far cry from being happy. She stacks the jars of jelly on a shelf in the pantry but keeps one on the counter. She pictures David now, and he's smiling. The image changes from David to Anthony. They have the same mouth, the same dimpled cheeks. Anthony smiling. It's an easy picture to sustain, an accessible memory, real. For all his frustration and aggression and inability to communicate, Anthony was mostly happy. It was his nature. Given time, it's David's nature, too.

She cuts a large slice of bread, slathers the jelly on it, and pours a glass of merlot. She gets comfortable in the chair in the living room in front of a glowing fire and takes a bite of the bread. Her homemade jelly is sweet and tangy, scrumptious.

She listens to David reading his letter in her head while she looks at Anthony's picture on the wall and decides she's done cooking. After two weeks of chopping and dicing and sautéing and sobbing, she's finally done with it all. She's done and left with a freezer stocked full of comfort food and a vague yet real feeling of hope.

If David can find happiness and begin again, maybe she can, too. Happiness. Shared happiness. Maybe it's human nature. And all she has to do is invite it in.

As she eats her bread and jelly and considers this new outlook, she gazes up at her photograph of Anthony on the wall. She drinks her wine and admires her collection of white rocks in the glass bowl on the coffee table in front of her—Anthony's rocks, plus the rocks she's collected here on Nantucket and the one Beth's daughter gave to her. She leans over, chooses a rock from the top of the pile, and holds it in her hand. It feels unexpectedly warm in her palm, as if someone had already been holding it.

Oh, my beautiful Anthony, why were you here?

The penetrating, hollow ache that usually follows this question doesn't come. Instead, a calm energy fills her heart with the assurance of a truth already known, more an intangible feeling, though, than a fact that can be verbalized. She sits still and listens but not with her ears.

She feels her attention being nudged elsewhere. She considers the new books on the table next to the fireplace. She gets up and squats in front of them, contemplating the spines, mysteries and memoirs and novels she's excited to get lost in. She lays her hand on the book at the top of the pile. *Not these.*

She walks into the kitchen, finds a red pen, and returns to her living-room chair carrying a thick stack of paper bound with red-and-white bakery string.

Untitled by Elizabeth Ellis.

She looks up at her photograph of Anthony on the wall and smiles at him with her eyes. She places the white rock back in the glass bowl, wraps a blanket around her lap, unties the bakery string, and begins to read.

CHAPTER 33

"Man, it's nasty out there," says Jimmy, parking his boots at the door before taking a seat on the couch across from Beth.

He blows into his hands, pink and wet from the cold rain, then rubs them together. The wind howls, sounding determined, as if the big bad wolf were roaming the neighborhood, bent on blowing every house down. One of the shutters rattles, and Beth feels a breeze whisper across her face, a current of uninvited air sailing into the living room through the many cracks around the old, warped windows. She cups her hands around her mug of cocoa, absorbing its comforting heat.

It occurs to her that this is exactly how everything started. A winter storm, a mug of cocoa, a fire in the fireplace, Grover asleep on the rug. Everything feels familiar, as if she's done this before, yet she has the sensation of standing tiptoe at the edge of a precipice, leaning out, about to free-fall into the unknown.

"You look good," says Jimmy.

She allows a self-conscious smile and picks a fleck of white lint off the front of her red shirt. "Thanks. You do, too."

The beard is gone, but he left the sideburns long, which she likes, and his face looks smooth and young. He smells nice, like citrus, an aftershave or cologne she doesn't recognize. He holds a piece of notebook paper folded into the size of a playing card in his hand.

"I'm glad we're finally doing this," he says, smiling, exuding excited anticipation, like a child about to unwrap a Christmas present, sure that it's the very thing he asked for.

Beth's paper, folded once, lies on the couch cushion next to her.

"How do you want to do this?" asks Jimmy.

"I don't know."

"You want to go first?"

"How about we just swap and read?"

"Okay."

Beth passes her homework to him, and he hands her his wadded piece of paper. Oily and worn on the folds, it's probably been in his pocket for two months. She unwraps it and reads.

WANTED
> Wait up for me every now and then and sleep late with
> > me
> Come to the bar for dinner some nights
> Initiate sex

HAPPY
> Be happy to see me
> Stop being mad at me all the time
> Don't talk to me like I'm one of the kids

SECURE
> Be proud of me

LOVED
> Tell me you love me

His list is short and reasonable, straightforward and simple. It's almost too simple, yet she believes him. His list is sincere, and she feels unexpectedly ashamed. This is all he needs from her, and she's been unwilling to give it to him, even before he began cheating on her.

Her list is similarly uncomplicated. She's not asking for diamonds and luxury vacations. She doesn't need roses and chocolates on her pillow. She's not asking for the moon. It should be easy. Love, happiness, security, feeling wanted, the most basic elements, like air, water, earth, and fire—missing for both of them. No wonder they're both sitting here with sorry pieces of paper in their laps, husband and wife, strangers.

When and why did they start withholding these basic needs? For her, was it in response to the changes in him after he stopped scalloping, before he started working at Salt? Was it a subconscious reaction to his affair? Did she unknowingly sense his infidelity and withdraw? Or did she maybe set aside too much of her creative and passionate self years ago, storing it in a box in the attic, not leaving her with enough love and happiness to share with Jimmy? Did she deprive him first, and he reacted in kind? It's a chicken-and-egg question, probably unanswerable.

She rereads his list, afraid to look up at him. On paper, it all looks so achievable, with the obvious exception of going to the bar for dinner. Not with Angela there. Not a chance. But it also confirms what she's suspected for too long. She looks over his piece of notebook paper and sees words that should've been spoken aloud, chatted about on this couch, whispered in bed, needs that could've been conveyed through a look, a note, a tap on the shoulder—all in uncharged, day-to-day moments. But none of that ever happened. They don't know how to communicate.

And even if they did, even if they worked on it and learned the tools, there is one item on her list, one nonnegotiable need as essential as the drafty air she breathes and that Jimmy can't give her.

She looks up, and Jimmy is done reading, waiting and grinning at her, and a heavy, hollow pit plants itself in the middle of her stomach.

"This is great, Beth. I can do this, all of it. And I want to. I want to get back together and give you these things. I've missed you so much."

He's still smiling, ready to celebrate, high atop the opposite end of her seesaw.

"We can't."

"What? I can, Beth, really. This won't be hard."

"Then why couldn't we do it in the first place?"

"I don't know, but we will now, we—"

"I can't, Jimmy."

His smile collapses, and the pit in her stomach expands. He stares at her and blinks.

"What are you saying?"

She swallows and tries to take a deep breath, but the pit in her stomach now feels like it's taking up all the space inside her where air goes. She looks at Jimmy, at that face she still adores, afraid of saying what she's about to say. But it's the truth, and she knows it. She leans forward and falls.

"I want a divorce."

"No. Beth, please. We can do this."

"I can't."

"You can. What part of that can't you do?" he asks, pointing to the piece of paper she holds.

"It's not your list, Jimmy. It's mine. I can't get past the cheating. I need to believe that you'd never do it again, and I can't. The kind of man I thought you were, the kind of husband I need, would never cheat on his wife."

"It was a mistake."

"Thinking it's Wednesday when it's only Monday is a mistake. Sleeping with her once, in the heat of the moment, I could even call that a mistake. But—"

"I'm sorry. It was stupid and wrong, and I swear, I promise it'll never, ever happen again."

"I can't believe you. I don't trust you anymore."

"Let's start over, and you'll trust me again because I won't give you any reason not to. Let me earn it back."

She shakes her head. Trust shouldn't be something he needs to earn. It should be a given. And he shouldn't need instructions on a piece of homework paper to remind him, DON'T CHEAT ON YOUR WIFE.

"I have something for you." He pulls a small, white cardboard box out from the front pocket of his jeans.

"What's that?" asks Beth, not wanting whatever it is.

"It's a gift."

"Jimmy—"

"Here, open it," he says, handing it to her.

Beth stares at him for an uncomfortably long moment. She lifts the lid and the square piece of tissue paper, revealing a necklace. A single, large, round moonstone hanging on a silver chain. She holds the gem in her hand, a shimmering, smooth, almost translucent bluish-white stone. It's beautiful.

"Jimmy—"

"When I saw you wearing the other necklace at the bar, I started thinking about when I gave it to you. It was the year we got married. That locket reminds me of our beginning and the commitment we made to each other. It reminds me of how much we loved each other. I know I ruined that. I'm so desperately sorry for what I've done, Beth. I want to start over with you, and I thought you should have a new necklace, something to symbolize a new beginning and a new commitment."

She clenches her teeth, swallowing down the urge to cry. Not now.

"Jimmy, it's beautiful."

"I noticed the ring you've been wearing and thought they'd look good together."

"And it's a beautiful thought. But I can't accept it."

She dangles the necklace back into the box, lays the tissue paper over it, closes the lid, and places the box on the coffee table. She looks up at Jimmy. All color and expression have drained out of his face. She suspects she looks the same way.

"Please," he says.

"I'm sorry."

"What about the girls? Don't they deserve their parents to be together?"

"Were you thinking about what they deserve when you were sleeping with that woman?"

"No." He looks down at his socks. "I wasn't thinking about anything I should've been. But I wish I had. Come on, Beth. We have to at least try to make it work."

"I have been trying this whole time, but I don't trust you anymore, and if I don't trust you first, then none of this other stuff can happen," she says, waving Jimmy's homework in the air.

"See, I think the opposite. I think if you have all the other stuff, then the trust will come. I can give you what you need, Beth. I love you. Let me earn it back. You can trust me."

She remembers attending a reception at one of the art galleries downtown with Jimmy when they were dating. They were there for the wine and to see some of Courtney's husband's oil paintings. Beth fell in love with one of his more abstract representations of a woman standing on the shore. The unexpected colors and strange lines captivated her interest and awe. She remembers the look of puzzled disgust screwed onto Jimmy's face as he studied the same canvas. She wanted to buy it, and Jimmy said, *Looks like something some kid did in kindergarten class*. She remembers feeling disheartened, that they could look at the exact same thing and experience something so completely opposite. And here they are again.

"I'm sorry, Jimmy."

"I can't believe you won't even try."

"I did."

"How?"

She says nothing.

"I think we should go back to Dr. Campbell."

"I'm done, Jimmy."

He reads her piece of paper again, shaking his head.

"You still love me, Beth. I know you do."

"This changed who you are to me."

She sees her words piercing him, his face pinching in pain, and she can't stand to be the cause of it. She looks away, over to the fireplace mantel, the piece of driftwood he knew would be theirs. The starfish and the nautilus shell are still there, but the old pictures are gone, replaced by a single framed photo of Beth and the girls in mismatched tank tops, arms around each other, laughing.

"I still love you, but it's not enough."

"It is. It has to be. I love you. If you still love me, that's everything. Please, Beth. Please forgive me. I know we can do this."

She looks down at her hands in her lap, at her diamond ring and wedding band she still wears.

I promise to be true to you.

A belief shattered into pieces too jagged and sharp, leaving her now holding what feels more like a weapon than a vow. She looks up at Jimmy, at the vulnerable desperation and love in his eyes, and unexpectedly, instinctively maybe, her guard drops and she mirrors his emotions with her own, with the reciprocal love and desperation she still has for him. An uncertainty niggles at her throat. She coughs and drinks a gulp of cocoa.

"I'm sorry. I can't."

She watches his eyes change, retreating into a familiar fortress.

"So this is it?"

The brutal enormity of what is about to happen hits her full on. This feels nothing like that morning last March when she found out about Angela and told him to leave, not truly wanting him to go, lost in crazed disbelief that he actually did. Today is different. This is their ending. She's losing Jimmy, and a deep and aching sadness fills her heart, but like witnessing death after a prolonged and ugly illness, there is also relief and peace.

"This is it."

He rakes his fingers through his hair and shakes his head.

"This is wrong, Beth. We should be together. We love each other. We deserve a second chance," he says, his words struggling against the oncoming force of unstoppable tears.

He gets up and rushes out of the room. She hears him putting on his boots, zipping up his coat. The front door opens and closes. She listens to his truck start and pull away. Her heart is pounding. She did it. It's over.

She walks into the kitchen, pulls a bottle of Triple Eight vodka from the cabinet, fills her mug of lukewarm cocoa to the rim, and returns to the couch. She listens to the storm, the fire, the radiator, the silence. She takes a sip of cocoa and notices that her hands are shaking. She stares at the white cardboard box left on the coffee table, afraid to pick it up.

The doorbell rings, and she startles, splashing cocoa onto her lap. She wipes her jeans with her hand and eyes his homework page, left on the couch. Maybe he came back for it. Or maybe he has more to say. She takes an apprehensive breath and heads for the mudroom.

She opens the front door, and she startles again, this time spilling cocoa down the front of her red shirt. It's not Jimmy. It takes her emotionally exhausted brain a few seconds to adjust her expectation and identify who is standing in front of her.

It's Olivia, soaking wet, holding a white cardboard box in her hands, looking as if she's just seen a ghost.

————— ❧ —————

CHAPTER 34

"Olivia, you're soaked through," Beth says. "Come in."

"Sorry to stop by unannounced," Olivia says, hoping to sound casual. She doesn't pull it off. Her voice sounds wired, tight, too high.

"That's okay, come in."

Olivia steps inside. She's in a mudroom—gray-tiled floor, a braided green-and-blue rug, girls' shoes and boots arranged in a tidy row under a long wooden bench, coats hung on hooks on the wall. The house is warm. It smells like cookies.

Beth hesitates before shutting the front door, looking out at the empty road. She appears distracted, shaken even. Maybe now isn't a good time.

There is no other time.

"I have your book," says Olivia, clutching the box she holds tight to her chest, protecting what's inside like it's a precious gift, a sacred offering, a beloved baby.

"Oh, great!" Beth's face lights up. "Let me take your coat. Come into the living room, and we can sit by the fire."

Beth hangs Olivia's drenched coat on an empty hook. Olivia removes her shoes and follows Beth into the living room.

"Sorry about the mess."

Olivia looks around the room, her senses heightened, raw and wide-open, trying to take in every possible detail. White walls, cream-colored Roman shades on the windows, a faded blue area rug on the hardwood floor, a modest TV set inside a white wall unit, all cabinets closed, firewood piled high in an iron trolley, a candle and a small, white gift box on the coffee table, two brown couches facing each other opposite a traditional brick fireplace, a single framed photograph taken by Olivia of Beth and her daughters sitting at the center of the mantel, leaning against the wall, flanked by a large shell on one side and a starfish on the other. A blue plastic laundry basket full of unfolded clothes sits on the floor next to one of the couches, but otherwise, the room is immaculate.

Olivia sits on the couch opposite Beth.

"There's one of your photos," Beth says, smiling and pointing to the mantel. "We have eight more framed in the hallway upstairs. We love them. I'll show you before you go."

"Sure. Glad you like them," says Olivia, trying to sound breezy, not knowing how much longer she can maintain normal, polite chitchat.

"Can I get you something to drink?"

"Uh, okay. Whatever you're having," she says, noting the blue mug in Beth's hands, assuming it's coffee.

But caffeine is the last thing she needs right now. When she starting reading Beth's manuscript last night, she began underlining and marking up words and phrases that reminded her of Anthony in red pen. She smiled as she read those first few pages, admiring Beth's depiction of a boy with autism, so similar to Anthony. She marveled at the coincidence, that Beth's book was about a subject so close to Olivia's heart. She applauded Beth's choice to tell the story from the boy's point of view, in his voice.

By the third chapter, the words she read and the voice she

heard began to feel uncanny, surreal, impossible. Her hands trembled, and her heart pounded. Goose bumps spread across her skin and stayed there. She switched to a highlighter, high-lighting whole passages she felt could only be about Anthony and no one else. By the time she reached Chapter 4, she was highlighting every word of every sentence on every page.

She devoured the words, finishing the book just after mid-night, breathless, stunned, her heart racing, tears streaming down her face. She sat still for a long while, staring at the last page, crying and smiling, believing and disbelieving.

Finally, she turned over the last page, gathered the rest of the manuscript, and held the pages in her lap, feeling the weight of it, believing. *These words written by Beth are Anthony's words. The voice of this boy is the voice of my voiceless son. The boy in this book is Anthony.*

She went back to the beginning and read it straight through twice more. She's been up all night, and yet she's never been more awake, every cell in her being on high alert, wide-eyed, plump full of adrenaline, ripe to the point of bursting.

"This is hot cocoa," Beth says, then hesitates. "And, don't judge me, a little vodka."

"Okay."

"Yeah?" Beth smiles and darts into the kitchen.

Olivia removes Beth's manuscript from the box and holds the pages on her lap, trying to contain what she feels for just a bit longer, imagining that she might actually explode into a million bloody pieces of flesh and bone if she doesn't soon say what she came here to say. She listens to the sounds of a mi-crowave cooking and Beth opening and closing cabinets in her kitchen. Any minute now. Her head buzzes, and her stomach is dizzy, like what an actor must feel before going onstage on opening night, or maybe like what a death row prisoner must feel on the day of execution, but like neither of these really. She hears the microwave beep. Beth returns with another blue mug and an eager smile.

"I can't believe you're here with my book. I'm so nervous."

She places the mug on the coffee table in front of Olivia, then sits, attentive and leaning forward, like a good student.

"Your book." Olivia's voice catches. Her heart is slamming against her chest like a fist pounding on a locked door, demanding to be let out. "Your book," she tries again. "How did you write this?"

"What do you mean?"

"This story. This is my son's story."

"Oh?" Beth raises her eyebrows and tilts her head, not understanding but not yet alarmed.

"My son's name is Anthony, and he had autism."

"Oh my God." Beth lowers her mug, floored. "That's unbelievable."

"Yeah."

"That's an amazing coincidence. I had no idea."

"No. Not a coincidence. You didn't just write a story about an autistic boy named Anthony. You wrote about *my* Anthony."

Beth knots her eyebrows and says nothing.

"The details. You knew everything. Barney, his rocks, the Three Little Pigs. He died when he was eight, almost two years ago."

"Oh my God, Olivia, I'm so sorry."

"Do you hear the sound of his voice?"

"Sorry?"

"Does he speak to you in words?" Olivia clears her throat and blinks back tears. What she wouldn't give to hear the sound of Anthony talking.

"I'm not sure I understand what you're asking me."

"I don't know how else to say this. Your book isn't fiction. This is my son's voice," Olivia says, lifting the pages.

Beth tentatively explores Olivia's face, like she's waiting for her to explain the punch line to a joke she doesn't quite get.

Olivia stares at her, waiting for her response. Olivia tunes in to the refrigerator humming in the kitchen, the wood popping and hissing in the fireplace. She's aware of her own eyelashes each time she blinks and water from her wet hair dripping down her neck and back.

"Look, I'm really so sorry about your son, but I didn't—"

"How did you write this?"

"I don't know what you mean."

"How do you know about autism? Do you know anyone else who has it?"

"No. But I've read about it—"

"You couldn't know this from just reading what's out there."

"And I've observed kids who have it. Even before I ever read anything, I think I've always been tuned in to the kids who have it."

"This is my son," Olivia says, raising the pages up off her lap.

"I'm sorry, Olivia. I didn't realize you had an autistic son named Anthony. I had no idea I'd be asking you to read something that's so personal. It's amazing that he reminds you so much of your own boy."

"This is my son's voice. I know I sound like I'm some desperate, grief-stricken mother who wants to believe someone is in contact with my dead son. But I'm not crazy. This is my Anthony," Olivia says, flipping the pages.

Beth's eyes widen as she notices all the red and pink ink on the sheets of paper.

"I'm sorry. I don't know what to say," says Beth.

"I know. I know I've freaked you out. Believe me, I'm freaked out, too. But there's no other way to explain this."

"It's a coincidence."

"It's not. This is my son," says Olivia, rubbing the top page with the palm of her hand. Her hand is shaking.

"Look, I'm sorry, I really am. But I didn't hear any voices. The book was inspired by a short story I'd written years ago about a boy I'd once seen creating a line of rocks at the beach. And then recently I read some books on autism that somehow seemed to fit the boy in my short story and the boy on the beach, and I combined them all into this character. Honestly."

A boy creating a line of rocks at the beach. Olivia used to take Anthony here, to Nantucket, to Fat Ladies and Miacomet Beaches, when he was little. The boy Beth remembers is Anthony. Olivia's sure of it. An electric chill runs through her.

"I don't know how or why, but my son gave you his story. It didn't come from you. It came *through* you."

Beth stares at Olivia in disbelief and says nothing. Olivia holds on tight to the pages on her lap. She can't leave this living-room couch without somehow convincing Beth. She exhales and regroups.

"Let me start over. I love your book. I do. It's beautiful and compelling and so real."

A smile breaks through Beth's guard, a small ray of light peeking through a pinhole in a concrete wall.

"But you didn't quite finish it. Where you ended the story, that's not the ending."

Beth's smile vanishes, but she's listening.

"We need to know what Anthony thinks about his time here, about his life and his autism. What does he believe was his life's purpose? This is the big, unanswered question in your novel. What did his life mean to him?"

Olivia's voice leaves her. She feels as if she needs the answer to this question more than she needs the air in this room. She's been asking this question, praying for an answer, for so long, and sitting in front of her is an ordinary but now completely spooked woman, a neighbor she barely knows, who somehow, for some reason, has access to the answer. Access to Anthony.

"Even if you think I'm completely nuts, please listen to me here. Go back to your story and write a little bit more. Trust me. You haven't gotten the right ending yet."

Beth still looks a little freaked, but she's listening. She nods. "I'll think about it."

Olivia searches Beth's eyes. This is as far as she can push.

"Thank you. I can't thank you enough. And trust me, you'll see. You'll know you have the real ending once you write it."

Beth chews the nail of her index finger and stares at her book on Olivia's lap. "You really believe what I wrote came from your son?"

"I know it did."

Olivia's eyes are brown. This book is Anthony. It's not similar to him or based on him. It doesn't remind her of him. It *is* him.

As Olivia stands up to leave, she notices Beth aiming with her eyes to pry the pages of her manuscript from Olivia's hands. Oh my God, she can't leave Anthony's words here. She can't.

"Can I please take this copy with me?"

Beth hesitates. She looks bewildered and exhausted.

"Okay."

"Thank you. I can't thank you enough for writing this. You've let me know my son in ways I was never able to know him."

Olivia slides the manuscript back into the box, and Beth walks her to the front door. Olivia looks Beth in the eye, making sure Beth really sees her, then embraces her in a hug.

"Thank you."

Beth nods and whispers, "You're welcome."

Olivia retrieves her still-soaked shoes and coat, says a reluctant good-bye, and leaves. As soon as she steps outside, the wind whips her hood off her head. She runs across the lawn to her Jeep but pauses before opening the door. She tips her head back, giving her face to the enormous gray sky, to the wind and the rain, and prays.

Anthony, I know it's you. Please, tell her more. Give me just a little bit more.

She stands in the road, exposed to the wind, vulnerable to the rain, to heaven, to God. She can't imagine why Anthony would choose to communicate through Beth and not her. But he did. She believes. She more than believes. She knows. This is Anthony, and the unwritten ending to Beth's novel is the answer to Olivia's prayers.

CHAPTER 35

It's early Sunday morning, and Beth is sitting on Petra's living-room couch, waiting for her to return from the kitchen with herbal tea. She pulls a speck of black fuzz off the couch cushion and flicks it to the floor. Petra's couch is white and many years old, but it still looks brand-new without a single stain, only one of many signs in the room of a woman who lives without a husband or children.

Opposite the couch sits Petra's meditation chair, a low, espresso-colored rattan seat with a high back and a white cushion (again, no stains). A beautiful, handwoven pink-and-gray blanket is curled around the seat, revealing the shape of where Petra was sitting only moments before. A lavender candle burns on the low, round coffee table next to a copy of *Cook's* magazine and a deck of tarot cards. The room is sparsely decorated—a black-and-white photograph of Petra with her siblings and parents, a painting of a sunrise over the ocean, a wooden carving of a sperm whale, a jade plant in a large, blue ceramic pot on the floor, its branches decorated with tiny gold-ball Christmas ornaments, a glass bowl filled with colored sea glass. There is no TV.

Petra walks into the room, still in pajamas, barefoot, toenails painted bright pink, and hands Beth a steaming-hot mug. She sits cross-legged on her chair, wraps the blanket around her, sips her tea, and leans forward, directing herself toward Beth.

"So this is incredibly cool," Petra says.

"This is crazy, not cool."

"Well, it's kind of mind-bending cool, but I think it's cool."

"Petra, this is unbelievable, impossible."

"It's a lot to process," Petra says.

"It's pure coincidence."

"Or not."

"It has to be."

"Why does it have to be?"

"So you believe in this kind of stuff?"

"What stuff is that?" asks Petra, knowing full well what Beth is referring to.

"You know, channeling dead people. Talking to ghosts."

Petra laughs and tucks her hair behind her ear.

"I believe in divine beings and spirituality."

"But what does that mean?"

"I believe that we're more than flesh and bone, that we are all spirits living here on Earth for a spiritual purpose."

Beth sighs and sips her tea. Her own experience with religion, with concepts and beliefs about spirituality and life after death, is extremely limited. Her mother wasn't a churchgoer. Beth's not even sure what denomination her mother might have belonged to. For a while when Beth was a teenager, she and her mother went to different churches on the weekends, sometimes even to other towns, with the purpose of at least exposing Beth to organized religion.

She remembers little about any of them. There were strange choral songs that she didn't know the words to and statues of Jesus nailed to the cross that gave her nightmares. That's about all. They usually went for jelly doughnuts after. She remembers the doughnuts. Then one weekend the church field trips stopped, and her mother left it up to Beth to choose. She was about sixteen. She chose to sleep in on Sundays.

When her mother died, Beth wished she hadn't made that choice. She assumed her mother was in heaven, but she had no religion to help her believe in heaven as a real place. She could only imagine heaven as a part of the sky filled with puffy, white clouds and chubby, naked babies with wings. And it was hard to include her mother in that image. It still is.

"Okay, what about what Olivia believes?" asks Beth. "Do you believe that's even possible?"

"Yeah, I do. I sometimes experience the presence of spiritual energy when I meditate."

"So do you hear actual voices?"

"No, but some people do, and some people see images, visual flashes. For me, it's not like hearing or seeing, it's more a sudden knowing, but the knowledge doesn't come from me."

"That's what we call *thinking*, Petra."

"It's not. It's different, it's information I wouldn't normally think, or it's communicated to me in a style that's not mine. It doesn't come from me, it comes to me or through me. It's hard to explain."

"Okay, but even if I believed in this, why would this boy's spirit choose me? I mean, why not communicate directly with his mother?"

"I don't know. Maybe his mother wasn't open to receiving him. Too much grief blocking the channel."

Beth looks around Petra's living room—the tarot cards, the rose quartz crystal in the shape of a heart hanging from a string, sparkling in one of the windows, the meditation chair. If the spirit of a boy named Anthony was looking to channel his story through a woman on Nantucket, why not use Petra? Why not choose someone who believes in this stuff?

"Yeah, but why me? Before writing this book, I had no connection to him or autism."

"We're all connected, even if we don't know how. Maybe his communicating through you gives you something that you need in this lifetime."

"Me? Like what?"

"I don't know. Maybe the chance at a new life, a creative life. Maybe it's a lesson, something in the story you've written that you need to learn."

Writing this book has given Beth access to a part of herself that she'd forgotten about, the creative dreamer she stored away in the attic so many years ago. But a lesson for her? Her book is about autism. It's not about her. She shakes her head.

"Did you ever feel like you were tapping into something or someone else while you were writing?" asks Petra.

"Not exactly."

Hearing the obvious uncertainty in her own voice surprises Beth. She never heard any voices. She didn't. But at times when she'd write, hours would go by, a whole morning and afternoon, and it'd feel like only a few minutes. And sometimes she'd read back what she wrote and think, *How did I come up with this? How did I know how to write this?* And there were the dreams. Those full and vivid dreams about Anthony.

"But, Petra, *I* wrote this book."

"I know you did, but maybe his spirit provided you with inspiration, guidance toward an intended path, some necessary truth."

Beth chews on her thumbnail and concentrates hard on what Petra just said. "Okay, but if I was going to be a conduit for someone's spiritual message, why would it be for this boy and not my own mother or my grandmother or my grandfather? Why this boy?"

"I don't know. Again, maybe there's a reason you're connected. Maybe there's something in what he's saying for you to learn. Or maybe Olivia's just a mother who really loves and misses her son, and there's something unresolved with him."

Beth sips her tea and thinks for a minute.

"She wants to know what purpose his life served."

"There it is. And your book reminds her so much of him, she sees the story you've written as her chance to understand why he was here and heal. What about that?"

Beth nods.

"I can live with that."

"Okay, then what do you think about her feedback? Do you think you have the right ending?"

There it is again, just like when Olivia was in Beth's living room, that electric, sick, sinking feeling.

"I don't know. I'm not sure of anything right now."

"I would go back to the library and try to write a little more. See if Anthony has anything more to say. It can't hurt."

"There's something else," Beth admits.

Petra raises her eyebrows and waits.

"Every time she said, 'You don't have the right ending yet,' I swear I felt a zap and my stomach dropped to my knees. I'd *just* ended things with Jimmy."

"Interesting." Petra taps her mug with her index finger. "Are you having second thoughts?"

"I don't know, but every time she said, 'You're not done,' it was like a lightning bolt. She was talking about me and Jimmy, not the book."

"So maybe you and Jimmy aren't done."

"Petra, she was talking about the book. She doesn't know anything about me and Jimmy."

"Yeah, she was talking about the book, but what you heard was Jimmy."

Beth sighs. She thought her book was done. She thought she and Jimmy were done. Now this woman she barely knows walks into her house and suddenly she's questioning everything.

"You can believe the spiritual stuff or not," says Petra. "Call it a wild coincidence if you want. I believe in it, and I believe in you. Go write. You don't have the right ending yet."

There it is again. Lightning bolt. Woozy stomach. Jimmy.

"I don't know, I'll think about it." Beth checks her watch. "I need to get going."

"Come here."

Both women stand and hug close, heart up against heart.

"Thanks for the talk," says Beth.

"Anytime."

Beth pulls on her coat, grabs her bag, and waves as she walks out the front door, still uncertain of everything, including the smooth, round moonstone necklace in her pocket.

CHAPTER 36

Olivia is sitting at her kitchen table, reading. She had planned to sit and read from one of her journals, but she opened the mail first, and she unintentionally got sucked into reading an advance reader copy sent to her from Louise, a book called *Believing in Bliss: Twelve Steps to Finding Happiness from Within*. She finishes the first short chapter, closes the book, and studies the cover, surprised by her interest in it. She sets the book aside for now.

She sips her coffee, thinking about Beth. Still no word from her. Every day, Olivia prays that Beth decides to write just a little bit more. Olivia can think of little else, consumed and desperate with the desire to read more of Anthony's words, to hear his voice, to have the answer she needs.

Why were you here, Anthony?

She sips her coffee and sighs. Her journal will have to do for today. She opens it and finds one of her favorite entries.

December 7, 2008

*Today we had David's father and brother over to watch
the Patriots game. Artie is really going deaf, but he refuses
to admit it and get a hearing aid, so the TV volume was
on screaming loud all day long. And they all yell a lot when
they watch the game, especially when it's against the Jets
(and it doesn't matter if they're winning or losing, they yell
either way). So with all that noise, I knew Anthony would
be avoiding the living room today.*

*I spent the first part of the afternoon in the kitchen. I
made an antipasto, chicken Parm, and lasagna for supper.
Anthony doesn't like being in the kitchen when I'm cooking.
I think it's all the noise I make banging pots and pans and
dishes, and maybe all my unexpected moving around, and
maybe even the smells. I don't know for sure why, but when
I'm cooking in there, he tends to steer clear.*

*So with the men hollering at the loud TV in the living
room and me busy cooking in the kitchen, I worried
Anthony would be out of sorts in the house. It was a nice
day, so after lunch I sent him outside.*

*I'm so glad we got that new, fancy Fort Knox lock for
the gate so he can be outside alone on the deck or in the yard,
and we don't have to worry about his bolting God knows
where. I don't ever want to have to search the neighborhood
for him again. It's the worst feeling, not knowing where
he is, if he's hurt or scared, if we'll be able to find him before
something awful happens. And I hated ringing some of the
neighbors' doorbells, watching their human faces change
to stone as I explained what was happening. He's a sweet,
nonverbal boy on the autism spectrum, not an escaped sex
offender.*

*So I knew he was outside and that he couldn't leave
the yard, but I didn't know what he was doing out there,*

and I didn't check on him for a long time when I probably should've. I would normally poke my head out every few minutes, but today I felt greedy—I just wanted a few more minutes of peace and quiet. A few more. A few more.

And it was interesting but of course not surprising to notice that David didn't get up off the couch once to see how Anthony was doing. He assumes I'll do it. I chopped and stirred and boiled and resisted the urge to check on Anthony in the yard, and I didn't tell David to do it or fight with him because he didn't think to do it himself.

I finished cooking the chicken Parm, had the lasagna baking in the oven, and even made the antipasto, all without interruption. No screaming from outside. That was good, but sometimes quiet that lasts too long is just as bloodcurdling as one of his screams, and I started to fear what he might be doing out there. He could be naked and playing with his own poop. This spring, he decapitated all the newly bloomed tulips. You never know. But most likely he's just swinging on his swing or playing with the sand in his sandbox or lining up his rocks.

I finally went outside, and he was lying on his back on the deck in a square patch of sun. His arms were by his sides, palms up, his feet splayed, his eyes open. He was just lying there, staring at the sky.

The square of sun was big enough for two, so I decided to lie down next to him. It was a crisp fall day, cold in the shade but warm enough to be comfortable without a coat in the sun. In fact, the deck boards were hot, and the heat felt like heaven on my sore back.

The sky was a perfect blue, not a cloud anywhere. I looked over at Anthony looking up at the sky and wondered, How long has he been lying like this? Has he been doing this the whole time? What is he looking at? There are no clouds, no birds, no planes. What could be capturing his attention for so long? What's going on in that head of his?

I started to feel antsy, like I should get up and do something. I thought, I can't just lie here. I should be accomplishing something. I still had a sink full of dirty dishes. I should pretend to care about the Patriots and join the men in the living room for a while. I should throw in a load of laundry.

And I felt guilty for ignoring Anthony for so long. I thought I should get him up, redirect him, get him engaged in doing something he should be working on. I thought (with dread) about his upcoming IEP meeting. He's so behind. He has so much to work on, so much to learn.

But luckily, for some reason, I stopped myself. I decided to continue to lie there and do what Anthony was doing, seemingly nothing, for as long as he wanted to do it. So we lay there on the deck, side by side, only a couple of inches separating his entire body from mine, and watched the unchanging blue sky.

My mind wandered all over the place at first. I imagined all those dirty dishes sitting in the sink, not even soaking in water, begging me to come wash them. I worried about his IEP meeting and thought about everything that I need to do to prepare for it. But I stayed. And I eventually let it all go. I did nothing, and I experienced simply being—the blue sky, the warm sun, the cool air, the hot decking, and Anthony next to me.

At some point, I looked over at him, and he had the biggest smile stretched across his face. God, his smile makes me so happy. And so there we were, the two of us lying on the deck together, smiling at the sky.

And then the sun moved on, and our square turned to shade. Anthony sat up and shot me a sideways glance and a pleased grin that I swear said, *Wasn't that AWESOME,*

Mom? Didn't you have the best time looking up at the sky with me?

And then he screeched and flapped his hands and ran into the house.

Yes, it was, Anthony. It was one of the best times I've ever had.

⌒○⌒

CHAPTER 37

Beth is sitting in her seat at the table in the library with Sophie's laptop opened to the last page of her book. She's rereading the ending. She likes it. It works, but she begrudgingly admits that it doesn't knock her socks off.

But how else would she end it? She taps her teeth with the chewed nail of her index finger and reads it again. She leans back and stares vaguely at the stage and the oil paintings of Thoreau, Emerson, and Melville on the wall behind it.

You don't have the right ending.

Why should she listen to Olivia? Endings are so subjective. She reads the last chapter again. It's a perfectly reasonable way to end this story.

What purpose did Anthony's life serve?

It is a powerful question, and if Beth is being honest, she can see how she skirted around answering it, how readers might be left wondering after turning the final page. But what's wrong with leaving them wondering? Isn't that a good thing? Leave the reader with something to think about. Resonance.

Beth sighs and pushes the laptop aside. She pulls out a brand-new notebook from her bag and opens it to the first blank page. She taps her teeth with her pen and stares out the window. No one else is here today except for Mary Crawford, who is sitting behind the circulation desk.

The library is hot and quiet and still. The clock ticks. She looks down at her notebook.

Blank.

She doesn't need to write any more. The ending she chose is good enough. Even if she does write another ending, it might not provide Olivia with the answer she wants. Beth can't guarantee that. She caps her pen and closes the notebook, but she doesn't leave. She stares out the window, debating with herself, listening to the ticking clock.

You don't have the right ending yet.

The ending you wrote is fine.

What was the purpose of Anthony's life?

Maybe there's a lesson in the story for you.

Jimmy.

Tick. Tick. Tick.

She stretches her arms up over her head and arches her back. She plants her feet on the floor, sits in her seat a little straighter, opens her notebook, and uncaps her pen. She stares down at the blank page.

Blank.

She hasn't bumped up against this kind of resistance since she first started writing here all those months ago. But here it is again, feeling bigger than ever, a fifty-foot brick wall standing between her and the possibility of a new ending. Maybe there *is* nothing left to write.

What was the purpose of Anthony's life?

Tick. Tick. Tick.

"Hey, Anthony. Do you have anything more to say here?" she whispers.

She holds her breath and listens.

Tick. Tick. Tick.

No voice from another dimension. She exhales, feeling relieved. But then something does come to her, a question asked in her own voice.

What's the purpose of my life?

And then a thought barrels through her mind, big and full of confidence, not composed of sound or an image in her mind's eye, but knowing, ethereal, yet as real and sure as the chair she's sitting in—the answer to her question.

They are one and the same.

She closes her eyes and breathes. She breathes to the rhythm of the ticking clock, and soon both seem to slow down and stretch out. She pictures the fifty-foot brick wall of resistance towering over her in her mind's eye, but instead of trying to scale it or knock it down, she imagines walking along it. She smiles as she assesses the wall from this new perspective. That impossibly tall wall is only a few feet wide. She strolls around it, and standing there before her in front of a pure blue sky, looking straight into her eyes and smiling, is Anthony. She mirrors his smile and nods.

She opens her eyes and picks up her pen, feeling suddenly and powerfully inspired as her hand flies across the page.

⸙⸙

CHAPTER 38

Olivia awakens still tired to yet another dark gray morning, not thinking yet, not realizing what day it is. She lingers in a steaming-hot shower, gets dressed, and then sits at the kitchen table with a book and a cup of coffee, like any other morning. Not until she drains the last sip does today's date slap her across the face.

January tenth. And any semblance of a normal day evaporates in that realization.

Like today, January tenth two years ago started as a typical morning. It was a Sunday. Anthony got up first, and Olivia followed him downstairs. He parked himself on the couch in front of Barney while she got coffee and breakfast started, and David took a shower.

She toasted three French Toast sticks and served them with maple syrup on Anthony's blue plate. She arranged his plate, his grape juice, a napkin, and a fork on the kitchen table at Anthony's seat and went back upstairs to take a shower while David was still home. By the time she dressed and came back downstairs, Anthony had eaten his breakfast and David had downed his coffee. David said good-bye and left for an open house at least a couple of hours before he really needed to go, part of his daily practice of avoiding her.

Anthony was now upstairs in the master bathroom, playing with water in the sink. It was their typical weekend routine. After breakfast, Anthony played with water in the sink while Olivia cleaned up the dishes, drank a cup of coffee, and read some of the *Globe*. She'd long ago stopped chaperoning him in the bathroom while he played. He knew not to use the tub without her there. Tubby time was at night, and he understood that rule. He liked rules.

And he was finally potty-trained. He typically peed before breakfast, and he normally didn't need to go again until after lunch. So while he played in the bathroom in the mornings, she didn't worry about his using the toilet or poop and all the unsavory adventures that often came with poop.

This was what they did every weekend. She drank her coffee and read the paper, and Anthony played in the sink. He loved to run the cold water over his hands. He loved to fill a large plastic cup and dump the water down the drain over and over and over. He also loved to close the stopper and fill the sink. Then he'd scoop some water into his cup and pour it back in, water into water.

He also loved shampoo. She bought lots of travel-size bottles of shampoo for him and made sure to keep her expensive bottles hidden and out of reach. He'd take off his shirt first. He liked to empty the entire bottle into the sink and make bubbles. He also liked to rub the shampoo on his arms and body. He liked the feel of his skin wet and slippery with liquid soap.

When she was done with her cup of coffee, she'd go upstairs to his room, grab his clothes, go into the bathroom, hand Anthony a dry towel, and tell him that it was time to get dressed. Then they'd go to the bottom step, and she'd help him get into his clothes.

On January tenth, two years ago, she drank her morning cup of coffee and read the paper while Anthony played with water in the bathroom and David hid from her at work. Maybe if she'd drunk her coffee faster. Maybe if David had stayed home longer. Maybe if she hadn't been absorbed in reading the paper.

The taste of this morning's coffee still lingers in her mouth, a taste she loves, but it's suddenly too bitter, foul, nauseating. She rushes to the bathroom and retches over the sink. She brushes her teeth, rinses her mouth with mouthwash, then sits on the cold bathroom floor.

She drank that cup of coffee two years ago in complete peace and quiet. She was reading the Arts section when something about the silence radiating from upstairs crawled under her skin and screamed. She put the paper down and listened. She heard nothing out of the ordinary, just the sound of water running in the pipes.

He's fine, she thought, then the second she finished thinking it, she heard a thud.

THUD. Too big, too heavy, too loud to be a travel bottle of shampoo or a plastic cup full of water. She doesn't remember anything between the kitchen chair and the bathroom. She remembers THUD, then instantly there was Anthony, lying on the tile floor, seizing.

She now peels herself up off the bathroom floor. She gets bundled in her winter coat, hat, and boots and heads outside for a walk, trying to evade the memory of what happened next. Maybe if she keeps moving, maybe if she's not sitting in one easily found, stationary spot, maybe the memories from the rest of that morning won't invade her.

It works at first. She focuses on walking, on bracing herself against the painful cold, leaning into the biting wind. But soon she is literally numb to the weather, and everything she walks past is gray—the houses, the streets, the trees, the sky. Walking becomes one long, familiar, gray, numb blur, not enough to keep her mind and body distracted. And the memories begin marching through her.

Anthony lying on the bathroom floor. Anthony's eyes rolled back in his head. His toes curled. Every muscle in his small, shirtless, pajama-bottomed body squeezing him, shaking him, distorting him.

She'd seen him like that once before when he was four. Just before it happened, he had an odd, blank look on his face. He was staring off at nothing, more so than usual, and he looked sort of washed-out. Then he dropped to the floor, unconscious, his whole body gripped tight and shuddering. It lasted about a minute, a completely terrifying, hour-long minute. Then it released him, and he came to about a minute later, drained but okay.

She and David were both there when it happened. David called 911, and she rode in the ambulance with Anthony while David followed in his car to Children's Hospital. Anthony had an EEG and some other tests she doesn't remember. The neurologist said Anthony had a seizure. He said that seizures are common with autism, that about a third of kids with autism also have epilepsy. He said that seizures are usually controlled well by medication and that Anthony might never have another one.

She watched him like a nervous hawk for a long time after that, but Anthony didn't have another episode. She relaxed and convinced herself that the seizing was gone for good, that it was a onetime fluke. Finally, they were lucky.

The experience of that first seizure when Anthony was four did nothing to prepare her for the sight of this one. This seizure was different. It kept going. One rolled into the next, each one gripping him tighter, shaking him harder. As if someone were adding kindling to a fire, the blaze kept growing bigger, hotter, brighter.

She tucked a towel under his head, unaware that he'd already banged it against the porcelain tile floor with way too much force, and watched in helpless horror. Then it released him. The seizing stopped, and he just lay there. His eyes were still rolled back. His feet were splayed. His lips weren't pink enough. His lips were purple. Purple turning blue.

Anthony!

As she wrapped her arms around him, she felt his limp wrists and his neck with her fingers. She couldn't feel anything. She put her ear on his slippery, wet chest. She thinks that's when she started screaming.

She called 911. She doesn't remember what she told them. She doesn't remember what they said to do.

She pinched his nose and began breathing into him.

Breathe!

She pressed on his small, naked chest with her hands the way she'd first been taught as a teenager on a lifeless doll named Annie.

Anthony, breathe!

Then there were two men. The firefighters. They took over. A bag on Anthony's mouth, a large man repeatedly pushing the heels of his large hands down on Anthony's chest. She remembers thinking, *Stop! You're hurting him!*

Then two more people. Anthony on a board. Anthony down the stairs. Anthony on a stretcher. Another man, bigger than David, straddled over Anthony, sitting on his knees, pumping Anthony's chest over and over with his hands. Violent. Unrelenting. A bag squeezed over Anthony's mouth. All while they were moving. Two men carrying Anthony and the big man on the stretcher out the front door to the ambulance in the driveway.

The images are surreal and all too vivid. Even as she's remembering each moment now, reliving that morning and crying as she walks, it still feels unbelievable, as if it couldn't have happened. She walks faster.

She sat in the front of the ambulance, facing backward, try-ing to see Anthony, to see what they were doing to him, trying to will him to breathe, to open his eyes.

Anthony, look at me.

She doesn't remember calling David, but she must've. Or someone did. He was there, standing next to her in the ER hallway when a short, balding, bird-nosed man, replaced in her mind's eye with the image of her grandfather who was simi-larly small and bald, approached them.

I'm sorry is all she remembers before the sound of her own voice screaming. The sound of her own voice screaming is the last thing she remembers with any clarity for the rest of Janu-ary tenth.

She's on her third loop through her neighborhood, circling the same gray, empty houses and gray, barren fields, with no intention of altering her route or going home. She pauses only once each time around, in front of Beth Ellis's house.

The black truck and blue minivan are both in the driveway, and the lights are on. Beth's home. Olivia stands in the street in front of the house, desperate to ring the doorbell. She hasn't seen or heard from Beth since that morning in her living room. But each time she passes by, she talks herself out of it. She's in no condition to talk sensibly to anyone.

Not today.

She walks the loop three more times and stops. She's freez-ing and exhausted. She checks her watch.

My God, it's only noon.

Twelve more hours of January tenth. She can't walk any-more. She has to go home.

On her way, she takes a quick detour over to her mailbox. She pulls out a couple of bills, a catalog, and a manila envelope with only her first name on it and no postage. She shoves the other mail back into the box, and with a scared and hopeful heart she opens the envelope.

In her hands, she holds a thin stack of printer paper, stapled together at the top left corner. The top piece of paper is blank, but a pink Post-it note is stuck to the middle of the page.

Olivia—

For you and for me.

Thank you,

Beth

She pulls the sticky note off the page, revealing a single word.

Epilogue.

CHAPTER 39

Today is a Sunday-brunch book club at Jill's house. It was Beth's turn, but Jill insisted on hosting. Beth is early, the first to arrive. Jill walks her into the dining room.

"What do you think?" asks Jill, beaming, anticipating Beth's reaction.

Beth surveys the room. Blue dinner plates on blue-and-white gingham place mats. A white bookmark lying on the center of each plate. A single, large, smooth, white rock placed on top of each folded blue linen napkin. A large glass-vase centerpiece packed with purple tulips sitting in the middle of a round metal tray covered with small, white stones. Skinny champagne flutes. A glass pitcher of orange juice and a pot of coffee. The food on the side table—a bowl of mixed berries, bagels and cream cheese, some kind of egg casserole, bacon, and French Toast sticks.

"It's spectacular," says Beth. "You're amazing. Thank you for doing this."

Jill waves off the compliment and excuses herself to tend to something still cooking in the kitchen. Beth chooses a seat and picks up the homemade bookmark on her plate.

Reading Group Guide followed by ten questions created by Jill, printed in an elegant calligraphy font. Beth smiles.

They were here in Jill's dining room for book club this time last year. This time last year, they talked about Jimmy's affair and her separation instead of the book. She remembers that night as if it were yesterday and a million years ago. She remembers feeling terrified, humiliated, sick with worry, and drunk on vodka. She thought that night was the beginning of the end of everything.

What a difference a year makes.

The front door opens.

"Hello?" someone calls.

"Come in!" hollers Jill from the kitchen.

A few seconds later, Courtney and Georgia come into the dining room. They pause for the slightest moment, taking in the spread and Beth. They look ready to burst, like children absorbing the sight of presents beneath the tree on Christmas morning.

"Beth!" says Georgia. "I just finished it last night! This morning actually, you kept me up till two a.m. It was *so* good!"

"I finished it weeks ago. Read it in three sittings. I've been *dying* to talk about it," says Courtney.

"Really?" asks Beth, grinning, her face flushed.

Jill made them all promise not to speak a word about the book until this morning, to save any discussion for book club, when they could all talk about it together. Even though Beth found this request to be more than a little controlling, even for Jill, Beth agreed. They all did. But she found sticking to her promise almost unbearable, as if she were stewing neck deep in a puddle of her own anxiety, every day for the past month battling the almost irresistible urge to ask each of her friends, *Have you read it yet? What did you think?* Every time she talked to Petra, she wanted to pepper her with at least a dozen questions, especially about the ending. But she held her tongue. It's been an agonizingly long thirty days.

Petra walks in next, carrying a thick stack of white paper under her arm. Instead of paperbacks or library books or e-readers, they've all come to book club today with 186 pages of printer paper. Beth's manuscript.

Petra plunks her stack of pages down on the table and smiles. "It's *beautiful*."

"Who knew you had this in you? How did you come up with this? Do you know a boy with autism?" asks Georgia.

"No," says Beth. "Not really."

"I just heard a question," says Jill, coming in from the kitchen with a bottle of champagne in each hand. "No questions until we're all here."

"Well, it's inspired, it really is. To get inside his head the way you did. I really understood him. I loved him," says Georgia.

Beth looks around the room. Jill, Petra, Courtney, and Georgia. It's usually just the five of them, but today, there's an extra place setting and one seat still empty.

As if on cue, the doorbell rings. Jill smiles at Beth and heads toward the front door.

"You look great," says Georgia.

"Thanks."

A book club held in her honor, discussing the book she wrote, her first novel, called for a new outfit. She made a special shopping trip to the Hyannis mall. Sophie came with her. Beth's wearing a red-and-orange, floral wrap dress, a new pair of cream-colored, open-toed wedges, a pair of dangly earrings that Sophie picked out, and even a little makeup.

"And I love your necklace," says Courtney. "Is it new?"

Beth places her hand just above her heart and rubs the shimmering bluish-white moonstone between her thumb and forefinger.

"It is," says Beth, smiling.

Jill returns to the dining room followed by Olivia. She's holding 186 pages in her hands. Beth gets up and walks over to her—her photographer, her neighbor, her editor, her friend—and hugs her.

"Thanks for coming."

With a hand on Olivia's shoulder, Jill guides her to the chair next to Beth's and introduces her to everyone.

"Ready? Let's raise our glasses," Jill says, waiting for everyone to lift her flute. "To Beth and her beautiful book!"

"Cheers!"

They all clink glasses and drink champagne.

"That's my only big problem with your book," says Courtney.

Beth swallows and waits, her stomach clenched.

"It doesn't have a title."

"I know," says Beth, relieved. "I can't decide."

"She was awful at naming her kids, too, remember?" says Jill.

She's right. Poor Gracie was still Baby Girl Ellis when they left the hospital. She was almost a week old before she had a name.

"How did you pick the name Anthony?" asks Georgia.

Beth glances over at Petra and then Olivia and smiles, like she's sharing a secret.

"I don't know. I just liked the name."

She doesn't know why she never considered any other names for her main character. And she doesn't know anyone named Anthony.

"I'm still crying over that ending," says Georgia.

"I cried, too," says Jill. "It gave me goose bumps."

Beth looks over at Petra with raised eyebrows, waiting, holding her breath.

"It's the perfect ending," says Petra.

Beth exhales, and she swears she can feel her heart smile.

"Thank you so much. I love the ending, too," she says, locking eyes with Olivia. "It's my favorite part of the whole book."

When Beth began writing this story, she remembers thinking how alien this character was to her, this boy with autism who didn't speak, who didn't like to be touched, who didn't make eye contact, who loved Barney and the number three and lining up rocks. But as she kept writing, as his autism became more familiar to her, she began to see more and more the ways in which they are similar—she chews her fingernails as a form of self-soothing, she feels calm when her house is clean and all the picture frames are level and centered, she can't stand the thought of someone else sitting in her seat at the library, she feels agitated when there's too much noise around her, and sometimes, she just needs to be alone.

But their real similarities have nothing to do with autism. As she continued to write, she began to realize that this story was more about Anthony the boy than Anthony the boy with autism. Autism became almost irrelevant, and eventually she was simply writing about Anthony, a boy worthy of happiness and safety, of feeling wanted and loved. Just like her. The more she wrote about Anthony, the more she realized that she was actually writing about herself.

She loves the whole book, but the last chapter, the one she almost didn't write, is without question her favorite. And the most essential. It was the lesson her heart needed, the advice her true self wanted to hear.

Now, her book is done. She rubs the smooth, cool moonstone on her necklace between her forefinger and thumb and presses it against her heart.

Thank you, Anthony.

"I think we should talk about the ending after we talk about the beginning," says Jill. "I've made a discussion guide for us on the bookmarks. Food is there. There's plenty more champagne, and coffee and orange juice, but please don't use the Moët for mimosas. Use the Korbel. Okay, let's eat and discuss the book!"

........•ᴐ﹒ᴐ•........

It's early in the day, and the sun feels soothing on Olivia's back as she walks along the water's edge on Fat Ladies Beach. It's a clear morning, no fog, and only a gentle wind. The sky is a pure, soft blue, and the air smells clean. Yesterday, when the sky was crowded with heavy, gray clouds, and the wind was fierce, kite surfers in black wet suits were all over this beach, riding parallel to the shore, playing on the choppy waves. Today, the thrill-seeking kite surfers have stayed home, replaced by the dog walkers. Olivia has already nodded hello and good-morning to at least a dozen people and their pets. So much activity on Fat Ladies Beach is unusual for April. But this weekend, it's to be expected. This weekend is Daffodil Festival weekend.

She feels done walking, but she won't leave until she finds one more. With her jeans rolled up to her calves and her shoes hanging from her peace fingers, she strolls barefoot on the smooth, packed sand, wet and cold from a recent high tide, a trail of her own sunken footprints following her. She walks with her head down, her eyes focused on the golden grains of sand in front of her. The beach is washed clean. It's mostly fine sand, only a few broken clamshells scattered here and there. She persists.

As she knew she would, she finds one, only partially exposed above the sand, white and glistening in the sunlight. She picks it up, then squats by the lip of the ocean, waiting for it to come and lick her rock clean. She beholds it in the palm of her hand. White and round and smooth. Anthony would love it. She smiles. She's ready to go now.

Back in her neighborhood, she walks in the middle of the road, taking notice of all the daffodils, bright, unexpected explosions of jubilant color, like three million yellow phoenixes rising above the ashen gray. Life returns. It's been unseasonably warm this year, and the daffodils bloomed two weeks early. They're everywhere. They're beautiful.

There are cars in many of the driveways now, windows open in many of the houses. As she walks, she hears a lawn mower nearby and someone hammering in the distance. She smells mulch and paint. Spring is here.

She stops in front of Beth's house. The driveway is empty. They're probably already out in 'Sconset. She said they'd be tailgating today. Two Adirondack chairs sit side by side on the front lawn, bright and slick white, freshly painted. Olivia smiles. She checks her watch. She won't have time to say good-bye to Beth before leaving, but she'll see her again soon.

Before turning to go home, she walks to check her mailbox one last time. She opens the door. No mail. Good.

She makes her way back to her cottage, a home that she and David bought for their future. It was a lovely and romantic plan, but it wasn't meant to be. For someone else maybe. She stands in the street before her house, its gray cedar shingles and white trim, the farmer's porch, the stone walkway. The FOR SALE sign staked in the front lawn by the edge of the road shines brightly, reflecting the sunlight. She sighs. For someone else.

She's already packed. She shipped most everything yesterday, and the rest is in the Jeep. Her load is actually lighter today than it was just over a year ago. There's no need to go back inside.

Before getting into her Jeep, she sits on the grass in the sun, already much higher in the sky than it was on the beach, and admires her daffodils. She planted a dozen more this year, so now there are eighteen. Eighteen happy yellow and white flowers, dancing in the gentle breeze, celebrating Daffodil Day.

The promise of a new beginning.

And they celebrate the day today above a bed of white stones, spread evenly over the earth around them. A rock garden and eighteen daffodils. The perfect home for Anthony's rocks.

She thinks about tossing the rock she found this morning, still in her hand, onto the pile but changes her mind. Instead, she chooses two more from the ground and holds all three in her hand. There. Three rocks. That's all she needs.

She picks a single daffodil, inhales its buttery-sweet fragrance, and tucks it into her hair over her right ear. Then she gets into her Jeep, takes one last look at her cottage, her daffodils, and Anthony's rocks, and drives away.

THE HIGH-SPEED FERRY to Hyannis isn't crowded, and she has her pick of window seats. People aren't leaving Nantucket today. They're here to see the daffodils. Olivia has seen enough. The ferry engine rumbles, and they begin to move.

She leaves her bag at her seat and walks up the stairs and outside to the back of the ferry. As the ferry approaches Brant Point Lighthouse, she pulls a penny from her pocket and tosses it into the ocean, a tradition symbolizing a promise to return to the island. She'll be back. She'll be back to visit Beth and Jimmy.

She's standing at the railing, facing backward, as more and

more ocean separates her from this tiny island. She watches the boats in the harbor, the two church steeples, the buildings in Town, and the gray houses dotting the shoreline shrink smaller and smaller. And soon, Nantucket is gone.

The ferry picks up speed. Olivia returns to her seat inside, facing forward. She's going back to work, back to Taylor Krepps, but as a fiction editor this time. She's ready and excited. Her first book will be the one she brought to Louise herself, the debut novel by Elizabeth Ellis. She can't wait for its publication, to see it in the bookstores, to hold it in her hands, to feel the cover and the weight of it.

She opens her bag and pulls out a thick stack of paper. Beth's manuscript. She holds it in her lap. This is why she came to Nantucket. For this. Her answer. Her peace.

As the ferry takes her back to the mainland, she flips to the last few pages and smiles as she rereads her favorite part, savoring each word, listening with her spirit to the beautiful sound of Anthony's voice.

CHAPTER 41

EPILOGUE

Dear Mom,

You already possess the answers to your questions. You already hold them in your heart. But your mind still resists. I understand that sometimes we need reassurance, to hear the words. A two-way conversation.

I wasn't here to do the things you dreamed and even feared I'd do before I was born. I wasn't here to play Little League, go to the prom, go to college, go to war, become a doctor or a lawyer or a mathematician (I would've been great at that one). I wasn't here to grow to be an old man, to be married, to have children and grandchildren. All that has been done or will be done.

And I wasn't here to help others understand immunology, gastroenterology, genetics, or neuroscience. I wasn't here to solve the riddle of autism. Those answers are for another time.

I came here to simply be, and autism was the vehicle of my being. Although my short life was difficult at times, I found great joy in being Anthony. Autism made it difficult to connect with you and Dad and other people through things like eye contact and conversation and your activities. But I wasn't interested in connecting in those ways, so I felt no deprivation in this. I connected in other ways, through the song of your voices, the energy of your emotions, the comfort in being near you, and sometimes, in moments I treasured, through sharing the experience of something I loved—the blue sky, my rocks, the Three Pigs story.

And you, Mom. I loved you. You've asked if I felt and understood that you loved me. Of course I did. And you know this. I loved your love because it kept me safe and happy and wanted, and it existed beyond words and hugs and eyes.

This brings me to the other reason I was here. I was here for you, Mom. I was here to teach you about love.

Most people love with a guarded heart, only if certain things happen or don't happen, only to a point. If the person we love hurts us, betrays us, abandons us, disappoints us, if the person becomes hard to love, we often stop loving. We protect our delicate hearts. We close off, retreat, withhold, disconnect, and withdraw. We might even hate.

Most people love conditionally. Most people are never asked to love with a whole and open heart. They only love partway. They get by.

Autism was my gift to you. My autism didn't let me hug and kiss you, it didn't allow me to look into your eyes, it didn't let me say aloud the words you so desperately wanted to hear with your ears. But you loved me anyway.

You're thinking, *Of course I did. Anyone would have.* This isn't true. Loving me with a full and accepting heart, loving all of me, required you to grow. Despite your heartache and disappointment, your fears and frustration and sorrow, despite all I couldn't show you in return, you loved me.

You loved me unconditionally.

You haven't experienced this kind of love with Dad or your parents or your sister or anyone else before. But now, you know what unconditional love is. I know my death has hurt you, and you've needed time alone to heal. You're ready now. You'll still miss me. I miss you, too. But you're ready.

Take what you've learned and love someone again. Find someone to love and love without condition.

This is why we're all here.

Love,

Anthony

As of the writing of this story, the neuroanatomical, neuro-chemical, and neurophysiological underpinnings of autism are poorly understood. While I look forward to the day, hopefully in the near future, when scientists have identified the causes, elucidating the neuroscience of autism wasn't the goal or within the scope of this novel.

About a third of children with autism also have epilepsy. For most of these children, seizures can be well managed with medication. However, managing the proper dosing and effec-tiveness of any medication with children who are nonverbal is particularly challenging.

Boy with autism or *autistic boy?* The specific use of language can powerfully influence how we perceive and treat people. I have read and understand the arguments for both choices here.

Boy with autism—the focus is on the person. The boy is a person first, not defined by and only by autism. On the other hand, *boy with autism* can be perceived to treat autism like a disease, like describing a person with Alzheimer's or a person with cancer. It can be perceived as something negative, a mal-ady to cure.

Autistic boy—the argument for this language asserts that autism is a trait to be accepted. It is part of the person, like being brown-eyed or blond.

Seeing the merits of both sides, I consciously used both ways of referring to autism in this book, as they are used in today's culture, aware of this ongoing discussion, respectful of both opinions.

When I began writing this novel in 2010, the incidence of autism in the United States was 1 in 110 children. A report released by the CDC in March 2012 states that the rate has risen to 1 in 88.

This is a fictional story about a boy on the autism spectrum. Over and over, I read and heard this statement from parents and professionals:

"If you've met one child with autism, you've met one child with autism."

Anthony, the fictional boy in this novel, is one child with autism. While he cannot possibly represent all autistic people, I hope that through the story of Anthony and his mother readers will gain an insight and sensitivity that can be extended to every person with autism.

After talking with parents, physicians, and therapists and reading as much as I could about autism for the past two years, here's what I've come to believe:

The spectrum is long and wide, and we're all on it. Once you believe this, it becomes easy to see how we're all connected.

ACKNOWLEDGMENTS

First, I need to thank all the amazing parents who so generously shared their experiences with me. I can't thank you enough for opening your personal lives to me, for teaching me what you know about autism, and for trusting me with this knowledge. I know that what you gave to me is extraordinary. Thank you Tracey Green, Kelly Gryglewicz, Kate Jacobson, Jackie Maust, Susanna O'Brien, Holly Shapiro, Ginger Shephard, and Jim Smith.

Thank you Dr. Barry Kosofsky, one of my first teachers, for your insights as a pediatric neurologist and for describing the current scientific and medical understanding of autism. It was great to learn from you again.

Thank you Corinne Murphy Genova, MEd, BCBA, for your insights as an applied behavioral analysis specialist.

Thank you Jennifer Buckley and Reine Sloan for your generosity, for helping me better understand what happens before, during, and after seizures. Thank you Dr. Jessica Wieselquist for explaining the clinical perspective.

Thank you to Jessica Lucas for sharing her expertise as an emergency medical technician.

Thank you to everyone who helped me come to know and love the quirky and beautiful island of Nantucket: John Burdock, Sarah Crawford, Michael Galvin, Dr. John Genova, Wendy Hudson, Tina and Richard Loftin, Jacqueline and Vincent Pizzi, Nancy and Peter Rodts, Susan Scheide, Dr. Louise Schneider.

Thanks also to Anne Carey, Sue Linnell, and Christopher Seufert for accompanying me on various trips to the island.

Thank you to Father Jim Hawker for providing information about the Catholic Church.

Thank you Mary Ann Robbat for sharing your insights about channeling.

Thank you Addie Morfoot Kauffman for helping me to imagine the details of Beth's professional life in New York City prior to moving to Nantucket.

Thank you Jill Abraham for role-playing a pivotal scene with me at Starbucks (Jill was Petra, I was Beth).

Thanks to my baristas and good friends at Starbucks for guarding "my seat" and for providing me with all the chai tea lattes I could drink: Lauren Fowler, Desiree Gour, Brandon Lopes, Erin McKenna, and Mary Trainor.

Thanks to Ann Hood for the glorious writing retreat at Spannocchia.

Thanks to the Peaked Hill Trust for the truly amazing artist residency in the Margo-Gelb dune shack in Provincetown.

Thanks to Danyel Matteson for providing me with the opportunity to spend some uninterrupted time writing in a stunning room at the Chatham Bars Inn.

For the time and space to write this book, I thank my parents, Mary and Tom Genova; my in-laws, Marilyn and Gary Seufert; Sue Linnell; and especially my husband, Christopher Seufert.

For reading each chapter, for sharing this journey with me, and for the many needed pep talks along the way, I thank

Vicky Bijur, Anne Carey, Laurel Daly, Kim Howland, Mary MacGregor, and Christopher Seufert.

Thank you to my incredible team at Simon & Schuster for believing in this story—Kathy Sagan, Jean Anne Rose, Ayelet Gruenspecht, Anthony Ziccardi, Jennifer Bergstrom, and Louise Burke.

Thank you to Vicky Bijur and Kathy Sagan for reading and rereading, for your invaluable insights. This book is infinitely better because of your input.

Thank you to Chris, Alena, Ethan, and Stella for your love and patience.

Finally, I thank Tracey Green. Thank you, Trace, for trusting me to write this story. I wrote this book for you, with all my love.

Lisa Genova

Love
Anthony

SIMON &
SCHUSTER

DISCUSSION QUESTION

1. How much did you know about this condition before starting *Love Anthony*? Do you know anyone who has autism or an autistic person in their family?

2. What significance does the setting of Nantucket play in this story? Would the story have been different if it had taken place in New York City or Chicago?

3. Beth pulls a box out of her attic, filled with remnants from her old life, and is reminded of the woman she once was. If you were to go through a box from your attic, what items might you find?

4. On the subject of marriage and fidelity, Beth's friend Courtney muses: "You're always at the mercy of the people you're in a relationship with, right?" (p. 151) Do you agree? What do you think of the advice she offers Beth?

5. Do you think the author accurately captured the voice of a young autistic boy in the Anthony chapters? Did these

sections enhance Beth's story for you? What about Olivia's journal entries?

6. After receiving David's letter about his impending engagement, Olivia ponders the concept of happiness: "He's right. She forgot about happiness. At first, it wasn't a priority. Anthony had autism, and every ounce of energy went into saving him. Her happiness was irrelevant . . . And then, just when she was starting to realize that happiness and autism could co-exist in the same room, in the same sentence, in her heart, Anthony died, and happiness was no longer a concept she could fathom." (p. 251) Do you think happiness is a conscious choice? Do you find it telling that Olivia uses the phrase "saving him" in reference to Anthony and his autism?

7. Towards the end of the story, Olivia has an epiphany when she realizes that "There was more to Anthony's life than his death. And there was more to Anthony than his autism." (p. 252) What do you think finally enables Olivia to have this realization? Was it a singular event or a process?

8. When Jimmy and Beth share their homework assignments given to them by Dr. Campbell, were you surprised by Beth's initial reaction? Why is forgiving Jimmy the one thing Beth can't do?

9. After reading Beth's novel, Olivia is convinced Anthony is speaking to her through Beth. Skeptical, Beth discusses the idea with the more spiritual Petra, who feels "we're all connected, even if we don't know how. Maybe his communicating through you gives you something you need in this lifetime." (p. 273) Do you agree or disagree with Petra?

10. Through writing her book, Beth realizes "this story was more about Anthony the boy than Anthony the boy with autism . . . she was simply writing about Anthony, a boy worthy of happiness and safety, of feeling wanted and loved. Just like her. The more she wrote about Anthony, the more she realized that she was actually writing about herself." (p. 295) How so?

11. Which character did you relate to the most and why? Where do you see these characters in five years?

12. What do you think of Beth's epilogue? Do you think it provides a satisfying ending to her story? To the novel as a whole?

13. Another recurring theme of *Love Anthony* is faith – having faith, losing faith and taking a leap of faith. Can you remember a time in your own life when you took a leap of faith?

1. Visit the website http://www.autismspeaks.org to learn more about autism and different fundraising or awareness-raising events your book club can participate in.

2. The author is a keen public speaker and tours often with her books. Check out the author's website, to see if she's speaking near you: http://lisagenova.com/

3. When out at Salt with her friends, Jimmy makes Beth a special drink – a Hot Passion Martini. Why not concoct a signature drink (with or without alcohol) for your book club gathering? Why not invent a 'Nantucket Knockout'?

1. You have said that Oliver Sacks, along with your grandmother's struggle with Alzheimer's, inspired you to pen *Still Alice*. Was there a particular person in mind when you started *Love Anthony*?

This book began with Anthony, a boy with autism who doesn't speak, inspired by my cousin's beautiful autistic son, Anthony. My cousin and I are close, and my oldest daughter and Anthony are the same age. We spent much of their baby and early childhood years together. So, as with *Still Alice*, this story sprang from a deeply personal place.

2. What kind of research did you undertake for this novel?

I did a lot of research on autism for this novel. I read as many books, blogs and research articles as I could both before and while I was writing *Love Anthony* – from fiction to memoir to clinical texts. A list of the books I read can be found at my website. I interviewed physicians, behavioral therapists, an EMT and people who've experienced seizures. The most important research involved talking with parents of children (age 3–17) with autism. These conversations were intensely personal, raw, honest and generous. I can't thank these parents enough for what they shared with me.

I also spent a lot of time researching the island of Nantucket. This involved reading many books about the island, interviewing people who live there (natives, summer people and wash-ashores), and hopping the high speed ferry from Cape Cod to Nantucket as many times as I could throughout the year.

3. Did you intend to make it a two-fold story (two characters whose lives intersect) or did that come organically?

This was the intention from the beginning. I did this for two reasons. One, both for the child who has it and for the families who love and advocate for them, autism can be incredibly isolating. When I talked with parents and professionals who know autism, I repeatedly heard the same words – isolated, disconnected, solitary, alone. While isolation is a very real aspect of living with autism, and I certainly needed to portray this in the book, I wanted to show people connecting (lives intersecting) through autism. Second, much of the focus on autism, especially among people who aren't all that familiar with it (like Beth at first), is on all the ways that autistic children are different from typical children. The focus is on what is strange or abnormal or even tragic. Again, that is there, but I also wanted to shed light on what is the same among all of us, whether you have autism or not. How do we connect as human beings with each other? Are we all capable of this? What happens when we can't or won't or give up on connecting? What happens when we find a way to truly understand and accept each other?

4. You have your degree in biopsychology and a PhD. in neuroscience. How has your education influenced your writing?

Neuroscience continues to be the first and foremost influence on what I'm interested in writing about. I'm definitely still a nerdy girl who loves learning about how the brain works. I love that I get to weave this passion for neuroscience into the stories I tell as a novelist. I get to ask the questions I care about most, questions about the brain and the bigger questions about life and then try to answer them as best I can through stories. I'm a lucky, nerdy girl!

5. What part of the writing/publishing process do you find the most challenging – the researching, the actual writing, the editing, or the public speaking at conferences and on book tours?
I honestly love all of those aspects of being a writer, even (and especially) the challenges. I think the most challenging part is when I have to do all of these at once! For example, many times in the past year while traveling on book tour for *Left Neglected* or on speaking tour for *Still Alice*, I would read a book about autism on the plane and then write some of *Love Anthony* in a Starbucks (Sydney, London, Montreal) before having to give a talk about Alzheimer's or a book event about *Left Neglected*. So on any given day, I might be writing about Olivia and Anthony and autism but also talking about Alice and Alzheimer's or Sarah and Left Neglect.

6. How was the experience of writing *Love Anthony* different from your two previous novels, *Still Alice* and *Left Neglected*?
When I was writing *Still Alice* and *Left Neglected*, I always felt like I could lean on my neuroscience background when I needed it. I could go to the textbooks and the medical community for scientific information about Alzheimer's or Neglect and traumatic brain injury, and, as a fledgling writer, I found this comforting. With *Love Anthony*, I was very much aware that I was writing without this safety net. There is no

neuroscience textbook on autism. And the structure of this story is far more complex than my previous two books. With *Still Alice* and *Left Neglected*, I was a neuroscientist writing a novel. With *Love Anthony*, I became a novelist.

7. Can you read other writers while you are working on a book, or do you take a sort of 'media-blackout' approach?

I'm always reading, typically two or three books at once. While writing *Love Anthony*, I was always reading a book about autism – *The Siege, Born on Blue Day, Making Peace with Autism, A Regular Guy, The Way I See It, Son-Rise, Thinking Person's Guide to Autism.* But I was also usually reading a novel or a memoir unrelated to autism. Right now I'm reading *Mapping Fate, One Hundred Years of Solitude* and *Maine*.

8. With *Still Alice*, you raised awareness to the insidious disease of Alzheimer's, and in *Left Neglected*, you shed light on traumatic brain injuries. Is it your hope that *Love Anthony* can do the same for autism?

Absolutely. Scientifically and clinically speaking, we're only beginning to understand what autism is. Most physicians were taught essentially nothing about it when they were in medical school. So in 2012, we're in the infancy of elucidating the neuroscience of autism. Yet 1 in 88 children are on the spectrum. And each one of those children has a mother, a father, grandparents, siblings, cousins, neighbors, teachers, student peers, friends – people who are touched by autism, connected to it, and need some better understanding of what it is. I hope that *Love Anthony* can contribute to an increased awareness and a much-needed, better understanding of autism.

9. Both of your female lead characters discover a strength they didn't know they possessed. Did you struggle with giving Beth a happy ending with Jimmy?

Yes! This was probably the most unanswered question in the book while I was writing it. Will Beth forgive Jimmy and take him back, or will she leave him? Right up until she decided, I honestly didn't know what she would do! My aunts, a friend, my husband, my editor and my agent were reading along as I wrote the book, and they all had different opinions. Thankfully, I realized that the answer Beth was looking for would have to come from Anthony. And then, her decision and her ending became obvious.

10. I love that Beth feels that she has to be in her ideal writing environment in order for the words to flow out of her: at the library, in her chair, etc. Where do you do the majority of your writing? Are you superstitious like Beth?

I write my books in Starbucks. I have three kids. The twelve-year-old is in school while I write, but her younger siblings are four and one, so they're home. If I'm home, and they're home, they find me. They'll come into my home office with a question or just wanting to play with their mom, and I can't resist. Plus there are all the distractions of home – laundry, phone calls, dirty dishes in the sink. So I remove myself and go to Starbucks.

This came in quite handy while I was traveling on book tour. I wrote some of *Love Anthony* in a Starbucks in Sydney, Montreal, and London. But mostly, I wrote the book at the Starbucks near my home. I'm not superstitious about it, but I did like to write everyday at the same table. One day, there was a couple sitting there, in my seat! I had to relocate. There's a scene from *Love Anthony* that came directly from this experience.

11. Can you tell us anything about your next novel? Do you already have something in the works?

My next novel is about a genetic, neurodegenerative disease and fate.

12. Are there particular authors who have inspired your writing? Who are the literary giants, past or present, that you esteem?

My "literary" giants are probably not on any other writer's list. Although I love Shakespeare and Hemingway, the writers who've inspired me most come from the neuroscience world – Oliver Sacks, Steven Pinker, Antonio Damasio, V.S. Ramachandran. I recently read *The Immortal Life of Henrietta Lacks* and really should add Rebecca Skloot to that list. Amazing story, brilliant writing!

13. It seemed as though Nantucket itself with all its natural beauty was a character in the novel. Which character was the hardest for you to write?

Discovering Beth's backstory was probably the hardest. Where was she before she came to Nantucket and why did she come and stay? How did she and Jimmy get together in the first place, and how did their relationship break down? Aside from that, the characters came quite easily. I loved writing about these women. And Anthony was already there – every one of his "chapters" came to me immediately and fully formed.

14. There has been a trend lately with authors who normally write adult fiction trying their hand at writing for young adults (i.e. Kathy Reichs, Philippa Gregory, Jodi Picoult). Have you ever thought of going this route?

Anything is possible.

Read on for an extract
from the *New York Times*
bestselling novel

Still Alice

by Lisa Genova

**SIMON &
SCHUSTER**

A lice sat at her desk in their bedroom distracted by the sounds of John racing through each of the rooms on the first floor. She needed to finish her peer review of a paper submitted to the *Journal of Cognitive Psychology* before her flight, and she'd just read the same sentence three times without comprehending it. It was 7:30 according to their alarm clock, which she guessed was about ten minutes fast. She knew from the approximate time and the escalating volume of his racing that he was trying to leave, but he'd forgotten something and couldn't find it. She tapped her red pen on her bottom lip as she watched the digital numbers on the clock and listened for what she knew was coming.

"Ali?"

She tossed her pen onto the desk and sighed. Downstairs, she found him in the living room on his knees, feeling under the couch cushions.

"Keys?" she asked.

"Glasses. Please don't lecture me, I'm late."

She followed his frantic glance to the fireplace mantel, where the antique Waltham clock, valued for its precision, declared 8:00. He should have known better than to trust it. The clocks in their home rarely knew the real time of day. Alice had been duped too often in the past by their seemingly honest faces and had learned long ago to rely on her watch. Sure enough, she lapsed back in time as she entered the kitchen, where the microwave insisted that it was only 6:52.

She looked across the smooth, uncluttered surface of the granite countertop, and there they were, next to the mushroom bowl heaping with unopened mail. Not under something, not behind something, not obstructed in any way from plain view. How could he, someone so smart, a scientist, not see what was right in front of him?

Of course, many of her own things had taken to hiding in mischievous little places as well. But she didn't admit this to him, and she didn't involve him in the hunt. Just the other day, John blissfully unaware, she'd spent a crazed morning looking first all over the house and then in her office for her Black-Berry charger. Stumped, she'd surrendered, gone to the store, and bought a new one, only to discover the old one later that night plugged in the socket next to her side of the bed, where she should have known to look. She could probably chalk it all up for both of them to excessive multitasking and being way too busy. And to getting older.

He stood in the doorway, looking at the glasses in her hand but not at her.

"Next time, try pretending you're a woman while you look," said Alice, smiling.

"I'll wear one of your skirts. Ali, please, I'm really late."

"The microwave says you have tons of time," she said, handing them to him.

"Thanks."

He grabbed them like a relay runner taking a baton in a race and headed for the front door.

"Will you be here when I get home on Saturday?" she asked his back as she followed him down the hallway.

"I don't know, I've got a huge day in lab on Saturday."

He collected his briefcase, phone, and keys from the hall table.

"Have a good trip, give Lydia a hug and kiss for me. And try not to battle with her," said John.

She caught their reflection in the hallway mirror—a distinguished-looking, tall man with white-flecked brown hair and glasses; a petite, curly-haired woman, her arms crossed over her chest, each readying to leap into that same, bottomless argument. She gritted her teeth and swallowed, choosing not to jump.

"We haven't seen each other in a while. Please try to be home?" she asked.

"I know, I'll try."

He kissed her, and although desperate to leave, he lingered in that kiss for an almost imperceptible moment. If she didn't know him better, she might've romanticized his kiss. She might've stood there, hopeful, thinking it said, *I love you, I'll miss you.* But as she watched him hustle down the street alone, she felt pretty certain he'd just told her, *I love you, but please don't be pissed when I'm not home on Saturday.*

They used to walk together over to Harvard Yard every morning. Of the many things she loved about working within a mile from home and at the same school, their shared commute was the thing she loved most. They always stopped at Jerri's—a black coffee for him, a tea with lemon for her, iced or hot, depending on the season—and continued on to Harvard Yard, chatting about their research and classes, issues in their respective departments, their children, or plans for that evening. When they were first married, they even held hands. She savored the relaxed intimacy of these morning walks with him, before the daily demands of their jobs and ambitions rendered them each stressed and exhausted.

But for some time now, they'd been walking over to Harvard separately. Alice had been living out of her suitcase all summer, attending psychology conferences in Rome, New Orleans, and Miami, and serving on an exam committee for a thesis defense at Princeton. Back in the spring, John's cell cultures had needed some sort of rinsing attention at an obscene hour each morning, but he didn't trust any of his students to show up consistently. So he did. She couldn't remember the reasons that predated spring, but she knew that each time they'd seemed reasonable and only temporary.

She returned to the paper at her desk, still distracted, now by a craving for that fight she hadn't had with John about their younger daughter, Lydia. Would it kill him to stand behind her for once? She gave the rest of the paper a cursory effort, not her typical standard of excellence, but it would have to do, given her fragmented state of mind and lack of time. Her comments and suggestions for revision finished, she packaged and sealed the envelope, guiltily aware that she might've missed an error in the study's design or interpretation, cursing John for compromising the integrity of her work.

She repacked her suitcase, not even emptied yet from her last trip. She looked forward to traveling less in the coming months. There were only a handful of invited lectures penciled in her fall semester calendar, and she'd scheduled most of those on Fridays, a day she didn't teach. Like tomorrow. Tomorrow she would be the guest speaker to kick off Stanford's cognitive psychology fall colloquium series. And afterward, she'd see Lydia. She'd try not to battle with her, but she wasn't making any promises.

ALICE FOUND HER WAY EASILY to Stanford's Cordura Hall on the corner of Campus Drive West and Panama Drive. Its white stucco exterior, terra-cotta roof, and lush landscaping looked to her East Coast eyes more like a Caribbean beach resort than an academic building. She arrived quite early but ventured inside anyway, figuring she could use the extra time to sit in the quiet auditorium and look over her talk.

Much to her surprise, she walked into an already packed room. A zealous crowd surrounded and circled a buffet table, aggressively diving in for food like seagulls at a city beach. Before she could sneak in unnoticed, she noticed Josh, a former Harvard classmate and respected egomaniac, standing in her path, his legs planted firmly and a little too wide, as if he was ready to dive at her.

"All this, for me?" asked Alice, smiling playfully.

"What, we eat like this every day. It's for one of our developmental psychologists, he was tenured yesterday. So how's Harvard treating you?"

"Good."

"I can't believe you're still there after all these years. You ever get too bored over there, you should consider coming here."

"I'll let you know. How are things with you?"

"Fantastic. You should come by my office after the talk, see our latest modeling data. It'll really knock your socks off."

"Sorry, I can't, I have to catch a flight to L.A. right after this," she said, grateful to have a ready excuse.

"Oh, too bad. Last time I saw you I think was last year at the psychonomic conference. I unfortunately missed your presentation."

"Well, you'll get to hear a good portion of it today."

"Recycling your talks these days, huh?"

Before she could answer, Gordon Miller, head of the department and her new superhero, swooped in and saved her by asking Josh to help pass out the champagne. As at Harvard, a champagne toast was a tradition in the psychology department at Stanford for all faculty who reached the coveted career milestone of tenure. There weren't many trumpets that heralded the advancement from point to point in the career of a professor, but tenure was a big one, loud and clear.

When everyone was holding a cup, Gordon stood at the podium and tapped the microphone. "Can I have everyone's attention for a moment?"

Josh's excessively loud, punctuated laugh reverberated alone through the auditorium just before Gordon continued.

"Today, we congratulate Mark on receiving tenure. I'm sure he's thrilled to have this particular accomplishment behind him. Here's to the many exciting accomplishments still ahead. To Mark!"

"To Mark!"

Alice tapped her cup with her neighbors', and everyone quickly resumed the business of drinking, eating, and discussing. When all of the food had been claimed from the serving trays and the last drops of champagne emptied from the last bottle, Gordon took the floor once again.

"If everyone would take a seat, we can begin today's talk."

He waited a few moments for the crowd of about seventy-five to settle and quiet down.

"Today, I have the honor of introducing you to our first colloquium speaker of the year. Dr. Alice Howland is the eminent William James Professor of Psychology at Harvard University. Over the last twenty-five years, her distinguished career has produced many of the flagship touchstones in psycholinguistics. She pioneered and continues to lead an interdisciplinary and integrated approach to the study of the mechanisms of language. We are privileged to have her here today to talk to us about the conceptual and neural organization of language."

Alice switched places with Gordon and looked out at her audience looking at her. As she waited for the applause to subside, she thought of the statistic that said people feared public speaking more than they feared death. She loved it. She enjoyed all of the concatenated moments of presenting in front of a listening audience—teaching, performing, telling a story, teeing up a heated debate. She also loved the adrenaline rush. The bigger the stakes, the more sophisticated or hostile the audience, the more the whole experience thrilled her. John was an excellent teacher, but public speaking often pained and terrified him, and he marveled at Alice's verve for it. He probably didn't prefer death, but spiders and snakes, sure.

"Thank you, Gordon. Today, I'm going to talk about some of the mental processes that underlie the acquisition, organization, and use of language."

Alice had given the guts of this particular talk innumerable times, but she wouldn't call it recycling. The crux of the talk did focus on the main tenets of linguistics, many of which she'd discovered, and she'd been using a number of the same slides for years. But she felt proud, and not ashamed or lazy, that this part of her talk, these discoveries of hers, continued to hold true, withstanding the test of time. Her contributions mattered and propelled future discovery. Plus, she certainly included those future discoveries.

She talked without needing to look down at her notes, relaxed and animated, the words effortless. Then, about forty minutes into the fifty-minute presentation, she became suddenly stuck.

"The data reveal that irregular verbs require access to the mental . . ."

She simply couldn't find the word. She had a loose sense for what she wanted to say, but the word itself eluded her. Gone. She didn't know the first letter or what the word sounded like or how many syllables it had. It wasn't on the tip of her tongue.

Maybe it was the champagne. She normally didn't drink any alcohol before speaking. Even if she knew the talk cold, even in the most casual setting, she always wanted to be as mentally sharp as possible, especially for the question-and-answer session at the end, which could be confrontational and full of rich, unscripted debate. But she hadn't wanted to offend anyone, and she'd drunk a little more than she probably should have when she became trapped again in passive-aggressive conversation with Josh.

Maybe it was jet lag. As her mind scoured its corners for the word and a rational reason for why she'd lost it, her heart pounded and her face grew hot. She'd never lost a word in front of an audience before. But she'd never panicked in front of an audience either, and she'd stood before many far larger and more intimidating than this. She told herself to breathe, forget about it, and move on.

She replaced the still blocked word with a vague and inappropriate "thing," abandoned whatever point she'd been in the middle of making, and continued on to the next slide. The pause had seemed like an obvious and awkward eternity to her, but as she checked the faces in the audience to see if anyone had noticed her mental hiccup, no one appeared alarmed, embarrassed, or ruffled in any way. Then, she saw Josh whispering to the woman next to him, his eyebrows furrowed and a slight smile on his face.

SHE WAS ON the plane, descending into LAX, when it finally came to her.

Lexicon.

LYDIA HAD BEEN LIVING IN Los Angeles for three years now. If she'd gone to college right after high school, she would've graduated this past spring. Alice would've been so proud. Lydia was probably smarter than both of her older siblings, and they had gone to college. And law school. And medical school.

Instead of college, Lydia first went to Europe. Alice had hoped she'd come home with a clearer sense of what she wanted to study and what kind of school she wanted to go to. Instead, upon her return, she'd told her parents that she'd done a little acting while in Dublin and had fallen in love. She was moving to Los Angeles immediately.

Alice nearly lost her mind. Much to her maddening frustration, she recognized her own contribution to this problem. Because Lydia was the youngest of three, the daughter of parents who worked a lot and traveled regularly, and had always been a good student, Alice and John had ignored her to a large extent. They'd granted her a lot of room to run in her world, free to think for herself and free from the kind of micromanagement placed on a lot of children her age. Her parents' professional lives served as shining examples of what could be gained from setting lofty and individually unique goals and pursuing them with passion and hard work. Lydia understood her mother's advice about the importance of getting a college education, but she had the confidence and audacity to reject it.

Plus, she didn't stand entirely alone. The most explosive fight Alice had ever had with John had followed his two cents on the subject: *I think it's wonderful, she can always go to college later, if she decides she even wants to.*

Alice checked her BlackBerry for the address, rang the doorbell to apartment number seven, and waited. She was just about to press it again when Lydia opened the door.

"Mom, you're early," said Lydia.

Alice checked her watch.

"I'm right on time."

"You said your flight was coming in at eight."

"I said five."

"I have eight o'clock written down in my book."

"Lydia, it's five forty-five, I'm here."

Lydia looked indecisive and panicky, like a squirrel caught facing an oncoming car in the road.

"Sorry, come in."

They each hesitated before they hugged, as if they were about to practice a newly learned dance and weren't quite confident of the first step or who should lead. Or it was an old dance, but they hadn't performed it together in so long that each felt unsure of the choreography.

Alice could feel the contours of Lydia's spine and ribs through her shirt. She looked too skinny, a good ten pounds lighter than Alice remembered. She hoped it was more a result of being busy than of conscious dieting. Blond and five foot six, three inches taller than Alice, Lydia stood out among the predominance of short Italian and Asian women in Cambridge, but in Los Angeles, the waiting rooms at every audition were apparently full of women who looked just like her.

"I made reservations for nine. Wait here, I'll be right back."

Craning her neck, Alice inspected the kitchen and living room from the hallway. The furnishings, most likely yard sale finds and parent hand-me-downs, looked rather hip together—an orange sectional couch, retro-inspired coffee table, Brady Bunch–style kitchen table and chairs. The white walls were bare except for a poster of Marlon Brando taped above the couch. The air smelled strongly of Windex, as if Lydia had taken last-second measures to clean the place before Alice's arrival.

In fact, it was a little too clean. No DVDs or CDs lying around, no books or magazines thrown on the coffee table, no pictures on the refrigerator, no hint of Lydia's interests or aesthetic anywhere. Anyone could be living here. Then, Alice noticed the pile of men's shoes on the floor to the left of the door behind her.

"Tell me about your roommates," she said as Lydia returned from her room, cell phone in hand.

"They're at work."

"What kind of work?"

"One's bartending and the other delivers food."

"I thought they were both actors."

"They are."

"I see. What are their names again?"

"Doug and Malcolm."

It flashed only for a moment, but Alice saw it and Lydia saw her see it. Lydia's face flushed when she said Malcolm's name, and her eyes darted nervously away from her mother's.

"Why don't we get going? They said they can take us early," said Lydia.

"Okay, I just need to use the bathroom first."

AS ALICE WASHED her hands, she looked over the products sitting on the table next to the sink—Neutrogena facial cleanser and moisturizer, Tom's of Maine mint toothpaste, men's deodorant, a box of Playtex tampons. She thought for a moment. She hadn't had her period all summer. Did she have it in May? She'd be turning fifty next month, so she wasn't alarmed. She hadn't yet experienced any hot flashes or night sweats, but not all menopausal women did. That would be just fine with her.

As she dried her hands, she noticed the box of Trojan condoms behind Lydia's hairstyling products. She was going to have to find out more about these roommates. Malcolm, in particular.

THEY SAT AT a table outside on the patio at Ivy, a trendy restaurant in downtown Los Angeles, and ordered two drinks, an espresso martini for Lydia and a merlot for Alice.

"So how's Dad's *Science* paper coming?" asked Lydia.

She must've talked recently with her father. Alice hadn't heard from her since a phone call on Mother's Day.

"It's done. He's very proud of it."

"How's Anna and Tom?"

"Good, busy, working hard. So how did you meet Doug and Malcolm?"

"They came into Starbucks one night while I was working." The waiter appeared, and each of them ordered dinner and another drink. Alice hoped the alcohol would dilute the tension between them, which felt heavy and thick and just beneath the tracing-paper-thin conversation.

"So how did you meet Doug and Malcolm?" she asked.

"I just told you. Why don't you ever listen to anything I say? They came into Starbucks one night talking about looking for a roommate while I was working."

"I thought you were waitressing at a restaurant."

"I am. I work at Starbucks during the week and waitress on Saturday nights."

"Doesn't sound like that leaves a lot of time for acting."

"I'm not cast in anything right now, but I'm taking workshop classes, and I'm auditioning a lot."

"What kind of classes?"

"Meisner technique."

"And what've you been auditioning for?"

"Television and print."

Alice swirled her wine, drank the last, big gulp, and licked her lips. "Lydia, what exactly is your plan here?"

"I'm not planning on stopping, if that's what you're asking."

The drinks were taking effect, but not in the direction Alice had hoped for. Instead, they served as the fuel that burned that little piece of tracing paper, leaving the tension between them fully exposed and at the helm of a dangerously familiar conversation.

"You can't live like this forever. Are you still going to work at Starbucks when you're thirty?"

"That's eight years away! Do you know what you'll be doing in eight years?"

"Yes, I do. At some point, you need to be responsible, you

need to be able to afford things like health insurance, a mort-gage, savings for retirement—"

"I have health insurance. And I might make it as an actor. There are people who do, you know. And they make a hell of a lot more money than you and Dad combined."

"This isn't just about money."

"Then what? That I didn't become you?"

"Lower your voice."

"Don't tell me what to do."

"I don't want you to become me, Lydia. I just don't want you to limit your choices."

"You want to make my choices."

"No."

"This is who I am, this is what I want to do."

"What, serving up Venti lattes? You should be in college. You should be spending this time in your life learning some-thing."

"I *am* learning something! I'm just not sitting in a Har-vard classroom killing myself trying to get an A in political sci-ence. I'm in a serious acting class for fifteen hours a week. How many hours of class a week do your students take, twelve?"

"It's not the same thing."

"Well, Dad thinks it is. He's paying for it."

Alice clenched the sides of her skirt and pressed her lips together. What she wanted to say next wasn't meant for Lydia.

"You've never even seen me act."

John had. He'd flown out alone last winter to see her per-form in a play. Swamped with too many urgent things at the time, Alice couldn't free up to go. As she looked at Lydia's pained eyes, she couldn't remember now what those urgent things had been. She didn't have anything against an acting career itself, but she believed her daughter's singular pursuit of it, without an education, bordered on reckless. If she didn't go to college now, acquire a knowledge base or formal training in some field, if she didn't get a degree, what would she do if acting didn't pan out?

Alice thought about those condoms in the bathroom. What if Lydia got pregnant? Alice worried that Lydia might someday find herself trapped in a life that was unfulfilled, full of regret. She looked at her daughter and saw so much wasted potential, so much wasted time.

"You're not getting any younger, Lydia. Life goes by too fast."

"I agree."

The food came, but neither of them picked up a fork. Lydia dabbed her eyes with her hand-embroidered linen napkin. They always fell into the same battle, and it felt to Alice like trying to knock down a concrete wall with their heads. It was never going to be productive and only resulted in hurting them, causing lasting damage. She wished Lydia could see the love and wisdom in what she wanted for her. She wished she could just reach across the table and hug her daughter, but there were too many dishes, glasses, and years of distance between them.

A sudden flurry of activity a few tables away pulled their attention from themselves. Several camera flashes popped, and a small crowd of patrons and waitstaff gathered, all focused on a woman who looked a bit like Lydia.

"Who's that?" asked Alice.

"Mom," said Lydia in a tone both embarrassed and superior, perfected at the age of thirteen. "That's Jennifer Aniston."

They ate their dinner and talked only of safe things, like the food and the weather. Alice wanted to discover more about Lydia's relationship with Malcolm, but the embers of Lydia's emotions still glowed hot, and Alice feared igniting another fight. She paid the bill and they left the restaurant, full but dissatisfied.

"Excuse me, ma'am!"

Their waiter caught up to them on the sidewalk.

"You left this."

Alice paused, trying to comprehend how their waiter might come to possess her BlackBerry. She hadn't checked her email or calendar in the restaurant. She felt inside her bag. No BlackBerry. She must've removed it when she fished her wallet out to pay.

"Thank you."

Lydia looked at her quizzically, as if she wanted to say something about something other than food or weather, but then didn't. They walked back to her apartment in silence.

"JOHN?"

Alice waited, suspended in the front hallway, holding the handle of her suitcase. *Harvard Magazine* lay on the top of a pile of unclaimed mail strewn on the floor in front of her. The clock in the living room ticked and the refrigerator hummed. A warm, sunny late afternoon at her back, the air inside felt chilly, dim, and stale. Uninhabited.

She picked up the mail and walked into the kitchen, her suitcase on wheels accompanying her like a loyal pet. Her flight had been delayed, and she was late getting in, even according to the microwave. He'd had a whole day, a whole Saturday, to work.

The red voice-mail light on their answering machine stared her down, unblinking. She checked the refrigerator. No note on the door. Nothing.

Still clutching the handle of her suitcase, she stood in the dark kitchen and watched several minutes advance on the microwave. The disappointed but forgiving voice in her head faded to a whisper as the volume of a more primal one began to build and spread out. She thought about calling him, but the expanding voice rejected the suggestion outright and refused all excuses. She thought about deciding not to care, but the voice, now seeping down into her body, echoing in her belly, vibrating in each of her fingertips, was too powerful and pervasive to ignore.

Why did it bother her so much? He was in the middle of an experiment and couldn't leave it to come home. She'd certainly been in his shoes innumerable times. This was what they did. This was who they were. The voice called her a stupid fool.

She spotted her running shoes on the floor next to the back door. A run would make her feel better. That was what she needed.

Ideally, she ran every day. For many years now, she'd treated running like eating or sleeping, as a vital daily necessity, and she'd been known to squeeze in a jog at midnight or in the middle of a blinding snowstorm. But she'd neglected this basic need over the last several months. She'd been so busy. As she laced her shoes, she told herself she hadn't bothered bringing them with her to California because she'd known she wouldn't have the time. In truth, she'd simply forgotten to pack them.

When starting from her house on Poplar Street, she invariably followed the same route—down Massachusetts Avenue, through Harvard Square to Memorial Drive, along the Charles River to the Harvard Bridge over by MIT, and back—a little over five miles, a forty-five-minute round trip. She had long been attracted to the idea of running in the Boston Marathon but each year decided that she realistically didn't have the time to train for that kind of distance. Maybe someday she would. In excellent physical condition for a woman her age, she imagined running strong well into her sixties.

Clustered pedestrian traffic on the sidewalks and intermittent negotiations with car traffic in street intersections littered the first part of her run through Harvard Square. It was crowded and ripe with anticipation at that time of day on a Saturday, with crowds forming and milling around on street corners waiting for walk signals, outside restaurants waiting for tables, in movie theater lines waiting for tickets, and in double-parked cars waiting for an unlikely opening in a metered space. The first ten minutes of her run required a good deal of conscious external concentration to navigate through it all, but once she crossed Memorial Drive to the Charles River, she was free to run in full stride and completely in the zone.

A comfortable and cloudless evening invited a lot of activity along the Charles, yet the grassy area beside the river felt less congested than the streets of Cambridge. Despite a steady stream of joggers, dogs and their owners, walkers, Rollerbladers, cyclists, and women pushing babies in jogger strollers, like an experienced driver on a regularly traveled stretch of road, Alice retained only a vague sense for what went on around her now. As she ran along the river, she became mindful of nothing but the sounds of her Nikes hitting the pavement in syncopated rhythm with the pace of her breath. She didn't replay her argument with Lydia. She didn't acknowledge her growling stomach. She didn't think about John. She just ran.

As was her routine, she stopped running once she made it back to the John Fitzgerald Kennedy Park, a pocket of manicured lawns abutting Memorial Drive. Her head cleared, her body relaxed and rejuvenated, she began walking home. The JFK Park funneled into Harvard Square through a pleasant, bench-lined corridor between the Charles Hotel and the Kennedy School of Government.

At the other end of the corridor, she stood at the intersection of Eliot Street and Brattle, ready to cross, when a woman grabbed her forearm with startling force and said, "Have you thought about heaven today?"

The woman fixed Alice with a penetrating, unwavering stare. She had long hair the color and texture of a teased Brillo pad and wore a handmade placard hung over her chest that read AMERICA REPENT, TURN TO JESUS FROM SIN. There was always someone selling God in Harvard Square, but Alice had never been singled out so directly and intimately before.

"Sorry," she said and, noticing a break in the flow of traffic, escaped to the other side of the street.

She wanted to continue walking but stood frozen instead. She didn't know where she was. She looked back across the street. The Brillo-haired woman pursued another sinner down the corridor. The corridor, the hotel, the stores, the illogically meandering streets. She knew she was in Harvard Square, but she didn't know which way was home.

She tried again, more specifically. The Harvard Square Hotel, Eastern Mountain Sports, Dickson Bros. Hardware, Mount Auburn Street. She knew all of these places—this square had been her stomping ground for over twenty-five years—but they somehow didn't fit into a mental map that told her where she lived relative to them. A black-and-white circular "T" sign directly in front of her marked an entrance to the Red Line trains and buses underground, but there were three such entrances in Harvard Square, and she couldn't piece together which one of the three this was.

Her heart began to race. She started sweating. She told herself that an accelerated heart rate and perspiration were part of an orchestrated and appropriate response to running. But as she stood on the sidewalk, it felt like panic.

She willed herself to walk another block and then another, her rubbery legs feeling like they might give way with each bewildered step. The Coop, Cardullo's, the magazines on the corner, the Cambridge visitors' center across the street, and Harvard Yard beyond that. She told herself she could still read and recognize. None of it helped. It all lacked a context.

People, cars, buses, and all kinds of unbearable noise rushed and wove around and past her. She closed her eyes. She listened to her own blood whoosh and pulse behind her ears.

"Please stop this," she whispered.

She opened her eyes. Just as suddenly as it had left her, the landscape snapped snugly back into place. The Coop, Cardullo's, Nini's Corner, Harvard Yard. She automatically understood that she should turn left at the corner and head west on Mass Ave. She began to breathe easier, no longer bizarrely lost within a mile of home. But she'd just been bizarrely lost within a mile of home. She walked as fast as she could without running.

She turned onto her street, a quiet, tree-lined, residential road a couple of blocks removed from Mass Ave. With both feet on her road and her house in sight, she felt much safer, but not yet safe. She kept her eyes on her front door and her legs moving and promised herself that the sea of anxiety swelling furiously inside her would drain when she walked in the front hallway and saw John. If he was home.

"John?"

He appeared in the threshold of the kitchen, unshaven, his glasses sitting on top of his mad-scientist hair, sucking on a red Popsicle and sporting his lucky gray T-shirt. He'd been up all night. As she'd promised herself, her anxiety began to drain. But her energy and bravery seemed to leak out with it, leaving her fragile and wanting to collapse into his arms.

"Hey, I was wondering where you were, just about to leave you a note on the fridge. How'd it go?" he asked.

"What?"

"Stanford."

"Oh, good."

"And how's Lydia?"

The betrayal and hurt over Lydia, over him not being home when she got there, exorcised by the run and displaced by her terror at being inexplicably lost, reclaimed its priority in the pecking order.

"You tell me," she said.

"You guys fought."

"You're paying for her acting classes?" she accused.

"Oh," he said, sucking the last of the Popsicle into his

red-stained mouth. "Look, can we talk about this later? I don't have time to get into it right now."

"Make the time, John. You're keeping her afloat out there without telling me, and you're not here when I get home, and—"

"And you weren't here when I got home. How was your run?"

She heard the simple reasoning in his veiled question. If she had waited for him, if she had called, if she hadn't done exactly what she'd wanted and gone for a run, she could've spent the last hour with him. She had to agree.

"Fine."

"I'm sorry, I waited as long as I could, but I've really got to get back to the lab. I've had an incredible day so far, gorgeous results, but we're not done, and I've got to analyze the numbers before we get started again in the morning. I only came home to see you."

"I need to talk about this with you now."

"This really isn't new information, Ali. We disagree about Lydia. Can't it wait until I get back?"

"No."

"You want to walk over with me, talk about it on the way?"

"I'm not going to the office, I need to be home."

"You need to talk now, you need to be home, you're awfully needy all of a sudden. Is something else going on?"

The word *needy* smacked a vulnerable nerve. *Needy* equaled weak, dependent, pathological. Her father. She'd made a life-long point of never being like that, like him.

"I'm just exhausted."

"You look it, you need to slow down."

"That's not what I need."

He waited for her to elaborate, but she took too long.

"Look, the sooner I go, the sooner I'll be back. Get some rest, I'll be home later tonight."

He kissed her sweat-drenched head and walked out the door.

Standing in the hallway where he'd left her, with no one to confess to or confide in, she felt the full emotional impact of what she'd just experienced in Harvard Square flood over her. She sat down on the floor and leaned against the cool wall, watching her hands shake in her lap as if they couldn't be hers. She tried to focus on steadying her breath as she did when she ran.

After minutes of breathing in and breathing out, she was finally calm enough to attempt to assemble some sense out of what had just happened. She thought about the missing word during her talk at Stanford and her missing period. She got up, turned on her laptop, and Googled "menopause symptoms."

An appalling list filled the screen—hot flashes, night sweats, insomnia, crashing fatigue, anxiety, dizziness, irregular heartbeat, depression, irritability, mood swings, disorientation, mental confusion, memory lapses.

Disorientation, mental confusion, memory lapses. Check, check, and check. She leaned back in her chair and raked her fingers through her curly black hair. She looked over at the pictures displayed on the shelves of the floor-to-ceiling bookcase—her Harvard graduation day, she and John dancing on their wedding day, family portraits from when the kids were little, a family portrait from Anna's wedding. She returned to the list on her computer screen. This was just the natural, next phase in her life as a woman. Millions of women coped with it every day. Nothing life-threatening. Nothing abnormal.

She wrote herself a note to make an appointment with her doctor for a checkup. Maybe she should go on estrogen replacement therapy. She read through the list of symptoms one last time. Irritability. Mood swings. Her recent shrinking fuse with John. It all added up. Satisfied, she shut down her computer.

She sat in the darkening study awhile longer, listening to her quiet house and the sounds of neighborhood barbecues. She inhaled the smell of hamburger grilling. For some reason, she wasn't hungry anymore. She took a multivitamin with water, unpacked, read several articles from *The Journal of Cognition*, and went to bed.

Sometime after midnight, John finally came home. His weight in their bed woke her, but only slightly. She remained still and pretended to stay asleep. He had to be exhausted from being up all night and working all day. They could talk about Lydia in the morning. And she'd apologize for being so sensitive and moody lately. His warm hand on her hip brought her into the curve of his body. With his breath on her neck, she fell into a deep sleep, convinced that she was safe.

Read on for an extract from the
Richard & Judy bookclub pick,

Left Neglected

by Lisa Genova

On a fateful day, while driving
to work, Sarah looks away from the road for one
second too long. In the blink of an eye, her chaotic life
comes to a screeching halt. In the wake of a devastating
accident, it's time for her to choose:

What does she *really* want?

'An inspirational book' Richard Madeley

SIMON &
SCHUSTER

Bob and I are standing in Charlie's empty classroom, on time, hands in our coat pockets, waiting for Ms. Gavin. Every bone in my body doesn't want to be here. However long this meeting lasts, I'll probably be late for work and can already foresee chasing the rest of the day and never catching it. I feel as if I'm coming down with a miserable cold, and I forgot to down a shot of DayQuil before we rushed out the door. And I really don't want to hear whatever it is Ms. Gavin is going to tell us.

I don't trust this Ms. Gavin. Who is she, anyway? Maybe she's a terrible teacher. I remember from Open House Night that she's young, in her twenties. Inexperienced. Maybe she's overwhelmed with her job and has been scheduling a meeting like this with the parents of every kid in her class. Maybe she has a thing against kids who challenge her. God knows Charlie can be challenging. Maybe she doesn't like boys. I had a teacher like that once. Mrs. Knight only called on the girls, only gave the girls smiley faces on their papers, and was always sending one of the boys out into the hall or to the principal's office. Never one of the girls.

Maybe this Ms. Gavin is the problem.

I look around the room for evidence to support my well-reasoned suspicion. Instead of the individual desks with attached chairs that I remember from my elementary school days, this room has four low, round tables with five chairs arranged around each, like little dining tables. Ideal for socializing, I'd say, not for learning. But my nice long list of things that the inept and unqualified Ms. Gavin is doing wrong ends with that single, lame observation.

Art projects line the walls. At the front of the room, printed-out photos of kids are taped onto two giant poster boards titled "Stellar Spellers" and "Math Olympic Champions." Charlie's picture is on neither. Five vibrantly colored, stuffed, kid-sized armchairs sit in a corner labeled "The Book Nook" next to a shelving unit packed with books. At the back of the room, there are two tables: one with a hamster in a cage and the other with fish in a tank.

Everything looks organized, cheery, and fun. I'd say Ms. Gavin loves her job. And she's good at it. I really don't want to be here.

I'm just about to ask Bob if he wants to make a break for it, when she appears.

"Thanks for coming. Please have a seat."

Bob and I sit in the kiddie chairs, inches from the floor. Ms. Gavin sits high in her grown-up teacher's chair behind her desk. We are munchkins, and she is the great and powerful Wizard of Oz.

"So, Charlie's report card must be concerning to you both. Can I start by asking if you were surprised by his grades?"

"Shocked," says Bob.

"Well, they're about the same as last year," I say.

Wait, whose side am I on?

"Yeah, but last year was about the adjustment," says Bob.

Ms. Gavin nods, but not because she's agreeing with him.

"Have you noticed if he has a hard time completing the homework assignments?" asks Ms. Gavin.

Abby starts the process with him in the afternoon, and Bob and I continue with him often past his bedtime. It's supposed to take only twenty to thirty minutes. He struggles, agonizes, stalls, complains, cries, and hates. Worse than broccoli hates. We threaten, bribe, implore, explain, and sometimes just do it for him. Yup, I'd call it a hard time.

In his defense, I know I didn't have homework at his age. I don't think kids, with the exception of a few precocious girls, are ready for the responsibility of homework at the age of seven. I think the schools are putting too much academic pressure on our little kids. That said, we're talking one page of "greater than or less than," or spelling words like man, can, ran. It's not rocket science.

"He does," I say.

"It's brutal," says Bob.

"What are you seeing here?" I dare to ask.

"He's struggling. He can't complete any of the class assignments on time, he interrupts me and the other children, and he daydreams a lot. I catch him staring out the window at least six times before lunch every day."

"Where is his seat?" I ask.

"There."

She points to the chair closest to her desk, which also happens to be right by the window. Well, who wouldn't get lost in thought when you've got a view? And maybe he's sitting next to someone who's distracting him. A troublemaker. A pretty girl. Maybe I gave Ms. Gavin too much credit.

"Can you try moving his seat to the other side of the room?" I ask, sure I've solved the whole problem.

"That's where he started the year. I need him right in front of me if I want any chance of holding his attention."

She waits to see if I have other bright ideas. I have none.

"He has a hard time following directions that have more than two steps. Like if I tell the class to go to their cubbies, get their math folders, get a ruler from the back table, and bring it back to their desks, Charlie will go to his cubby and bring back his snack, or he'll bring back nothing and just roam the room. Are you seeing anything like this at home?"

"No," says Bob.

"What? That's Charlie," I say.

He looks at me like he can't imagine what I could be talking about. Is *he* paying attention? I wonder what Bob would get on his report card.

"Charlie, go get dressed and put on shoes. Charlie, put on your pajamas, put your clothes in the hamper, and brush your teeth. We might as well be speaking Greek."

"Yeah, but he just doesn't want to do those things. It's not that he can't. All kids try to get out of doing what they're told," says Bob.

I sneeze and excuse myself. My congested sinuses are killing me.

"He also doesn't participate well in activities that require taking turns. The other kids tend to shy away from playing games with him because he won't follow the rules. He's impulsive."

Now my heart is breaking.

"Is he the only one doing these kinds of things?" Bob asks, convinced that he's not.

"Yes."

Bob glances around at the eighteen empty little chairs and sighs into his hands.

"So what are you saying?" I ask.

"I'm saying Charlie is unable to focus on all aspects of the school day."

"What does that mean?" asks Bob.

"It means that Charlie is unable to focus on all aspects of the school day."

"Because?" challenges Bob.

"I can't say."

Ms. Gavin stares at us and says nothing. I get it. I envision the policy memos stamped and signed by the school lawyers. No one is saying the words I think we're all now thinking, Ms. Gavin for legal reasons, Bob and I because we're talking about our little Charlie. My mother would be great at this conversation. Her next words would be about the nice weather we're having or Ms. Gavin's pretty pink shirt. But I can't stand the unspoken tension.

"Do you think he might have ADD or something?"

"I'm not a physician. I can't say that."

"But you think it."

"I can't say."

"Then what the hell can you say?" asks Bob.

I put my hand on Bob's arm. This is going nowhere. Bob is gritting his teeth and is probably seconds away from walking out. I'm seconds away from shaking her and screaming, "This is my boy! Tell me what you think is wrong with him!" But my business school training kicks in and saves us all. Reframe the problem.

"What can we do?" I ask.

"Look, Charlie's a sweet boy and he's actually very smart, but he's falling way behind, and the distance between him and the other kids will get worse if we do nothing. But nothing can happen fast enough here unless the parents initiate an evaluation. You have to ask for it in writing."

"Ask for what exactly?" asks Bob.

I half listen while Ms. Gavin describes the red-tape-lined mountain climb to an Individualized Education Program. Special education. I remember when Charlie was born, checking him for all ten fingers and toes, studying his delicate pink lips and the conch-shell curviness of his ears. *He's perfect*, I thought, amazed and grateful for his perfection. Now my perfect boy might have Attention Deficit Disorder. The two thoughts refuse to hold hands.

Kids are going to label him. His teachers are going to label him. What did Ms. Gavin call him? Impulsive. The kids are going to throw names that are sharper and uglier than that at him. And they're going to aim for his head.

"I want him to see his pediatrician before we start doing anything here," says Bob.

"I think that's a good idea," says Ms. Gavin.

Doctors give kids with ADD Ritalin. That's an amphetamine, isn't it? We're going to drug our seven-year-old son so he doesn't fall behind in school. The thought flushes the blood out of my brain, as if my circulation won't support the idea, and my head and fingers go numb. Ms. Gavin keeps talking, but she sounds muffled and far away. I don't want this problem or its solution.

I want to hate Ms. Gavin for telling us any of this. But I see the sincerity in her eyes, and I can't hate her. I know it's not her fault. And I can't hate Charlie. It's not his fault either. But I feel hate, and it's growing massive inside my chest and needs a place to go, or I'll hate and blame myself. I look around the room for something—the innocent faces of the kids on the "Stellar Spellers" board, the painted hearts and moons and rainbows, the hamster running on its wheel. The hate stays trapped inside my chest, crushing my lungs. I have to get out of here.

Bob thanks Ms. Gavin for informing us and promises that we'll get Charlie whatever help he needs. I stand and shake her hand. I think I even smile at her, like I've enjoyed our conversation. How ridiculous. Then I notice her feet.

In the hallway, after Ms. Gavin has shut the door to her room, Bob hugs me and then asks me if I'm okay.

"I hate her shoes," I say.

Baffled by my answer, Bob decides not to ask any more

questions of me at this point, and we walk to the gym in silence.

Before the Bell is just about over, and the kids are lining up to go to their classrooms. After saying hello and good-bye to Lucy, Bob and I find Charlie in line.

"Hey, bud, gimme five!" says Bob.

Charlie slaps his hand.

"Bye, honey, see you tonight. Do what Ms. Gavin says today, okay?" I ask.

"Okay, Mom."

"Love you," I say and hug him hard.

The kids ahead of Charlie begin to walk, following one another in a line, inching out of the gym like a single caterpillar. The line breaks at Charlie, who doesn't move.

"Okay, bud, get going!" says Bob.

Don't fall behind, my perfect boy.

FRIDAY

"One, two, threeeee, shoot!"

My fingers are a pair of scissors. Bob's hand is a piece of paper.

"I win!" I yell.

I never win the shoot. I snip the air with my fingers and dance a ridiculous jig, a cross between the moves of Jonathan Papelbon and Elaine Benes. Bob laughs. But the thrill of my unexpected victory is short-lived, stolen by the sight of Charlie now standing in the kitchen without his backpack.

"The Wii won't save my level."

"Charlie, *what* did I tell you to do?" I ask.

He just looks at me. The strings of my vocal cords wind a little tighter.

"I *told* you to bring your backpack in here twenty minutes ago."

"I had to get to the next level."

I grind my teeth. I know if I open my mouth, I'm going to lose it. I'll yell and scare him, or cry and scare Bob, or rant and throw the damn Wii in the trash. Before yesterday, Charlie's inability to listen or follow the simplest instruction annoyed me but in the typical way that I think most kids annoy most parents. Now, a tidal wave of fear and frustration rises inside me, and I have to fight to contain it, to keep it from spilling out and drowning us all. In the few seconds that I struggle to stay silent, I watch Charlie's eyes become wide and glassy. The fear and frustration must be leaking out of my pores. Bob puts his hands on my shoulders.

"I'll take care of this. You go," says Bob.

I check my watch. If I leave now, I can get to work early, calm, and sane. I can even make a few phone calls on the way. I open my mouth and exhale.

"Thanks," I say and squeeze his piece of paper hand.

I grab my bag, kiss Bob and the kids good-bye, and leave the house alone. It's raw and raining hard outside. Without a hood or an umbrella, I run like hell to the car, but just before I throw myself into the driver's seat, I notice a penny on the ground. I can't resist it. I stop, pick it up, and then duck into the car. Chilly and drenched, I smile as I start the engine. I won the shoot and found a penny.

Today must be my lucky day.

Rain is coming down in sheets, splashing onto the fogged windshield almost faster than the wipers can keep pace. The headlights click on, its sensors tricked by the dark morning into thinking that it's nighttime. It feels like nighttime to my senses, too. It's the kind of stormy morning that would be perfect for crawling back into bed.

But I'm not about to let the gloomy weather dampen my good mood. I have no kids to shuttle, buckets of time, and traffic is moving despite the weather. I'm going to get to work early, organized, and ready to tackle the day, instead of late, frazzled, grape juice stained, and unable to kick some inane Wiggles song out of my head.

And I'm going to get some work done on the way. I fish

in my bag for my phone. I want to make a call to Harvard Business School. November is our biggest recruiting month, and we're competing with all the other top consulting firms, like McKinsey and Boston Consulting Group, to pluck the best and the brightest from this year's crop. We never lure in as many graduates as McKinsey does, but we usually beat out BCG. After our first round of a hundred and fifty interviews, there are ten particularly impressive candidates whom we plan to woo.

I find my phone and begin searching for the Harvard number in my contact list. I can't find it under H. That's odd. Maybe it's under B for Business School. I glance up at the road, and my heart seizes. Red brake lights glow everywhere, blurry through the wet and foggy windshield, unmoving, like a watercolor painting. Everything on the highway is still. Everything but me. I'm going 70 mph.

I slam on the brakes. They catch the road, and then they don't. I'm hydroplaning. I pump the brakes. I'm hydroplaning. I'm getting closer and closer to the red lights in the painting.

Oh my God.

I turn the wheel hard to the left. Too hard. I'm now outside the last lane of the eastbound highway, spinning between east and west. I'm sure the car's still moving very fast, but I'm experiencing the spinning like it's happening in slow motion. And someone turned off the sound—the rain, the wipers, my heartbeat. Everything is slow and soundless, like I'm underwater.

I hit the brakes and turn the wheel the other way, hoping to either correct the spinning or stop. The landscape bends into an unmanageable slant, and the car begins to tumble end over end. The tumbling is also slow and soundless, and my thoughts while I'm tumbling are detached and strangely calm.

The air bag explodes. I notice that it's white.

I see the loose contents of my bag and the penny I found suspended in air. I think of astronauts on the moon.

Something is choking my throat.

My car is going to be totaled.

Something hits my head.

I'm going to be late for work.

Then suddenly the tumbling stops, and the car is still.

I want to get out of the car, but I can't move. I feel a sudden crushing and unbearable pain on the top of my head. It occurs to me for the first time that I might've wrecked more than my car.

I'm sorry, Bob.

The dark morning gets darker and goes blank. I don't feel the pain in my head. There is no sight and no feeling. I wonder if I'm dead.

Please don't let me die.

I decide I'm not dead because I can hear the sound of the rain hitting the roof of the car. I'm alive because I'm listening to the rain, and the rain becomes the hand of God strumming his fingers on the roof, deciding what to do.

I strain to listen.

Keep listening.

Listen.

But the sound fades, and the rain is gone.